Foreword by the Editor

Horror.

Scares.

Boo!

From the time we are small there are things that frighten us. As children we have the monster under the bed, the monster in the closet, and the monster that is *this* close to snatching us from behind when we're on our way up the basement stairs alone, and we can't look back because if we saw him he'd be *real*, and he would get us.

Does any of this sound familiar?

I thought so.

But we don't *stay* children, do we? And as we grow and change the things we are afraid of change with us: in grammar school the monster has moved out into the streets, and we fear "Stranger Danger"; in high school the monsters are inside of us, and we fear failure, and the possibility that we might not fit in; as adults our fears are everywhere, from worry about our jobs to the guy who's driving erratically in the lane beside us to the silent return of "Stranger Danger"—this time fearing for children of our own.

As new fears filter into our lives we *try* to forget the old ones. But, though they might not *frighten* us any more, they are never quite forgotten. We all *remember* the monster under the bed; the monster in the closet.

I'm forty-five years old and I *still* won't look back on the basement stairs, because I swear to God that son of a bitch is getting closer every time.

What you hold in your hands is the combined work of fifty people who won't forget, who *refuse* to forget, who have opened up that dark door in their hearts and minds to offer you one thing—just one thing each—that frightens them, selecting from the gamut of fears they've had in their lives, from childhood to now.

Disappearing children, ghosts, road rage, mental instability, vampires and more: somewhere in this book, possibly *many* places in this book, you'll find the things you are afraid of—even some things you thought you'd forgotten. You'll find fears so familiar you'll say "Yes. *Yes. That's* what scares me!"

And no matter how many times you say it, you'll be right.

We hope you enjoy *Demonic Visions 5*, a book filled with frightening thoughts and boogeymen so numerous and familiar you'll put it down knowing you are not alone in your fears.

Especially on those basement stairs.

Whatever you do, don't look back.

—*Rob Smales*

Cover art by Grant Cross, artwork on Facebook: *Grant Cross Artwork*

Table of Contents:

Other Works by the Authors

~ ~ * * ~ ~

Shaun Avery—*Spectre Show*

Max Booth III—*Toxicity, The Mind is a Razorblade, How to Successfully Kidnap Strangers*

Rick A. Carroll—*Dead Man's Skin*

Shenoa Carroll-Bradd—*The Minstrel Angel, The Widow's Painted Room*

Christopher Conlon—*Savaging the Dark, He Is Legend: An Anthology Celebrating Richard Matheson, A Matrix of Angels, Midnight on Mourn Street, The Oblivion Room*

Patrick Freivald—*Twice Shy, Special Dead, Blood List* (with Phil Freivald), *Jade Sky*

Robert Friedrich—*The Darkness Within: A Novella, Enlightened by Darkness - Vol.1 First Encounter, Enlightened by Darkness - Vol.2 The Invasion, Enlightened by Darkness - Vol.3 As Darkness Spreads, Enlightened by Darkness: Complete Trilogy, The Book of Metal Lyrics, Seed of Evil: An Ancient Evil Rises, Deathmongers: Where the Light Dies, Blessings from the Condemned: A Horror Legacy, Welcome to your Death: Part 1*

S.C. Hayden—*Rusty Nails Broken Glass, Kill Your Idols*

William Holden—*Words to Die By, Clothed in Flesh*

Justin Hunter—*Nostalgia, Chet & Floyd vs. the Apocalypse: Volumes 1 and 2*

K. Trap Jones—*The Sinner, The Harvester, The Drunken Exorcist, One Bad Fur Day, The Crossroads*

Naching T. Kassa—*The Venihi, Master of the Shade*

Chris Leek—*Nevada Thunder* (Snubnose Press), *Smoke Em If You Got Em, Gospel of the Bullet*

Mike Leon— *KILL KILL KILL, Rated R,* and *Supervillainous!: Confessions of a Costumed Evil-doer.*

Vince Liberato—*Redshifted: Martian Stories, After the Fall: Tales of the Apocalypse, What Has Two Heads, Ten Eyes, and Terrifying Table Manners?:*

An Anthology of Science Fiction Horror, Master Minds (Third Flatiron Anthologies Vol 3)

Ken MacGregor—*An Aberrant Mind*

Rick McQuiston—*Twelve Days of Christmas Horror, Giant Book of Nightmares, To See as a God Sees, Where Things Might Walk, In the Dark They Hear Your Screams: A Cthuhlu Anthology*

Adam Millard—*Only in Whispers, Dead West, Dead Cells, Dead Frost, Dead Line, The Susceptibles, Deathdealers, Skinners, Olly, Chasing Nightmares, The Marionnettiste of Versailles and Other Oddities, Peter Crombie, Teenage Zombie, Peter Crombie Vs The Grampires, Vinyl Destination, The Human Santapede, Larry, Caniba, Wanderlust, Rue, Soul of Dust, Hamsterdamned!, Zoonami, Milk*

James Pratt—*Cthelvis and Others, Horrible Stories for Terrible People, Vol. I: Monsters, Horrible Stories for Terrible People, Vol. II: Obscura*

Jeani Rector—*Shrieks and Shivers from The Horror 'Zine, Pestilence: A Medieval Tale of Plague*

Chris Robertson—*Death Dreams Deluxe*

Peter Adam Salomon—*Henry Franks, All Those Broken Angels, Prophets*

J. T. (Troy) Seate—*Valley of Tears, Tears for the Departed, And the Heavens Wept, Something About Sara, Connor House, A Resting Place*

Marc Shapiro—*Lindsay Lohan Fully Loaded: From Disney to Disaster; An Unauthorized Biography, Annette Funicello: America's Sweetheart; An Unauthorized Biography, Legally Bieber: Justin Bieber at 18; An Unauthorized Biography*

Mark Slade—*A Six Gun and the Queen of Light, Hellspeak: A Pete Chambers Book, Electric Funeral*

Rob Smales—*Wicked Seasons: The Journal of the New England Horror Writers, Volume II; The Ghost IS the Machine; Dangers Untold; Coffin Hop: Death by Drive-In; Dark in the Limelight; Dark Bits; Zombies Need Love, Too; The Best of Dark Eclipse*

Julianne Snow—*Days with the Undead: Book One, Glimpses of the Undead, The Carnival 13, (collaborative novella for charity)*

Marc Sorondo—*Aurora*

D.J. Tyrer—*The Yellow House, Acting Strangely*

Jay Wilburn—*Loose Ends, Time Eaters, Zombies Believe in You, The Rip and the Rhythm, Zombies: More Recent Dead*

Trisha J. Wooldridge—*Bad-Ass Faeries 2: Just Plain Bad, Bad-Ass Faeries 3: In All Their Glory, Epitaphs, Wicked Seasons, The Unicorn & the Old Woman, Mirror of Hearts, UnCONventional, Holiday Magick, Doorways to Extra Time, Once Upon An Apocalypse Volume 1.* As T.J. Wooldridge— *The Kelpie, Silent Starsong, The Earl's Childe*

1. CARRION MAN BY NACHING T. KASSA

The Carrion Man perched on the body like a scavenger bird, his arms sleeved in blood. He plunged his hands into the corpse once more, pulled out a piece of flesh and placed it in his mouth. Mara turned her face from him, squeezing her eyes shut. Her whole body began to tremble, and she clutched at the nearby door jamb for support.

"Please … not now," she whispered through gritted teeth.

A soft whimper sounded from her right. Mara identified it as a sound a child would make, but could not tell if it was real or not. Sweat broke out along her brow, beading at first, until it grew so heavy it trickled down. She moaned.

"Shut up, you little brat!" a muffled, male voice commanded. The whimpering ceased as fast as it had begun. Mara cracked an eye open, and from her kneeling position saw an elderly man cradling a young girl against him. Like her, they knelt upon the floor.

Mara avoided Carrion Man's gaze, as she surveyed her surroundings once more. She was still in the bank, and the five men dressed in black and wearing ski masks were still robbing it. Four members of the bank staff still knelt before all of them, their hands crossed behind their heads. The murdered security officer was still dead and lying in a pool of his own blood. Carrion Man was feeding on him.

Mara's purse still lay on the table across the room. The man who had silenced the child had taken it from her when the robbery had begun. She had tried to keep hold of it but he had torn it from her, breaking the strap as he did so. He had no way of knowing that when he had taken that bag, he had taken her sanity with it.

"Ma-ra," a sing-song voice called.

Mara refused to turn. Of all her hallucinations, the one she called "Carrion Man" was the worst. Her stomach churned as nausea flooded in.

"God, please, let it be over," she whispered.

"It will never be over," Carrion Man said. He was closer now. Mara squirmed.

"You shouldn't have listened to that quack. You weren't getting better, you were getting worse. By cutting your medication down, he has allowed me in," the monster said. He smiled. "And there are worse things than me."

Mara shuddered.

"Five minutes," one of the masked men announced.

Mara looked up, hoping to distract herself from her hallucination. Two men were trying to break into the vault with the unwilling help of the bank manager, while two watched from guard positions in the lobby. The fifth man stood watch at the entry doors. Since it was nearing five o'clock, no other patrons had entered the building. Mara, the old man, his granddaughter, and an elderly couple were the only ones unlucky enough to be caught inside.

The little girl began crying again. The dark, braided hair framing her face enhanced her pitiful expression. The old man patted her back and whispered, but could not quiet her.

"I said, shut up!" the bank robber said, nudging her with the toe of his boot.

The girl's grandfather looked up into the masked man's face, his eyes windows to his suppressed rage.

"Whatcha gonna do, ya old fart?" the robber taunted.

"Creep," Mara muttered under her breath.

The old man pushed the little girl aside and tried to rise to his feet. As he did so, the robber struck him with his rifle, driving him back to his knees. The Creep didn't stop there, clubbing the old man once more, knocking him to the floor. The little girl screamed.

Alerted by the girl's cries, the other masked man approached. "What are you doing?" he hissed.

"Had to put him in his place," Creep sniffed.

"Leave him alone and shut that girl up. We gotta move in two minutes."

Creep pointed the muzzle of his firearm at the girl, his finger on the trigger.

"Not that way!" the second criminal cried, pushing the weapon aside. "Jesus! You know Alpha doesn't want any more casualties!'

"Delta!" the man at the door called. "Cops!"

The two men hurried through the lobby toward the third. Mara took this opportunity to join the girl and her grandfather.

"Grampa!" the girl cried.

Mara checked the man's pulse, alarmed by how weak it felt. Nonetheless, she turned to the girl and forced a smile.

"Shh, Honey. He's going to be fine. He'll wake up soon."

"He's going to die," Carrion Man whispered. "They all are."

Gooseflesh arose on Mara's arm. Her breath shortened. The voice was closer now. Soon, he would caress her with blood-slick fingers, and when that happened she would scream and scream, unable to stop. Her eyes strayed toward her purse.

All she needed was one pill and Carrion Man would disappear.

"He is not going to die," the girl snapped. "He will live. All of them will live."

Mara looked up from the elderly man's body, her eyes wide. She stared at the girl, whose eyes were focused on something behind her.

"What?"

"The bloody man is wrong," the girl said.

"You … you see him?"

"He's right behind you," the girl pointed.

"Describe him."

"He's very white, and his skin is peeling off. His teeth are black and sharp."

"His eyes—what about his eyes?"

"They're black in the middle, but yellow all around."

Mara closed her eyes, a smile tugging at her lips though tears spilled down her cheeks.

"She sees you!" she cried, turning to Carrion Man. "She sees you too!"

The monster was squatting directly behind her. He grinned.

"How do you know she is real?"

Mara looked at the girl. She reached out, grasped her by the arms and pulled her forward.

"Who are you? What's your name?"

"Lori. Lori Smith."

"How old are you, Lori?"

"Eight."

Mara fingered the girl's dark braid. It was silky to the touch, as was the dress she wore. Silver braces adorned her teeth and she smelled like bubble gum. A little piece of purple gum was caught in the brace covering her front tooth.

"She's real!" Mara argued.

"Creep will come back soon, and when he does, he'll be in a panic. He'll start shooting. I think he'll shoot you first, just 'cause you're there. You're going to taste so good!" The monster licked his lips.

"You're not real," Mara said, shaking her head.

"Then take this. Take your pill and make me go away."

In his decaying hand lay a bottle, her bottle. The label bore the name of her drug as well as her personal and physician's information. She reached forward, then hesitated.

"You don't need it," Lori said.

"I do," Mara said, choking back a sob.

From the corner of her eye, Mara saw Lori walking into view. She held something in her small fist, and when she opened her hand; a small stone was revealed. It was a river rock, smooth and grey, polished for centuries by fresh running water. Mara stared at it in wonder.

"Take it," Lori said.

"A rock?" Carrion Man laughed. "Yeah, like that's going to work."

"Trust me," Lori said.

"He's coming," Carrion Man said. "And he doesn't look very happy."

Creep had stripped off his ski mask, disheveling his hair and revealing his rugged face. His eyes were wild and he was arguing with the man called Delta.

"Put your mask back on!" Delta was saying. "They'll see your face!"

"It doesn't matter now," Creep said, raising his gun.

"Trust me, Mara," Lori said, thrusting the stone at her. "Take it before it's too late!"

Mara stared at the girl, her eyes wide with fear. "My name! I never told you my name. How do you know my name?"

Carrion Man smiled in triumph. "I told you there were worse things than me."

"No!" Mara wailed.

"Hear me, Mara!" the girl cried. "It doesn't matter. You can still save them. You can save all of them. All you have to do is believe!"

Creep was approaching. Mara heard his booted footsteps on the marble floor. She looked from the small hand to the large, pale one.

"Choose," Carrion Man hissed.

"Choose," Lori said.

The cold muzzle of the rifle was pressed to the back of Mara's head. She heard the soft click as the trigger was depressed.

She chose.

Pain seared through the back of her head. It ricocheted about her brain, her entire body spasming in agony. Blackness clouded her vision. She squeezed the object in her hand, and knew no more.

~ ~ * * ~ ~

When Mara awoke she was reclining on a gurney. The interior of an ambulance surrounded her, and she felt the unpleasant tightening of a blood pressure cuff on her left arm. The dizzying scent of pure oxygen filled her nostrils, and she pulled the mask which covered her face down to her chin. Her head ached.

The paramedic tending to her smiled as he stripped the pressure sleeve from her arm.

"You've got a nasty scalp wound, but otherwise you're fine. You're very lucky."

Someone outside called the man's name and he hurried out of the ambulance. He had left her alone, or so she thought.

A soft cough sounded beside her. She froze.

"Are you okay, miss?" a male voice said.

She turned her head painfully to the right, and saw Lori's grandfather seated beside her. His forehead was bandaged and concern was evident in his eyes. She favored him with a wan smile.

"You're all right!"

"Yes. When I came to, the paramedics had arrived and the police had already arrested the bank robbers. I saw you lying on the floor, and I was sure you were dead. I guess the bullet only grazed your scalp."

Mara touched her head and winced.

The old man was peering out of the doors. "They're moving the bodies now," he remarked.

"Bodies!" Mara cried, rising to a sitting position. Her head pounded with the effort. "But, there was only one body! Where is she? Where is your granddaughter?"

"My granddaughter? I don't have a granddaughter, only grandsons."

Mara closed her eyes and slumped back on the gurney.

"He drowned you know," the elderly man said.

"Who?" Mara murmured.

"The one who knocked me down."

Mara rose to her elbow. "How? How did he drown?"

"I heard a paramedic talking to one of the police officers about it. They said he just collapsed. Said his lungs were full of water. They can't explain it."

Something cold filled Mara's hand. She felt the smoothness of it and squeezed it until her knuckles whitened.

"What happened to Lori—the little girl?"

"Oh! The girl!" he chuckled. "Did you think I was her grandfather? No, though I wish I was. She was waiting outside when I got here. I just kept her near me when the robbery started. I tried to keep her safe."

He touched his forehead and smiled sheepishly.

"Anyway, she was here a little while ago, checking on us. Said for me to give you a message when you woke up."

"What is it?"

The paramedic suddenly appeared. He bore Mara's purse in one hand and her medication in the other.

"Do you need this, miss?" He handed her the bottle.

Mara studied the label and asked her question again.

"What was her message?"

"She said: 'He won't bother you anymore'."

Mara squeezed the stone in her hand. Then she threw the bottle away.

2. BEHOLD THE HURRICANE by Chris Leek

I hadn't thought about home in a long time, maybe in years. But now the dirty cotton sky and the moody swell of the gulf made it hard for me to think about anything else. The wind buffeted my truck, pushing me into the northbound lane. I fought the wheel to keep the old girl in a straight line. Not that it mattered. I hadn't passed another car since Clear Lake. The television had been warning everyone south of Freeport to get out while the getting was good. Most of them had, packing up those pieces of their lives that could be carried in the trunks of cars, running from a storm toward a future that would be no more certain than the fate of the hastily boarded homes they left behind.

The only living soul I had seen all morning was a man about my age. He had been sitting on a plastic chair outside of a rust-streaked singlewide, just waiting. He wore a red checkered shirt unbuttoned to the waist and as the wind tugged it open I caught sight of a long puckered scar in his pasty skin. I had one just like it—triple bypass two years back. They told me I died three times during the surgery. I told them just once would have been fine. The man in the red shirt had nodded to me as I rolled past; the gesture both determined and resigned all at once. I returned it with one of my own, acknowledging the bare-ass truth of it all. Running is for the young. Sooner or later you have to make your stand.

Wind-blown sand scuttled across the cracked asphalt and the first drops of rain wetted the insect splatter on my windshield. I flicked on the wipers, which only made things worse. Through the smeared bug-guts I saw a police cruiser parked at the spot where county road 27 split from the coast highway. There used to be a gas station and a motel there too; all that remained of them now was a jungle gym of salt-encrusted rebar and smashed concrete.

I made the turn and the cruiser pulled out behind, cherries spinning. I coasted over to the shoulder and cranked down my window, wincing as the arthritis in my elbow set about its bitching. When I looked up there was a stern-faced female county deputy watching me. She looked so much like my Mary I almost stalled out the truck.

"The road is closed, sir. You'll need to get back on the highway."

The cancer took Mary from me in '95, although in truth it had been taking her for a good while before that. She barely weighed 60 lbs when she passed. I don't know what's worse, having a thing like that kill you from the inside out, or having to watch while it does it to someone you love.

"Did you hear me, sir?" The deputy asked raising her voice a little. The wind played with her coal-black hair, pulling it down across her face. She brushed it away with a flick of her hand that felt like a memory.

"I hear you all right, miss, but I've got to get home."

"The water is already up over the causeway, you can't get through to San Luis this way."

"I ain't trying to get to San Luis, just to the Higgins place."

She smiled uncertainly, her face taking on a look of puzzled sympathy. I get that a lot. You get old as me and you'll get it too. "Nobody lives at the old Higgins place. It's been a derelict for years," she said.

"I know, but I've got to go see it anyway."

"Sir, I drove past there not half an hour ago and there's nothing to see. The only things you'll find are vacant lots and Hurricane Ellie."

I never understood why they named the storms after people. Call them thieves and murderers if you want, but not Tom or Edna, and definitely not Ellie. Ellie was my sister's name. That's why I had to go back.

"Look Mary, I—" I cut myself off, but not before the name had escaped my thoughts. For a moment it hung there between us like an untaken breath before being snatched away by the wind.

"How do you know my name?"

My mouth had gone dry, the old familiar taste of salt air on my tongue. I leaned out the truck window to spit and then remembered my manners and swallowed hard instead.

"I didn't," I said, gooseflesh prickling on my arms.

I glanced at my watch. It was only a little past noon, but the light was already leaching away, the sky appreciably darker than it had been only a few minutes ago. I'd been waiting sixty years for this day without even realizing it and now suddenly I was running out of time.

"Look miss, I don't expect you to understand, but seeing as this is America, I do expect you to honor my God-given right to be an idiot." I gave a smile, trying for the reassuring kind and ending up with something that felt a little manic. "This is just something I have to do."

The look on her face told me she already had me pegged as an old fool and she was probably trying to decide now if I was a danger to anyone other than myself. She looked me over, weighing that up and balancing it against the fact she wanted to be gone from this place as much as I did.

"You drive safe, sir," she said at length, "and don't linger too long, they say this one is going to be the worst since '52."

"Thank you, miss," I said and started the long job of rolling up my window again before she could change her mind.

She looked at me like maybe she wanted to say something more; in the end she only nodded and walked back to her cruiser, leaving me alone on the rain-soaked highway with nothing but regrets for company.

~~ * * ~~

The timber frame house I grew up in was long gone. The big blow of '52 had carried most of it away, and what remained was now buried under decades of trash, weeds, and neglect. It's funny, there are days when I can't remember what I had for breakfast, but I can still remember every last detail of that house. In my mind I can count every nail in its white-washed boards. Maybe it was a trick of the storm, but as lighting flickered overhead I thought I could see the blue-green sparkle of the ocean glinting in its windows again, just like it had when I was a boy.

I parked the truck alongside the carcass of a fishing boat that had been tossed into the bramble snarls of our old front yard by the last big storm, or maybe the one before that. Its hull had rotted away, leaving only the ribs, thrusting out of the wet dirt like a skeleton trying to pull itself from a shallow grave. Behind the boat was a vine covered hump, at the bottom of the little rise where the house had once stood. That was where Ellie and me hid, in the root cellar. I screwed up my eyes, but it didn't help. I could still remember every damn detail of that night too. I hadn't been back to this place since. Ellie … she had never left.

~~ * * ~~

The rich earthy smell of the root cellar groped at my nostrils. Rain drummed on the tin roof like the hoof beats of the apocalypse. I tilted the candle, dripping wax into the bottom of a Mason jar and settled the candle on it, only burning my fingers a little. I put the jar up on one of the shelves with dozens of others filled with Momma's pickles and preserves. I glanced over at Ellie. Her wet nightdress was plastered to her skin and her face full of all kinds of worry.

"When's Momma coming home?" she asked in a small voice.

"Soon," I said, not knowing if she would be. It was eight miles to town and the cannery where she worked. "We'll just sit tight here 'till she does. It'll be okay." Being the eldest I felt like I had to say something reassuring.

Ellie looked at me like she wanted to believe it. "You sure, Tommy?"

"Sure I'm sure," I said and shot her a smile.

I had just about convinced myself too, when the jars started rattling and clinking, jostling against each other on the shelves. The ground under my feet thrummed like it was full of electric cables. The air in cellar got syrupy and hard to breathe. Something was wrong. Something was coming.

"What is it?" Ellie asked.

"I dunno." I went up the steps to the cellar door and hesitated, my hand resting on the latch.

"Don't go out there, Tommy. Don't leave me," she said her eyes all big and scared.

"Wait here. I'll only be a minute," I said.

I drew back the bolt and peered out. The candle guttered as the wind caught hold of the door. I tried to haul it shut again, but a powerful gust wrenched it wide open pulling me with it, out into the night. Behind me in the cellar I heard the sound of glass smashing on the packed dirt floor as the door crashed back on its hinges. Ellie screamed. I called out to her, but my shout was lost in the roar of the storm. That's when I saw it; a wall of foaming black water as tall as our house surging up from the beach, swallowing everything in its path.

~ ~ * * ~ ~

"Ellie!"

The sound of my own shout shook the memory loose. I opened my eyes. The road outside was underwater. The truck rocked violently on its springs as the ocean slammed into it, throwing a dirty white spume up over the windshield. I had no idea how long I'd sat there. It was probably only a few minutes, but it felt more like hours. Time likes to play tricks on the old.

I don't know why I was spared that night. If it was for some higher purpose, God had never let on, at least not to me. A fishing boat found me the next morning, better than a mile offshore, still clinging to the splintered door of the root cellar. My leg was broke and I'd cracked my head open, but somehow I had survived. They never found Ellie though, said she must have been swept out to sea. Maybe she was, or perhaps she was still here, waiting for me to come back, just like I'd told her.

I reached into the glove box and took out a flashlight. Slipping it into my pocket I opened the door and plunged my feet into the swirling, knee-deep surf. I worked my way around the hood holding on to the truck for support, head bowed against the stinging rain. Through it I could just see the dim outline of the root cellar. I let go of the truck and waded across, the water getting shallower as the ground began to slope up.

The wind howled like a wounded animal, rain washing the blood from my hands as I tugged at the brambles covering the cellar's entrance.

"I'm coming, Ellie." I yelled and pushed my way inside not feeling the thorns tearing at my flesh; not feeling anything at all.

I lost my footing on the crumbling steps and half-fell into the cellar, landing on my knees in the musty darkness. I cussed and fumbled out the flashlight, my heart racing as the shadows jumped back from its light. The beam bounced around in the long narrow chamber, showing a line of rusty holes in the tin wall, which marked the place where the shelves had been fixed, and a few shards of broken glass that twinkled in the dirt. But there was nothing else to see. I was alone. That's what happens when you live too long. Everyone you care about dies and you end up alone, torn apart by the guilt of it all, chasing ghosts. I knew now I hadn't come here for Ellie. I had only come for myself.

"I'm sorry, Ellie. I never meant to leave you," I said. The words sounded hollow, all meaning stripped away by the long years in between now and then.

I heard something move off to the right and swung the flashlight around, expecting to find a rat, or some other piece of meanness lurking in the shadows. Instead, I saw Ellie. She was standing at the far end of the cellar, water dripping off the hem of her nightdress. She looked exactly as I remembered her, wet hair stuck to her face, scared eyes blinking in the light.

The years shuffled away as I shuffled toward her. In that moment I was ten years old again. Momma was working the evening shift at the cannery and there was a storm coming. I dropped the flashlight—which wasn't a flashlight at all, it was a candle in a mason jar. I reached out and took hold of Ellie's hand. It felt cold and clammy, as if she was coming down with a fever. Momma would have my hide if she got sick.

"Let's get out of here," I said.

"But I have to wait for Tommy."

Her voice sounded strange, like it was coming from far away; a recording playing in another room or another time.

"C'mon we have to go," I said gently tugging on her hand.

"No, I have to wait," she said and tried to pull free.

The skin on her hand came away with a noise like wet newspaper tearing, leaving me clutching a mottled glove of rotting flesh. I screamed then; a scream that echoed down through eternity and rattled the glass jars on my momma's shelves.

Ellie just stood there, in this place, but not in this time. She raised her arm and pointed behind me, tendrils of slime dangling from her skeletal fingers. I turned just as the wave crashed in through the doorway, flooding down the steps, pulling me under, filling my lungs with cold black water.

Thank God, I thought I was going to have to live forever.

George picked up the knife, an antique stainless steel surgical blade from a bygone age, and drew it across his fingertip. He winced as blood welled from the cut, the black fluid writhing with near-microscopic worms, filaments of flexible glass given form and dark purpose.

He sucked the blood from his finger, pulled it out of his mouth, and sighed, his hunger unabated.

"Mom?" He raised his voice, blasted it through the speakers to carry through the house.

"What is it?" Her shrill voice warbled with age.

"I need another drip."

Her exasperated sigh carried through the wall without amplification. She thumped around the corner, her six-ton exoskeleton shaking the floor with every step. A withered crone more jaundiced wrinkle than flesh, her stringy, dull gray hair hung in tangled, listless clumps from her liver-spotted head. Bruises showed under her paper-thin skin, yellow to blue to black. The wires and tubes connecting her to the machine pierced every bruise, a thousand-thousand tendrils carrying nutrients, fluids, and data to and from the World-Stream. A cable snaked from her back to disappear into the darkness above.

She pointed a yellowed, jagged fingernail, crusted white with mold, square at the space between his eyes. "Young man, you've had four already today, including those breeders, and you're going to put us in the poor house."

He rolled his eyes. "Mom, I'm two hundred and eighty-seven."

She put her fists on her hips. "Which is relevant how? Will your advanced age put food in our streams? Will it pay for another drip, and who knows how many more before dinner? The answer's no."

He rose up, the bed articulating and morphing around his limbs to raise him to his full robotic height, fourteen feet not counting the massive cable that wound upward from his back into the ceiling. He stepped forward, and the house rumbled. Glaring down at the crone who'd birthed him, he clenched robotic fists where his arthritic, frail fingers could not.

"I've warned you not to defy me." Integrated speakers poured all the malice and hate and subsonic undertones designed to cause fear in his human subjects straight into his voice, and the house shuddered with his warning.

She threw up her hands and rolled her eyes, then whirled in defiance of her decrepit body. Her fingers stabbed the air, pointing behind him, to the side of the bed. "Look at them! Just you look! Do you know how hard it is to find good drips these days?"

He looked down at the pile of drained corpses, the bloodless holes where tubes had pierced their bodies, screams of agony frozen on their desiccated faces.

"A fortune in good breeding stock," she raved, "gone. Just gone! With nothing to show for it—no money, no babies, no nothing—because you can't control your appetite. Well, god or no, we can't *afford* your appetite, so you're going to have to wait."

He sulked, his titanic bulk sagging toward the floor. "The other gods will laugh if I get too skinny."

She chuckled and closed her eyes. "Have you looked out the window lately, dear?"

He closed his eyes and called up the feeds, transforming the world outside into a panorama of sensation.

Dust scoured the skies, the never-ending storm stripping the flesh from anything stupid or unlucky enough to be caught in it. Gods plodded through the decaying streets, metal monsters lifting rotted-out cars, their search-lights piercing long-shattered windows, hunting, searching for drips. The city stank of diesel and burning rubber and dry, rotting technology.

A rusty god, patches of armor hanging from loosened rivets, lifted a bus with one hand. A drip, suddenly exposed, bolted for cover, the nano-rubber suit clinging to her body and augmenting her reflexes while protecting her from the harsh environment. The god lunged, clumsy, and she dove through grasping fingers to escape down a side alley. Instead of giving chase the god raised its head to the sky and howled, a desperate cry of hunger and despair.

George froze in shock. He knew this god, had played with him before they'd ascended, hunting drips for their fathers and uncles under a sky remembered blue. They'd used knives back then, knives and harpoons to make it fun. His heart had swelled with pride when his father had presented them with their first praise, for a scrawny brown-haired boy no older than ten. George had laid the trap, but Benny had chased down the boy, just managing to harpoon his ankle before he escaped through a hole in the brick wall.

And now Benny moaned at the sky, a pale shadow of a shadow, a god in form and name but no longer in spirit.

"What … what happened?" He opened his eyes, returning his consciousness to the room. "Benny, he looked so good just last year."

"Not last year." She shook her head without opening her eyes. "You haven't left that bed, haven't looked outside, in seventeen years. It's 2430, sweetie. The storm's been raging three decades."

He looked at his feet, as if the marble floor might offer an explanation. "But he looked so hungry."

Her eyes snapped open and she scowled up at him. "Why do you think I've always harped on you about livestock management, huh? Breeding programs?"

He groaned. "But Mom, farming is so *boring*."

"Those four you stole this morning—"

"I can't steal what's mine!"

"—were the only fresh-caught stock we had. The rest are inbred and nasty; it's no coincidence they don't fill you up as they should. Now our stock is compromised, again—"

"We've always made do."

She snarled. "You idiot fool! Will you even listen? We're under two thousand drips in the pens, none of them children under five, less than a quarter breedable females. Do the goddamned math."

He did, and a sob escaped his throat before he could contain it. He clasped his hands over his mouth—his real hands, his real mouth—and forced himself to speak. "Mom, what are we going to do?"

She shrugged. "You're the god. You figure it out."

He closed his eyes, fleeing into the World-Stream, away from his mother's demands, away from the hunger and need and want, to the infinite expanse of pure data, sensation divorced from the cold, harsh reality of the flesh. After she'd left he returned to his body, and picked up the knife.

Another taste couldn't hurt.

4. WHAT'S THE MATTER WITH KIDS TODAY? BY
WINIFRED BURNISTON

The TV drones on while a low throbbing seeps through my eyes, and spreads slowly to the back of my skull. I'm unable to focus on anything other than my uninvited guest on the back porch.

The police aren't coming. After calling multiple times and not even getting a recording, I knew I was on my own. And I can't call anyone on the street. I'm a New Englander, for God's sake! I only know my neighbors to wave at while driving by or to shout an occasional hello to during a walk around the block. All I have are a few first names scattered up and down the street. No last names, no phone numbers, and none friended on Facebook, so no getting in touch unless I walk up to a door. And there's no way I'm going out there.

This morning started out as a typical suburban Sunday. Snuggled deeply under the covers, a chink of sunlight and birdsong filtering into the room, I was jolted awake by the delightful sounds of kids next door yelling and screaming out back. Giving up on sleeping in, I dragged myself out of bed and shuffled downstairs. I'd just turned on the coffeemaker when the screaming changed. The high-piercing screeches were now those of pain and fear, not kids screwing around. I opened the slider and poked my head out. No adult voices, just frantic noises coming from the side of my house. I was pissed. The kids were cutting through my yard again. I slapped on a pair of slippers and a bathrobe, lumbering out there, ready to be the big, bad adult in charge.

There were four boys out there: Billy and Jake, who live behind me, their friend Matt, and some bigger kid I didn't know. The big one had Matt in a headlock, Matt's feet dangling about eight inches off the ground. Matt struggled, bulgy-eyed and panicked, as the other two ran around, screaming and throwing rocks at the older boy.

Rocks. That's what snapped me out of it.

"What the hell is going on here?"

Four pairs of eyes were suddenly on me. Using this distraction, Matt managed to break free, landing directly on his face. There was the snap of cartilage and the whoosh of air being slammed violently from the kid's lungs, and the world came to a halt for a moment. Nobody moved, nobody spoke. It was just Matt fighting to breathe.

Billy and Jake finally stepped over to Matt, careful to keep as far away from the other kid as possible. Matt tried to push himself up, purple and gasping, blood spouting everywhere from his twisted, broken nose. He whimpered like a hurt dog as his friends dragged him away.

And the whole damned time the other kid just stared at me, all slack-jawed and stupid, rather than the kids he'd been torturing. He kept his eyes on me, not wavering for a second. The boys pulled Matt to his feet and started back to their homes. They babbled away, checking each other over as they went. Matt suddenly stopped and turned back. Pale and panic-stricken, he kept his eyes on his foe as he wheezed at me.

"Get back in your house, Mrs. Burniston," he said. "David's one of them."

I was just about to ask, "One of whom?" when David finally opened his mouth wide. Wider than should have been possible, unhinging his jaw like a snake … and what rose from the hollow depths within was a bone chilling, soulless moan that grew to a roar that shook his entire frame.

The boys bolted, but my legs betrayed me as though they'd turned into bits and pieces of rubber. I landed on my ass in the moist patch of petunias. I sat there, the new slack-jawed fool, staring at this thing, no longer a child. The creature before me began to writhe, shaking violently. The gaping maw continued to expand, exposing ring after ring of viscous little teeth. Slowly, sliding up from within the purplish gullet emerged a mass of milky tentacles. Hundreds of these spewed forth, growing longer, taller than should have been possible, a weeping willow of twitching appendages sprouting from the human shell, each snaking out, probing the air and the grass before them.

Every nerve and fiber screamed out for me to move, to run, but I just sat there, staring, forgetting to breathe. When I finally remembered to draw a breath, the tentacles became frenzied, thrusting frantically in my direction. One struck my left calf, slicing a wicked gash that splashed blood across the flower tops and grass. The intense burning and sight of my own blood finally got me moving. Sliding in the muck, I managed to get to my feet. Tentacles whipped through the air, slicing my wrist, forehead, and neck as I skidded around the corner of the house. The creature lurched forward on its human legs, arms and tentacles stretched out and searching.

Tripping up the deck stairs, I dove head first through the open door. Scrambling around on the floor, I managed to slam the door just as the beast reached the deck. The creature stopped in its tracks after several steps, tentacles dancing about its body. I stared for a moment, then drew the curtain closed and began to shove furniture in front of the slider.

I've checked many times over the past hour, peeking out at what's standing on my back deck. Whatever is out there looks like David again, the boy from down the street. And he's just standing there, staring at the door. The tools are out in the shed, so my kitchen knives are lined up on the table, one duct-taped to a broom handle—eventually he'll decide to come in.

It's beginning to rain out now, and I've seen no one else out on the street. In the distance, I've heard sirens several times and I'm betting it has to do with others discovering Davids of their own. Why? Because the boys said *them*, he's one of *them*.

5. THROUGH THE MASK BY JEFF McFARLAND

Originally appeared in *The Siren's Call #17 - Trick-or-Treat*, revised for *Demonic Visions*.

"I hate it," Todd said with a scowl. "I hate everything about it."

"What? Come on, it's adorable!" Jane said, a toothy grin showing through the hole of the mask's mouth.

"That thing is nightmare fuel," he muttered, pretending to look at the wigs. It had been a long time since he actually saw a mask that scared him, especially in a two-bit seasonal shop like this.

"Oh, come on." She laid a hand on his shoulder and took a step closer. "What if I was wearing this … and nothing else?" He shuddered and shook his head. The thought sent lightning down his spine. He imagined her beautiful hourglass figure, soft skin, long legs—all exposed, save for a smiling pig mask with tiny crescent moon eye holes and ears that stuck out comically from the sides. There was even a little tuft of black hair on top.

"If I could get it up while you were wearing that thing, I'd need to be thrown in the loony bin."

Jane pulled the mask off and laughed, putting it on her hand like a ventriloquist's puppet. "Why does it bother you so bad?" she asked, wiggling her hand, causing the mask's flesh to ripple.

He stared at it for a while. It was easier now that there was no one inside. The mouth was a wide open grin that would have been at home on the face of some deranged clown. The eye holes were barely there at all; he had no idea how she had seen out of them. With the right costume, there would be no telling who was inside.

"I have not the slightest clue," he said, continuing to stare. Maybe it was because it was the color of human flesh. Whatever it was, it made the hair on Todd's arms stand. "Something about it just … ugh. It's way too 'dueling banjos' for me." She laughed again and put the mask back in the bin with the others on clearance.

"So, is that a 'no' to making me squeal, then?" she asked. He shook his head and slapped her ass. She jumped and hurried away with a giggle. He turned to follow her, but as he did, he found that the mask's gaze met his. He stopped. The way it folded and laid on top of all the others had turned its grin into a large frown, like some sort of Comedy / Tragedy cliché. He shoved some of the other masks aside, burying it deeper in the bin.

"Darlin'! Are you coming or what?" she called from a few aisles over. He stood there, looking into the bin.

"Yeah, I'm coming."

~ ~ * * ~ ~

It had to be coincidence. There had been hundreds of goofy masks in that shop, and it was Halloween on a Friday night for Christ's sake. He and Jane hadn't been the only ones last-minute shopping. But it *wasn't* a coincidence. Todd knew that. Of *course* he was wearing that mask. How else could it have gone down?

Todd sat alone in a booth with duct-taped seats and stared across the room. Lights of every color pulsed in time with the DJ's music, painting the zombies and serial killers on the dance floor every imaginable color. Behind the bar, a sign lit by a black-light read *"Show up in Costume, Drink Half-Off!"* with a crudely-drawn pumpkin beside it. He was watching Jane over at the bar. She was smiling big and laughing at whatever the man wearing the pig mask was saying. Todd swished his drink around, staring into the glass and drumming the fingers of his other hand on the table. All he could hear was the music thumping around him, some crappy remix of the Monster Mash.

The guy in the pig mask had been taking advantage of the half-price drinks. Todd had watched him from the booth as he bought Jane and himself a shot. Then another. Now she was giggling about something, her hand on his shoulder. Todd continued to swirl his drink. The guy put his arm around her waist. Todd finished his drink in one gulp and bolted up from his seat.

He shoved past the people on the dance floor, his steps in time with each thump from the bass of the music. The other side of the bar felt a lifetime away as Todd's vision swayed back and forth. The music, the lights, and the room's movement made Todd feel like he was outside of his own body: he was watching a movie of his own life.

"Oh, Todd! We were just—"

Todd shoved the man in the mask against the bar. The guy sprawled backward, his back shaking the counter, and his drink flew from his hand.

"Todd! What the hell?" Jane shouted.

The guy in the mask had already recovered. He stepped forward, nose-to-nose with Todd. Todd couldn't see anything past the mask. There were no eyes in the slits, the mouth only a dark cavern. Todd stood and stared for what felt like forever, fists clenched tight. His heart pounded in his ears. Jane was shouting, tugging on his shirt sleeve, but

28

he didn't hear her. Todd was craving it; itching for this guy to say the wrong thing, to make the wrong move. But he didn't. He just smiled. Smiled big. His teeth shone a sickly yellow in the black light, giving the pig's face an uncanny human grin.

"What?" Todd shouted over the music. "You got a problem?" The guy stared a minute longer, then turned and walked away without a word.

Todd's whole body relaxed. He was suddenly aware that the room was spinning faster than before, and Jane wasn't shouting anymore. Only glaring at him.

"What?" he asked again, plopping down on one of the stools. "Did I interrupt something?" He could tell by the look on her face that was the wrong thing to say.

"You know what?" she started, getting nose-to-nose with him herself. "Yeah, you did. We were just talking about how I already have a boyfriend that I love very much." He felt his shoulders slump.

"You have a boyfriend you love very much, but you'll happily keep taking drinks from some guy?" Todd said, avoiding eye contact with her.

"Duh!" she said, with a laugh he knew was more frustration than good humor. "Free drinks are free drinks! It's, like, the one good thing about being a chick at a bar. I was starting to tell him to step off when you stormed over like some fucking macho man."

"Gee, I wonder where he would get the idea you were available. It's not like your boyfriend was sitting alone across the room while his girlfriend was being hit on," Todd said with a sneer.

I can't even talk to you right now," Jane said, her eyes misty. "I'm going home." She stormed away, cutting through the dance floor full of werewolves, vampires, and guys in banana suits.

"Seriously?" he slurred. He gritted his teeth and spun on his stool to face the counter. He threw his wallet down on the bar and waited for someone to notice him.

~ ~ * * ~ ~

The bartender, surprisingly, hadn't cut Todd off. Now, he wished she had. He was taking some very cautious steps to the parking lot behind the bar, bracing himself against the building's brick exterior. The alleyway leading to the parking lot was decorated top to bottom with city-sanctioned graffiti that glowed eerily in the dim orange streetlight. The shadows danced to the music still pounding in Todd's ears. All the scantily clad women and strange monsters on the alley's walls watched him stumble though, doing nothing to help him. When he heard another set of footsteps echoing his, he knew who they belonged to immediately. He didn't turn around. He didn't need to.

By some miracle, he had made it to his car. He fumbled around his pockets, looking for his keys. The footsteps grew louder. He didn't have them. He tugged on the handle of the door anyway, and to his surprise, it opened. He stooped and reached under the driver's seat, searching frantically. The steps drew closer. He thought he heard someone speaking, but his own breathing was too heavy for him to tell. They were behind him now, echoing through the alleyway. His hand found a handle under the seat. Someone else's hand was on his shoulder.

Todd stood and whirled with a cry, plunging a three inch blade into the guy's neck. He still couldn't see any eyes—that pig's stupid fucking smile was all he could see. But the person underneath wasn't smiling now. Todd was. The man grasped Todd's wrist and at his face, gurgling, gasping desperately for air. Blood drizzled down the front of the guy's shirt, leaving a trail of crimson down the once-white fabric. Todd shoved him, and he fell against the car behind him. Something shimmered in the guy's free hand, and Todd stooped to look. It was a set of keys.

The man pressed a button on the keyring, and the alarm on Todd's car began to go off.

Each honk from the car exploded into Todd's head like a set of church bells. The man had pulled the knife out of his throat and was pooling blood on the dirty alleyway ground. Between the car's honking and the alarm's wail, Todd heard the stuck pig wheeze out a few final words.

"W … wanted, ap-p-pologize," it gurgled. "Dr … dropped … keys …"

6. THE ORIGINAL SULLIVAN BY S.C. HAYDEN

In the movies, career criminals (gangsters and Mafiosos, hit men, spies, secret agents and sundry characters of ill repute) always have a go-bag stashed someplace. When times get tough, when your number's up, you grab the go-bag and run.

A typical go-bag might contain a few grand in cash, maybe a passport and a driver's license with a new identity, and a handgun. Everything a fella might need if he has to disappear fast.

Eddy "Sully" Sullivan always thought that was a piece of Hollywood fiction. First off, where were you going to keep it? Not at home. How likely was it you'd be home when the shit hit the fan? And if someone was after you, they'd be clocking your address, right?

He'd seen one movie where the guy had his go-bag stuffed up in the rafters in some airport parking garage. *No way*, Sully thought. How could he be sure some jack-off maintenance guy wasn't going to find it and spend all his getaway money on hookers and blow? He wouldn't be able to stop thinking about it. He'd be checking on it twice a week.

Then there's the passports and stuff. Those things expire. Was he going to update his go-bag every ten years? Would the cash stay clean and dry for that long? Would the gun still fire? No, go-bags were a movie thing.

Right then though, Eddy Sullivan really wished he had one. Instead of making a clean escape in the dead of night, go-bag in hand, he was tossing a hastily packed duffle into the trunk of his Lincoln Townie in the middle of the afternoon. He didn't even have a gun.

Not so smart after all, are you, Sully? he thought.

When he slammed the trunk shut, he heard a voice behind him. "What's the rush Sully? Where you headed?"

Sully didn't need to turn around to see who the voice belonged to. Mickey Finn's voice was unmistakable: It sounded like a whisper, yet you could always hear him over everyone else in the room.

Sully turned back slowly; sudden moves around Mickey were bad for your health. "Hey there, Mickey," Sully said, trying—for whatever it meant—to sound like he wasn't scared shitless. "What's up?"

Mickey didn't say anything. He just stood there, one eye locked and loaded, the lazy one staring into the abyss. Some people thought they called him Mickey Finn because he put people to sleep, but Sully was one of the few who knew it was actually his real name.

"Not much Sully, but say, why don't you come with me?" Mickey said after what seemed like an eternity.

"Yeah Mickey, sure." Sully knew there was no point in arguing. When Mickey Finn tells you to do something, you do it.

Mickey ferried Sully into the passenger side of a pristine light blue Mercury Grand Marquis, double parked across the street.

"So, where we going?" Sully managed once they were rolling.

"We're going to see Frank," Mickey said in his weird, loud but quiet voice.

Sully didn't say anything. There was nothing to say. It was becoming increasingly likely that he wouldn't survive the day.

A few weeks ago, Frank had sent him down to Providence to talk with a couple of numbers guys about a potential business transaction. Turned out one of the guys was an undercover cop. Of course, it wasn't Sully's fault. He hadn't set up the meet. But they'd all gone out to a strip club, and he'd had too much to drink and said more than he should have, and now the Feds were crawling up Frank's ass.

Sully sank down a little in his seat. If only he could go back. If he could just go back in time and un-fuck what he'd fucked, everything would be okay. Sully closed his eyes and pictured himself standing on a great stone precipice. Stars and worlds wheeled and collided in the void beyond … and then, without thinking, he *jumped*.

Sully's eyes popped open but he couldn't see anything save a whirling blur of color. He felt like he'd fallen right through the bottom of Mickey's car. His stomach lurched and he felt himself tumbling backward through space.

When he landed, he was standing on his feet, staring at a cracked brick wall. Gasping, he spun. Another wall. Sully heard the sound of traffic to his right. When he turned toward the noise he found himself looking at a familiar street. He was standing in the alley beside his apartment building. Sully took a tentative step forward, his wingtip crunching on broken glass. He quickened his pace, reached the street and saw himself being stuffed into the passenger seat of Mickey's Grand Marquis.

"Holy shit," Sully said. He'd done it. He'd gone back in time. He just hadn't gone far enough. The Grand Marquis cut into the D Street traffic and headed off toward Dot Ave. Sully felt a sense of relief that he wasn't in the car with Mickey … but he was in the car. The other him was in the car.

He eyed his Townie and reached into his coat pocket. For a moment, he wondered if his keys would be there, or if the *other* him had them, but there they were. When he popped the trunk, his duffle bag was right where he'd left it.

Go, Sully thought, *just get in the car and go.* What else was there to do? There was no time to think about what the hell was going on or what the hell it meant. He'd been given a gift, and he'd be damned if he wasn't going to take it.

But then, what about the other him? What about the Sully in the car with Mickey, the one on his way to see Frank? What was going to happen to *that* Sully? *But I'm me*, Sully thought, with less certainty than that thought would typically elicit. If they whacked the other him, would he die too? It was certainly a conundrum.

Sully fired up the Townie. He wasn't sure what he was going to do until he actually started doing it, but once he started rolling, rather than peel the fuck out of Dodge, he went after Mickey. He still didn't have a gun, and he certainly didn't have a plan, but when you travel through time to rescue yourself from South Boston's coldest killer, what kind of plan could you possibly have?

Once he was behind them, Sully stomped on the gas pedal like he was trying to kill a rat with his wingtip. The Town Car launched forward, smashing into the back of the Mercury. Sully's world flashed blinding white. When his airbag deflated, he was looking through a shattered windshield and a curl of rising steam.

Mickey got out of the Mercury and strode toward him. "Da fuck's the matter with you?" he said in his loud quiet voice, then stopped short when he realized who he was talking to. He shook his head and looked back at the Mercury just in time to see the other Sullivan bail from the passenger side and take off running.

Mickey pulled a black semiautomatic pistol from his coat and leveled it. Sully blasted his horn and Mickey flinched. The shot missed its mark and the other Sully ducked into the back of a taxi.

Mickey, his face a twisting scowl, spun about and leveled the gun. Sully closed his eyes and *jumped*.

Once again, the bottom fell out of the world and Sully felt himself pinwheeling backward through space and time. When he landed, he found himself staring at the same cracked brick wall in the alleyway beside his apartment building.

Sully didn't hesitate. He sprinted to the end of the alley but the Mercury was already rolling down D Street. Sully saw himself climb into his Townie and take off after Mickey and the other him—and then another Sullivan rolled after the Townie in the back of a taxi.

Holy shit!

This was seriously fucked up. Somehow he'd created a time paradox straight out of a science fiction movie. Pretty soon he'd be popping up all over the place. He'd be everywhere. The world would be full of Eddy Sullivans.

Sully paused. Maybe that wasn't such a bad thing. Maybe he could get them all together, organize them. He was the original Sullivan after all. He could have a private army. An army of Sullivans. He'd like to see what Frank Salemme, that ginzo fuck, had to say then.

An army of fuck ups, Sully thought, shaking his head. No, he had to take care of this. Sully understood numbers. They were, after all, how he made his living. As far as he could tell, each time he *jumped* he came back about ten minutes before. If all the Sullys kept *jumping*, they'd keep on doubling. If you double Sullivans every ten minutes, you'll have a million Sullivans in a few hours. It was a simple exponential growth curve. It had to stop.

There was another kind of time paradox he'd seen in science fiction movies. The Grandfather Paradox. What happens if you go back in time and kill your grandfather? You don't exist, that's what, because if you kill your grandfather, you'll never be born. But if you were never born, who went back in time?

It gave him a headache just thinking about it.

Either way, he needed to put a stop to this. Sully tried to wrap his head around the order of events. What would happen if he *jumped* again and killed his other self before his other self had a chance to *jump*? Would all the other Sullys wink out of existence? Not the Sully in the car with Mickey: if he killed that Sully, he might wink out of existence too, like the kid who kills his grandfather. No, he had to kill the second Sully, the one following Mickey. If he did that, all the others would disappear, leaving him and the original Sullivan.

No, Sully shook his head, *I'm the original Sullivan.*

As soon as he finished the thought, Eddy Sullivan heard his own voice speaking behind him. "I'm afraid I can't let you do that, Sully."

Sully spun around and saw himself, looming. But it wasn't him, not *really*. The other Sully looked completely unhinged. He had a cuckoo for Cocoa Puffs look in his eyes and his face kept twitching, like a booze brain at half past dry. Two more Sullys stepped up behind that one, each looking crazier than the next.

"Fuck me," Sully said.

Without warning, the other Sullivan punched him square in the nose and Sully found himself flat on his back blinking up at a rectangle sliver of slate gray sky. In an instant, the other Sullivan was on him, hands wrapped around his neck.

Fuck, Sully thought, *I didn't know I was that strong.*

"Out with the old, in with the new," the other Sully said. "You might not have the stones for it, but an army of Sullivans sounds pretty good to me."

Sully *jumped*. This time, the drop was painful. Rather than tumbling backward through space, it felt as though he'd been hurled out of a moving car.

When he opened his eyes he was back on his feet but he wasn't alone. The alley was packed with Sullivans, and they were waiting for him. *Not so smart after all, are you, Sully?*

One of the Sullivans hit him from behind and he was on the ground again. *Oooof*, another Sullivan shoed him in the gut. Sully rolled onto his back and one of the Sullivans straddled him. Impossibly strong hands wrapped around his neck and squeezed. Sully's vision darkened. His bile rose and he could hear himself gurgling.

Sully tried to *jump* again but he couldn't do it. The vice around his neck tightened.

But I'm the original Sullivan, Sully thought.

"Are you sure?" someone said. Everything went black.

He stands on the stage looking out at an audience of thousands, but all he can see is the face of the living dead girl.

Not all the ones out there in the crowd either, the ones that just dress like living dead girls. Not all those cheering him and the rest of the band on, waiting for him to strike his plectrum to the strings of his guitar and bash out the opening chords of "Zombie Town."

He looks back to Peter.

His friend and bandmate shrugs from behind the drum kit, as if asking him, "What's up?"

Mark looks back to the audience.

Then steps through his fear and toward the microphone, ready to sing.

~ ~ ** ~ ~

Five years ago.

"So this is it?"

"Yep." Mark slapped a hand against the side of the van, a wave of pride surging through him as he did so.

"It's second-hand, right?" Peter asked.

"More like tenth or twelfth hand," Cliff commented.

"So is your bass," Peter told him.

Cliff blushed slightly at this reminder, but still shot back with, "Yeah, but my bass still *plays*." He looked to Mark. "Are you sure this thing even *works*?"

"It drove me over here," Mark replied. "And it'll get us out on tour."

That was the magic word, and suddenly all three of them were too excited to bitch about the shortcomings of their new band vehicle.

So they went back home and packed what they needed, quit their temporary jobs, then got in a few last minute practices as they learnt their songs and loved their songs and got ready to show those songs to the world as they hit the road.

Stopping along the way to play a town called White Beach.

~ ~ * * ~ ~

"Great show tonight," their manager, Norman, tells them after the concert.

"Yeah," Cliff replies. Then looks to Mark, a slightly sour look on his face. "We should have had something new to play them, though."

"Cliff …" Peter says, a warning in his voice.

"I'm just saying what everyone is thinking," Cliff goes on. "We need a new hit."

And both band members look to Mark.

I'm trying, he wants to tell them. *I really am. I want to write another song that millions of people will love.*

He shivers.

But I don't think I can pay the price anymore.

~ ~ * * ~ ~

They knew that the only way for a band like them—punky, dreaming of being the next Green Day—to gain popularity, to get noticed, was to tour relentlessly. That meant playing lots of towns. So many towns that they eventually all seemed to blur into one.

Then they reached White Beach.

"Big houses," Peter commented as they drove through it, sitting in the passenger seat whilst Cliff slept in the back with all the instruments. "Fancy cars." He grinned. "Place looks far too good to be letting *us* play here."

Mark was inclined to agree.

Up on the stage, though, it was just like any other place. They were playing an alternative bar called *The Suck Spot*, and despite its name, it was actually pretty jumping.

Afterwards, the crowd dissipated.

Except for those people that were throwing parties.

You got used to those. In fact, Mark had found, you began to actively seek them out. Why not, when you had a few hours to kill before heading off to the next town, the next show? Better to do it in bed with some chick that loved your music than in the van with your two—male—bandmates, right?

Mark had always thought so.

The girl that came over to him this time was a pretty, white-faced Goth girl.

"Hey," she said. "Great show!"

"Thanks," he said, checking her out. And there were a lot of good things to check, from the chest that seemed to scream at him to let it free from the tight black corset restraining it, to the lips that were painted oh so black and yet looked oh so inviting. "What's your name?"

She looked away shyly. "My name's Cheryl."

He was just about to reply when a third party entered the scene: the manager of The Suck Spot, a guy called Dean.

"Good show tonight," he said, putting an arm around Mark's shoulder.

"Yeah," Cheryl added. She nodded vigorously as she said it, and Mark could not help but notice the way her breasts heaved with the movement. "I just told him that!"

Dean smiled at her. Then looked back to Mark and asked, "You coming to party with us?"

Mark glanced back at his two friends, still gathering up their gear on the stage.

"Not them," Dean told him. "You."

Mark thought about asking why, but now Cheryl was giving him the eye.

So in a moment that changed Mark's life forever, he followed.

~ ~ * * ~ ~

He returns to the hotel alone.

The band didn't fight about his inability to craft them a new hit, but it's coming. He can feel it. He walks through the reception area of the hotel, and he sees there a few other musical acts staying there.

Big acts.

They all give him that nod of recognition—that "we have a secret" look that he's come to loathe—and Mark feels close to tears as he reaches the door of his room.

He has to stifle a scream when he sees what lies inside.

~ ~ * * ~ ~

Cheryl pushed him back onto the bed and reached behind her back to undo her bra.

Mark stretched out with his own hands, eager to help with this task, but she shook her head.

He laid back, waiting. Watching the bra drop, seeing what it released when it joined the corset on the floor.

Mark was feeling pretty horny by now.

Suddenly she was running out of the bedroom, away from him.

"Hey!" he cried.

Her giggle came from somewhere down the hall.

"Come and get me!"

His erection leading the way before him, he did so.

She stood just outside the door of another room, hands stroking her breasts, pulling at her nipples, moaning for him to come and join her.

He obeyed, but she stepped back, entering the room behind her.

Mark followed—

—and stepped into the nightmare that was about to engulf his life.

~ ~ * * ~ ~

There is a row of eyeballs laid out on the bottom of the bed. All facing him, all—though he knows they can't *really* be—watching him.

He looks past them, glancing further up the bed.

A knife has been jammed into the headboard with what looks like tremendous force.

He falls to the floor, weeping.

Message received.

~ ~ * * ~ ~

Mark came into the room, mouth agape.

"Is she dead?"

Dean and Cheryl—the latter still partially undressed—stood looking down at the bed.

Mark came closer.

A naked woman was laid out atop the covers, arms crossed across her body, palms touching her bare shoulders.

"Is she?" he said again.

Dean shook his head.

"Not dead," he said. "But not alive, either."

"We're really not sure what she is," Cheryl added.

Dean nodded. "Only what she *does*."

Mark peered down at the woman. She really was very beautiful, he saw. All that fine blonde hair on display. And not just on her head.

He couldn't help it. His erection, already pushed to almost unbearable limits by Cheryl's sudden departure earlier, began to throb.

"You want her, don't you?" Cheryl said.

He looked at her.

"Don't worry," she said. "I'm not jealous. I was never even all that into you. My job was just to lure you here."

"That's right," Dean said. "It's her you really want, isn't it?" He pointed at the woman on the bed. "But you don't know why, do you? You don't know why you came into this room to look at her, when any sane person would have run away screaming."

Mark looked up at him.

"You're not the first band to come through White Beach," Dean went on. "No, sir, not by a long fucking shot. But not all of them get to see our friend here. Only the special ones. Only the ones that we know can make it to the top."

"Guys like *you*, Mark," Cheryl said, placing a hand on his shoulder.

39

"Those ones," Dean told him, "we bring here."

"But why?" Mark wondered.

"Didn't you notice the big houses?" Dean asked. "How much … nicer our town is than any of the others you've been to?"

Mark remembered his earlier conversation with Peter. "Yes," he said. "Yeah, I did."

"Well," Dean said, "why do you think that is?"

Before Mark could reply, Cheryl took his hand, placed it on the other woman's breast, and—

"*Zombie Town they keep on knocking, Zombie Town I can't stop rocking, Zombie Town it drives me mad, feels so good to act so bad—*"

Mark fell to the floor as if struck by lightning.

"What the Christ was *that*?" he shouted.

"That," Dean told him, "was your first taste of the Muse."

"Want more?" Cheryl asked.

Mark rose to his feet, groggily, the lyrics and the music and the ideas, oh God a full series of *albums* worth, burning up inside of him.

He looked at the woman.

Licked his lips.

"You got all that just *touching* her," Cheryl said. "Imagine how much more you'll get when you're inside her."

"But there's a price," Dean said.

"Price?"

"Yes." Dean looked at him. "She'll help you make millions. But you'll owe some of it to the town."

"How much?"

Mark hated himself for asking the question, but he couldn't help it. He had to know.

Dean smiled. Named a figure.

Mark stared down at the woman. Had her face changed? Was she beckoning him now? Did she *want* this?

He wasn't sure. But the songs he suddenly saw himself singing—the success the band could have—that was all that mattered.

He took his erection in his hands and climbed atop the girl.

Stuck it into her.

And that was when everything changed.

Her eyes popped open, and the face that he been looking at for the past few minutes, the one that had seemed so beautiful, became something else. Something rotten, mouldy and green, a diseased, wart-ridden tongue suddenly lolling out of her mouth. Mark realised she did not feel right *down there*, that the inside of her vagina felt cold and damp—*mushy*—and he wanted to pull out, he *went* to pull out, but she was gripping him now, and laughing, her breath cold and rancid in his face, and he was just about ready to scream—

—but then they were back, the ideas, the chords and the melodies, flowing through his system telling him he could do this, he could be *huge*. He looked into her eyes, and God help him she revolted him, she did, but her power was surging through him, he could feel it, and he lowered his lips and kissed that mouth, sucked her vile tongue into his, so thick it filled his mouth, making him gag, but he couldn't help it, he could not stop, and he rode her until he came and they both screamed but for different reasons.

Suddenly she was normal again, was beautiful, and he was lying on the floor, his rapidly deflating penis now sticky with ejaculate and other moistures he did not even want to think about. He looked up and saw Dean looking down at him. The man smiled and said:

"I think we can call that a hit."

Mark started to weep.

~~**~~

Five years later, he is still doing so.

Tears of bitterness. Tears of rage.

See, when he returned to the van that next morning and found Cliff and Peter waiting for him—the former sulking, wondering where he'd been, the latter concerned, worried about him—he'd been filled with anger. Wondered why it had been him alone that had been invited to meet the Muse. But he knew the answer: he was always the one who'd put the most into the band. Even going so far as to buy the tour van himself, with no help from the others.

He was the frontman.

And "Zombie Town"—the song birthed in that dark bedroom—had been, as he'd always known it would, a massive hit.

The money had come rolling in and, through fair means and foul, he had seen that the required amount of it went to White Beach.

But Mark hadn't been able to follow up the first set of hits.

That was when—hating himself for it but unable *not* to—he had returned to the town.

To that bedroom.

The Muse was still waiting. She had not aged. Not until he entered her, and she became the horrible hag once more—laughing her vile breath in his face.

She had given him another hit album.

But that had been three years ago, and now he sits in his hotel room with his back against the door and looks at the eyes. Takes them in his hand and rolls them about in his palm.

Sales from the band's back catalogue are steady … but he gets the message. It's been too long since he produced a hit. He has to produce something that will bring the town of White Beach some more money.

Because they're greedy.

He wonders which one of the acts that are beholden to them left this little surprise in his room for him. It could have been one of hundreds.

And what will happen next time, if he doesn't do what they want?

He looks to the knife, and before he is even aware of doing so, he has pulled it from the headboard and holds it in his hand.

Could he do it himself, Mark wonders? Does he have what it takes to write a hit on his own? Or is his only chance another visit to White Beach?

He doesn't know.

He places down the knife and heads to his suitcase anyway, pulling out his pen and notepad. Then, on second thought, puts the pen back.

"You want a song?" he says to the empty room, to whoever else might now be listening. "Okay, I'll write you a fucking song."

He starts to cry once more, visualising that room and cursing the moment that he made the wrong choice, that he let it all go wrong.

"It's called 'Fuck You'," he says.

Then he grabs the knife.

Places his wrist above the notepad.

And writes the last song of his life in blood.

8. A PLACE OF FEAR BY WILLIAM HOLDEN

"Bless me father for I have sinned." Gian trembled as he sat in a tiny booth. He could smell the years of frankincense and myrrh etched into the wood. It surrounded him, suffocated him, and terrified him. "It has been over five years since my last confession." He braced himself against the priest's reply.

"It's been a lot longer than that Gian," Father Gregory said. "Why…"

"How did you know it was me?" Gian wrapped his arms around his shoulders to quiet the nerves that rattled his body.

"You have the voice of an angel, Gian. I knew it was you from the first word spoken. I have not seen you in church since your parents died. Why did you stay away? You should have known this is where you belong, among our congregation."

"My parents made me come to church Father." The words spilt from his lips before he could stop them. "I am terrified of this place, of all places holy. I feel as if I will burn in hell for being a part of it. When they died, I vowed never to set foot in a house such as this again."

"Obviously, fear is no longer holding you prisoner. Your presence here today proves that."

"The fear has not subsided Father. My eyes are closed to block out my surroundings. My hands are shaking, and I'm covered in my own sweat." Gian heard the faintest creak of old wood as if something next to him had shifted. Then a heavy breath filtered through the confessional.

"Then why come back?" The priest's voice was closer.

"My therapist said I must face my fears."

"But why a confession? Could you not just sit in the church as an act of facing what you seem to consider the place where all your fears hide?"

"Because of you, Father."

"Me?"

"Yes. And the nightmares."

"Tell me about these night visions."

"As a child I had terrible nightmares. Even before I understood about Christianity, I would dream that I was walking up to the altar with my mother and father on either side of me. We would stand before the cross to pray, and as I began to recite the Lord's Prayer, the cross would be covered in blood. I would turn, seeking my parents for help, but the people holding my hands were no longer my parents, they were the decomposing bodies of the priests. They would turn to me with their hollow eyes and mouths, which swirled with darkness. Their flesh, cold and slimy, would peel from their bones and fall on me; the sweet smell of rotting flesh penetrating my nose and mouth stealing every breath. I tried to run, but they wouldn't let me go. They just stood there, holding me and laughing. Oh God, their hideous laughter would pierce my ears and make them bleed. It was as if they wanted to get inside of me, to tear out my soul and devour it." Gian gasped for breath as the visions of his tortured nightmares replayed in his mind.

"Yes, good, very good."

"Father?"

"It's good that you are confiding in me. Yes, very good indeed. I take it that you feel I am somehow connected to these nightmares as you call them."

"Yes."

"Can you see the priest's face in your dreams?"

"No, they are featureless, but I know you are there. I can feel it Father. I've always been able to feel your presence."

"You should be careful, Gian where you lay blame."

"I was not laying blame Father, yet you seem eager to accept it."

"You know not what you are saying my child; this fear you have has clouded your judgment."

"It is not my judgment in question. The dreams I had as a child were the same as other children in this parish."

"And how would you know such a thing."

"Children talk, Father. We confide in one another when our parents dismiss our thoughts as immature and fanciful. They were as afraid of you and this place as I was, and still am."

"Childhood fears are not real, my child. They are the product of imagination, and lack of understanding."

"Our fears were real back then, but no one listened to us. The only difference is, I'm still alive."

"The difference is your parents listened to you, unlike the others in my congregation. They believed you when you told them about the dreams. When you told them that I was not who I pretended to be."

"They were going to leave your order weren't they?"

"Yes, and we couldn't allow their betrayal. You see, it's not just me—it's everyone here. They believe so strongly in the words of our dark Lord that they will do anything to protect one another, including sacrificing their own children."

"You killed my parents, didn't you?"

"You seem to have already figured that out, so there is no use in my answering that question."

"I was supposed to die with them, wasn't I?"

"No, you were meant to live."

"Why not kill me like the others?"

"We came looking for you, Gian, but you ran from the hospital."

"I ran so that you couldn't find me."

"So why have you come back now?"

"To stop you."

"I don't think so, Gian. You see, you can't stop me any more than your parents could. As I said, it's not just me. Take a look outside the booth. They've waited over five years for this day. We knew you'd come back."

"Why?"

"You don't know? You are the son of our beloved saint. You were born from the blood of those sacrificed in his name."

"I don't believe you."

"Believe it or not, it doesn't matter. They are out there, waiting to welcome the new priest to their church."

"I won't do it. You can't force me."

"Yes I can, and I will. You see, every one hundred years a new leader must rise. You shall take my place as I transcend into our Lord's realm. You will lead the congregation as I have."

"No."

"Open your eyes Gian. Let go of the fear, and see me standing before you."

"Our Father who art in Heaven …"

"Prayers will not help you, Gian. Open your eyes and see me as I am, as you will soon be. Yes, that's it. Accept your destiny. Feel our Dark Savior enter your body. Yes, give Him the invitation He needs to enter your soul. Take Him in, Gian. Revel in His dark glory forever and ever. Amen."

9. A MOMENT OF SILENCE BY MAX BOOTH III

When somebody lives alone, they don't really pay attention to the sound of their own voice. They barely even talk. Especially when they work from home on the computer, where all their conversation comes from typing on the keyboard. And even when they do talk, it isn't significant enough to give it a second thought.

Richard discovered he had lost his voice early in the morning, along with the rest of the world. He had just finished outlining his next column due to *Dark Moon Digest*, and was heading into the kitchen for a quick refill on coffee. His pinkie toe had always been an issue, ever since infancy; so had the bottom corner of the wall, separating the living room and kitchen.

Whoever had designed that goddamn apartment was a masochist.

The coffee mug escaped his grasp, shattering into a million little pieces all over the floor. His neck bent back, adam's apple poking strongly against his neck, and his mouth opened wide as it released a scream similar to that of a banshee. Afterward he stood there for a moment, looking at all the broken glass, wondering if he'd startled any of his neighbors. He hoped nobody came knocking at his door—or worse, called the police. He had deadlines to meet. There wasn't time for any of that nonsense.

Limping, he gathered a broom and dustpan and cleaned up the mess. He decided to forget the coffee. It was obviously cursed.

Richard sat back down at his MacBook and began reviewing his outline again, making sure he hadn't missed any glaring plot holes. He was still a little tense about a possible knock or phone call regarding his obnoxiously loud screaming. He didn't want to deal with that. Maybe nobody heard it. Maybe nobody cared.

It was then that he realized that he hadn't actually screamed. Sure, his mouth had opened, and his vocal cords had strained with pressure, but no sound had left his mouth. Was he sure, though? Maybe, maybe not. It seemed ridiculous that the scream wouldn't have been audible.

"Ridiculous," he tried to say, but he did not *hear* himself say it.

What the hell?

The words only traveled as far as his thoughts could take them.

This is wrong, something is wrong.

He opened his mouth again, tried to say *"Testing, testing,"* but heard nothing.

Am I deaf? Oh my God, I'm deaf.

No. That was impossible. He'd heard the coffee mug shatter. He could hear the traffic outside. Birds at his window. Planes in the sky. He could hear it all.

All but himself.

So I'm mute, then?

His lips parted, tried to say "*Hello? Help! HELP!*" but he only hurt his lungs from trying too hard.

This is fucked, this is so fucked.

He stood abruptly, pushing the chair to the ground behind him, and made for the cell phone plugged in at the counter. He held it in his hand for a moment, just staring at it. What was the point? He couldn't talk. Nobody would be able to hear him. It'd be like trying fill a bucket with water, only the bucket was missing a bottom.

Who would he call, anyway? He didn't know many people, and those he did know didn't particularly care to speak to him anymore. He was divorced, his parents were dead, and all his friends had taken his ex-wife's side. He could call his agent. His agent always knew what to do. It was why Richard hired him.

Only the problem still remained: no voice, no way to use the phone.

He was left with three options. He could hang out, and try to wait whatever weird affliction this was out. Maybe it'd just go away after a while; kind of like hiccups. Second option: he could get on the MacBook, email his agent about what was going on. But who knew when he'd get a response? He could always try Facebook, make a random status declaring his lack of a voice—but how many of his social network friends would actually take him seriously? Besides, what would they know? The total intelligence of all his media contacts could be summed up with a badly spelled photo of an adorable kitten wearing a hat.

So that left the third option: he would have to leave his apartment, find someone else and try to pantomime the situation. One of his neighbors, maybe; just keep pounding on the door until someone answered.

It was times like these that Richard felt like a lazy, horrible human being. He'd lived the last year and a half in this apartment, the whole time sharing the same hallway with a deaf-mute. Not once had he ever bothered to even *attempt* to learn sign language. If there was anyone that would know what was going on, it'd be Hautala down the hall. Trying to converse with him now would just be useless.

It's always the actions you neglect that end up killing you in the end.

Richard paused for a moment, standing there in his empty apartment. On the street below traffic carried on like normal. Everything continued. Nothing ever stopped.

Suddenly a loud bang, like metal smacking metal, killed the tranquil silence. Richard jumped back, bumping his head against the wall. What the hell was that? He ran across his apartment to the open window overlooking the city. He stuck his head out and scanned the streets below.

"*Holy shit*," he failed to say.

Car after car had flipped over and crashed into other cars, piled up on top of one another. Drivers, passengers and random pedestrians ran around the wreckage like chickens with their heads cut off. They stood in front of each other waving their hands like crazy.

It occurred to Richard that even though he could hear car alarms barking like mad, he couldn't actually hear anything else. Even from how high he stood in his apartment, he could still see everyone's mouths opening and closing but, nothing came out. They were just as silent as he was.

What the hell is going on?

Richard was done staying in his apartment. Either he had been stricken with a strange disorder that blocked all human vocals from entering his ears, or everybody had gone mute. It would be impossible to further self-diagnose until he had determined which one it was. Plus, that pile-up outside looked really bad. Somebody was bound to need some help.

He slipped on his shoes, threw a shirt on and headed out the door. He didn't even lock it behind him; suddenly, possessions no longer mattered. There were a few other people in the hallway, just walking around aimlessly, but Richard didn't pay them any nevermind as he pushed past and ran to the elevator.

It was the longest ride of his life. His heart beat loudly against his chest with every nauseous movement the elevator made downward. For a moment, he found it amusing that he could hear his own heart but not his voice. The humor in it quickly diminished, however.

Outside, the alarms of the wrecked cars were much louder. The noise pierced his eardrums; it made his teeth hurt. People were running past him in both directions, hands waving in the air, mouths open wide yet absent of voice. Blood stained the streets. Corpses hung limp through shattered car windows. This was madness. What had happened? Where were the police, the ambulances? Hadn't anyone called them?

Of course nobody had. Phones were useless now. Conversation had suddenly become obsolete.

Without their tongues, everybody had become helpless.

Dear God, how many people is this affecting?

An Asian man with a messenger bag stumbled up to him, mouth going a mile a minute. Richard shrugged. He didn't know what else to do. The Asian began tapping his wristwatch furiously. Richard shrugged a second time and the man gave up, angry, and ran away.

A woman lay in the street, half her body pinned underneath a flipped car. Her stomach was smashed to hell and her guts were spattered all over the street around her. She reached toward God, mouth unhinged in a silent scream.

How the hell could this pile-up have happened? This was utter insanity. He was surrounded by corpses and obliterated metal. Richard tried to imagine it: maybe two people had been conversing in their car when suddenly they both realized neither could hear the other. In the midst of the confusion, the driver took his or her eyes off the road and ran a red light, getting plowed by traffic. Maybe the same thing happened to two dozen different cars at the same time. Three dozen. A hundred. A thousand.

Or maybe something else happened. There was an infinite number of possibilities, and Richard would never know the truth. He didn't *want* to know the truth. He just wanted it to end.

A crying child tugged at his shirt. He looked down and tried to smile, but failed. Instead, he waved sadly.

The child was asking him something, but he didn't have any idea what it was. Maybe asking where her mother and father were. He looked back at the dozens of corpses littered across the street and quickly turned back to the child. He brushed a finger through her hair, and she flinched back, biting his hand.

Richard pulled away quickly, holding his bitten hand and watching as the confused child fled the scene.

This was all happening so fast, and he had no idea what to make of it.

Richard approached a woman sitting on the curb. Her face was covered in blood and she wept. Tears fell down her cheeks, mixing with the blood, but no sound escaped her lips. She made no effort to hide her despair. Why should she?

He leaned down and placed a hand on her shoulder and she let her head fall into his chest. He wrapped his arms around her, embracing her with his warmth. It didn't matter that her blood and tears rubbed against his shirt. With a hundred humans surrounding them, panicking without making a sound, nothing at all mattered.

Richard watched as two men attempted to argue with each other. They each opened their mouths, trying to scream at the other, but nothing came out. Their faces strained with stress and frustration. Their bodies trembled with pure rage. Richard had no idea what had sparked the argument; maybe they had crashed into one another during the pile-up, or maybe they were just trying to figure out what had happened to their poor, precious voices. Either way, no solution was being made, and it didn't take long for one of the men to lash out physically at the other.

Flesh against flesh, violence upon violence, the two men tumbled to the bloodstained street, fists whirling like murderous perpetual motion machines. The sound of their faces being brutalized was louder than Richard could have ever expected; it made his stomach nauseous, and if he hadn't been holding a strange woman, he would have surely vomited, yet he couldn't take his eyes off the scene. One of the men stayed on top of the other, repeatedly pounding his knuckles into the man's face, despite the fact that the man on the ground was long dead. He kept trying to scream at his corpse, and the more he failed, the more he cried, the more he lashed out.

He got up from the dead man and approached someone else who was trying frantically to talk on a cell phone. The man grabbed a hold of Cell Phone Man's neck and began to squeeze, again screaming something nobody else could hear.

Richard imagined he was saying, *They can't hear you, you stupid fuck! Just hang up already, because nobody can hear you! Don't you REALIZE that? WE ARE ALONE!*

Richard looked away and held the woman tighter against his chest.

This is crazy, he thought, *this is so goddamn crazy, I don't even know where to begin.*

What were they supposed to do? Life as they knew it was crumbling beneath their feet, faster and faster, destroyed as each second ticked by. How could anyone be expected to continue as they had before? They couldn't talk, they couldn't communicate. They couldn't call an ambulance, they couldn't call a loved one.

Five miles away, Richard watched two airplanes collide. There was a bright, vibrant explosion that made everyone stop what they were doing and watch it, eyes wide with horror. The flames lingered in the sky for what felt like eternity.

The whole world had completely shut down.

Why?

Richard shook his head, discouraged. Wondering "why" about something as insane as this would be useless. He might as well have wondered what brought them to this planet in the first place. How could anyone possibly answer something like this?

This was …this was lunacy.

And lunacy had no answer.

~ ~ * * ~ ~

Richard led the woman back up to his apartment. She did not seem hesitant to follow—if anything, she was eager to escape the massacre happening on the streets. Any place would be safer compared to that hell. He showed her to the couch and she sat while he fetched her a soda. She nodded her thanks and gulped half of it down, like she'd been dying of dehydration. Her body shivered violently. Richard handed her a blanket and she took it, smiling sadly. The woman watched every move Richard made, as if afraid of what he'd do when she wasn't looking.

He didn't blame her. After what had happened outside, anything was possible.

He sat on the sofa next to her, wishing he could tell her that it was okay, that they were safe up here. But all he could do was just sit there like an idiot. How long could they stay like this, he wondered, before they would have to begin thinking of a plan of action?

How long would she stay?

Richard grabbed a notebook laying on the coffee table and wrote at the top of a new page: *Hello, my name is Richard.*

He handed her the pen, and she wrote below: *What is happening?*

I don't know, Richard wrote.

Why can't we talk? she asked, and he tapped the line above for an answer. Then she wrote, *I'm scared.*

Me too.

He looked the woman deep in the eyes, sharing the same tears. Her face was still smeared with dried blood. It looked awful. He felt so bad for her; there was this urge in him that wanted to take care of her forever.

Is it going to stop? she asked.

God, I hope so.

I want to go home, she wrote.

51

Richard placed a hand on her thigh, and wrote, *It is safe here. I promise.*

He leaned forward, kissed her lightly on the lips. She flinched.

She was still scared. No doubt still thinking about the madness out on the street. How could you not?

He picked the notebook back up and wrote, *DON'T LEAVE,* underlining *"LEAVE".*

He headed for the bathroom and closed the door behind him, which was a rarity when you lived alone. Richard took out his phone and stopped again, reminding himself that he couldn't call anyone. Would he ever be able to again? He wished he knew the answer.

He logged onto FaceBook briefly to see what everyone else was saying about this most unfortunate event. His news feed wall was corrupted with picture after picture of overused memes; cats in humorous positions, children smoking cigarettes, dogs with sunglasses on their tails. The only actual status that he found was an old co-worker saying that he was hungry. Richard sighed and returned the cell phone to his pocket.

He took care of his business quickly, then found a washcloth in the cupboard that he damped with hot water. He grabbed a box of bandages and headed back into the living room to take care of the woman's head wound, only to find that she was gone from the couch and now heading for the front door.

Where the hell was she going?

He tossed the washcloth and bandages on the table and rushed over to stop her, grabbing her shoulder and spinning her around. He smiled innocently, shrugging as if to ask what was going on. What was she thinking, trying to go back out in that chaos?

She opened her mouth to loose a soundless scream. Richard held her tighter, trying to understand what she was trying to convey.

Goddammit, if we could just talk ...

The door to his apartment suddenly burst open, having been kicked in by the murderous madman from the street. The one who'd brutally beaten the men outside. Why, of all apartments, why had he chosen this one?

There was no time to question the situation; the situation had already arrived full-force.

The woman leaped out of the way and the madman tackled Richard to the floor. The air was pushed from his body and he desperately tried to reclaim it with little success. The madman was on top of him, just as he had been on the man down on the street—the dead man he had brutally slaughtered with his bare hands.

The madman raised his fist and slammed it into Richard face, and a stream of warmth flowed down his cheek. Jesus Christ, what was wrong with this guy?

Richard watched in horror as the madman raised his fist again, only this time Richard managed to move his head out of the way just before contact was made. He used this slight advantage to grab a hold of the madman and fling him to the floor. Richard scrambled to his feet, picked up a barstool by the kitchen counter, and swung it around just as the madman was standing back up. The hard wood of the seat cracked loudly against the side of the madman's skull, and he immediately collapsed to the ground, body limp. A puddle of blood quickly formed underneath his head.

"Holy shit, holy shit," Richard tried to say, *"I just killed him."*

He dropped the stool and just stood there for a moment. He had never killed someone before. He had gone his whole life thinking he would never have to, and yet now he had, and it could never be taken back.

Dear Lord, what has happened to the world?

The woman slowly walked out of the kitchen, leaving her hiding spot, looking at the corpse in utter horror. Her whole body was shaking. In her hand she gripped a large steak knife.

It's okay now, Richard wanted to say, *the bad man is gone.* He held out his arms, hoping that she'd embrace him.

Embrace him she did.

He didn't realize the steak knife was in his stomach until he was laying on the ground, looking at the ceiling. Suddenly there was a pain deep in his gut, and everything felt warm and wet.

What? Why?

No ...

The woman stood above him for a moment, crying. Then she turned and ran out of the apartment, leaving him to die with the man he had just killed.

Had he frightened her that badly? Jesus Christ, he was just trying to protect them. Why would she do such a thing after he'd saved her life? What was *wrong* with her?

Now he was going to die, too, and for *what?* How utterly meaningless of an ending. He hadn't done anything wrong. He was a good person, dammit. He didn't deserve this.

Body growing numb, he discovered a cell phone on the carpet beside him. Weakly, he picked it up and looked at the screen. It must have belonged to the dead madman next to him. He wouldn't need it any longer.

Richard looked at the screen. It was a series of text messages from the madman and a woman named Laura.

ME: Where the hell did u go?

LAURA: A man took me

ME: What man???

LAURA: Idk. He just took me.

ME: WHERE??

LAURA: The building outside. Apartment 5B.

ME: I'm on my way.

LAURA: Help me. He's in the bathroom but I think he's going to rape me. Please hurry.

Richard threw the cell phone across the room. It exploded against the wall. His gut felt like it was on fire.

He began to laugh, and he did not stop for a very long time, despite the fact that no sound left his mouth.

~ ~ * * ~ ~

He passed out. When he came to he heard singing. A man—not on the radio either, but somebody inside his apartment.

Somebody was singing.

Richard stirred into a sitting position, grabbing at his bleeding stomach. The pain was immense, like the ocean.

There was a man in the kitchen, going through his cabinets. The man took out a bag of sugar and turned around, startled to see Richard awake.

Richard looked at the man a good while. He recognized him.

It was the deaf-mute from down the hall. Hautala.

And he'd been *singing*.

What in the hell?

"Oh, hello there," the deaf-mute said. "I hadn't realized that you were actually alive, sorry about that. You see, I made tea, but clumsy me forgot to buy sugar this week. I trust it's okay if I go 'head and borrow some?"

Richard shrugged. Nodded.

Hautala grinned from ear-to-ear. "Excellent! Thank you very much, friend. I went ahead and called an ambulance for you, but there wasn't exactly much of a response on the other side. It sure is quite the day, is it not?"

Richard just looked at him. This wasn't happening.

Hautala grinned again. "Well, I guess I'll be off. There is just so much left to accomplish, now that … well, you know. God, for the first time in my life, it feels *good* to be alive!"

He didn't just walk out the door, but skipped. Singing the whole time.

Just as he entered his own apartment down the hall, Richard heard the deaf-mute shout, "Thanks again for the sugar!"

10. FALLING IN LOVE BY CHARLIE JACK JOSEPH KRUGER

Sprawled near the middle of the muddy ravine was an old television. Not old enough to be completely obsolete, and not cracked or shattered. A television like you might find in any number of living rooms throughout the world. Except this one was half buried in muddy water.

I thought about the story it could have told me.

If it could have talked I am sure it would have told me about how it was thrown out before its time, and now it sits here in mud, collecting the general filth of nature, waiting for its next chapter to begin. Maybe it cries every night, wishing someone would clean it and watch it lovingly again. Or maybe it is happy to be free from the shackles of slavery that appliances are forced to live in while in use.

Who knows …

The television just lay there. Caked and crusted with months of rest and slumber.

Rust. Beautiful.

A little ways away there were some tires. Only two. Neither one looked similar—they were clearly from different cars—and the mud and grass built up around one of them showed that they hadn't arrived at the same time, either. I looked at them with the same sort of adoration and confusion as I had the television. Who had dropped off the first tire? Who had thrown a tire into the mud and tall grass? And more importantly, who had thrown the second tire there some time later? Why here? Why here behind the industrial buildings of this run-of-the-mill city?

I didn't have an answer, even though I was dumping something here.

I just stood and thought, next to the little ravine. It was a picture that I didn't dare take. It was too real. Too beautiful. No camera could capture the feeling of the place. The concrete sewage pipe jutting from the cold wet ground; the cracked pallets stacked in the tall grass; the strange refuse that found its way to this rubble burial ground. This wasn't the kind of thing that I could take some pictures of and then show people. This wasn't my beauty to take pride in. Maybe that was why I liked it so much … maybe that's why I chose it.

As someone who lies to the world daily, and tells everyone I am a healthy human, it is important for me to understand just what you do as one. I have always seen it in looking at things and finding normalcy through them. Getting used to the limitations, and adjusting happily. Being okay with your lot in life. You look at a child eating ice cream and you find beauty in it. You look at a wildfire and find revulsion. You look at good things and you feel good, but then you look at bad things and you are supposed to feel bad about them. Learned behavior. You look at the world and catalog the emotions that you see. But you don't notice you are cataloging it at all—you just do it. That is what being healthy is. Doing everything I do to fit in, but not doing it to fit in … doing it because it comes naturally. When I do it, I'm painting pictures to show the world. I love to do that. I love to find things that are so simple, and so astounding. But here, this location, this wasn't something I couldn't show anyone. I could never capture the smell of the cold air, the wet concrete, the mud, and the grass. I could never capture that brisk taste of broken glass and industrial paint that filled the muddy ground. I could only take pictures. Take. That is the word that made it impossible. I couldn't create this. I couldn't even get credit for it. I could only *take* the credit. I could only *take* the picture. *Take* the beauty …

Everything I added to the place helped make it all grow, but I didn't make it. I never brought the television, I didn't make the place a burial ground for hopeless refuse. I just came to adore it.

So I just looked at it.

It looked so calm and gorgeous. It looked just like I imagine my heaven will.

I felt guilty for the first time ever. Just looking at the beautiful scene, I just kept taking from it. I never gave anything back. I didn't make it more than it was.

That was why I brought Alia.

I walked through the tall grass, looking at the cigarette butts and foil gum wrappers. She didn't think it was as beautiful as I did. But she was so young, she couldn't understand. She thought those shows on the television in her house were beautiful. She hadn't wanted to leave them when I came to get her. She was too young to appreciate such beauty. She didn't understand it yet. But I thought she could make it all better.

And look at how right I was.

I looked at the occasional liquor bottle. I smelled the stones and shattered concrete that swam in the mud and thick waters. I tasted the grass, those thick, straw-like strands. I felt the wet floor under my feet. I took the whole place in, little by little. This was my childhood and this was my future. This was my city and this was the home I had run from.

This was all at once, what I left and what I had come to. Alia turned her nose up at it. She didn't see the beauty in this dumping ground.

I took a seat on a huge concrete slab that had been dropped partially in the ravine. It was cold and moist with rain and dew. I let it soak into my faded jeans. She asked to go home. She wanted to see her parents. I told her this place was home now. I told her she would have everything she needed here.

She cried. So I hit her.

The sky above me was the same color as the concrete that surrounded the mud and grass, all one blended canvas of grays, browns, blacks and greens. It was brightly dark to look at. And it was darkly bright too. You could say. Her voice was so loud for a second. Then she joined the bright darkness. My hands were wet against her face. I wrapped her up in the garbage bags I brought and weighed her down with stones. Just knowing she was there, in the water next to that rusted bike … it made the place even more beautiful. I gave back to the photograph I loved.

I sat until time found me. Until I could hear the creak of the rest of the world grow to a deafening roar. Until the painting started to crack and curl. It is hard to gauge just how long that is … but it felt long. That is something I am sure of. In the distance a siren wailed. It must have been looking for Alia. She must have been missing. I would have missed her. It wouldn't find her though. She was my gift to the Mecca in front of me. I had given this beauty such a thoughtful gift.

This place, complete with me watching it all, was beautiful. This was more than a simple nude photograph, stolen from a dream. This wasn't another picture: this was the only picture. This was the memory that had to live on.

A faint neon glow over the tops of the trees far in the distance was a constant reminder that a bowling alley and strip mall waited for your money and time just over the mud and scum. A sort of post it note that reminded you there is even more scum once you pass this place.

This place was my own little living picture. So I stayed for longer than I should have. I looked at the black water where Alia was. I looked at the things the mud and concrete held secret. I looked at the different shards of glass: the green and brown, the clear, the thick, and the thin. I looked at the plastic cigarette pack wrappers dancing in the light wind around with the tall yellowing grass. I looked at the television in the water again. I looked at Alia again. She was the girl I had always wanted. You know that beauty and figure that you create in your little boy mind? That sadosexual smell of desperation? The shape of eroticism, made cold? The one that had breasts and lips just the way you like them. The one in that sweater. The one that has the smile you have never seen on a real woman. The one with the perfect form, which she somehow still thinks is fat. That garbage bag-wrapped girl in the mud and water was the perfect girlfriend.

And the tires were the bride's maids.

And the old television was the priest.

I continued to survey. The rain that crept around the clouds and jumped down at me didn't stop me. The cold wind and the lowering sun didn't deter me. I was on my honeymoon.

Then my phone rang.

Just like an alarm clock in the perfect relationship, my dream was ruined. I woke up and looked at who was calling me. I was told to make sure I brought home milk. It is always milk. It always seems to need to be brought home. Like a runaway dog. Like a rebellious teenager. Milk is a constant reminder that things don't work out.

I looked back at the black water, holding the bride I had wanted to spend the night with, and her decaying castle, built around her. She was no goddess now. The tires were muddy and cold. The television looked like every ex-girlfriend: a little too cracked in the wrong places, mean, confused, alone, and heartless. It was just a shell that baked itself in mud and scum.

I said goodbye to my bride. She was just another woman now.

… The bus ride home would have been beautiful if I hadn't already seen it all.

I wanted to try again. Alia wasn't right. Neither was Nicole. Or Donna. Or Tessa. Or Elisabeth. Or Annalisa. But I would just try again. Wait a few days, let Alia settle down with the others. I would find the right queen for my castle. In the meantime I would go home to my wife and children, pretending I was normal. Painting pictures for everyone else. Dreaming about my castle.

I felt like a whore.

11. DEATH COMES TO US ALL BY JULIANNE SNOW

I wake to the smell of smoke, claustrophobia washing over my senses. I cough, trying to expel the acridness from my lungs; my body only succeeds in sucking more of it in.

I reach up to cover my mouth, my left hand coming up short against a hard surface. As I slide my palm upward, I feel the roughness of it and smell the subtle scent of pine over the smoke.

As I panic, I wonder where I am. I can tell I'm lying on my back, but have no idea how I got this way. My hand reaches my face and I clamp it over my mouth and nose, trying to filter the smoke through my trembling fingers.

My lungs don't cooperate, sucking in heaving lungfuls of tainted air. I know I'll likely die from its inhalation, but I make the choice to not give up. Yet. Even with all the cards stacked against me, it might not be my time…

My right hand begins to explore my prison in an attempt to find some means of escape. I pull the neckline of my dress over my nose, thinking to use both hands in my search, and am surprised to find myself wearing my most formal of outfits. My mind wanders for a moment as I remember the last time I wore it: my father's funeral.

The day had been a sad one for some, but I look back on it fondly; an odd reaction, some might say, but my father and I never got along. And it was for good reason. I had felt the force of his fist at the bottom of a bottle more times than I cared to remember.

Bringing my brain back to the moment, I try to figure out why I'm wearing it. The dress that is. Too formal for a night out or a day at my menial job, it made no sense.

I move my legs, hearing the clack of heels on the surface beneath my feet. Nothing makes sense to me. My mind feels foggy, and isn't helping me figure out why or where…

I feel it for the first time. The heat washes over me and while it's not uncomfortable, it warms my panic-stricken nerves. And it makes sense given the smoke crowding the air from the space around me.

At least my powers of deduction are still working. Heat typically accompanies smoke. Not that it makes me feel better. In fact, it triggers the opposite effect as my panic rises. I smile. A peculiar reaction for sure, but one I cannot seem to help. I feel like I've lost my mind.

What is going on? Nothing is making any sense. Why am I dressed for a funeral and trapped inside a box?

It hits me like a ton of bricks. I'm in a box. And it is probably on fire. But why?

The question niggles at the back of my brain as I struggle in earnest against the sides of the box. My mind might be playing tricks on me, but I swear the sides are getting hotter. They burn as I push and scratch.

I hear the crackle and think I'm going crazy. If only I could wake up, all of this would be over. I would find myself at home, in bed, hazy from a night spent tossing and turning in a nightmare. I plead with my mind to rouse my body, but from the lack of light peeking through now open eyelids, I know I'm not dreaming.

The brightness blinds me for a moment. Then realization sinks in. My prison is getting brighter and I can now see the confines of the box. I can make out the rough surfaces, the splinters primed for attack if the opportunity arises.

I start to fight against the boundaries of my confinement, feeling the heat begin to rise. The first lick of flame on my ankle causes my legs to recoil toward the farthest side of the box.

The searing pain imprints on my mind, singing my already frazzled nerves. The agony robs a few breaths from me as I struggle to pull my legs away from the blinding heat. But I cannot pull them far enough away and I feel the painful lick of each flame as they climb up my legs.

My mouth opens and I scream—a terrified, pained howl of anguish. It sounds foreign to me, like I am removed from the situation but I feel the strain in my throat as I swallow more of the blistering smoke. Tender tissues scorch, ending the shriek in short order.

The wooden surface below me becomes unbearable, and I squirm in response. But I can't get away. There is no room, no place to go. I'm trapped.

I continue to fight, tears vaporizing before they can fall down my cheeks. The pain is intense, growing monstrously until it consumes me—until that moment my brain hides the agony of it from me. Then, blissfully, it's over. I feel the fire bubbling my skin, but I can't feel the pain. It's peaceful, and euphoria swims over me. My arms drop back to my sides and I feel an odd sensation akin to wind, but I know it's the flames. Eating me. Consuming the flesh I need to exist.

I smell my hair, an awful burnt smell I will never forget. My lips feel chapped and when I try to wet them, my tongue dries in response to the flames.

Then darkness. I am aware of myself and then idyllically unaware. I wish I could tell you the moment I ceased to exist but I can't.

It's just over.

12. PIECES OF GOD by Chris Robertson

"I thought this only happened in movies," said Dan.

"Not today," replied the dark-suited man behind him.

Dan turned from the closed and powerless elevator doors and looked toward the fellow trapped with him: a stranger approximately his own age. "No offense, but after the day I've had, this is hell."

Dan looked at his watch: 6:50 p.m. Not good. The building would be nearly empty at this hour on a Friday.

"I was looking forward to a martini, not this." He gazed at the stranger, looking for shared frustration at their improbable circumstance.

"No, Hell is different than this." The stranger paused to chuckle. "Have you ever wondered why the powers of both good and evil traffic in human souls? Doesn't it seem like an odd *modus operandi* to you?"

Dan was in no mood for ridiculous conversations, but did not feel he could ignore this man trapped with him. "I suppose," said Dan. "I've never really thought about it. I just went to catechism like they told me to. Can't say as though I found it particularly stimulating."

"I have a theory," said the stranger. "Would you like to hear it?"

Dan grew slightly uncomfortable at the man's stare. A kook, surely, but what was the harm in talking to a kook while trapped in an elevator?

"Yes, I suppose. But hadn't we better try to call for help or find an alarm button?" Dan ran his hands over the panel, pushing and pulling at corners. "No, there's nothing. We'll have to use our cells."

The dark man neither moved nor spoke. Dan dug out his phone, then paused. "911 do you think? This is an emergency, right?"

"I've seen worse," said the peculiar man, his smug tone suggesting a stifled chuckle.

~ ~ * * ~ ~

"There," said Dan, triumphantly returning the phone to his pocket. "They're going to phone building management and maintenance. I predict twenty-five minutes."

"Phoning your wife?" asked the stranger.

"Not married," said Dan, but his companion barely let him speak before starting in again.

"It is peculiar, don't you think? That God should want the souls just as badly as Satan? Perhaps it's all a ruse."

"I wouldn't know," said Dan, not hiding exhaustion.

"I'm totally fucking serious," said the peculiar man, and the new emphasis in his tone seized Dan's attention. He looked upon the stranger fully for the first time. They were approximately the same height, both dark haired, with similar body types and dress. The odd doppelganger leered back at him with that same smug stare.

"Souls. It's all so logical if you think about it. They are *pieces of God*. Each one of them. Every person walking the earth carries a miniscule fragment within them of the strongest power in the universe. That is why they are desirable."

Discomfort filled the air between them. "That's an interesting theory," said Dan, staring at the stranger and forcing a smile as the hairs on his arms and neck stood on end.

"Oh, it's more than a theory. There is an occasional empty vessel launched. There have been births in which the fragment of God was inexplicably absent from the tissue. True sociopaths—some of the worst rapists and serial killers to ever walk the earth. But why does God want them returned to his possession? I'll tell you. With each soul he obtains, his strength is reinvigorated. Perhaps launching them in the first place was out of his control. Some sort of rule of nature … "

Dan stared, his exhaustion forgotten. "And Satan?"

"What of him?" replied the man with that peculiar smile.

"What, then, is his motivation?"

"Why, the same as God's of course: the attainment of power." The smug face altered a bit, the gleam in the man's eyes brightening. "With each soul he too becomes more than he was. And perhaps one day his power will exceed that of the creator."

Dan swallowed, sensing an unseen abhorrence churning beneath the skin of this handsome stranger.

"Like your ex-wife, Linda. She might be coming my way. In fact, she's working on cumming right now." The Evil leaning against the elevator wall looked upon Dan with intense satisfaction. "And do you know what she's thinking at this very moment, as she's penetrated by new cock? She's feeling joy from the fact that it isn't *you*."

Intensity lingered in the closed elevator, hanging thickly in the air.

"What are you?" asked Dan. The question was little more than a whisper.

"You know." The stranger smiled, his teeth repugnantly dry and white. "And what about you, Dan? Would you like to make the bitch feel regret like she has never known? You could experience such pleasure and attain such power that she would yearn for nothing but your return. Would that suit your desires?"

"Lies," whispered Dan through his confusion and fear. "I can't believe anything that you say."

"Not true—in fact, I'm not allowed to lie. Not while bartering for souls. Do you know what heaven is like? It's like being emasculated. Like swallowing four Valium and lying around feeling neither pleasure nor pain. Heaven lacks all semblance of true joy."

"And Hell?"

"It's where the fun people are," remarked the devious being leaning against the wall.

"And the serial killers and rapists too I suppose," said Dan.

"They are the vast minority."

"But they are there."

"You're on the path there anyhow," said the stranger. "Why not commit yourself ahead of time, and feed all of your deepest desires before you go? Linda's pretty, but she's an aging brunette. When is the last time you had blond pussy?"

The thing across the elevator peered at him with interest, awaiting reply. Perhaps he was not omniscient, thought Dan. Perhaps he truly did not know.

"Seventeen years, at least, but then some I suppose …" Dan's gaze meandered to the floor in thought. "… It seems like such a distant dream, like something I imagined."

"You can do much more than imagine it tonight," said the stranger with that familiar tone of enticement.

"This is all so overwhelming," said Dan, and he heard the note of pleading in his own voice.

"I cannot lie," said the embodiment of evil. "Not while I barter. Here …"

It reached out its hand, palm facing the silver ceiling. Dan stared, heart pounding in horror and anticipation, as the skin between that thumb and forefinger bulged, then protruded; the mass of flesh elongating and darkening in color. Soon a thin black disc seemed to hover over the hand. The stranger plucked it, detaching the disk from the skin where it had emerged, and held it aloft.

"Communion," said the strange and handsome thing. "Partake of my flesh and every thirst you have now will be quenched."

Dan hesitated. It was all so much to absorb … and then he thought of Linda, feeling joy from a touch that was not his own. Heat suffused his face as his heart beat faster and faster—and suddenly he relented, extending his right hand to take the dark communion. The smug face leered at him as his thoughts extended beyond his ex-wife, to new pleasures soon to be had. With uncertainty Dan placed the disc upon his tongue …

The elevator suddenly shook with restored power and Dan turned numbly to the doors. He chewed the sinuous material and realized a question he had not yet asked.

"When does my soul transfer ownership?" he said, then swallowed the unholy offering.

A chill came upon him, as though a great breeze blew right through his skin and left him chilled to the bone. His exhaustion was gone … along with something else he could not place. It seemed to him as though he now perceived … the imitation of something he had once known. Some sensation he had once felt.

The silver doors parted, revealing the beautiful blond hair of Beckie from Marketing.

"Oh, hi," she said, and then smiled. He did not remember her ever smiling at him before, and it seemed to him this should have made him feel … something.

"Hello," he said with newfound confidence and charisma. "We were stuck for a bit, but it seems to be fine now."

"We?" she said, then looked at him, slightly puzzled.

Dan turned and saw, without surprise, the three vertical walls of an empty silver box.

"A figure of speech. Come on, it's Friday. I've got a martini to get … can you join me for a round?" He said this with the imitation of a smile, and pushed the button for the lobby once she had entered.

They waited out the summer storm in the basement. Three table lamps with tall, aged linen shades created warm circles of light in the dark, farmhouse cellar. One sat on the small bookcase next to Aunt Amy, rocking in the corner. Her reading glasses teetered on her hawkish nose while knitting needles clinked a counterpoint rhythm to the creaking chair. The second shone from the end table between Uncle Roy's afghan covered leather recliner and the boy on the couch upholstered in a faded weave of burnt orange, harvest gold, and avocado green. The third lamp stood on the heavily polished walnut, HiFi stereo console, guarding the doorway to the "Off Limits" part of the basement.

Bobby licked the last bit of chocolate from his fingers and brushed crumbs off his flannel shirt. Aunt Amy's fresh baked cookies masked the dank cave smell coming from the forbidden side of the cellar. "Uncle Roy," he scolded, trying to make his seven year old voice sound more grown up, "that doesn't go there!"

"Oh really?" teased Roy. "And where do you think it should go?" He gave his favorite nephew a comical, befuddled look and buttoned his blue cardigan against a chill.

Bobby grabbed the puzzle piece and placed it in the upper right portion of the nearly completed picture on the coffee table. He bounced back on the couch with a triumphant smile. Uncle Roy winked, touching the side of his own upturned nose with his pointer finger. The whiff of burlap from the sofa spurred childhood memories; wrestling matches with his older brother, Wayne, on this very sofa until Dad threatened spankings, tornado warnings on the radio while Mom cuddled his little sister, Kathy, in the rocker to keep her from crying, playing Monopoly and card games with his brother through long, thunder filled nights. Bobby reminded him so much of Wayne, he reminisced. The way Wayne was before that one storm, before the troubles.

Lightning flashed and the radio belched like a ravenous grizzly bear, disguising sparks from the wall socket under the stereo cabinet. Rain slashed at the tiny windows. The whole room shuddered with the rolling thunder. Bobby's face paled, accentuating the smattering of freckles across his upturned nose.

"That's getting closer." Aunt Amy grinned, readjusting her yarn and needles. "I counted three Mississippi, what about you, Bobby?"

"I—I—I forgot to count," he said sheepishly, his color coming back but his wild eyes darting around the room like a cornered rabbit. Odd clunking sounds came from the dark, restricted area, louder than the static and local news from the old speakers. Bobby steadied his fingers enough for a sip of hot cider from the grown-up coffee mug. There was always one big thunderstorm that sent them to the cellar, every time he visited the farm, he thought.

"Maybe you should check the furnace, honey?" Amy said, resuming her rhythm. That stubborn gray lock of hair escaped her braided bun and swung like a pendulum across her soft jaw line. More thuds and hoarse mechanical barks echoed from "Off Limits."

"Give it a minute, dear," sighed Roy. He winked at Bobby again and reached for his steaming cider under the lamp. *Thump, thump, puff-**woof***, bellowed from the back. A hint of sulphur and stale dryer lint crossed the basement bonus room. "There, you see? Nothing to worry about," he said slurping sips through his graying mustache.

Earlier that evening, Bobby had peeked from the doorway as Roy lit the finicky pilot light on what the old man called the "cantankerous crusty contraption". Bobby had heard it called many other things when his uncle didn't know he was eavesdropping. That side of the cellar still had a river stone wall behind the black iron furnace and corroded sump pump. The bare bulb swinging from the sagging wood beam didn't reach beyond the laundry corner and tottering stacks of tools and chests. He'd caught the glint of wet rocks from the glow of Uncle Roy's long match and furnace flame.

Bobby placed his cup under the lamp, just as another round of lightning flared through the windows. Two seconds later, the foundation shook. The radio announcer rattled off county names, severe weather alerts, tornado warnings, and lightning strike sites. The boy wiped his sweaty palms on his jeans.

"Gonna be a long night," Roy said tousling the boy's brown curls. It reminded him of another night in the basement years ago.

That was the Tornado of '54. Their township took all the lightning strikes while Jefferson City caught the tornado. Wayne had a blackout, then seizures during the furious climax of the storm. He babbled all night about people dancing and jumping rope around a huge bonfire with train cars for logs. Wayne swore on the family bible with cold, steady hands and bulging eyes, like steel bearings on bone china plates, that the lightning told him. "Sky talk" was what he called it. Roy could still see the sweaty brown curls framing that fragile, ashen face. The next day they learned a power line had fallen on the local diner. The newspaper ran a photo of volunteer firemen grappling with hoses around the flame engulfed converted railroad car. Every thunderstorm brought more wild stories from the boy. Mom and Dad took Wayne to special doctors, at least once a week, until just after the New Year. Preachers from every church in the county came to the house and examined Wayne like doctors. One time, two grim priests came to the house and talked about exercising demons. Roy had laughed at the idea of horned devils with pointed tails doing sit-ups and push-ups, but Dad actually shoved the priests out of the house and bolted the door. They even had visits from a couple of psychics in colorful silk turbans with scary black eyes. Neighbors stopped coming around and avoided anyone in their family when they went to town.

The next summer, Wayne had to stay three months in the asylum, but Mom and Dad told everyone he was visiting Uncle Joe in Minnesota. No one talked about his time away, or the scars on Wayne's temples, but he wasn't quite the same after he came home. He never smiled or joked or laughed anymore. He always seemed half asleep, with sad, hollow eyes. Roy had been scared and shied away from this empty, soulless version of his older brother. Roy quit sharing the bedroom with Wayne, sleeping on the living room sofa instead, and still felt pangs of guilt. He was devastated by what the family insisted was "Wayne's deadly barn accident" one year later.

A crackle of static brought Uncle Roy back to the present. "You ready to keep watch with me?" he said, shaking off the memories. Bobby straightened up like a little soldier and nodded. "Amy, darling, do you have the candles and everything ready?"

Click, clank, growl, p-purr emanated from "Off Limits." Bobby jumped.

"All ready, honey," she sang, needles and rocker never missing a beat. She winked at the boy, "One day that sump pump is going to give me a heart attack!"

Bright, blue-white light blinked with the radio's scratching static like Morse code. The lamps flickered off beat, and a second later the rumble rattled in. "Better finish this cowboy puzzle before the lights go out," Roy said steadily, waving at Bobby before placing another piece in the puzzle.

The males hunkered over the incomplete rodeo scene, taking turns to fill the shrinking gap. The sump pump shut off, and Amy's steady rocking soothed the stereo's squelching stutter.

"I've got it! The last piece!" Bobby proclaimed, beaming like he'd won first prize at the county fair. Uncle Roy cheered and Aunt Amy silenced her needles to lean over and watch the grand finale. "Here it goes!" Bobby snapped the piece into place with his pudgy pointer finger.

Blinding lightning strobed into the room. Everything shook like an earthquake.

Bobby froze.

The basement looked like a frame by frame, slow-motion, black and white movie, flickering from Uncle Roy's rickety projector on a rain streaked wall. Bobby couldn't move his arms or legs. He couldn't speak or scream. It was as if he was, and yet was not, part of the movie. He could only move his head and eyes. It was the basement, but not exactly the same, somehow silent and frozen in black and white blinking bits of time. The puzzle picture was different! Now it showed a burning house with firemen and fire trucks. He jerked his head, searching for Aunt Amy. The broken, burnt rocking chair was toppled on the floor. The stereo cabinet shimmied like a rocket ship, sparks shooting out from underneath. He looked through the doorway into "Off Limits." A wild, black wolf with flaming eyes was barking and dancing around a rattlesnake in a puddle. Bobby searched the flashing scene; he couldn't find Uncle Roy or Aunt Amy. Then he saw a pair of skeletons sprawled on the smoking, charred staircase.

Suddenly, everything went black. Bobby counted three shallow, raspy breaths before he could see again.

He was still touching the final puzzle piece with his fingertip. The basement was in color again. Everything was normal. Aunt Amy smiled and resumed her knitting. Uncle Roy's weathered hands gripped the worn arms of his brown leather recliner, "Better get the camera, we want to show off this one!" It was as if the strobing scene in the quaking lightning had never happened. Panic filled the boy like an explosion.

"We gotta get outta here!" Bobby shouted, his steel-blue eyes wide with fear. "NOW!" he screamed, grabbing his aunt out of the rocker. Uncle Roy sprang from his chair. Bobby drug Amy toward the stairs. She struggled like she was tethered to a raging bull.

"Now wait a minute, boy!" growled Roy, wrestling his wife free from the wild child.

Bobby scampered up the stairs, backwards like a crab, staying just out of reach. "NOW! We've gotta get outta here! NOW!" He roared the commands.

He turned and ran up the steps, bursting through the bolted door as if it was a curtain. The old couple scrambled after the frantic boy all the way out into the freezing rain.

Lightning blasted the corner of the old farmhouse. The running trio were knocked off their feet as the ground rolled with the shock wave. Hail pounded down from the angry sky as they rose from the mud and huddled together. Flames exploded from the tiny basement windows, blending shards of glass into the hailstones, and knocked Aunt Amy off her feet again.

Half an hour later, they were wrapped in saddle blankets in the barn. Approaching lights from the firetrucks twinkled up the road. The wailing sirens barely audible against the storm and raging fire.

"S-s-sorry I g-grabbed you, Aunt Amy. Did I h-hurt you?" Bobby offered, his timid voice breaking.

"No, child," Amy crooned, fingering wet brown bangs away from his tear swollen eyes. She gave him a little hug and kissed his forehead. "Don't you worry about me."

Roy kneeled down, eye to eye with his nephew. His large, gentle hands steadied the boys trembling shoulders. "How did you know, Bobby?"

The boy's face went white, "The lightning showed me. I swear, Uncle Roy, the lightning showed me. Kinda … kinda like sky talk."

"All right my young apprentice, let's get a move on!" Professor Nickels shouted as he leapt from standing pillar to standing pillar, ignoring the darkened recesses far below them. The portly man, as miniature as he was in stature, never seemed to have any problem moving along in the strange halls of ancient architecture. Jake, on the other hand, was hardly happy with jumping between the wobbly stone pillars over who knew how far a drop.

"Professor Nickels, how exactly are we going to get out of here?" Jake called, sweating as the column he stood upon shifted beneath his weight.

"That's the thing with most ruins of ancient Olmec origin m'lad, they often have two entrances, one on each side. Supposedly the ancient Olmec, and to a lesser extent the Aztecs, believed this place to be the nine hells, better known as Mictlan. At least, that's what the bottom is called. That's where all of the souls were supposed to reside at the very least."

"And we want to descend into Aztec hell, why?"

Professor Nickels backed up, giving Jake plenty of room to land. "Elementary my dear Watson! The Olmec and Aztec were renowned goldsmiths, and they would no doubt decorate their final resting place with some pretty convincing artifacts to a couple of curious explorers such as us."

"So we're coming down here on the hope that these long dead people left gold lying around?"

"It is a fair assumption. A good number of Aztecs fled into these very tunnels when Cortes came about, fearing he was a vengeful god coming to bring about the end of an age. In a way, they were right."

"Fat lot of good it did them," Jake grumbled, holding his electric lantern high to shed light down the rest of the tunnel. Cobwebs and intricately carved stone floors and walls were all that greeted him. "Is it strange that we haven't come across a single skeleton yet?"

"What's that?" Professor Nickels asked, walking forward as he pulled a pipe from his inner jacket, slowly packing it with some leaves.

"I mean, you said a lot of people came down here right? Well, where are they?"

"I imagine they died of starvation deeper in, or fell into the depths we just traversed." Professor Nickels replied, pulling a match from his breast pocket and lighting it along the roughened edge of his pipe before sticking it into the bowl. Puffing a few times, he heaved a sigh. "Let's keep moving, shall we?"

"I guess …" Jake said a bit uncertain. The bulky, short-haired student had little choice in the matter as he was doing this to maintain his scholarship with Texas State University. He'd taken Professor Nickels' course and had somehow flunked it, but the diminutive man had offered him a choice: either retake the class or go on an expedition into Central America, all on the professor's dime.

It'd seemed like a no-brainer at the time.

Now it seemed like it would have been better to have just taken the class in the coming fall, as exploring the ruins of ancient civilizations with this man was maddening! He had almost no regard for personal safety, carried a pistol on him at all times, and seemed to find a way to irritate almost every person he spoke to, all in their native tongue. How many languages the small man spoke, Jake couldn't even begin to guess.

He gave up counting when he heard the fourth one.

The long hall slowly turned into a slope, gradually on the decline. After a while the slope turned into rough-hewn steps that the professor took two at a time. Jake was having trouble keeping up with the little man, huffing and puffing, when he first heard it. The tinkling of stones falling on each other, of slate grinding against slate.

"Professor!" Jake said in a hushed whisper.

"What?" the professor replied in an equally hushed tone, blowing smoke rings slowly.

"I think I heard something."

"Oh you most definitely did."

"You heard it too?" Jake asked, surprised.

"No, but I know there has to be something down here guarding whatever treasure there is to be had."

"Guarding? Like some kind of monster?"

"Well, monster is kind of stretching it … I suppose you could call it such a thing, but that is such a broad characterization I don't think it's exactly fair."

"What?"

"Fair. You know, giving the creature due justice for its own unique status in the world? I went over all of this in class. See, this is why you failed, you never listen!"

The tinkling echoed once more, slate stones falling from someplace high and breaking on their way down. The tinkling was joined by the clack of something hard upon stone. Looking behind them, Jake could just make out the edges of a shadowy lump crawling out of sight, back down the corridor from which they came.

"Professor … what did you say about guardians in class?" Jake asked slowly.

"If you'd managed to listen, I said they were generally the remnants of the civilization, be they undead or constructs left behind to keep people at bay. Now in this region, you have to worry more about the undead than anything else—and with the Olmec, whoo boy did they get creative."

"Creative?" Jake said, dreading the word.

"I went into a set of ruins once where some skeletal archers had been sealed on a second floor, and rained down rusty arrows on any that tried to pass through the atrium. Damn good aim too, I have a scar on my shoulder if you'd like to see …"

"No Professor, I don't want to see your scar. I want to know what is behind us."

The small man smiled, puffing on his pipe, giggling as smoke drifted down around him. "The same thing that's in front of us, my boy. A very grisly demise followed by a decidedly painful reanimation into the guardian that patrols these halls."

"How can you possibly say that and stay calm?"

"Because I'm smoking coca leaves, that's why. Very soothing."

Jake stopped, turning to look at the man with wide eyes. But his eyes didn't stay on the professor for long, as they soon beheld something far worse than a drug-using midget.

Clacking and clambering down the hall was a roiling wall of spinning, twisting bones of hundreds of humans, none of which formed a whole skeleton. Instead, the swarm roiled like a tidal wave down the narrow tunnel, dozens of skulls bubbling up to the surface to scream with unholy delight, their eyes blazing red as they surged onward. Long arms, made from multiple tibias and ending in long fingered hands drug the mass along, while clattering maws of ribs with snapping tongues made from elongated spine snapped at the very air around them, seeking something soft to sink their sharpened edges into. Hundreds of individual hands crawled like spiders along the wall ahead of the swarm, scouting out as they leapt from wall to ceiling to floor.

Jake screamed, pulling the pistol from Professor Nickels' holster, aiming into the oncoming swarm of calcified bone, firing three rapid shots. Nickels continued to smoke, watching this all passively as he adjusted his glasses and smoothed back his brown-and-grey hair.

The shots blasted apart a skull, fractured a rib, and shattered a spine, which sank into the swirling mass of animated bones—only to be replaced seconds later with unbroken pieces. The skulls howled in their ancient language, the noise echoing down the long tunnel.

"Come on Professor," Jake said, reaching out and grabbing the man's hand, dragging him along as he ran from the advancing onslaught of stretched bones and sharpened claws.

They pelted down the steps, coming out into an open cavern, high enough to where they couldn't actually see the floor. The steps were held aloft by high columns of decorated stone, while great spires rose up around them. Hearing the chittering of the creatures behind him, Jake grabbed the professor around the waist and began running down the steps as quickly as he could, hoping to find an area where the swarm of bones wouldn't go. Looking back as he turned along the crumbling stairs, he watched as the opening to the tunnel they just exited exploded with a flurry of movement, the grasping claws and packs of skulls chattering as the massive centipede of bones surged forth like a skeletal tsunami, coiling around the stairs and the columns as they moved along the path. Great fans of interlocking hands and wrists allowed manta-like wings to flap up and down as the swarm steered itself along the narrow pathway.

"Professor, I think I see the landing just below us!"

"Indeed you do my boy, keep running!"

Sprinting down the stairs as fast as he could go, Jake only looked over his shoulder to stare at the swarm of bones as they swirled ever closer, countless skulls snapping at his heels while hands raked softly along his back, desperately trying to get a hold of him. The landing was in sight, a small passageway leading deeper into the tomb that was what Jake was looking for!

Leaping from the last three steps, he landed just at the opening with a sickening crunch, his ankle snapping like dry timber. Tumbling forward, dropping the professor in the process, Jake turned onto his side, aiming the pistol at the writhing storm of bone as it reared up like a serpent ready to strike.

"Move back Professor," Jake said, casting a sidelong glance at his diminutive friend as he stood up, brushing off his slacks as he did, pipe still smoldering between his teeth. "Try and get in the tunnel where they can't reach you."

"Oh they'll be able to reach me, but they won't try." Professor Nickels said with an air of authority, walking out and toward the swarm, garnering its attention.

"What are you doing, get away from there!" Jake yelled, aiming the gun and firing two more shots into the mass, to no effect.

The swarm focused on the professor, several spines lacing out sinuously to pat him down as skulls leaned forward and gazed at him with their ember filled eyes. Roaming hands moved around him, poking at him as they hopped to and fro. Slowly, the swarm moved up into its coiled position, the skulls casting a baleful glance at Jake.

"What?" Jake said, amazed that the undead terror hadn't attacked the professor.

"The Olmec and Aztec would never attack one of their own. The easiest thing to do was smell like royalty, or one of their priests. Thus, the coca leaves," the professor explained, puffing on his pipe as if to showcase his point. "This thing has yet to attack me."

"What do you mean 'yet'?" Jake asked, staring at the mass as it slithered closer, bony arms dragging the mass forward.

"Oh, I come down here once a decade or so, and return with a few choice artifacts that I can use to write papers on for a few years … you know, keep up the academia and whatnot."

"So you knew what was down here?" Jake demanded, looking at the professor with growing hate.

"Oh yes. I didn't expect you to last this long to be honest, but that bit where you grabbed me must have gotten some smoke on you as well. The creature is mostly docile at the moment … though I doubt that will last much longer."

"And why is that?" Jake spat, holding himself up on his elbows in order to stare at the professor, his eyes darting to the eldritch horror crawling ever closer.

"Oh, the Olmec and Aztecs believed in blood sacrifice," Professor Nickels replied, pulling a knife from his pocket and expertly throwing it into Jake's leg, causing the young man to yell out in pain. With blood bubbling from his wound like water from a font, the swarm moved swiftly, slamming into him with the force of a train, a multitude of arms pulling Jake up into the center of the mass, surrounded by skulls, their crackling ember eyes glowing faintly enough to create a dome of bright red light.

As he hovered in the air, arms holding him from all directions, Jake groaned as he saw a maw of ribs open up before him, hundreds of hands pouring forth, chittering in anticipation of the meal they were about to have.

"God I hate graduate school …" Jake muttered just as the arms pulled him in, spearing him with sharpened ribs, hands roaming over him, stripping him of flesh and muscle. Below, Professor Nickels puffed on his pipe, casually watching the blood dribble down over the yellowed bone, chunks of red meat falling through the cracks of the swarm.

"Hmmm … now what to take home this time," Professor Nickels said, leaning down to pick up the electric lantern and his pistol, holstering it as he checked over the dropped items Jake had left behind. Looking up, he smiled as he watched the red skeleton slowly get split into separate parts, being pulled around in the swarm to fit the needs of the host creature. "Pity … that was one of my favorite blades."

15. THE BALLOON MAN by Justin Hunter

Steve stood, swaying drunkenly, then turned his head, slumped forward, and ran through the open bathroom door to crash full into an immense, heavily muscled black male. The man was clothed in a rumpled brown suit, stained down the front with flecks of vomit. Ham-sized hands hooked Steve under the armpits and hefted him to his feet.

"Are you here for me?" Steve was so terrified he could barely mumble the question. The man said nothing, half-carrying, half-dragging Steve out of the bathroom and dumping him on the living room floor. Steve watched as the man bent forward and tore a large section of carpet up with his bare hands. Under the carpet were lengths of carpet tack board and plywood. Stabbing blunt, sausage-sized fingers through the board as if it were nothing, the large man tore away the layer of flooring.

Steve gazed not at his destroyed living room, but at the floor. Removing the plywood revealed a trap door, ancient and grey with mold. Steve hadn't known his home to have any sort of basement. He hadn't known anyone to place a trap door in the middle of their living room, let alone have a floor built over it. The door looked antique. Not beautiful, by any stretch, but very old.

"This house was built in the fifties," Steve mumbled. Curiosity for what was within battled, head to head, with his dread of the door.

"This is much older." The deep bass voice of the black man startled him. The man reached into his suit coat and brought out a medium sized hempen sack which he put over his own head, pulling the drawstring tight. The trap door opened with a bang, revealing stairs leading down into darkness. Steve found the strength to run, terror overwhelming his shock, but the black man caught him before he'd managed a step, grabbing him by the hair and slapping him so hard Steve felt his brain dash against the inside of his skull, then fell limp in the man's arms. The man cradled Steve like a child and walked down the cellar stairs, the light from the living room fading from view as they went down and down. Soon all light was gone, but the man holding Steve moved with sure steps down the stairs that never seemed to end. Finally the descent was over. The man knelt and laid Steve on the ground, then Steve heard him stand and move back up the stairs. The footsteps receded, leaving him in complete silence and darkness.

"Would you care for a balloon?"

Candles flickered to life in all directions across the floor. A myriad of soft flames flickered from candles suspended in the air for endless miles above. Steve covered his eyes even though the candlelight was soft. A low laugh emitted from bruised lips, and he wondered if he were going insane. A monstrously large and starkly white-skinned man stood ten feet away, his back turned. He was nude except for thick straps about his ankles and wrists. Thrust through one of the straps was a slip-knotted webbing of strings attached to a cloud of balloons hovering over his head, a cluster of colors, shapes and sizes.

"Would you care for a balloon?"

"Please let me go," Steve pleaded. Sweat streaked the balloon man's back and ran down his pasty, moderately hairy skin.

"Selling balloons has always been how I made my living." The balloon man plucked a yellow oval from the pack and held it aside. "My father sold them before me, and his father before him. While growing up I balked at what my father did, especially as a teenager. It was embarrassing to me. But with age came wisdom. I couldn't find work, so I grudgingly worked alongside my father. What I expected to be a long and boring experience was actually filled with happiness. Everyone smiled at me. People who bought my wares left happy. Children flocked to me with unabashed joy. Who would have thought a bit of latex and pennies worth of helium could bring so much happiness to so many? It's just a balloon after all. Right?"

"Let me go."

"Do you remember Michael?" The balloon man queried, and Steve's mind flooded with images of a freckled college student with wispy blonde hair. How many years ago did he hook up with Michael? Two? Three?

"I remember."

"He was the first one you slept with after you knew you were HIV positive."

"He was." Steve clutched his chest. It was beginning to burn.

"Michael died a year ago." The balloon man let go of the string holding the yellow balloon. Steve watched it fly up into the galaxy of flickering candlelight above.

"He did?"

"Yes," The balloon man said. "There were many more. Remember Tim?" The balloon man pulled a small blue balloon from the glut and allowed it to float away. "You infected him. He's dead too." Before Steve could reply, the balloon man tore more balloons away from the large cluster and sent them flying. "Remember Don? How about Joel or Nicholas? Do you remember that one night you took that homeless guy home after you had too much to drink and couldn't score a trick for the night? You gave him a bed, but he didn't get it for free, did he?" The balloon man ripped balloons from his arm in a frenzy. The string knotted and coiled. He rent the strings from him as if they were a nest of rattlesnakes. "Do you remember Titus? Jeremy? Brian? Debra? Whoa, how did she get in there? What about Thomas? What about Ryan?"

The balloon man ripped so hard three of the fingers tore off his right hand as he removed the last glut of balloons from his arm. Blood poured to the floor. The balloon man's eyes were wide with fury as he shook the pack of balloons in Steve's face.

"What about all of these? These are all the people that slept with those that you infected. They didn't know they were killing these people. Did you think your actions ended with one fuck at a time? All of these belong to you. All of them. And you didn't even get the pleasure of fucking them before you killed them with AIDS. What a fucking loss this must feel for you!"

The balloon man turned and faced Steve. Pressed against his body, strapped to wrists and ankles, like a spread-eagled, sore-ridden living skeleton, was a man. The man's open eyes stared wildly all around. Huge, scabbed, pus-leaking wounds covered the man from head to toe. He seemed to have lost all flesh on his bones.

"Phil." Steve stared at his last mark in horror.

"I thought you'd remember Phil," The balloon man said. "After all, he is the most recent of your victims. He's special to us as well. Open your hand Phil." Phil opened the claw-like fingers of his left hand and dropped a deflated balloon. The balloon man nodded to the flaccid piece of latex at his feet.

"Would you like a balloon?"

"No," Steve said. "Please, God no."

"This one is yours," The balloon man said. "Phil doesn't want it."

"No," Steve groaned. The balloon man walked forward, bending to pick up the green balloon on his way toward Steve. Phil quivered against the large man's chest as he moved, jouncing like a marionette made of plague. Behind him and all around Steve, other men came. They wore suits of black, brown and grey. They came in staggered lines through the darkness and into the candle light. Their shoulders pressed together. Each wore over his head a tied hemp sack. None could be distinguished from the other. Gloved hands lifted Steve from the floor, shoving him toward the balloon man. He fell hard against Phil, who writhed against his bonds. The balloon man shoved the green balloon into Steve's mouth.

"Blow it up," The balloon man said. "It's yours."

Steve began to blow up the balloon. After inflating the balloon slightly from his first breath into the musty latex, his lips clamped down and he couldn't release. The balloon inflated more with each breath. As it grew, Steve felt his body weaken. His flesh sank rapidly. His muscles deteriorated. His lungs burned and threatened to fail. Sores ripped along his skin all over his body. He felt his spine contract and he was bent forward. When the balloon was fully inflated, the balloon man leaned forward and plucked it from Steve's mouth, tied it off, and gave it to one of the hooded men, who walked back into the darkness, the crowd parting before him.

Steve looked up from the floor, in an all-consuming hell of torment and pain. The balloon man smiled down on him. Phil, fully whole and healed, buttoned up his suit coat and pulled a hemp sack over his head, tying it off with a pull-string around his neck. He stepped into the crowd of others and was lost among them.

Slowly the men dispersed. The balloon man turned and walked after them, his flaccid penis bouncing against his left thigh as he went. The candles flickered out one by one. Steve lay on the hard, earthen cellar floor and wept. He wept for his sickness. He wept for himself.

16. THE HERO, THE FAIR MAIDEN, AND THE LUNATIC BY PETER ADAM SALOMON

The bride lifted the veil to wipe a tear away. She smiled.

She was always smiling. Laughing. She had a wonderful laugh. She even laughed during his vows.

I laughed as well, there in the shadows where I watched.

"Bobbi," he said.

I didn't know his name. No, I knew his name, I'd just forgotten. On purpose. It began with a B, I think. Didn't matter.

"You've made me a better man," he said. Still talking. He talked too much.

She wiped another tear away. She smiled. The light reflected off strands of hair escaping around the pristine white of her veil.

"You are the other half of me," he said. "The better half." She laughed.

I laughed, there in the shadows.

She smiled.

It was time for her to say his name.

I covered my ears, long enough to miss his name on her lips.

"You've made me a better woman," she said. "I never thought I'd find myself again." She wiped her eyes. Deep blue, full of love and laughter.

I'd drowned in them once.

I was still in there somewhere. Lost in her eyes.

"And then you rescued me," she said.

He laughed. She laughed. The people filling the church laughed as well. They all knew the story. The brave police officer rescuing the fair maiden from the lunatic. The reporters called the officer a hero. Politicians pinned a medal on his chest.

~ ~ * * ~ ~

The lunatic had stalked her, the story went. Stalked her for days and weeks and months and years.

Then, one dark and stormy night—it was always dark and stormy in stories, it made them more terrifying—on that dark and stormy night, the lunatic had broken in. Had to have broken in. The fair maiden would never have opened her door to the lunatic. Would never have invited him in. Would never have given her heart to the lunatic.

The lunatic broke in one dark and stormy night. The lunatic threatened. The lunatic attacked. The lunatic raped. The fair maiden cried out. She screamed his name.

The hero broke down the door—which, of course, should already have been broken down if the lunatic had broken in, right? But dramatic tension required the hero to break down the door in order to rescue the fair maiden. And the fair maiden needed to be rescued. After all, the lunatic was threatening. The lunatic was attacking. The lunatic was raping.

The hero broke down the door. He never called the crime in, never waited for backup. There wasn't time. The fair maiden was screaming. The hero climbed the steps, his flashlight beam cutting through the dark and stormy night. Gun in hand.

The lunatic drowned in her eyes. The lunatic never returned, lost in the waves.

The hero rescued the fair maiden. Shot the lunatic in the back. The lunatic collapsed, blood dripping down to land on the curls of her hair, her laughter nothing but a memory.

~ ~ * * ~ ~

"With this ring," the Priest said.

~ ~ * * ~ ~

The wound had never healed. Still hurt if I moved too quickly in the time since I'd been shot. I'd been warned it would hurt. He'd told me it would hurt. I couldn't remember his name. I'd blocked it out.

It had hurt, when he'd shot me. Even knowing it was coming, even expecting it, tensed up against the sting of the bullet, it hurt. I'd been so focused on her eyes, drowning in them. I was never supposed to notice her eyes. Or the way the light caught the curls of her hair. Or the way she smiled when she laughed.

I was only supposed to scare her. Just a little, enough so she needed rescuing. He'd paid me to scare her. He'd paid me to threaten her.

He knew every detail of her life. Where she'd be every moment of every day. He'd stalked her for days. For weeks. For months. For years.

He watched her every movement, wherever she went. He watched her at work. He watched her at home. He watched her take baths every Saturday night. Studied the way she liked the water temperature just right. Dipping just a couple red-painted toes into the water to test it. Then sinking in. She'd sigh, he said. She'd sigh and she'd smile and, best of all, she'd laugh.

Her whole body flushed red when she'd laugh. He showed me thousands of pictures. Her skin wet and soapy-shimmery from the bath. Thousands of videos. Her bedtime ritual of lotion and creams. The special occasions when she'd entertain a guest. The really special occasions when she'd entertain herself.

He'd follow her guests, he told me. Ticket them for speeding or for failure to use a turn signal or a broken taillight. He knew where they lived. He ruined their lives when he could. He sent pictures to wives or arrested for trumped up charges or, once, poisoned the tomatoes growing in their garden.

She never knew why so many of the men in her life seemed to have problems, shrugged it off to her terrible taste in men. What else could it be, to have everyone she dated turn out to have arrest records or horrific divorces or secret lives they kept hidden not only from the world but, apparently, from themselves as well. Of course, no one believed them when they claimed innocence. After all, who would frame someone for poisoning his son with arsenic-laden vegetables?

He told me where she'd be. He told me what to say to get close to her. He told me what she looked for in a date. He told me what she liked to do at night. Where she liked to go. What food she liked to eat. Her taste in wine. Her favorite dessert.

He paid for the first date. He paid for every date. He never told me that what she was really looking for was me. How could he have known we'd be right for each other?

She was delightful. Glorious. Beautiful, yes, she was that. But she was vulnerable and curious and talented and more. But that was just a part of her.

She was brilliant and sweet. Kind and independent, precious and perfect.

He never told me to drown in her eyes. I did that on my own. I couldn't help it. She was everything I'd ever wanted. And she was, for that one brief moment, mine.

After the hero shot the lunatic, he showed the fair maiden the photographs and videos and computer files of the lunatic's obsession. The lunatic had stalked her. The lunatic had been obsessed with her. For days and weeks and months and years. The hero had saved her. Had rescued her.

And she believed him. The lunatic was just one more terrible choice in her history of terrible choices in men.

The hero was different. He was always there, supportive as she cried on his shoulder all those lonely nights after the lunatic had been shot. The hero helped her find the truth. He found proof, entered it into evidence.

The lunatic was arrested.

~ ~ * * ~ ~

"I do," the fair maiden said, wiping away a tear with the sweetest laugh I'd ever heard.

"I do," the hero said.

"I do," the lunatic whispered in the shadows, yet more pieces of his heart dying with the words. Still drowning in her eyes. Still hearing her voice tell him she loved him, still remembering the way she smiled when he said "I love you, too."

~ ~ * * ~ ~

The bullet missed his heart, but killed it anyway. They diagnosed him with depression and a dozen other lunacies. They strapped him down. They medicated him. They found him not guilty by reason of insanity.

The hero spoke at his sentencing. Asked for leniency.

On weekends they'd let me out for good behavior. I'd stay in a halfway house filled with criminals and junkies. They all looked at me funny. Kept their distance. They called me a lunatic. Shot in the act of raping the woman I'd spent my life stalking. They knew the story. They're even making a movie of it, the greatest love story ever told. A real life hero saving the fair maiden from the lunatic.

I wonder who they'll get to play me?

~ ~ * * ~ ~

"You may kiss the bride," the Priest said.

The hero—I can't remember his name—lifted her veil. She smiled. It lit up her eyes.

Her lips were always shiny. Shiny and soft. It's hard to explain. She was so soft.

Probably from all those lotions and creams every night. He watched the videos over and over again. Ten, fifteen minutes of spreading lotion over her arms and legs and everywhere else. A different cream for her face. Every night.

He laughed. Told me that someday he'd be the one applying the lotion. I didn't believe him.

The hero kissed the fair maiden.

People clapped. A thousand people or more. The greatest love story ever told.

~~**~~

Depression isn't the proper word. I'm not depressed. I'm too numb. I would have to be able to feel something to feel depressed. I feel nothing. I'm still drowning.

No.

I drowned.

Yes, he paid me to seduce her. But, I'd have done it for free.

She loved me. I know she did. She told me so the night she took me to bed for the first time. The night I was shot.

Now I'm nothing but her stalker, her rapist. Her lunatic. She testified against me.

I never broke down her door. The hero did that. I never forced her. The hero did that, too, didn't he? She fell in love with her rescuer so I guess it's not rape.

Is it?

Is there a term for what he did? Fraud? Is it even illegal to win the fair maiden's heart by saving her from being raped?

Who'd ever believe the hero set it all up?

I'm not depressed.

I just have nothing left to live for.

I know what she does every night. I remember everything he taught me. All the notes he showed me. I remember her schedule. I remember where she lives. I remember the tree branch he used to stand on every night.

I never stalked her.

So help me God.

Until now.

~~**~~

I watched him take her wedding gown off. Piece by pure white piece. She laughed. He smiled as he rubbed her lotion on.

~~**~~

The lunatic knew things about the fair maiden the hero never knew. He knew the way she whimpered when kissed softly, the softer the better. He knew where she wasn't ticklish. And he knew where she hid her house key.

The lunatic never broke the door down.

~~**~~

The house smelled like her. It felt like home. The couch where we'd
sat after our first date. Where we kissed for the first time after our
second date. The kitchen table we'd had a dozen dinners on.

I reached her bedroom door. No need for a flashlight, I knew the
way.

The door was unlocked. The hero reached for his gun but I'd passed
his holster on a chair downstairs. I smiled when I showed him the gun in
my hand.

The fair maiden screamed.

I think they'll have to change the ending of the movie. No one wants
to see the lunatic kill the hero. No one wants to watch the groom die on
his wedding day. No one wants to remember the way he died, begging
for his life and telling a truth the fair maiden refused to believe.

~ ~ * * ~ ~

She cried at his funeral.

She laughed when they sentenced me to die.

"Money's on the dresser," Mark Coolidge said, lighting up a cigarette.

Clarissa put on her red cocktail dress and grabbed the money, leaving a trail of scent hanging in the air. He recognized the scent—something cheap, he recalled, but with a pretty name that he just couldn't seem to remember. She glanced over at Mark, her brown eyes robotic. Mark laid on the bed. His skinny chest was bare and he wore socks and dress slacks.

"How long you been married?" Clarissa asked, bending to grab her high heels.

"Twelve years," Mark answered, as he gazed straight up at the ceiling.

"Any children?"

"No." He hesitated. "She's barren."

"Do you love her?"

"Of course."

"I see." Clarissa rolled her eyes. "How do you think she'd feel if she knew you were fucking call girls in cheap hotels?"

Mark looked over at Clarissa. His eyes flashed a bit of rage but soon filled with remorse. "She'd divorce me."

Clarissa gave a nod and left the hotel room. He sat up, placed the cigarette in the ashtray and called his wife in Chicago.

"Hello?" said Jill.

"Hi, sweetheart." Mark's voice shook.

"Baby, how are you, my sweet?"

"I'm good." Mark's voice lowered.

"I'm so excited you'll be coming home tomorrow; I've got a surprise set up for your birthday."

"Oh." Mark choked. "Really?"

"Yeah, I can't wait to give it to you."

"Can't wait," Mark mumbled.

"Bye baby," Jill replied.

"Bye."

"Thou shalt not commit adultery," the pastor on television shouted.

The television had clicked on, right as he was saying goodbye to his wife. "To save yourself, you must repent, or burn in the lake of fire!"

He walked to the television and clicked it off. He was walking back to the bed when the set turned back on. "Repent, sinner," the television hissed. It was Clarissa's voice. Her face appeared in the static. Her eyes were red. Her tongue was forked, like a snake's. He let out a base-filled scream and lunged at the television. He fumbled around for the knob and tried clicking it off.

It would not turn off, and Clarissa continued cackling. "Sinner, repent or die!" Over and over she taunted Mark.

"Shut up, shut up, shut up," Mark insisted, frantically fighting with the knob.

The knob would not budge, as though the damn thing were suddenly made of cement. After what seemed like twelve years, the television clicked itself off. Panting like the dog he felt he was, he shuffled toward the bed and sat on the edge of the mattress. His cigarette still burned in the ashtray on the nightstand. He remembered his wife clutching his hand while the two waited in the hospital waiting room. "You're mother's passed away," Dr. Brown said. "We did all we could, but the cancer spread too quickly."

Mark still felt the warmth of Jill's hand, as she gently muttered, "I'm so sorry."

He remembered her kissing his cheek and then the back of his hand. He'd remained stoic then, but now his eyes began to mist. "What have I done? Am I stupid? How could I cheat on Jill? She's the best woman any guy could have."

His chest heaved and ached. The tears flowed. "I'm so sorry, my God, I'm so sorry, Jill. I'll never do anything this stupid and reckless again."

There was a *click* and the door swung open, revealing a figure in the doorway. Nine feet tall, though the black wings made it appear even taller, the thing crouched to thrust itself through the open door, crowding into the room. Long hair, blonde, though matted with blood, framed a grinning, faceless skull. The body, huge and distorted, was wasp-waisted and huge bosomed, female to the point of being cartoonish but for the giant scorpion's tail visible over its shoulder, weaving about slightly, twitching as if eager to strike.

Pushing into the room with the thing came an invisible cloud of scent, a smell that arrowed right into his brain's recognition center— something cheap but with a pretty name he still couldn't remember.

"Clarissa?" The word was a croak.

The figure nodded, the sockets in the skull no longer containing eyes but burning with a reddish inner light, and raised an axe. "Repent sinner," she hissed. Her tongue, of course, was forked. "Or die! Ha hah!"

"Please, let me go! I'm a changed man. I won't do anything like this again, please let me go!"

Mark leapt off the bed, backing away from the terrifying creature.

"Likely story, but once a cheater always a cheater," she growled, raising her axe and stalking toward her prey.

"You fucked me too," he shouted. "You're just as responsible for me cheating as I am!"

"I'm a succubus," she said. "It's what the devil does."

"You mean, you …"

"No, I'm just his bride."

"Oh shit," Mark mumbled.

He let out a terrified scream, ramming back against the window as the giant creature cornered him. She swung her ax at Mark's head, the blow throwing Mark backward, through the glass. He fell, and the succubus continued to hack away on the poor old sinner.

18. A TRUTHFUL REPORT CONCERNING THE RECENT EVENTS AT SERPENT'S HILL BY CHRISTOPHER CONLON

The recent events at Serpent's Hill have led to a thousand wild, unsubstantiated, and mischievous rumors which have inflamed rather than quelled public passions. It is in the interest of *TRUTH*, therefore, that the present author's efforts, poor though they may be, are directed. In this report shall be found no falsehoods, no exaggerations; nothing but that which is *VERIFIABLY ACCURATE* is included, said verification to have come either from the author's own eyewitness experience or from that of other serious, sober individuals known personally to him. In short form, then, the following represents *THE FACTS OF THE CASE* in the matter of the recent events at Serpent's Hill.

Everyone agrees, certainly, on how the thing began. A gang of coolies, under the direction of the estimable Mr. Leary (known to villagers in this part of the country for his admirable tenor, his rendition of such standards as "My Wild Irish Rose" and "Danny Boy" an event not to be missed at local parties and soirees and surely the equal of such entertainments as are to be found in New York or Boston), was working on clearing the land in and around the abandoned cemetery on Serpent's Hill when a worker named Old Chang—not to be confused with Young Chang, Tall Chang, or Gimpy Chang, all of whom are distinct individuals—plunged his pickaxe into an apparently indifferent heap of brown earth only to find it opening up under his feet, gaping wide and exposing a vacancy which proved to lead into what later became known in the more sensationalistic press articles as the *Devil's Cavern*.

Yet, at first, there was nothing Devilish about it. Further efforts at expanding Old Chang's hole led to the creation of a round opening some eight feet in circumference. The curious Mr. Leary and his coolies stared down into it; initially it simply appeared to be a natural sinkhole—of unusual size, certainly, but otherwise of no especial interest. But this misapprehension did not last long, for one of the coolies—there is disagreement among the Chinamen as to which one it was—soon discovered *steps* that led into the darkness below. There was no mistaking these steps for naturally occurring outcroppings of root or stone; their smoothness and evenness left no doubt that they had been *manufactured*.

Some have claimed that since it was not in the responsible Mr. Leary's billet to investigate obscure subterranean worlds but rather to clear the graveyard and its environs, he should have immediately ordered the coolies back to their work stations, ignoring the admittedly interesting but nonetheless irrelevant discovery. But consider the matter from the perspective of the intelligent Mr. Leary. This was a *completely unprecedented occurrence*; surely to expect him to turn away blithely, and to expect his Chinamen to do the same, conflicts with any common understanding of human nature. Too, headquarters for the Steam Corporation, the hard-working Mr. Leary's employer, lay nearly ten miles back on roads rough for even the best of horses. The new telegraphic devices of which we in the provinces have read so much in the press have certainly not made their way here. No, the resolute Mr. Leary had to make an *immediate decision*; and he decided to investigate the opening in the earth, with the expressed logic that such an opening might severely compromise the safety of the Steam Corporation's proposed Deluxe Hotel & Spa to be located there, or else might prove to be a boon of sorts—perhaps a "Mystery Cavern" could be added to the list of attractions to be found on Serpent's Hill, for which he, the enterprising Mr. Leary, could claim credit along with some small financial compensation.

When the group descended the steps—the brave Mr. Leary manfully in the lead—they found themselves engulfed in darkness. Matches were ignited, and soon enough the coolies discovered a mossy substance upon the walls which, when wrapped around a makeshift torch of root, would burn smokily for some minutes. In that way they made their way down—one hundred and seventy-seven steps in all.

When they arrived they discovered that which the entire world has seen, if dimly, through photographic reproduction in the world's newspapers. Photographs, however, give no idea whatever of the *feeling* of the place. It was a completely manufactured subterranean world, of immense size. The floor appeared to be of some smooth metallic substance, though every effort then and later to break off part of it to take up to the surface for analysis failed. The wall was constructed of this same substance, marked occasionally with strangely shaped fixtures of no discernable purpose. There were other shapes dotted here and there along the floor; long and low, they resembled small metal huts of some sort, but despite the efforts of our best scientists and engineers, no entrance was ever found for these structures which nonetheless seemed to be hollow.

Under the direction of the competent Mr. Leary, the coolies fanned out in twos in order to ascertain the dimensions of this extraordinary structure. They completely failed to do so, for none of them ever reached a far wall. They could walk as long as they liked in any direction and yet never come to the end of the immense chamber, or indeed to any obstruction whatsoever besides the aforementioned metallic huts. The steadfast Mr. Leary bellowed a mighty English "Halloo!" into the darkness, but was greeted by only a long echo. The coolies called out in broken English and in their own language; dozens of echoed reverberations sounded throughout the chamber for some minutes afterward, but no other response came.

It was then that the wise Mr. Leary made the decision to leave the chamber. The coolies were frightened and, as the honest Mr. Leary later told the press, "The place gave me the willies, as well." They climbed the steps again and were relieved to come out again onto the surface of the earth. Darkness had fallen during their time away, but walking around in an abandoned graveyard in the dark of night was infinitely preferable to the bizarre underworld from which they had emerged. Their satisfaction, however, was not destined to be long-lived. Inventorying his work force, the diligent Mr. Leary quickly discovered that two of his Chinamen were missing.

Much discussion ensued between the concerned Mr. Leary and Tall Chang, who served more or less as foreman of the work unit. They called down into the hole and waited hopefully for a response, but none came. Some of the Chinamen, terrified now, gathered together and prayed quietly to their God. It began to rain, and after some time the reluctant Mr. Leary felt he had no choice but to return his workers to the village. This he did, and when the offices of the Steam Corporation opened the next morning he immediately filed a full report of the events on Serpent's Hill.

Needless to say, the officials found the report grotesque and fantastic. Nonetheless, knowing the erstwhile Mr. Leary's reputation for seriousness and sobriety, an investigatory unit was deputized to return to the abandoned cemetery on Serpent's Hill. These half-dozen good and true men accepted their duty with the appropriate solemnity, and made their way thence. They returned with exactly the same tale of an immense manufactured cavern under the earth. It should be noted, however, that only four of the six returned.

The news spread like the proverbial wildfire, and within a day the abandoned cemetery on Serpent's Hill was thronging with onlookers, curiosity seekers, news reporters, and photographers. As there is as yet no proper police force in this frontier village, visitors behaved in all manners. There was no controlling them. Many made the journey down and returned with wondrous tales, some of which were clearly exaggerated. Some claimed, for instance, to have wandered off in a certain direction where they heard *indefinable sounds* of a low, wet, chewing nature. Others claimed to have seen a dim light in the distance of another direction, a light some saw as the deepest blue and others claimed was dark green, a light which made them feel frightened and sickly and caused their vision to be somehow *wrong* afterward. But let it be said now that *NO INDEPENDENT VERIFICATION OF ANY KIND* was ever produced for such stories, and the author suspects that they were the creation of overactive imaginations combined with the intake of alcoholic beverages and the desire to be celebrated as witnesses to something more extraordinary than merely a stupendously gigantic, profoundly mysterious cavern which was nonetheless—empty.

Still, it was undeniable that men had disappeared within the cavern—three more vanished in those first days after the discovery went public, making a total of seven disappeared souls. Theories abounded. They had fallen off a cliff impossible to see in the darkness. There was a noxious gas in portions of the cavern to which they had succumbed. Men took to exploring the cavern only while keeping lines tied to each other with thick, heavy rope. And yet even then, three additional men, securely tied, vanished together soon afterward.

In the meantime the respectable Mr. Leary had been undergoing something of a disintegration. He was seen at the local taverns mumbling about monsters in the darkness and when he was called upon to offer his classic renditions of "My Wild Irish Rose" or "Danny Boy" he would either ignore the entreaties or else get to his feet unsteadily and sing, if singing it could be called, only the first line or two before collapsing in a heap and returning to his drinking. This behavior was extraordinary for the stolid Mr. Leary, and caused much consternation among the townspeople.

As the world now knows, if only in fragmentary and partially inaccurate fashion, matters came to a head on the storm-strewn night of October 31. This was the night that numerous explorers of the cavern are said to have come running pell-mell up the steps, breathlessly gibbering upon their re-emergence of strange sounds, lights, and vibrations in the cavern, the likes of which none had ever experienced and which were, as one such is claimed to have said, "Not right! Not *right!*" One or two of these possibly intoxicated individuals are even believed to have suggested having seen the missing men, all of them, shambling about in the darkness below with their mouths agape and their eye sockets empty of all but the strange blue-green light. But again I must caution the reader that there is *no independent verification for any of these stories.* Those who supposedly told them all left the village that night, and none has been seen again.

That an explosion occurred at Devil's Cavern in the wee hours of October 31 is not in doubt. That its originator was the now deranged Mr. Leary is similarly certain, as is the fact that an extensive collection of dynamite intended for use in his occupation with the Steam Corporation was the method of ignition. What has not been known until now was the unhappy Mr. Leary's motivation—for, as we all know, he died in that same explosion which buried for all time the mysteries of Devil's Cavern.

Yet it was this author who was present not far from the blast and who saw the hysterical Mr. Leary charging up the hill with his burden of explosives, crying, "It got my boy! It got my boy!" The unmarried Mr. Leary was not known to have had children, but this author has engaged in research which strongly suggests that one of the lost Chinamen from that original investigation into the cavern was in fact his son by a Chinese laundress who once worked for his household. As the young man was commonly known about town as "Danny," villagers now find their memories of the talented Mr. Leary's rendition of "Danny Boy" inexpressibly touching.

The foregoing is a *TRUE AND COMPLETELY ACCURATE ACCOUNT* of the recent events on Serpent's Hill. All rumors concerning this grim and tragic matter should be considered highly suspect and are greatly to be doubted, including those rumors that in the weeks since the explosion some villagers have seen strange lights shining up at night through the solid ground on Serpent's Hill, lights which, it is said they claim, are "not right" and cause them to feel nervous and nauseous. Similar reports of some townspeople claiming that the earth itself seems to quiver at times, to shift mysteriously, should be confidently dismissed for the sensationalistic nonsense they doubtless are.

Waiting was the worst. Days turned into years and still the work wasn't finished. There were always more, no matter how many of them were slain. They crawled through sewers and slinked through the ruins of one city after another. As the skies dried out and the land turned arid, they continued to find more to drink and more to eat, sometimes preying on each other. They found new ways to hide, and to fight back. They had started traveling by night to make themselves harder to track. They found ways to lay false trails and even set out decoys to lure the hunters away from their lairs.

Every day there were more to find and kill to clean the Earth.

So they continued to roam the land, until their work would finally be finished.

"What are you thinking about, Ramiel?" he heard his partner ask.

Despite himself, Ramiel was startled. "Why, Forcus, I happen to be thinking about our next day off. How about you?"

Forcus answered, "I was thinking maybe we should start mapping out our kills. We could see if there's a pattern and we might be able to hunt more effectively. This is our third time in New York since Armageddon. We have to be missing something."

Ramiel snorted. "Yeah, we're missing a lot of somethings. That's why we keep getting sent back. Let's go while we still have daylight."

Forcus followed his partner over the ledge and down into the street. He landed next to the hulk of a city bus, tipping it over with a satisfying crash. A cloud of ash and dust wafted up around their heads.

Ramiel cleared his throat even though the dust had no effect on him. "Doesn't your name mean 'Invisibility' or some such thing?"

"And yours means 'Judgment'," Forcus retorted, "Now we just need to make a friend named 'Irony' and we'll be a threesome. Stop asking me questions you already know the answer to. It is tiresome."

"Let's get this over with," Ramiel said as he turned and raced up the deserted avenue.

Almost immediately they came across one walking along eating the uncooked carcass of a rat in the middle of the road. He was so caught up in the ecstasy of his meal he hadn't reacted to the clamorous entrance the pair of hunters had made entering the city.

Ramiel reached out and pulled the pitiful creature's head up away from his rodent feast. Without a word he jerked the skull around backwards, nearly twisting it off as the spine snapped clean. The body dropped dead to the dusty street and they continued on.

"Should we wait?" Forcus asked. "Sometimes they come for the bodies when they are hungry."

Ramiel groaned, "I know they come for the bodies sometimes. Why would you tell me they come for the bodies sometimes? How many years have we been doing this same thing day after cursed day? If there were any around to come for the body, they would have already been fighting him for the rat. Let's keep going."

"Since Armageddon," Forcus said.

Ramiel stopped under a light post in front of a shattered storefront. "What are you talking about now?"

"You asked how long. We've been doing this since the final battle. That's how long."

Ramiel just stared. "That's been years, you realize?"

"Yes," Forcus answered flatly.

"How can it be a final battle if we spend years roaming the Earth cutting down the leftovers?" Ramiel questioned.

"That's the Master's will," Forcus stated. "That's how, and that's why, and that's that."

Ramiel paused and looked into the collapsed department store.

He reached in under the stone slabs as he spoke, "Forcus, you can't possibly be fine with this arrangement. You can't possibly enjoy this perpetual winding down."

Ramiel pulled one out by its ankles, squealing as it struggled against what seemed to it to be an invisible force.

Forcus responded as he assisted by driving his heel down onto the back of its skull: "We've been doing this job since the Great Fall. We were assigned this work since shortly after the first battle. If we were able, we would have long forgotten how many we have taken. Why is it so different for you now?"

The creature's brains painted the sidewalk as the head burst into red soup. Forcus lifted his dripping foot out of the slosh.

Ramiel dropped the feet and started walking again as he responded: "The World is done. The work is done. We've been working clean-up for longer than the Tribulation. You realize a day is 31 hours now because the Earth is slowing down? You realize the average summer temperature is 50 degrees Fahrenheit because the sun is burning itself out? What is the point of this?"

Forcus grabbed Ramiel's shoulder and pointed down an alley. Ramiel heard the voice before he saw the man ranting just around the corner of a dumpster. They started walking down toward him.

Forcus said, "God's will is the point. Everything that lives must die is the point. That's always been the point."

"So die already!" Ramiel shouted. Bricks in the walls on both sides of them cracked at the sound.

Forcus whispered, "He sees us. Get ready."

The man stared right at them and held up his fists in defiance as they approached.

Ramiel continued, "Why all this long, drawn out whimper before the Final Judgment?"

"All must die, and then the Judgment."

"You first, assholes," the man growled and then swung at Forcus. The angel dodged the left hook despite himself.

Ramiel chopped his hand through the man's throat before turning around to exit the alley again the way they had come. He didn't even watch his handiwork as blood gushed out through the man's clamped fingers. He bled from his eyes, ears and mouth as he stumbled into the dumpster before falling to the concrete.

Forcus watched briefly before following his partner again.

Ramiel was saying, "Yeah, I got that. It was all planned since the Creation, God knows all things, it is to the Father to know the day and the hour, mysterious ways, et cetera. My point is that the climax should be approximate to the ending. Why not show us where they are? Or better yet, sweep the Earth clean with fire making way for construction of the New Heaven and New Earth I keep hearing so much about? Or give us a running head count so we know if we're getting close?"

"Maybe your faith is being tested to purge you of your great impatience, Ramiel," Forcus suggested.

"Angels are not creatures of faith, Forcus," Ramiel reminded.

"Clearly not."

They heard the noise of a vehicle and they took flight. The armored car bounced off the wall as it turned the corner with too much speed before regaining the road. They flew along both sides.

Ramiel drew his sword and drove it into the front axle causing the entire vehicle to flip over forward, sliding to a halt on its roof. Forcus drew his blade and began sawing into the metal plating. People were crying and moaning inside.

Ramiel leaned next to a tire that was still spinning.

He said to Forcus, "You do realize all the comforting angels are off duty now while we're doing this every day."

"No one is off duty," Forcus corrected. "They are all praising. Would you rather be doing that?"

Forcus drove his fist down into the opening he had made. The sounds of bones cracking and organs bursting was followed by a dead silence.

They waited by the overturned truck.

Forcus finally added, "Did I ever tell you that I took Jim Morrison?"

"Yes," Ramiel moaned, "you told me."

"Did you ever do anyone famous?" Forcus asked.

"Are you just trying to change the subject?" Ramiel asked.

"Desperately so."

Ramiel actually smiled. "No, not really. I took Mozart's mother, but she was just some girl and he was just a baby. I think it was Elemiah that pointed it out to me later."

"Isn't he the one that always said, 'I send thee to thy maker!' every time he did someone?" Forcus asked. He used a dramatic, inflected voice for the line.

"No, that was Gazardiel. Michael made him stop because some of his kills ended up in hell, so it was bordering on crediting Creation to the Evil One."

"That's right. What was the line Ongkanter always used?"

What they were waiting for finally arrived. A fourteen year old boy crawled out to inspect the wreckage for something to eat. He froze and then turned to run.

Forcus said, "He sees us."

Ramiel drew his sword and flung it. It sliced through the boy's back, spilling his bowels into the street.

Ramiel said, "I hope you and Jesus have it all worked out."

"What?"

"That was it," Ramiel explained as he went to retrieve is sword. "That was Ongkanter's big line."

Later in the overlong day, they followed the sounds of screams to a bridge in the center of the barren clearing that used to be Central Park. There was a gang of thugs standing around a girl that was pinned to the ground under the sweaty body of a man with a bandage over one eye. He continued to thrust while heads began exploding all around him and everyone started fleeing.

"Wraiths! Scatter!"

The angels spiraled out from the bridge, picking off the men trying to flee in the open ground. The screams and grunts under the bridge continued.

"This is the problem, right here," Ramiel declared.

"You mean that they still won't acknowledge the wrath of God even in these final days?"

"No," Ramiel said, "the procreation. Humans are still reproducing despite the slow death of the Earth. It is taking us years to purge them and more young are being conceived and born in their hiding places. We'll never be done."

"I'm not sure this counts as procreation."

They approached the bridge again.

Ramiel said, "The result is the same. Do you want to wait around ten months to see the result?"

"Nine months," Forcus corrected as he stood on the opposite side of the struggling couple. The pace and the tone of the scarred man's grunts increased.

Ramiel said, "Come on, Forcus. They start counting at the women's first missed cycle; not from the moment of conception."

The man took a bite out of the woman's cheek as he continued unaware of the discussion above their naked bodies. The girl screamed and gagged on her own blood as it ran into her mouth. The man chewed his snack and groaned with pleasure.

Forcus said, "No, they count from the last period before conception and it is nine months from then."

Ramiel groaned in unison with the man who was getting louder underneath them. The woman passed out. Ramiel finally drew his sword and stabbed down through both bodies. They ceased in mid-coitus. The bodies bucked one last time as the sword was withdrawn.

"We'll just have to agree to disagree," Ramiel concluded

As they prepared to leave the city, Forcus pointed down at movement in an open doorway.

Forcus said, "You're not going to like this."

Ramiel growled. "Exactly, there is another one born after the end and growing up in the age where all should be dead and judged. That's ridiculous. Where's the justice in that?"

As they swooped down toward her, Forcus said, "She sees us."

~~*~*~~

The seven year old that had been called Lolly saw the shadow monsters coming down from the sky. They had taken her mommy and then the old lady that used to find food for her. Now she was alone hiding from the evil that hunted her.

She ran back into the building and closed the door to the closet. She pushed her tiny body back deep into the corner behind the dead furnace and held her breath as her heart tried to beat out of her chest.

Lolly never heard the door open, but she did feel the cold hand close over her tiny heart. It beat twice more before it was crushed inside her.

She heard the shadow monster whisper, "You should have never been born," and then she was no more.

Crisp, long-dead leaves crunched under Daniela's feet as she made her way through the empty parking lot outside the convenience store. She burrowed her chin into the scarf wrapped around her neck, holding her hair down.

The lights blared from the little shop, sending shivery reflections off her glossy black hair and making her pale, grey eyes fill with neon color. She shook the rainfall from her shoulders and stepped into the heated interior of the store.

Shelves full of bright foil-wrapped snacks and chocolate bars glared down at her, but she deftly maneuvered around them. She either ignored the cravings or had none to begin with.

The sliding glass doors on the refrigerators stood open at one corner of the store, where Daniela stopped short. Nothing to be seen here. She looked about, up and down the long aisle of cold drinks and milk. Nothing to be seen.

Daniela shut all the sliding doors and leaned against the cold glass, eyes dark and brooding despite their unearthly pallor.

She glanced about the store, to either side, and saw no other patrons other than a tiny old woman in grayish, over-sized rags, standing next to the Christmas card display.

The pictures on the cards were pretty and bright, all snowy and glittering in the moonlight, but Daniela had never seen something so white and wintry in reality. Georgia isn't known for excessive snowfall.

Daniela left the store with a pack of cigarettes and a new lighter— one to add to her collection of cheap Bic lighters, long-lost.

She crossed the parking lot and the street in front: no cars, no moonlight because it had slipped behind a cloud.

The girl ducked under the round spotlight of a street lamp, into a yellow circle that flattened the planes of her face and heightened the blackness in her long hair. She fluttered out into the shadows again, drawing her coat around her narrow shoulders.

In an empty hallway with an ugly green-and-gold-threaded runner, Daniela opened the slick plastic wrapping on the cigarettes and slid one out onto her palm. She ducked into her room, locked the door behind her, and let out a sigh of relief. She held her breath then, opening her ears to the household, listening for signs of life.

Nothing.

Good.

They were asleep.

She sank to the floor and stretched her legs out before her, digging her heels into the carpet. She'd shed her coat and shoes in the front room and now wore only a black long-sleeved t-shirt and well-worn jeans.

At nineteen, she looked fourteen at the oldest; though she was almost painfully skinny, her face had never lost that baby roundness, with soft pink lips and thick black brows arched slightly.

The window stood propped open, so she didn't hesitate to flick the Bic lighter on, watch the little flame dance for a moment, then hold it to the cigarette perched between her lips. Another long night.

A few minutes later, something caught her attention outside the door. Clattering noises. She listened intently, ears pricked up, but the sound ceased almost immediately. Daniela held her breath again, not daring to make a sound. She waited like that for many long minutes, until an owl's screech outside made her jump.

Her heart thudded in her chest, making it harder to breathe, and she lay on the floor with one eye glued to the slit between the door and the carpet. Nothing moved in the hallway, but she didn't trust the silence.

She knew they were awake now—that clattering had been a sort of trap she'd set up just outside their bedroom door: aluminum cans strung together on a laundry line and hung where an unsuspecting walker would trip on them.

So they were definitely awake. All her senses were heightened to a painful extent—she could even hear the *drip-drop-drip* of the downstairs bathroom faucet and the barest scraping of the cats' nails on the garage floor. She kept the side of her face pressed to the bedroom carpet so she could catch any sign of movement in the hallway.

For a long while, nothing happened—then they left the room. One by one, the two creatures who had been her parents exited their bedroom, then her brother and sister. She could see only their bare feet and lower legs.

The mother—or the thing that had been a mother in a previous life—crossed before Daniela's door with little sister in tow the rest following after. The hallway lights flicked to life, bathing the carpet with pale fluorescent light and making it white.

They finally moved on, through the hall and down into the stairwell. They'd be going out to hunt, each to a different corner of the city.

Little sister would be with her friends this evening, although the other little girls might not survive the night.

Her father would be in the hospital building—he'd worked as a nurse on the night shift before his death, so he continued his regular work hours, though deaths increased significantly.

Older brother would disappear into whatever part of the city he'd formerly inhabited—gods knew where.

And their mother, more beautiful in death than in life, would haunt the bookstores and the university campus library. Daniela didn't know why, but her mother loved those places—so many abandoned corners, dim lighting, lonely students and book-browsers.

She loved emptiness and solitude.

They were like zombies, but conscious. Every movement was voluntary, even the breathing; Daniela knew they looked nearly perfect, utterly human if you ignored the dead look in their eyes and the rotting stench coming from their mouths.

Yes, they were dead—she knew it well. She'd watched them die, one by one, on a Monday night last month.

Since then, they hadn't rotted much—not on the outside, at any rate. On the inside, gods knew what they looked like. Rotting, organs squelching, falling to bits and eaten by grave bugs.

When the house was silent again, Daniela got to her feet. Her legs were unsteady—they felt like pudding—but she kept her footing. She took the back stairs and slipped out into the night again, onto the back porch. Her family was long gone, disappeared into the night, and she was once again alone with the house.

It was only a matter of time before she would join them, join the walking dead on their quiet rampage through the city.

It was a simple pie that had caused all the trouble. A creamy, pumpkin cheesecake, decadent and a little sickening. Too sweet. They'd all had a share of the pie, taken a little slice and eaten it with a glass of milk.

Daniela had refrained because she'd had such a huge dinner; her family laughed and told her she should try just a little mouthful, but she wouldn't.

And the next morning, they were dead.

Now more than a month had passed while she lived in the same house as those walking nightmares, and she was alone—completely alone.

And the cravings were starting at last, cravings for—pumpkin cheesecake. Creamy, rich, decadent and only half-eaten, it sat in the kitchen downstairs, on a shelf in the refrigerator. When Daniela had woken up that morning, she'd had this uncontrollable craving for pumpkin cheesecake—or any kind of cheesecake, really—and she'd gone down to the kitchen.

Standing in front of the open fridge, she'd gazed longingly at that half a cheesecake.

She knew she shouldn't have touched it, but it looked so appealing and there were only two days left until the expiration date on the box. She couldn't really let it go to waste, even though she knew it would turn her into one of those things.

All day she'd suffered a loss of appetite. Even when she'd forced herself to eat, she'd only made herself sick afterwards. The too-sweet taste coated her mouth and tongue and she could barely drink a glass of water. She'd gone to the convenience store, hoping that seeing all those snack foods might trigger an appetite, or at least a craving, but it didn't work.

Now, alone in the house and knowing that her family could be killing innocent people at this very moment, Daniela felt the first spine-tingling effects of the contaminated cheesecake.

Her insides twisted and churned, growling, and bile rose in her throat. Tasted awful; tasted bitter; she spat out a thin orange trickle and it hung from her lip, pumpkin flavored. It dribbled down her chin and she felt a cold sweat break out all over her back and arms. The jeans and t-shirt clung to her skin, and a chill ran down her neck.

The night closed in on her, consuming her, ruining her mind; visions of cheesecake and gore danced before her eyes in spinning, bright colors. She vomited and it streamed down her leg onto her bare feet— she'd forgotten her shoes when she went outside.

So it was finally going to happen; she was finally going to change.

It came in her mind first, like a pinprick of light, and then this warmth and white, blinding light spread down through her chest and extremities until she bathed in a wash of brilliant light. The tears of anger and humiliation dried on her cheeks, and her lips moved, making helpless sounds.

"I don't want to," she said, but when the energy from the contaminated cheesecake finally let her go, and she fell in a heap to the porch floor, she felt her first craving.

It started like a dull ache in her gut, followed by shivers all over her, under her skin. Then a chill set into her bones and her head swam.

The smell of human flesh rose in the distance, and she went out into the night to seek her prey.

A young girl wanders the streets alone, quiet as a shadow. The night swallows her up. The only sounds that comes from her lips are a soft moaning and the occasional burp, scented with popcorn and lip-gloss and raw meat.

An older woman, grand and elegant despite her years, walks straight-backed up the hollow-sounding stairwell in the east wing of a university library. Her high heels *click-clack* on the stairs. She wipes a red spot from her chin, and it isn't lipstick. One lonely, dead student waits below for a rescue that will come too late, books in her arms and a grimace of pain plastered across her face.

An aging man with a grim expression pushes a gurney down an empty hospital corridor, whistling low and tunelessly while the fluorescent lights flicker overhead. The wheels of the gurney *scritch-scratch-scritch* while they turn, spitting metallic creaking noises into the air.

A teenage girl, black hair in tangles down her back, bare feet scraped and torn with loose gravel, stalks through the night. A long white cigarette dangles from her right hand, caught in a death grip, trailing smoke until it burns up into an ashy cylinder. She smells faintly of pumpkin and cheesecake.

The throbbing, incessant pulsing of his hand reeled him back from unconsciousness.

The world was blurred shades of brown and yellow. Several rapid blinks sharpened his vision, however did not offer any real clues to his whereabouts. He sat facing a wall of knotty pine, old and weathered, with enough gaps between the boards to see it was night outside. Light came from an old hurricane lamp perched on a milk crate. The distinctive smell of kerosene wafted through the air.

Dave looked down at himself. A thick leather strap transected his chest and held him fast against a wooden chair. Thinner straps bound his forearms to the armrests. The *pound-pound-pound* of his right hand demanded attention. Dirty strips of material had been wound around his wrist. They cut into his flesh and turned his hand a mottled purple. Now aware, his brain registered pain in time with the throbbing.

Struggling proved futile. He whipped his head to either side to examine the scant surroundings. It was a small, wooden room, like an old garden shed. A workbench sat to his left, an iron vice the only thing on it he could see. His chair had been bolted to the floor. Although the fixtures looked old, they held fast as he tried to tip the chair over.

"Help!" His cry sounded dull within his wooden prison. "Help! Somebody! I'm in here!"

"Ain't no help for you, boy" a voice rasped behind him. "Not the sort you're thinkin' of anyway."

Wide-eyed, Dave tried to turn to see who the voice belonged to. "Who's there? Who the fuck are you?"

A figure moved in the periphery. A dark man-shape, large, wearing some sort of coat. "Don't matter who I am," a gruff male voice answered. "Only matters who you are." A grunt. "Who you're gonna be."

Dave thrashed against his bonds. "Let me outta here! Let me outta here man!" He stopped struggling. "I won't say nothin', just let me go. Please man, I got nothin' you want. Just let me go, okay?"

His captor stepped closer. The light revealed a leathery, wrinkled face, with dark, glassy pits for eyes. A long, black raincoat ended in a pair of steel-capped boots, so worn Dave could see the dull metal peeking out through the toes. His heart hammered against his ribs like a frightened, caged bird. The man's left hand held a scythe-like, serrated blade, much like one Dave used to prune thick branches in his garden. The right was tucked away in a pocket.

"Oh please man, no. God—what the fuck—God, no, please no!" His words became almost unintelligible as he began to weep. "No man, don't—oh God, please don't hurt me—please!"

"Birth is painful, boy," the old man said. "You're being reborn tonight." He withdrew his right arm from its pocket. A large, black, iron hook emerged where a hand should be.

Dave's terror turned to realization, and he barked a short, nervous laugh.

"Oh, man! You're supposed to be that urban legend? The 'Hook Man', or whatever it's called?" Dave blinked back tears as a smile grew on his face. "Oh shit, am I on some TV show? Like *Scare Tactics* or something?" He looked around. "Who put you up to this? Was it Mitch?"

Expressionless eyes regarded him. Dave laughed. "Damn, you scared the shit out me man!"

The man raised the hook above his head. Dave smirked. "Okay, I get it. You've got a role to play."

The suggestion of a smile played over the Hook Man's face. "My role's finished. You'll pick up where I've left off."

"Seriously dude, I get it. You don't have to—"

Dave choked on the rest as the hook slammed down through his throbbing hand and embedded itself in the armrest.

There was no immediate pain, not even any blood. Dave's mouth open and closed without sound, like a fish out of water.

"Forty years I've been the legend," Hook Man said, bringing the handsaw up. "But my time's over." The saw's wicked teeth rested on the rags round Dave's wrist.

"I'll teach you though. I'll train you."

Sharp points pressed into flesh that was very much alive with sensation. Dave's eyes grew large, staring first at the saw, then at the face of the man who wielded it.

He shook his head, his eyes pleading.

"The legend must live on."

There was a stinging sensation as the saw drew back against the skin, then the white noise of intense pain as its teeth chewed through flesh and bit into bone. Dave howled into the night.

"Don't worry, boy," Hook Man said, grunting with his efforts as Dave screamed. "You'll come around to the idea."

The blade cut through the last strands of tissue. He wrenched his hook free of the chair. Dave's hand remained skewered upon it, its fingers curled in on itself like a speared animal. Hook Man held it before Dave's face.

"I did."

The kitchen was like the rest of the house: small but neat, the counters cleared and clean, the cupboards organized. Even through my annoyance I was aware that everything was just as I remembered it, right down to the elephant cookie jar in the corner and the ink marks marching up one side of the doorframe—an annual record of my growth, from the time I learned to walk all the way through my teens. So many times as a kid I'd sat right at that kitchen table, squirming while my mother administered a stern dressing-down. Who'd have thought, thirty or forty years ago, the positions would someday be reversed?

Though Mom was definitely *not* squirming. I fought down my irritation and tried for a placating tone.

"Look, Mom, you can't keep doing this."

"Yes I can. Of course I can. *She's* the one who needs to stop. We're paying her, aren't we? She needs to do what we say. Aren't those the rules?"

To my right, Joan gave a theatrical sigh as the coffee cup rose to her lips. I shot her a look, trying to convey *I'm sorry*, and *just be patient* with my eyes, trying not to let her see the *you know, you could help here, instead of sitting there drinking my mother's coffee* that I was feeling. She watched me over the rim of the cup, dark eyes unblinking, then put it down and sat back in her chair. She folded her arms and crossed one leg over the other in a very obvious *You're on your own here, Danny. You don't pay me for **this** shit.*

My eyes flicked back to my mother, who, not having missed a thing, raised her eyebrows and gestured, actually *gestured*, toward the visiting nurse. Her own message was clear: *You see what I'm dealing with here?*

Joan sighed again, her dangling foot bouncing with impatience. *Terrific.*

"Mom, Joan needs to assess you when she gets here. That's part of her job, to make sure you're all right. You need to cooperate."

"She can 'assess' me with my eyes closed." Mom's tone was matter-of-fact. "She took my pulse and blood pressure, and everything was just fine until she stuck me with somethi—"

Joan's legs uncrossed and her bouncing foot hit the floor as she stood abruptly. Her deep, rich voice with its slight island lilt was just as matter-of-fact as Mom's.

"I have to go. Your mother is not the only one who requires care, and I have other clients to see this day."

She was already shouldering her bag as I got to my feet, chair scraping across the slightly yellowed linoleum. Part of me wanted to shout *This is ridiculous!* but I knew that would accomplish nothing. Instead, I put a hand behind Joan's back as if to guide her to the door, though I dared not make actual contact, suspecting she would take affront at such familiarity.

"I *am* sorry about this, Joan," I said as we approached the front door.

"It is not you, Mr. Chesterton. Your mother, she is a stubborn one at times."

Quick, harsh words leapt to my lips in my mother's defense, but I managed to keep my voice level, and chose my words with some care.

"She's just having … trouble. Dealing with Dad's death. I'm sorry."

I put my hand on the knob to open the door, but paused a moment, standing a little straighter.

"Joan? One thing. She said you 'stuck her' with something?"

Joan's large eyes, liquid and usually quite beautiful, went flat at my tone, and she held my gaze as she rummaged in her shoulder bag. She brought out an object, small and white in her strong mahogany hand.

A plastic spoon.

"I touch with the bowl of the spoon or the handle's end, they tell me if the contact is blunt or sharp. It is a nervous sensitivity test you may have had yourself at your doctor's office." Her tone was even flatter than her gaze. "No harm was done, I assure you."

I nodded, embarrassed, and opened the door. Without another word, Joan strode through, back noticeably stiff. I closed the door, then took a deep breath that stretched my cheeks as it came out in a frustrated *pufffff*. I turned back toward the kitchen, where Mom waited.

~ ~ * * ~ ~

"Mom, please, you can't keep doing this!"

I realized I was whining as I came through the door. I tried to shift my voice to "firm," and opted to stay on my feet, standing next to my chair to look down at her.

"Joan is the fourth visiting nurse we've had since Dad died—we're running out of options here. I'm sorry if you don't like her, but she's seriously all we can afford right now."

"We," I thought. *"We" is good. Same team. Us against them. Now if I can just get her to stick to the business part of this instead of—*

Mom shook her head, the gesture quick and birdlike coming from her small, spare frame.

"It's not that I don't like her, Danny, but if she thinks I'm going to just drop everything and jump whenever she says jump, especially when I'm with your father—"

"You're *not* with Dad, Mom!" I said, the words sudden, boiling out of me. "He's been dead almost a year!"

So much for "we."

I sighed and closed my eyes, ashamed at having all but shouted at her about this. Especially about this. I opened my mouth to say something—I have no idea *what*—but her voice filled the sudden silence, her tone quiet and so, so serious.

"Ten months, seventeen days. No one in the world knows how long your father's been gone better than me."

I opened my eyes to find her staring at me, not quite crying, though her large blue eyes were filled with pain. I had inherited those eyes, what my father used to call her "smilin' Irish eyes," like in the song. His pet phrase popped into my head, catching me off guard: I had worked so hard to put my own grief behind me, but dealing with Mom when she was like this brought it all back, and I missed him very much at that moment.

I looked into her eyes again. It hurt me to the bone to think my words had put that pain into them, but something had to be done. I steeled myself, preparing to take the hard line despite the lump in my throat, and felt an odd *deja vu*: I was bucking myself up the same way I did when I needed to give my daughter "a talking to." The feeling was confusing, and my next words came out more harshly than I'd intended.

"Well, then you should damn well know he's not coming back."

Her eyes cleared a little at that, and her jawline firmed.

"He always said he'd come back." Her own tone had sharpened, matching mine. "You heard him say it yourself, many times. You can't say you didn't."

My resolve to stay on my feet fractured—it felt like I was scolding her, and that was just too much. I slipped into my chair and pressed my palms to the table, leaning toward her, my voice cajoling.

"Mom, it was a romantic thing to say, that's all. Dad was a romantic guy. I heard him say lots of little things to you over the years. He called you his queen, he bought you flowers for no reason, he opened doors for you all the time—old-fashioned, romantic stuff. You don't think you're really a queen, do you?"

"No, don't be silly."

"*That's* silly? Saying you're a queen is silly, but saying Dad's coming back to visit from beyond the grave isn't?"

"No." Her voice remained deadly serious as she stared at a spot on the table. "It's not silly. Because he is."

"Mom ..."

"He *is*."

I blew out air in exasperation.

"They're dreams, Mom. I asked Harvey about them, and he said it's a natural part of the grieving process. People dream about loved ones that they've lost. Look, I dreamed about the old man myself a few times since he's been gone, but with you it's what, every night?"

I paused to let her answer, but she just stared at that table, her lips a tight line.

"Every night," I repeated, nodding slowly. "I asked Harv about that, too, the every night thing. He said that was less common, but it happens, especially with what he called 'long term couples who were very close.' I think that describes you and Dad to a T."

She nodded slowly, still staring at a spot on the table halfway between us.

"It's a pretty good start. But there's a difference between us and all those people your Harvey keeps talking about."

She finally met my eyes.

"He's coming back. Slow but sure, he's coming back."

I managed not to throw my hands in the air, but I couldn't do anything about the words that popped out of my mouth, high and whiny.

"Awww, Mom!"

She held up a palm, and her eyes made me fall silent.

"It's not just dreams."

I stared at her.

"He still comes to me in dreams; sure he does. We relive some of the best times we had in the past, but we have new good times too, just like I told you. It's not just memories. He takes me to new places, and he shows me new things. We spend time together and talk, and laugh, and do, oh, just everything we used to do while he was alive. None of that's changed, and a lot of times it makes me wish I could just stay asleep, so I can be with him."

"I know that," I said. "That's why we keep going through nurses like this. They all have schedules, Mom; they all have other people to see. I chose Joan because she can fit you into her schedule later than anyone else I could find, to let you stay in bed as long as possible. You said that was a good thing, remember? You said that was what you wanted."

She nodded.

"Yes, I remember. And it *was* what I wanted at the time, but it's not enough now. It's … it's not just dreams anymore, Dan."

I felt my brow furrowing, my face pinching in confusion. I waited a beat, hoping for some sort of explanation, but she simply held my gaze.

"What're you talking about?"

"He's still here, after I wake up. Like he's following me out of the dreams to spend more time with me. Like he's trying to stay. I can feel him."

"Feel him?" Panic rose in my chest, my mind leaping to thoughts of a confused, abused old woman. "What do you mean, like someone's *touching* you or something?"

A shake of the head. A tiny smile.

"No, nothing like that. At least, not yet. But I can *feel* him."

I stared at her, unable to think of anything to say.

"You know," she said, "how every once in a while you can just tell there's someone in the room with you without looking? The room just doesn't *feel* empty? Or how you can be in a crowd and just know someone's looking at you, you feel eyes on the back of your neck or whatever, and turn around to find that someone *is* looking at you?"

"Yeah," I nodded slowly.

"It's like that. But more."

"More?"

She nodded too, hard and fast.

"Yes. More. More … oh, specific, I guess. I can tell it's him. I can *feel* it's him."

She spoke faster, smiling, warming to her topic.

"I wake up from my dream of us being, oh, at the Polar Caves in New Hampshire, for example, and I can feel someone there, lying in the bed next to me. I can lay there with my eyes closed, feeling your father next to me, and I can reach out and almost touch him."

"But you said—"

"I know what I said. Listen to what I'm saying *now*. I can *almost* touch him. I reach out my hand and there's nothing there but the sheet and blanket, or the pillow, but I always have the feeling I *just* missed him. Like the sheets are almost warm. Like if I reach out just a little farther …"

She stretched out a hand as she trailed off, in my direction but not toward me. She reached toward a memory only she could see. I felt tears in my eyes, and though I cleared my throat, my voice was still rough.

"And then?"

Her eyes focused, hand dropping to the table as she sighed.

"And then I open my eyes and he's gone. I can feel him there, *right there*, until I open my eyes … and then he just slips away."

Her hands slid across the table to enfold mine, though she could never completely cover my larger hands with her small fingers. I was struck again by the reversal between this day and so many in my childhood, when this woman's hands would have engulfed my own, and *she* would have been caring for *me*.

Oh my God, I thought. *I'm losing you, too. You're not dying, not like Dad, but it's … what? Dementia? Alzheimer's?*

"That's why I was lying there with my eyes closed when that nurse came in to check on me. That's why I refused to open my eyes. I wasn't ready to let him go for the day. Can you understand that? He's coming back to me; a little more every morning, I think, and I just wasn't ready to let him go for the day."

Her face hardened.

"Then that *woman* stuck me with something! It surprised me, and my eyes just popped open, and *poof*, he was gone. Is it any wonder I was upset? Is it?"

She wiped at an eye gone suddenly wet once more.

"I didn't have the chance to say goodbye this morning."

I swallowed hard as I took all this in and tried to think. She wasn't confused. Well, not about anything but my father. *It's **not** dementia or Alzheimer's,* I thought. *Take Dad's passing out of the equation and she's sharper than me. She just can't bring herself to say goodbye.* I tried to consider everything: what Mom had said, what Marty had said, and the fact that we were down to the last visiting nurse in the area.

Then, quietly, I made myself say what *I* thought had to be said.

"Mom, you said goodbye to him months ago. We all did. Now, I'm not going to tell you you have to get over this—you will or you won't, and you'll do whatever you do in your own time, I know that. What I *have* to ask is for you to cooperate with the people I send to help out, okay? Joan's the fourth nurse in ten months, and if she leaves I don't know if I can get anyone else to come out here. She gets here every day at ten thirty, and that's as late as she can give you. If you haven't said goodbye to Dad by then, well, it's not her fault. For the past three weeks she's been calling me at about ten forty-five to tell me you're still in bed and uncooperative. Please, Mom, I'm asking you to *please* try? For me. Work with her, work with me, *something*, but we have to find a way to make this work, okay? Please."

She sat silent, letting me make my little speech until I was wound down, then sat a few seconds longer, making sure I was all done. When she finally spoke, her voice was resigned.

"All right, Danny. I understand what you want, and I know what I have to do. I'll do it, okay?"

I stared at her, trying to gauge her sincerity. As far as I could tell, she was being as serious as I'd ever seen her. I nodded.

"Okay then. I'm glad everything's sorted out. Thank you. I have to get back to work now. I'll call you tomorrow afternoon and see how you're doing, okay?"

She nodded, tight-lipped and silent, looking at the tabletop again.

I started out, but paused at the door and looked back, trying for a smile.

"And no phone calls to my office tomorrow morning, right?"

She looked up from the table, moving slow and dreamily once more, though her voice still sounded as focused as a laser beam.

"I told you. I know what I have to do."

I left.

~ ~ * * ~ ~

"So I was firm with her, like you said. Gave her boundaries and she said she knew what she had to do. I can't thank you enough. You sure I don't owe you anything?"

I was elated, but Marty just smiled and waved a dismissive hand.

"I've never had an actual patient in my life. I got the psychology degree twenty years ago and went straight into advertising, doing mass-market psychological analysis. I never hung out my shingle—I was just giving you advice as a friend, not as a mental health-care professional."

"Well, pal," I said, "whatever you did, it worked. Worked like a charm, as far as I can tell."

I pointed at the clock on my office wall.

"It's ten fifteen now. Joan gets there in about fifteen minutes. I'd say I'll know how it worked by eleven o'clock, latest. If she hasn't called me by then, everything's gravy."

Marty pulled the small visitor's chair closer to the desk.

"I don't have anything imperative until then. I'll wait with you, if you don't mind. Like I said, I've never had an actual patient before, and

I have to admit I'm curious as to how all this turns out. So tell me …
how, exactly, did the conversation go yesterday?"

Fifteen minutes later I had told Marty the whole story. He'd asked a
few questions, and I'd gone word-for-word as best I could remember.

"So she said 'I told you, I know what to do,' and I left," I said. "I
mean, how perfect is *that?*"

I was all smiles, but Marty was frowning.

"Hmm … I dunno about 'perfect,' Dan. I mean … look, I don't want
to sound harsh or anything, but that doesn't sound all that positive to me.
In the beginning of your talk she sounded very into being with your
father, and there at the end … you're seeing her as saying she knows
what you expect of her, and that's what she has to do. But what if it's
not that simple?"

I sat up a little straighter in my chair, a cold feeling in the pit of my
stomach.

"What do you mean?"

Harvey shifted a bit, still frowning.

"Look … I don't mean to scare you or anything, but all she said was
she knows what she has to do. She never said what she wanted to
accomplish, just that she knew what to do in order to get it done, and
she's obviously having a little disconnect with reality. What if … look,
this is just a thought, okay? But what if her goal is to be with your dad?
Not just for the dreams, or the time afterward, but, like, now and
forever?"

"Wait … you mean …'?"

"Yeah," he nodded, looking unhappy. "What if she means to kill
herself?"

"Ohmigod!" I fell back in my chair like my bones had all clocked
out and gone home early. My eyes flew to the clock. Ten thirty.

"Well," I started, but my voice hadn't gotten the rest of the message
yet and faltered. I swallowed and tried again. "Well, Joan should be
getting there right about now. I'm sure she'll call if there's a problem.
Right?"

Marty didn't answer. We sat there in my office and looked at each
other as the time crept past, silently marking the seconds until the
minute hand pointed straight up: Eleven o'clock.

"Well," said Marty sounding hopeful. "There. You said you'd know
one way or the other by eleven, and it's—"

The phone on my desk rang. Neither of us actually jumped, but we
did stare at it for the second ring, then the third, each unable to move.

My hand shot out at the beginning of the fourth ring, and I jerked the receiver to my ear.

"Mr. Chesterton! I'm so sorry sir, but—"

There was more, but my mind was shutting down by then. I recognized the voice immediately as Joan's, though I had never heard her sound like that before: agitated, almost distraught.

And apologizing?

I forced the world back into focus.

"What? I'm sorry, Joan, start again, please."

"Mr. Chesterton, I got here and the door was still locked. I didn't bother knocking, but let myself in as I have gotten used to doing. I found your mother … sir, I'm so, so, sorry … I don't know what happened, but—"

"I'll be right there!"

I slammed the phone into the cradle and started for the door. Halfway there I remembered Marty, still sitting in the visitor's chair by the desk. I turned to him, opened my mouth to speak, but nothing came out.

"Go." He waved a hand. "I'll tell Jim you're out for the rest of the day—call when you know what's going on, okay? And Dan … I'm sorry, man."

I don't remember the drive to my mother's place. There was a lot of honking—some of it may have even been me—but I got to her place in record time.

I saw the flashing lights from more than a block away, and screeched to a halt behind the ambulance and two police cars. Joan sat on the front steps, an EMT at her side.

"Where is she?"

Joan looked up in surprise, not having noticed my approach. I tried again, louder.

"Where *is* she, Joan?"

She pointed over one shoulder with a shaky finger. "In the kitchen."

I went through the door to find a police officer standing in the living room. He raised a hand is if to stop me, but I kept moving.

"That's my mother in there."

"Sir," he began, when suddenly, to my shock, Mom's voice came through the kitchen door.

"Is that Danny? Let him through, please. Danny? Would you come here?"

I shot the cop a look as I hurried by, feeling the surprise register on my face as I muttered, "What the hell is going on here?" The officer looked away, but dropped his hand to let me pass.

I entered the kitchen to find an EMT kneeling to either side of Mom's chair, her back to me as she sat at the kitchen table, which was set for two. The EMTs glanced up at me, then one went back to pumping up the pressure cuff around Mom's upper arm, while the other shone a penlight at her eyes.

"Mom? Are you all right?"

"I'm fine, dear. Better than fine if I could just get these nice young men to stop hovering over me."

"I'm not worried about them, Mom." I started around the table to face her. "What's going on?"

"I told you. I knew what I had to do, so I did it. It was hard, but so, so worth it."

"What are you—" I began, then recoiled, my hand shooting up to cover my mouth in horror as her face came into view.

The worst part, I remembered afterward, was that she was smiling— actually *smiling*—her teeth showing in a wide grin beneath the red, raw sockets where her smilin' Irish eyes had once been. Blood, both fresh and dry, stained her cheeks as she followed the sound of my whispered "Oh my *God*," tracking me with those terrible red holes.

"It worked. I can still feel him, Danny. You understand? He's still here."

She stretched out a hand, blindly reaching across the table, toward the empty place setting.

"I can almost touch him, and now I never have to say goodbye again!"

23. THERE WAS NO BODY BY MICHELE TALLARITA

Brenda dressed slowly for the funeral, moving around her bedroom like her joints were clogged with sand.

When at last she'd finished putting on the black dress, the black stockings, and the string of white pearls, she stopped in front of the mirror to slather on some makeup. She needed it—badly. Brown half-circles sagged beneath her eyes, which were sunken deeply into her grayish face. She'd spent most of the last two days either crying or sleeping.

"You almost ready?" Andrew said softly, poking his head into the bedroom. He wore the thin, hole-riddled slacks she'd told him time and again to throw away, along with his slightly wrinkled black sports jacket. He'd always been laid back. It was one of the things Brenda liked about him: the way his lax disposition could offset her panicky one.

She smiled sadly, shrugging, as she rubbed white cream beneath her eyes. "I guess."

Andrew came into the room and laid his hand on one of her hips, turning her until they faced each other. Beneath his crinkling forehead, his brown eyes found hers with concern.

"Maybe you shouldn't do this," he said.

"She was my best friend."

"I just think … maybe it's more than you can handle."
"I'm doing this," she said. "I can handle it."

He seemed to take a deep breath. "Okay."

If only Brenda were certain she could handle it. The truth was that she expected to completely lose it when she saw the coffin.

When they were kids, Katie had been Brenda's whole world. They'd done everything together. When Brenda's parents had gotten divorced, she and Katie had stayed up all night crying. When Brenda got dumped by her first boyfriend, Katie and Brenda had had a great time burning everything he'd ever given her. They were soul sisters, partners in crime. Brenda had thought it would always be that way.

But Katie's life had slammed into a tragic end. Death at twenty-seven. A terrible death, Brenda thought. There was no body.

Brenda and Andrew made the slow, heavy walk to the car, then set out toward the funeral home in silence. When they got there, Brenda found her body unwilling to move, as if a heavy lead blanket lay atop her. Sunshine impaled the dirty windshield as they sat in the parking lot with the doors locked. How could the weather be so beautiful on a day like today?

Andrew gave her knee a squeeze. "Don't do this," he said again.

Brenda shut her eyes, inhaling the scents of Andrew's trash-ridden car: stale pizza, cigarette smoke, a hint of mint from the dangling air freshener. The world seemed a wonderland of sensations to experience. But Katie would never experience anything ever again.

"Where do you think she is now?" Brenda said.

"Who, Katie?"

Brenda nodded.

Andrew shifted, the page of an old magazine crinkling beneath him. "Nowhere, I guess."

Brenda's eyes popped open. "You don't believe she could experience any kind of afterlife?"

Head bowed, Andrew shook his head. Brenda sighed and unlatched the car door, stepping out.

The viewing was as awful as Brenda expected: the waxy flowers, the polished wooden coffin, the horde of mourners in black. Brenda cried hard, while Andrew kept his arm draped heavily over her shoulder. Though he'd known Katie just as long as Brenda had, Andrew did not cry, but stared off into space in a detached way. The whole time, the couple spoke to no one, except an acquaintance Brenda did not particularly like—a quiet, awkward man Andrew had had over for dinner a few times. Afterwards, Andrew and Brenda left, heading to the car beneath the infuriatingly bright sun.

"I want to see the grave," Brenda said, once they were back in the car.

Andrew stared forward, gripping the steering wheel even though he'd yet to start the engine. "You know there won't be one, Brenda."

"Then take me to see a grave. Any grave."

"This is ridiculous."

"Take me to a cemetery, Andrew."

Sighing, he started the engine. His features—his thin, fine brows and broad forehead—were tense. Brenda knew the truth: Andrew had never liked Katie. He had resented her, how much Brenda loved her.

After driving for a few minutes, Andrew pulled the car to the side of the road beside a small cemetery: about a hundred tilted gray slabs right there beside the rushing traffic. The grass was overgrown, several old flower arrangements in tatters beside the stones.

Brenda set out into the cemetery without waiting for Andrew to follow. When he'd finally caught up to her, she was staring at a crumbling gray marker whose engraving was too smudged to read.

Hands thrust deep into his pockets, Andrew stared at the ground.

"How could you do this?" she said.

In a barely audible voice, he said, "I had to."

"You hated her."

"I didn't."

"You did."

More silence passed. When Brenda spoke again, her voice was hard with rage.

"I wish you could pay for what you've done."

Andrew laughed, but it was an unhappy sound. "You can't go to jail when there's no body."

She hit him, then, but it was so pathetic—a weak, floppy slap delivered with a thin hand—that Andrew barely felt the sting against his cheek. Did not feel it at all, in fact.

She shoved her face close to his. "I would rather die than spend another second with you."

She stalked back toward the road, her body a collection of jagged angles beneath her baggy black dress. She'd been getting so weak lately. With sorrow, Andrew watched her leave. He would miss her. A lot.

"What are you looking at?" someone said.

Andrew jumped.

But it was just Dr. Graff, whom Andrew had talked to back at the funeral home. Andrew guessed his doctor had followed him here and walked up without Andrew noticing.

"Brenda," Andrew said. "Walking away."

"You're still seeing her?" Dr. Graff said.

"Yes." Andrew laughed. "Guess your meds aren't totally effective, doc."

The doctor scanned the rows of old graves with a glum expression. "I guess not. I don't know if it was the best idea, Andrew. Going to a random person's funeral. I showed up because I was worried about you."

"Katie may not have been real to you, but she was real to Brenda," Andrew said. "Brenda had to grieve somehow, after … I willed her best friend out of existence."

Dr. Graff placed a hand on Andrew's shoulder. "Brenda isn't real either, Andrew. They were both figments of your imagination. Complicated, elaborate figments, but figments nonetheless."

Andrew sighed, nodding. "Anyway, Doc, I don't think I'll be seeing Brenda anymore."

"Why do you think so?"

"Because she just walked in front of a car. I can see her body lying flattened in the road."

Overhead, the sun blasted its brightness down onto the black asphalt, where there was no body.

24. ONE LAST DRAG by Bruce L. Priddy

It was three days after he emptied the last smoke from the last pack of his last carton that Mike realized where the last remaining cigarette on Earth was hidden. The memory competed for space in his skull with a headache that was trying to punch its way out through his eyeballs. It was at his favorite dive, dangling from the lips of a faux-brass bust of Dionysus hung over the back of the bar.

The corner gas station was dry. Mike checked a few days after half the world fell asleep, died, and woke to start killing the other half. Someone else had the same idea—but this someone had a gun. When Mike tried to join him behind the counter, raiding the stacks of cigarettes, the dude jammed the weapon in Mike's face. Damn near broke his nose.

 Mike ran.

He wasn't even to the gas pumps when he heard the dude shout from the broken automatic doors. Mike turned, hands to a Heaven he wasn't sure he believed in anymore, convinced he was going to catch a bullet. Instead the dude tossed Mike a carton, leveled the gun at him, and ordered him to get moving.

How long ago was that? He couldn't remember. No more room in his head. Mike had the idea of keeping track of the days, three cigarettes at a time. But the end of the world has a way of driving a man to smoke. Every day he sat on his balcony in nothing but his briefs—it was so hot, almost too hot to breathe—and chain-smoked until he coughed up the contents of his stomach and lungs. From his balcony he watched everything die, then watched everything that died crawl, walk and dance. Whiskey Shambles' blues provided him company in the first days, then the power went out and never came back. Only took a couple of days after that for the batteries in the CD player to join the dead.

His cell phone died the same day as the power. Not that it had been much use to him, before or after the world died. He tried calling a few drinking buddies, but every call beeped busy. Mike wondered what happened to his favorite bartender, the petite blonde with the aftermarket chest. She gave her his number once, when her good sense spent a night drowned in alcohol. He tried giving her a call a couple of times before the world went to shit, but she never answered. The extinction of humanity did nothing to change that situation.

There was a son, with a wife, and a couple of grandkids Mike had only seen a handful of times. Lived on the other side of the city, though he might as well have been on the other side of the country. Mike sent a text when things went south: *You guys okay?* Mike checked for a response, over and over, for days and days. None came before the power went. Mike ran down the battery checking. Hoping.

Once, he thought he saw his favorite hooker out there among the dead, the one he often pretended was the petite blonde. He shouted her name—he couldn't help himself. She came to stand under his balcony, bringing other dead things with her. If it was her. Closer, it was hard to tell from the weather and rot. The dead brayed and reached at him for days, until they and Mike got bored with one another.

Sometimes, before the dead wandered away, Mike would lean over the railing when the fits came, loosing the contents of his lungs on the crowd. "Fuck you," he'd laugh at them, then spit out the remains caught in his mouth. They picked bits of him from themselves. Ate them. But that was not enough to sate them, and they resumed their reaching.

Desperate want drove him out into a world no longer alive.

The big plate window in the front of his favorite dive lay broken on the sidewalk and the floor inside. Mike stepped over the low windowsill, gently lowering his boots onto the shattered glass, lest something dead inside hear. Every bottle of booze that once crowded the wall behind the bar was gone, snatched or knocked to the floor, broken. The refrigerators hung open: empty. But Dionysus still sucked that cigarette, smiling at the end of history.

Mike could hardly believe it. "Son of a bitch," he laughed, then clamped a hand over his mouth. He waited a moment, standing still. If anything was hiding in the bar, it didn't hear him. "Hello?" he tried to call out, but nerves made his voice a harsh whisper. He waited, to be certain. There was a hope, however slight, that the petite blonde would emerge from some hidden, secure storage-room or basement, inviting him to escape the world. And they'd drink and smoke and fuck like the last two people on Earth, because as far as he knew, they were. This they'd do until the end of their days, his much sooner than hers.

His very soon.

But no one, living or dead, came looking for him. No one had for a very long time.

He slid over the bar. As he did, the lighter in his back pocket squeezed out, falling between two overturned stools. "Shit," he muttered. The floor behind the bar was a jagged mess of glass, cemented to the tile with dried booze. Mike stretched a hand up and snatched the cigarette from Dionysus. "Give it up, you greedy bastard," he said, just a whisper. The cigarette hadn't survived the apocalypse unscathed—there was a bend at the filter—but it had survived. Mike had never seen anything so beautiful.

Somewhere down the street, dead things howled and wailed and screamed. Mike dropped to the floor, glass biting at his hands and the backs of his legs. He gritted through the pain, chewing on the sounds trying to escape him, swallowing them down. Crouched with his back against the bar, he ripped the filter off, flicking it away. A hundred things outside, dancing and cavorting in ways they could never in life, would kill him long before the cancer.

Mike reached to his back pocket, then remembered the lighter. "God damn it." He risked a peek over the bar. The dead were passing the big window, babbling in an alien language, but none were looking in. He swung himself over the bar, grabbed the lighter, and jumped back across. The movement stole his breath. As he sank back down, hand to his chest to calm his lungs, something outside let out a harsh howl. Over his ragged breathing, Mike heard bodies fall through the window, glass crunching, nails and bone-exposed fingers scrabbling against the floor.

Mike lit the cigarette and put it to his lips. Pulled in one last drag despite his protesting lung. It was stale as hell. The smoke smelled, tasted, like rot.

But, God damn, was it good.

25. THE BREAK UP by Mike Leon

Allison opens her eyes to the bright sun shining through the gaps in the blinds. She sweats under the heavy sheets; the upstairs room is like this every morning during the hot summer. The sun pours in through the front of the house and the second level becomes a sauna compared to downstairs where the thermostat is mounted. She peels back the sheets and steps out of bed, her right foot making contact with the cool wood floor.

"It's so gross up here," Daniel says. He remains in the bed, on the left side, where he always sleeps, as if it makes much difference on the tiny twin mattress. They always end up entangled in some back breaking position. "We need to move somewhere that doesn't get hot."

"Well, if you get a real job," she sighs, covering her svelte frame with a worn, frayed bathrobe and throwing her long hair behind her.

"I know," he says, rolling over to face away from her.

He works in a call center. Everyone they know seems to work in a call center. Banking, or technical support, or generic customer support—if they're not a teacher or a nurse or an engineer, they work in a call center. Daniel was supposed to be an engineer, but that never happened.

"My parents already said they would help us out if you go back to school."

"We talked about this already."

"So are you going to go?"

"I feel so itchy."

"Itchy? What does that mean?"

"I don't know," he says. "I just feel itchy."

Allison frowns at him as he climbs out of bed, walking across the room to start the Xbox on the dresser. He'll lie there for a few hours before he even puts pants on, just like he does any day he doesn't have to get up for work.

She quietly makes her way down the old, creaking stairs from the bedroom, actually feeling the bowed wood sink under her feet as she steps on some of them.

In the kitchen she opens the pantry for a can of Folgers and notices the abundance of Lucky Charms boxes on the top shelf. There are four. She picks up each and shakes it, finding only one actually contains any cereal. She disposes of the empty ones.

"Hey, babe," he calls from upstairs. "While you're down there can you grab me a Mountain Dew?"

She rolls her eyes. Once she thought it was cute that he ate like he was still a teenager. He had hardly been out of his teens then, and they had money and time and not a care in the world. Now they don't have money or time, and with each passing day his love handles grow less loveable.

As she waits for the coffee to finish, she goes out to the yard behind the house. It is not large, but is poorly kept and messy with weeds. The grass is weeks overdue for a mow, and she'll have to do that herself if it's going to be done at all. Next to the rusted propane grill Daniel never uses she finds the thing that she came looking for. She takes it into the house, carrying it through the living room and down the hall. She leaves it at the bottom of the steps and returns to the coffee maker.

She looks at a foil wrapped Nutri-Grain cereal bar, but puts it back in the box without opening it. She snatches a Mountain Dew can from the refrigerator before pulling out the coffee pot. Black liquid drips onto the hot burner, sizzling as she pours a cup. She replaces the pot before trekking up the stairs with the soda can and her coffee in a cheap Mickey Mouse mug they got at Disney World years ago.

She sets the can on the chipped black-panel nightstand next to him and sits on the foot of the bed.

"So, are you going to do anything today?"

"Nothing big," he says. "Probably play this for a couple hours. Maybe shotgun some Netflix later."

"The yard really needs somebody to cut it."

"I'll do it tomorrow."

"You said that last Saturday. It doesn't stop growing because you don't feel like cutting it."

"I'm too tired. I was up until like five last night."

"Why?"

"I was trying to beat Battletoads. Seriously, I'm so itchy. Do I have a rash or something? Do I look okay?"

"You don't have a rash, so no to the first question, but you're still playing video games in your tightie whities at noon."

"Could you just lay off me? It's Saturday."

"I told my sister we would come over and see the baby."

Daniel grimaces.

She sighs. "What? You don't want to do that either?"

"I'm just tired of babies. Everybody we know is having babies. All they do is eat and poop and throw up and I just don't understand."

"I thought you wanted to have kids?"

"I don't know. I guess. Just not now—what the fuck?" he growls at the TV angrily. "How did that hit me?"

"When?"

"Just a second ago! The lag is retarded. I need to call the cable company or something."

"I meant when do you think you want to have kids?"

"I don't know." He shrugs. "Like, after we get married."

"Yeah? Are we setting a date?"

"Come on, Allie. You know I need to finish school before we can do that."

"Yeah," she says, tipping back the mug to finish the last of her coffee. She sets the empty mug down next to his soda can silently and goes to take a shower.

Allison opens the door to the bathroom and walks inside, pushing it shut behind her. The lopsided old door does not close all the way and remains cracked open just a tiny bit. She turns the knobs to run the water and pulls the shower curtain closed before sitting on the hamper. She doesn't want him to hear her crying.

A noise from the bedroom draws her attention, but she disregards it. He's yelling at the TV again. She wishes he cared about *her* that much. She thinks he might have once, but not anymore. It has been two weeks since they last made love and if she caressed him now he would likely chastise her for the interruption.

Sounds again from the other room, this time louder than the first. It rings out over the shower spray quite clearly. The mirror quakes in the aftershock. Allison lurches from her seat and rips open the door.

The sight in the bedroom is one of terror beyond her wildest nightmares. Standing atop the bed, Daniel wrestles with something, like a person struggling out of a tight jacket, but this is not a jacket. It is his own skin. His bare bloody skull turns to face her and she sees into empty sockets and a clicking jaw. Her legs feel weak and she stumbles back against the wall. She curls against it until the floor meets her and she remains there, crying out in panic as she watches the wicked horror in front of her reach into its chest flesh, opening it like a coat to pop a shoulder socket free and and draw a bony arm from the sleeve of skin and muscle it once wore. Then it moves on to the other with its free skeleton hand, as the skin of his other side hangs limp. When the skeleton pulls its flesh down its ankles, she screams.

The skeleton steps out of its skin and leaps down to the floor. Bald metatarsals clatter against hard wood and a rope of intestines flops out of the chest cavity that leads all the way back to the sloppy sheath discarded on the bed. A whole liver splats against the floor, speckling Allison with red slime. The skeleton holds out a hand to her, as if offering to lift her to her feet. Its jaw chatters relentlessly, though it has no tongue with which to speak and no muscles for it to move. It drools blood onto her bathrobe as it pulls her up.

"Get away from me!" she shrieks.

The skeleton chatters more as it reaches out to spread her robe open. It takes hold of her hip with pointed fingers that feel like arrowheads and pinches at the flesh around her waist, stretching it away from her body. It wants her skin.

"No!" she shouts. "No! You can't!"

The skeleton nods.

"No!" she screams, slapping the horrible thing in the slimy crimson cranium. The skeleton rears away, possibly surprised though it has no way to make facial expressions.

It steps back slowly, continuing to stare at her with those black, empty sockets, as though it can see her with no eyes. It turns pointed fingers upon itself, digging into its ribcage to empty out the remainder of its entrails the way someone might scrape leftover food from a dish into the kitchen trash. Lungs, heart, kidneys, all land at her knees as she cowers on the floor.

Then it turns away slowly, toward the dresser where the television sits. It reaches out, wrapping bone fingers around the Xbox, and lifts it off the dresser. It rips the cables free and tucks the big black machine squarely under one arm. With its other hand, it snatches up a controller and stomps out of the bedroom. It gives her one last look back before it walks down the stairs.

She hears the front door open and the storm door swinging wide; then comes the slow hiss of the pneumatic piston, drawing the outer door gently closed. For a brief moment, there is silence.

Then comes the sound of something left on the bed.

"I- I-" it starts, each time choking off into a gurgle of blood.

Allison crawls over to the side of the bed and places a hand on the nightstand next to her. She is afraid to touch the bed—afraid to touch whatever might be on it. Warily, she rises to inspect the awful thing on top of the soaking sheets.

The sloughed off skin of him is like a broken balloon, or a spent condom, rubbery, deflated and dripping with oozing muck. She can't explain how, but somehow he continues to make noise. He continues to speak.

"I- I strt skl," the shed skin rasps. "I guh."

She takes the ooze covered hand that is closest to her in her own and holds it to her chest.

"It's better this way," she whispers. "It's better this way."

She untucks the corners of the contour sheets from between the mattress and box spring as the limp rubbery creature continues to gurgle out words that are mostly nonsense to her. Mostly. She finds it too difficult to label them anything else.

She picks up each of the corners and throws them over the pile of gore. She closes her eyes to collect the separate organs that lay on the floor. They squish in her hands in ways she hoped they would not. The intestines she winds onto the bed after leaving the other parts on top of the skin.

"Guh," the skin says. "Guh."

"Shush," Allison says, holding a finger to her mouth to sooth the blob.

When the whole of the solid parts are collected there, she wraps them in the sheets with the flesh sack and hoists it up from the bed. She strains to lift it, as most of the weight of his body remains even without the bones. She sees that it soaked through the bedding and the mattress is wet with a ring of brown stain that makes her cringe. She will leave it for later.

She tugs the red bundle toward the door, smearing a path through the lake of carnage on the flooring. Then she goes down the stairs, the sack slushing against each step as it smacks into them. At the bottom of the steps, she places the entire bag into the hefty brown plastic trash bin.

It continues to speak to her from inside the can. The muffled groaning becomes inexplicably clear as she drags the bin through the kitchen.

"I really need to start working out," it says.

She checks the bottom of the bin for blood before dragging it across the few feet of carpeted living room on the way to the sliding glass doors that lead out to the yard behind the house. She sees nothing that will be left on the carpet.

"Allison, do you think you would want to get married someday?" the skin says.

Allison pulls the back door open on its sliding frame and then fights to unlatch the cheap screen door on the other side. She prevails after several attempts pushing the door different directions while simultaneously picking at the latch.

She steps out on the patio, and glances out over the length of weeds they call a lawn to the little rotting tool shed where they keep the mower.

"I really should cut that eventually," she hears the skin say.

She can't listen to it anymore. She walks to the shed and undoes the padlock with the combination—her birthday. Inside, she retrieves the heavy red gasoline can. She carries the gas can out to the garbage bin and pops the cap from the long black nozzle. She tilts the can over the lip of the bin and showers the contents with gasoline.

"We should start thinking about having a baby," the skin says, as Allison lifts up the vinyl grill cover to get the long stemmed butane lighter from the rusted tin cabinet below the burners.

She closes her eyes as she flicks the grill lighter and ignites the vile remnants wrapped up in those sheets.

26. ONE OF GRANNY'S TALES BY JAMES PRATT

In the Old Woman's mind, the entire world consisted of two mountains and the valley in between. The first mountain held the long-abandoned shack where she had spent her brief childhood, trying to help her family eke a hardscrabble existence from the rocky soil. A bride at the age of fifteen, she had moved across the valley to the second mountain, where she would spend the rest of her life. She knew there were other slopes and valleys than those that constituted her world, but they were places she would never set foot, which made them mysterious and exotic. As a girl she had imagined them the gatekeepers to distant lands filled with wonder she couldn't even imagine. Even in her adult mind they remained inscrutable sentinels, marking the farthest edges of existence.

It was a hard life, living among the mountains. They made you a part of them, in life as well as death. The Old Woman's face was as jagged as an outcropping of weather-forged rock, her bony brow a shelf upon which sat several lifetimes' worth of misery. The edges of her cheekbones seemed sharp as razors, her complexion as red and raw as a freshly plucked chicken.

Time and misfortune, the Old Woman's only real companions, had gobbled up her children one by one. Each had come out of the womb red and shrieking as if already aware of its lot in life. One died minutes after birth, and two more after only a few short months of life. Three made it past their fifth birthday and two of those three past their tenth. Only one survived to the ripe old age of fifteen, the youngest, who was the seventh child and perhaps lucky for it. The Old Woman hadn't seen him in years. Like his father, he had simply gone out into the woods one day and never returned—not bound for war like his pa, though, just out hunting for meat.

The mountain giveth and the mountain taketh away.

Over a year had passed since the Old Woman had heard the sound of another human voice, and four months since she'd heard the sound of her own. Whether by choice or circumstance the Old Woman wasn't exactly a social creature, but even she wasn't immune to the occasional want for companionship. Deep down she was still human, after all.

The Old Woman used to get the occasional caller: Jessup, her husband's no-account brother would drop by every now and again, usually under the pretense of seeing if she had any chores that needed attending. He rarely did anything more strenuous than fetch wood for the stove, but always found the time to stay for supper. The last she'd heard, somebody had found Jessup's frozen corpse in a ditch one winter morning, and now he lay in a pauper's grave. Then there was Abe Lowe, a trapper who'd gone off to war with her husband and come back minus a hand. Abe would check in on her once in a while, but he hadn't been by in quite a spell. The Old Woman figured the mountain finally got him too.

And of course there was Granny, the old squaw who was all that was left of either the Nakota or Chinnacook Indians—the Old Woman wasn't sure which—that used to live in those parts. Though it seemed ages had passed since the last time she'd seen her, Granny crept into the Old Woman's memory every now and again.

Still, the pangs of loneliness were few and far between. Even in the early days of her marriage, the Old Woman had preferred to keep to herself. Truth be told, her husband hadn't been a particularly gentle man, and her fleeting recollections of him were often more bitter than sweet.

The infirmities of old age also figured into it. There were still familiar faces at the general store but it was a long trek that seemed as uphill going as coming back. Making do with less, the Old Woman soon discovered the general store's manufactured goods weren't a necessity after all. She had learned at an early age how to provide for herself. It was either that or starve. On her last trip, she had stocked up on coffee and flour because she had no intention of coming back for a very long time.

Deeply entrenched in her own inner world, the Old Woman barely noticed when things began to change. The transition was subtle, and at least in the beginning could be attributed to the feebleness of an aged mind. It started with familiar things becoming unfamiliar. The Old Woman would reach for an item and find herself holding some inexplicable thing, an artifact as alien to her frame of reference as a carrot peeler to a caveman. She marked time by the passing of the seasons, and thus noticed when the weather became unreliable. Within the space of a single week, drifts of snow would be swallowed up by summer heat, followed by spring showers washing over colorful autumnal displays. This played havoc with her garden but, knowing how to make a little stretch a long way, she endured. The Old Woman began to suspect something might have happened in the mythical world beyond the sentinel peaks. For all she knew, she was the last human being on Earth, which suited her just fine.

One night, faces from the past came tumbling through the Old Woman's dreams. They were just kaleidoscope flashes, random vignettes lacking context, but every single one stirred something within her. She was soon moaning in her sleep, suffocating, buried under an avalanche of forgotten emotions. The Old Woman woke the next morning feeling something indescribable, and for the first time in her life lay in bed until well past dawn.

When she finally rose, the Old Woman started a pot of coffee brewing and went to feed the chickens. She hadn't had fox trouble in quite a while, but the mere thought still made her anxious; without the eggs and meat the chickens provided, the mountain would have claimed her long ago. Every morning she expected to find the coop empty save for a few bloody feathers, and couldn't breathe easy 'til she'd verified that the chickens were safe, at least for another day.

The Old Woman stepped out into the cold air, the weather deciding to be winter that day, and was met with silence. Noisy, uninhibited creatures, chickens were in no way subtle when it came to their breakfast, or any other aspect of their brief lives. The Old Woman swallowed, hands clenched so hard her jagged nails dug into her palms. Then she noticed the door to the corn crib was open.

The corn crib had a simple but cunning latch intended to thwart even the cleverest and most persistent critter, so the Old Woman's mind went in another direction. The mountains had their own mythology. It started with the Indians that had lived in those parts before the white man drove them off with guns and smallpox. They told tales of lean, hungry shapes that prowled in the dark of night to the first white men, who then added their own tales to an ever-expanding body of lore.

A natural-born skeptic, the Old Woman brushed the thought aside. Besides, the corn looked untouched. The Old Woman inspected the ground in the vicinity of the crib. The only tracks in the morning frost were her own. Even the birds had left the corn alone, strangely enough. The birds …

Craning her neck, the Old Woman searched the roof of the shack, the chicken coop, the outhouse, and the barn. No birds were in sight. Then she noticed the silence didn't just extend to the chickens: the morning should have been alive with the sound of a world waking up, but all she heard was the crunch of the frozen earth beneath the galoshes she wore over three pairs of wool socks.

Reaching into the corn crib for an ear of corn whose kernels she would feed to the chickens, the Old Woman cried out and quickly withdrew her hand. The corn was covered in some sort of viscous goo that burned to the touch. Stranger still, the ear she'd picked up had practically liquefied in her grasp. If the goo was some sort of mold or fungus, it was one she'd never seen.

Ignoring the silence in the chicken coop, the Old Woman was determined the chickens be fed. She returned to the shack, crumbled up some old biscuits, and paused long enough to grab the double-barreled shotgun she kept by the door. When she opened the coop, she wasn't surprised by what she found. The chickens were dead: not brutalized, half-eaten, or torn to shreds, just still and lifeless, like a pile of feathery rag dolls.

The Old Woman would have cried if she'd remembered how—not that there was any point to it. Crying about the unfairness of things never did anybody any good. It hadn't brought her children back, and chances were it wouldn't work miracles on the chickens, either. The Old Woman picked up one of the chickens and examined it. The thing was as limp as a bag of sawdust.

"Stone dead," she said, speaking for the first time in almost half a year.

The Old Woman squinted. Beneath its feathers, the chicken's skin quivered. Putting her ear to its beak, she heard a sound, faint but definite, a wet, gooey sound not unlike her fourth child's labored breathing as he lay dying of pneumonia. It was an awful sound, the sound of a body turning on itself as it rots from within.

Even worse was the smell.

The Old Woman knew what death smelled like, and the smell of death was there, but so was something else: the fecund tang of refuse, of compost heaps, garbage dumps, and those other places as brimming with rot as they were life. Admittedly, said life tended to be of the buzzing, crawling, and verminous kind, but it was life nonetheless.

The chicken corpse jerked in her hand and the Old Woman tossed it away. Hitting the ground, it split like a rotten melon. Something wet and yellow oozed out. Shapeless, it was a glistening mass that gathered into itself then collapsed, like a fist clenching and unclenching.

As the Old Woman backed away, she noticed her shadow fell in the wrong direction. The sun was in motion, crawling slowly but perceptibly across the heavens. By the time she reached the shack, the sun was touching the horizon and the first stars had become visible in the night sky.

Once inside, the Old Woman closed the door and latched it behind her. Hanging on the back of the door was a dream catcher, an intricate lattice of twine set in a round wooden frame. The sight of it reminded her of Granny, who had given her the dream-catcher as a gift. In earlier days when the Old Woman was wont to go calling on her scattered neighbors, she would drop in on Granny who would tell her the stories of her tribe whom she simply called the People. One time they were discussing the Book of Revelations and Granny told her how the People thought the world would end.

The Old Ones were, the Old Ones are, the Old Ones will be, Granny had said. *They were here before everything, before the sun and the moon, before the mountains and the seas. Their medicine was so mighty even the Great Spirit feared them and so he killed them in their sleep and buried them in a stony lodge deep beneath the earth. But the Old Ones are not like us. They cannot really die, so they sleep and wait. When the stars are right, they will wake and run wild and free. It is the way of things because time is a wheel which is the wheel of life but also the wheel of death. The Old Ones are not a friend of the white man or the People. They hate the Great Spirit and all his works. When the last day comes the sun will die and the dead will rise, for in the age of the Old Ones there will be no difference between death and life.*

The Old Woman opened the door a crack and peered out. The sun sat close to the western horizon, painting the sky the fiery shade of orange. Silhouetted against the fierce glow was a disheveled figure.

"Who's there?" the Old Woman demanded, stepping out of the shack shotgun-first.

Swaying, the figure took a clumsy step toward her, then another, and another. Likewise the Old Woman advanced a few steps, finger on the trigger.

"Mama?" the shape asked in a voice the Old Woman hadn't heard in years but instantly recognized. "Mama?"

"C … Caleb?"

The shotgun fell from nerveless fingers. Her third child and secret favorite stood before her, looking surprisingly well for someone dead and buried twenty years or so. There was color in his cheeks and his right eye sparkled with mischief just like the Old Woman remembered. But it was an incomplete resurrection; his left eye and part of his skull were still missing from the day his brother carried him home after some fool mistook him for a deer.

"I'm back, Mama," Caleb said, reaching for her.

The Old Woman ran across the yard. She didn't notice how the frost was turning to steam, or how the landscape was melting around her, the rich greens and organic browns oozing together into a syrupy black. She didn't notice when the mountains began to fragment and tumble up into the sky like leaves scattered by an autumn wind. She didn't notice how the stars were winking out one by one, or the sun was slowly vanishing like the closing of a great, burning eye. She was holding Caleb in her arms when a darkness, black as sackcloth, swept them both up into its unexpectedly warm embrace. And still the Old Woman didn't notice. She was too busy savoring the smell of earth and living blood and the quiet, steady sound of her son's breathing. A contented sigh, however, was the last sound she heard, though whether it was Caleb's or her own, she couldn't tell.

27. BROKEN GLASS BY KERRY G.S. LIPP

Knock. Knock.

I opened the door and stared at the kid in front of me. I was expecting him. Preteen or early teen, I didn't know. He wore sunglasses, a florescent green hat—backwards and cockeyed—and a Lebron James basketball jersey. Heat, not Cavs. Mismatched black and white socks pulled halfway to his knees. Air Jordan shoes. I didn't know much about fashion, but I picked it all up easily. He was a walking billboard.

"Hey man, shit happens right? My bad. Can I get that back?" the kid said, his insincere words a formality.

"No," I said. "Get off my porch."

His jaw clenched. Tightened. His mouth opened.

"Now," I hissed, and he turned and walked away.

Random vandalism started shortly after our interaction that day. Sometimes my windows, sometimes my trees, sometimes my garden, a couple of times he even went after my car. But he never came back to my front door.

I started keeping an eye on that spoiled, entitled little shit.

I didn't want to harm a child, not even a shitty one like that, so I found out when he turned eighteen …

… and I planned a little birthday party.

I had five years to make my plans and five years to change my mind, but the pranks and vandalism never stopped.

My drinking started again, though, and I saved all the empty bottles.

~ ~ * * ~ ~

I snatched him on his eighteenth birthday, just after he got home. Some friends dropped him off and he ducked into the backyard to smoke a cigarette before he entered his house as he always did. I'd been watching. When I saw the car pull up, I left my house and ambushed him with a rock to the head. He smelled like booze and offered no resistance. His knees buckled and his body crumpled into the grass. I cuffed him, taped a burlap bag over his head and threw him in my trunk.

We went for a little ride.

I knew a quiet, abandoned field and forest about an hour away. For some reason it had stayed relatively undiscovered since I was the kid's age. I used to grow pot out there. Never got caught. Never had a close call.

That land was like a loner in high school. There, but forgotten.

For those five years I brought my empty bottles out here—I'd usually bring full ones too. I liked to drink while I prepped.

First thing I did was dig a pit, maybe five feet deep and eight feet around. Kind of like a swimming pool, but a circle, not a square. A big project, but when you chip away at it, not so bad.

I lined the bottom with broken bricks and jagged cinder blocks to shatter the bottles I tossed in, and dead in the center I stood up a nylon tube, like one of those little tunnels toddlers like to crawl around in. Like you see in gerbil cages. I reinforced the tube with wooden planks so the weight of the glass pressing in from the sides wouldn't cave it in. I wasn't sure if the glass would cut right through the nylon or not, but it didn't. Maybe I got lucky or maybe science forbids it. Doesn't matter.

I spent the rest of my time out there at the pit drinking and smashing bottles. Breaking glass is fun. I brought in load after load. Mostly beer and wine and liquor bottles, but food jars too. Whatever I could get.

Every few loads I brought some salt—rock salt, water softener, whatever—and dusted the layers of broken glass like I was pitching pennies in a fountain. I even made a few wishes. The pit was open to the rain, and in time a crusty white film coated the jagged pieces.

I'd been working on it for years, like an artist I guess you could say; considering what passed for art these days, maybe this was pretty damn good. Call it *Justice*, by Clyde Heavenshaw.

Dressed in coveralls, gloves, a mask covering everything but my eyes, and composite toe boots, I stripped the kid—a man now, I suppose, at least according to the law—and threw him over my shoulder.

I stuffed him into the little nylon toddler tunnel like the pissant child he was. I'd worried a bit about pulling the tunnel up and out of the pit, concerned that it might snag, or get stuck, but one good jerk and it came out fast as a spent dick.

With a sound like television static, the glass spilled in against his body, burying him to the neck. Sparkling waves of pain in the moonlight. The screams started right after. He screamed as if I'd set him on fire, but I thought this was worse. I enjoyed those screams as I carried the ragged tunnel to the edge of the pit. I dropped it, shed my mask, and picked up two beers. I walked back to the center of the pit, twisted one open and dumped icy coldness on his face.

"Shut up," I said.

His face lit in shock for just a second as he jolted into coherence. Then the sensation of salt-crusted glass cutting his skin kicked in again.

I twisted the top off my other beer and savored it. I took a long gulp while I watched him struggle, and enjoyed the moment. When he realized he was buried neck deep in broken glass, he started to fight. I'll give him credit for that. He struggled to raise his arms through the glass.

"Help me! Fuck. It burns, it burns, it hurts, somebody help!" he shrieked as I placed his hat, backward and cockeyed, on his head.

Eventually his arms came up, a mess of blood and flecks of skin. Hundreds, hell maybe thousands of tiny cuts lacerated him. I couldn't imagine how heavy that glass was and how hard he fought to free them, but he got them out.

I remembered the salt and shuddered.

He stared at me, his raised torn arms red and dripping, dots of skin and clotted blood plopping onto the top layer of the glass.

I reached into my pocket.

"Here's the ball that you put through my window you little shit. After I tasted your attitude that day I stared into the glass from my broken window and got a crazy idea," I said, finished my beer and smashed it in the pit.

He stared at the baseball gripped in my hand.

I threw it.

He gaped, and I could see in his glazed, almost-dead eyes that he wanted to live.

"It's a long way to that ball, but if you get there, I'll let you go."

With wild eyes he screamed, pushing his hands down into the glass, trying to force his lower half free. His palms tore.

His naked body slowly slid up, revealing shredded flesh, his body coated red.. Pieces of skin dangled, some even flapped, and I saw salt-coated glass embedded in the raw flesh beneath his skin.

But he didn't quit. He bit his bottom lip off as he focused through the pain, and it shocked me to see that he was going to actually make it to that baseball.

Good thing I'd only told him that I'd let him go. I didn't say I'd get him to a hospital.

And we were in the middle of nowhere.

28. THE JANITOR BY JEANI RECTOR

Craig parked in the empty lot and got out of the car, his windshield reflecting the glare of the brightly lit school sign. He was tired. Somehow his Monday night shift had come too soon.

He studied the school as he walked toward it. High school kids had to be the messiest people on the planet. He knew if he had paid attention and worked harder during his own high school days, he'd have a better job than this by now. But he hadn't, so this was the result.

"Make the best of things," his mother always said. "Being a janitor is an honest living." Yeah, and all good dogs go to heaven.

Craig took the large yellow cleaning can out of the closet, and began to lug it toward the first classroom. It was about the size of an urban garbage can, made of hard plastic, and it was on wheels. It contained all the supplies he needed to do his job.

He cleaned the brightly lit classrooms first. They were the easiest; the teachers always watched the students and made sure they didn't disrupt the rooms too badly. He moved on to the gymnasium, another fairly easy clean.

After he did all he could in the gym, he knew it was time for the rest of his job. He stepped out into the night air, locked the gym door behind him, and started walking across the grassy quad toward the bathrooms, still lugging his cleaning supplies behind him.

He hated cleaning the bathrooms the most. They were in their own small building, boys on one side and girls on the other. Who knew what he would find there; sometimes things he didn't even want to look at, much less touch, so he always left the bathrooms for last.

Everything was locked at night, even the bathrooms. He started fumbling with his key ring as he walked, not finding the right key, when suddenly he understood why he was having so much trouble: he couldn't see the keys very clearly.

Craig hesitated and glanced around. Why was it so dark? He looked ahead and noticed all the poles containing fluorescent lights that surrounded the freshman bathrooms were black. None of the lights were working.

Everything seemed quiet—too quiet. The sense of stillness was overpowering. There was simply no sound, no motion, as if all the night creatures were silently hiding; watching and waiting. No crickets chirped; no owls screeched.

The intense stillness was finally broken, and movement began again, as though the world was releasing a held breath. A slight wind picked up. A creak sounded as two twisted limbs of an old, gnarled tree rubbed together in the soft breeze. The seedheads of ornamental grasses fluttered with a sighing sound. Clipped boxwood shrubs rustled as branches shuddered in the wind.

Craig felt spooked. He wished he had a flashlight, more for cold comfort than for the visuals it would give him. Everything seemed threatening in the dark: everyday things seemed to take a sinister undertone. It was more of a mood than a lack of sight.

He wanted to turn around and go home, but knew he couldn't. He needed this job, as lousy as it was. He couldn't afford to lose it.

You're not a little kid, afraid of your own shadow, he told himself. *Buck up and be a man.*

So he started walking toward the bathrooms once again, resolving to clean them and then move on. It was what he did five nights a week. This night would be no different. So what if none of the lights were working?

When he reached the overhang of the building, it seemed even darker under there. The roof shaded what little light the moon delivered. The bathroom building was brick, and felt cold to his touch as he leaned against it, fumbling with his keys. God, why couldn't he find the right key?

Finally he felt it, the small one with the knob on the tip. Next he had to feel the door to find the keyhole. As his fingertips glided over the metal door jamb, he noticed how cold it was, colder than the brick. Maybe he had never noticed the temperature before, since he could normally see it and didn't have to feel it.

The key connected with the lock, and Craig pushed the door open. He reached to the wall for the light switch. He found it and flipped it up.

Nothing happened. The bathroom remained dark.

No way was he going into that pitch black bathroom. He would have to call the school office in the morning and explain the situation, that he didn't feel safe because none of the lights were working. They couldn't fire him for that, could they?

Craig began to turn around when he dropped his keyring. He cursed as he heard it bouncing into the bathroom, jangling as it tumbled and rolled the keys end over end.

Oh my God, I can't go in there!

But his car keys were on that ring. Unless he retrieved them, he had to spend the night in these dark school grounds. Which fate was worse?

He needed the keys. He knelt to the cement floor of the bathroom, feeling the coldness of the stone on his knees all the way through his pants. He held the door open with his foot as he leaned over and began feeling around the cement floor, his fingers doing what his eyes could not, searching for the keyring.

He realized that the keys must have fallen further into the room than he initially thought. He crawled forward, and his foot slipped from the door and it slammed shut with a *bang*. Craig could not suppress a small scream before he realized that the door only locked from the outside. From the inside, it could be opened. He was not locked in.

He noticed he was panting. Trying to slow his breathing, he gathered his wits about him and once again began feeling over the cement floor for the keyring.

I can do this. I am not afraid of the dark.

His fingers groped the cement and he felt something on the floor that gave a little at his touch. Craig hesitated, then touched the thing again. It felt wet and … did he feel it move?

A sour scent of musty brine assaulted his nostrils. Craig jerked his fingers back and decided to get the hell out of the bathroom, keys or no keys. He tried to rise to his feet, but his legs were like rubber beneath him. He staggered; his body rocked with fear, and made an attempt at reaching the door.

He heard the thing slam against him more than he felt the blow, and understood that whatever was with him in this bathroom was big. He could hear someone sobbing and realized it was he who was doing the crying.

Please God, get me out of here! Please God please God …

The creature dragged him down to the floor with its weight. He tried to push it off, but he couldn't seem to grasp it. Its surface was slimy and his hands slipped off.

He tried again to shove the wet, cold bulk with all his might and finally made solid contact. His hands seemed to sink into rubbery flesh that enveloped his fingers and didn't slow the assault. The stench of rotted seaweed and polluted ocean filled his nose, and his panic rose to desperation.

He pulled back his arm and landed a punch on what he hoped was the face. The thing grunted, then made a growling sound.

Craig tried to jerk his forearm backwards, because he knew that a sharp elbow could be an effective weapon, but he was disoriented in the dark and didn't know where to aim. He was aware of intense, searing pain. It felt like the creature was attacking him for an eternity, though what was left of his rational thought said surely it had only been for a few seconds.

He managed to roll out from the creature's grasp. He hoped with all his might that he was rolling in the right direction—toward the door. He honestly didn't know.

And suddenly he felt the door, and he cried out loud with relief and renewed hope. He shoved the door and it opened and the cool outside air slapped his face. He staggered to his feet and began to run across the grassy quad; a loping, lopsided gait because his left leg wasn't functioning properly.

He felt an adrenaline surge as he realized he was going to make it. He was going to escape whatever beast had been in the bathroom; he was going to survive!

And then, behind him, he heard the bathroom door open again as the thing came out.

It had begun as the faint sensation of pressure, of something within her that didn't belong, taking up room where there was none to spare. Now—distinct and undeniable—there was a sensation of movement.

Something writhed inside her.

She tried to ignore it while the doctor spoke. Doctor Richman's clinical gaze was cold and distant. She felt crazy when he looked at her. She felt worse when he caught her not paying attention.

"I can think of nothing else to recommend to you," he said, his hand out, offering her a business card.

"I'm sorry?" she said. She winced when his brow furrowed. There came the sensation again. It felt like a slurping sound.

"We've explored every strictly biological possibility. I simply cannot explain what you are feeling. I'm recommending that you speak with a colleague of mine." He extended his arm further, stretching it by a matter of centimeters, the business card between his index and middle fingers.

Joan reached out and took it the same way—between the same two fingers. She flipped it over and read it, all but ignoring Richman as he went on.

"Doctor Feversmith is very good. He's incredibly well respected … he's helped a lot of people."

"I'm not crazy," Joan snapped.

The volume of Doctor Richman's voice fell slightly; it took on a hushed tone, a comforting quality that she hadn't thought the man capable of. "No, no, of course not. That's not what I think and that's not what I mean to imply." He looked down at the pen on his desk for a long moment. "I believe you are sick … legitimately sick. Whatever it is that plagues you, however … well, we've run every test that could possibly be applicable to your complaint. I am hoping Doctor Feversmith can find something, some thread that we can pull on to unravel this whole thing. He's got a lot of experience. He's seen some pretty unusual stuff." Richman smiled and leaned over the desk a bit, as if sharing a harmless secret with her. "He just might be able to point us in the right direction."

She nodded. "I read about this parasite or worm or something. It gets up into your brain if you go swimming in lakes or ponds, it goes through your nose and …"

The doctor nodded. He smiled, but it was the sort of smile one reserved for terminal cases—hope in the face of hopeless odds, optimism in the very clutches of death herself.

"That kills in a matter of days, and the symptoms are flu-like. Nothing at all like what you've described. Then there is the obvious: when is the last time you went swimming in a lake or pond?"

Joan looked down at her hands, clasping the business card like it was the heart in a claddagh. Her face twisted; tears blurred her vision momentarily. She fought it back. Crying, she knew, would only make her seem weak and unstable. She needed to appear rational if she were to be taken seriously.

"Okay," she said finally. "I'll call him."

That thing inside her slithered. She pictured something thick and sinuous coiling up behind her eyes.

~~ * * ~~

Joan pulled her phone from her purse and stared at the caller ID. It was Richman's office again, the third time in as many days. She watched it and waited. Finally, the phone fell silent. A moment later a tone indicated that she had a voicemail.

A throbbing headache pulsed behind her temples. It had come the day after her last appointment with Richman. It never faded, never responded to any medication.

She punched in her code and held the phone to her ear: "Joan, this is Doctor Richman." He spoke in that compassionate tone again—somewhere between regular conversation and a whisper. "I've spoken with Doctor Feversmith. If you don't feel comfortable seeing him, perhaps you would come back into the office so we could discuss other options. Please call and I'll make sure you get an appointment as soon as possible."

Joan hung up. Then she turned the phone off.

She hadn't called the shrink. She wouldn't.

She had nothing against psychiatrists, and believed many people could benefit from talking to one…just not her. She wasn't some hysterical woman imagining things; she knew what her problem was, and she recognized that psychiatry could do nothing to remedy it.

Things were only getting worse. She could taste it, high in the back of her throat, like some infected postnasal drip, one with the flavor of blood and rot.

She snorted and felt that thick stuff collect at the back of her throat, strands of it pulled down from some place right behind her eyes. It hurt

147

to pull all of that stuff into her throat, as if she were using little loops of barbed wire to lobotomize herself.

She hocked and spat. The wad made a satisfying *splat* when it hit the ground, and for a moment she almost felt better. Then the thing in her brain nestled in and got comfortable, spreading and settling into that place behind her eyes.

Joan crouched down to examine the lump she'd spat onto the sidewalk.

The bulk of it was thick, rusty brown mucus. Small chunks of gore—partially coagulated blood and bits of tissue—hung suspended in it. A filament of glossy black slime was woven into it, a gelatinous swirl that clung to the bits of tissue.

She tried to look at it with detachment, to infer—with the most scientific part of her mind—all that the splatter could tell her.

Instead, she fell back on her artistic training: rusty brown for illness; reds and pinks for weak and tattered flesh; and black for evil, decay, sin…

Joan stood. She'd been unsure of the proper course of action, but seeing that mess, knowing that it represented what was going on inside of her, hardened her. She settled on a path, one she now realized had been inevitable from the start.

~~**~~

She'd given it a lot of thought. There was no cure; there was only the truth. Proving to the world that something had invaded her body was all she had left.

She'd spent quite a while considering method. Anything too damaging would destroy evidence. Jumping from a great height or putting a gun in her mouth could obliterate all trace of the parasite. She worried about the effects of chemicals on the thing.

She decided that only one method would do. It would, she hoped, preserve all evidence without tainting it with drugs or booze.

She scribbled a quick note: *I am so sorry. I was left with no choice. Please conduct an autopsy and pay close attention to my brain. There is something in there.*

She placed the note on the bathroom counter, just beside the sink where she brushed her teeth and washed her face. She looked at herself in the mirror over the sink one last time.

She got into the bathtub with all of her clothes on. She refused to suffer the indignity of being found pale and nude after several days.

At the last second, deciding she deserved some level of comfort, she opted to pull off her shoes and socks.

That thing in her brain wriggled—she hoped it understood, and was afraid.

She made sure to do it correctly. This was not some cry for help, after all. She needed to die. It was the only way.

The first cut hurt, and she gasped as she forced herself to drag the razor up, further and further, until it hit the meaty part of her forearm.

When she switched hands, it was hard to hold the blade. Her fingers felt weak and fuzzy, like there were cotton balls stuck to the end of each one.

The second slice stung, but it was distant. She only pulled the razor a few inches before it fell from her grasp and pinged against the inside of the tub before being lost in the growing pool of blood.

She looked down at her toes and tried to wiggle them. It was like watching someone else's toes on her feet—they moved at the wrong pace, and she could hardly feel them.

She thought she smiled. She couldn't see the mirror from where she sat, so she couldn't be sure. Either that thing had stopped moving or she had stopped being able to feel it.

Joan looked at the blood collecting in the bathtub, glossy and near black. She thought of Richman's voice—that soothing voice that seemed so incongruous with his cold stare. She wondered—when they cut open her skull and pulled out her brain—what would they find?

Richman's voice, softer than she'd ever heard it in reality—barely audible, even in her mind—whispered, "Nothing."

The blood kept coming. It seemed unending, as if she would die but the stream of crimson would go on until it overflowed the tub and ran across the bathroom tile.

Then she felt it again, a twitch, as if that thing were dying too. She smiled at that, and she didn't need to see her reflection to know it. She smiled still when she gave in and closed her eyes. She smiled still when she rested her head against the back of the tub.

Her smile fell away.

30. THE TREEHOUSE by Rick McQuiston

You'll see, boy, one day that treehouse will save your life. You are the Chosen One, the one deemed fit to survive.

The words rolled around in Tommy's head like fallen leaves in a thunderstorm. He tried to ignore them but the frightening image of the weird old man who'd spoken them made it impossible to do so. The man's eyes hadn't been right. They'd been elliptical and had a yellow tint to them.

Tommy rubbed his eyes to clear his head. His treehouse loomed before him, suspended in what seemed like midair. His dad and uncle had built it so well it looked as if it were part of the tree.

A cool morning breeze wafted up his nose … it was laced with the underlying scent of something rotten.

Tommy stopped and sniffed the air. "What's that smell?" he mumbled.

Again, the words from the strange man echoed in his mind.

"You need to get a hold of yourself," he whispered, walking to the tree. "The police must've found that guy by now."

A rumble dented the otherwise peaceful morning.

Tommy froze where he stood. He held his breath. His heartbeat slowed. He waited, too afraid to move.

Another rumble, this one with ground-shaking force. Overhead, the sky began to darken. Tommy turned to go back to the relative safety of his house.

"Mom? Dad?"

His cries went unanswered.

He ran to his house. Behind him he felt the ground split open, stretching into a vast chasm. He sensed a deep hole, reaching out for him, wanting him to lose his balance and fall into it.

The sliding glass door wouldn't budge so Tommy did something he'd never dream of doing: he picked up one of his mother's decorative stones lining the yard and threw it with all his might at the glass.

Nothing happened.

He snatched the rock up again and flung it at the slider a second time.

Same result.

He threw it at a neighboring window.

Not so much as a crack.

And when the entire house began to pulsate as if it were alive, he realized there were forces working against him that he couldn't possibly avoid.

"Mom! Dad!"

Despite the chaos, Tommy heard something that sapped any remaining strength he had: growls.

Growls right behind him.

He spun around and saw the eyes.

Dozens of red-rimmed eyes glared up at him from the gaping chasm, glowing with hatred.

But that wasn't the worst of it.

The eyes were *detached*. They weren't in pairs, as if they were in someone's head, but singular and seemed to float in the black rift.

And they were all looking at him.

Tommy lurched away without another thought. He had to reach the back fence. If he could get over it then maybe, just maybe he'd be able to escape. He could only hope that the rest of the neighborhood wasn't compromised as well.

As he skirted around the hole, trying not to look at the eyes, Tommy saw his idea of scaling the fence was not a good one.

There were … *things* past it. Horrible things with writhing tentacles and squirming bodies that he couldn't even begin to describe.

Standing in the purgatory between his house and the fence, Tommy's mind was racing. His options were extremely limited, and he knew it. He couldn't climb the fence. He couldn't go back to his house. And he couldn't stand and fight.

Hell was opening up.

One day that treehouse will save your life.

The treehouse! He could climb to his treehouse!

Having no time to wonder just how a treehouse would protect him from the things crawling toward him, Tommy ran to the huge tree and began to scuttle up the mismatched wooden planks nailed to its trunk. Behind him the stench rose from the undulating ground, almost a tangible thing.

It threatened to overtake him.

His treehouse never seemed so far away. The trapdoor loomed high in the tree, beckoning to him. Offering a chance at survival.

Tommy took the planks quickly, pulling himself up one at a time. He felt the presence of the things behind him, but resisted looking back, focusing instead on reaching the treehouse. On the other side of the fence things rustled back and forth, and these too he tried to ignore.

"Please, God, let the boards hold."

No sooner had the words left his mouth then the plank he was holding dislodged from the tree. His arm flung backward, taking the board with it.

The creatures, now swarming across the ground, squealed in delight that their prey was so close to falling into their clutches. Their twisted visages (those that had faces) tightened in hungry excitement.

Tommy hugged the tree. He steadied his breathing, letting the reassuring words of the old man calm his nerves.

The treehouse will save your life. You are the Chosen One.

Was it the end of the world? Is that what the old man meant by calling him the Chosen One?

Feeling air swish across his feet, Tommy glanced down. The beasts that had managed to crawl a few feet up the tree were swiping at him, only four or five planks below.

Tommy immediately increased his pace, and in a few seconds had put a comfortable distance between him and the creatures.

When the trapdoor to the treehouse was just above his head. Tommy swung his arm up and deftly unlatched the pitted brass lock holding it closed.

The creatures were now crawling over one another, creating a living pile that quickly grew in height. Some fell off, only to be replaced by others, who in turn would fall themselves, but their sheer numbers more than made up for their lack of coordination.

They were right below Tommy as he crawled up into the treehouse and slammed the trapdoor shut.

Heavy silence settled over the treehouse.

Tommy fell into a folding chair and weighed his options: he couldn't go anywhere, there was no guarantee the things outside wouldn't get in, and the neighbors were nowhere to be seen. And to top it all off, he had no food or water.

In short, he was trapped.

Looking out a small window, Tommy stared at the sky. It was angry red, fiery and swallowed any normalcy.

But that wasn't the worst part.

Tommy looked down at the neighborhood.

Houses, the ones that still stood, wallowed in a burning magma. Acrid smoke drifted up from the devastation, completing the nightmarish vision of Hell.

Squirming everywhere were the creatures.

Tommy looked away. The entire world had transformed into a sickening mess.

Then something happened.

He felt powerful. He felt like a superhero. He felt invincible. Gone were all the doubts and fears a kid his age harbored, to be replaced with sheer, unbridled strength and wisdom.

He glanced at his hands and was amazed to see they shone with a pure white light. He looked down at his chest, his legs, his feet; they too gleamed as if made of brilliant light.

The creatures thudded against the trapdoor. A screw popped loose from the impact. Hinges bent from the pressure. Steady growling seeped, along with a bitter smell, into the treehouse.

Unconcerned with the danger, Tommy let his gaze wander back to the window. If he was to be the One, the survivor deemed fit to survive, then would he be alone? How could he carry on the human race without the company of another?

More thudding on the trapdoor, but deeper, with more force.

Tommy saw her.

At first, it was just a pinprick of light, but as he watched, it grew into a dazzling white flash that took on the unmistakable shape of a young girl.

Jessica? Jessica DeWill?

She lived a few blocks away from him. He occasionally saw her in school, and once even worked up the nerve to talk to her.

Jessica. What a beautiful name.

The creatures broke through the trapdoor. Instantly, a dozen clawed hands, each one dripping with slime, grasped for purchase.

Tommy hardly noticed. He simply waved a hand in their direction, washing the beasts away with light.

"Jessica, come to me."

Jessica responded. She lifted off the roof of her house, her body bathed in light, and floated toward the treehouse. Below her, Hell's creatures squirmed in vast numbers, though neither she nor Tommy noticed. Their eyes were locked on one another, wholly aware of their destinies and embracing them.

They were prepared for each other.

With a wave of his hand, Tommy flooded the sky with light. Gleaming clouds of luminescence expanded to full-blown geysers, erupting in torrential downpours that showered the simmering landscape.

The creatures screamed in rage and pain. They fell back into the ground, swallowed whole by the scarred Earth.

Tommy greeted Jessica when she reached the treehouse, and they fell into each other's arms, fusing together in a gentle flash of light. They became one. They completed each other.

Far below, pushing his way through the smeared landscape was the old man.

He stopped.

He looked up.

He locked his yellow eyes on the young couple. "Good," he drawled. "Humanity is safe." He ran a long hand over his head, stopping momentarily to rub the stubby horns that pushed their way through his greasy hair. "Their test is complete. They will be my new apprentices. They will lead the armies of Hell for me."

And with those cryptic words the old man walked away on cloven hooves, his forked tail dragging along the ground behind him.

It started out as a normal drive, until they decided to take a shortcut down Old Creek Road.

They left home just before seven, headed for the town of Luton around thirty miles away. The sky was already growing dark. The first ten minutes were fairly uneventful until Jenny forgot to pay attention to a stop sign— luckily, there was no other traffic around. She apologized profusely, but James still scolded.

"Just be more careful! I don't want to die picking up concert tickets."

"You know," Jenny said after they had gone on for a while, "just because I only have a learner's permit doesn't mean you can treat me like crap."

"Do you want me to teach you or not? This isn't exactly fun for me."

They reached a crossroads, and he instructed her to turn right.

"But the Google map said to go straight on," she protested.

"They never tell you the best route on the internet," he responded as patiently as he could manage. "I've been driving around here for seven years. I know all the shortcuts."

Jenny sighed, exasperated, then made the turn.

"We better be back before nine," she muttered.

"Why? Got a sexting session planned with your boyfriend?"

"Screw you."

"I think I'm the only guy you haven't screwed."

"Gross!"

This road was littered with potholes, and had fewer streetlights than the one they had traveled previously. Withered trees stood under the pale half-moon. The only sounds were the engine and the blow of the heater. It grew increasingly dark, and the road surface became more uneven. There was no sign of life ahead or behind.

"How much longer is this *short*cut?" Jenny emphasized the last word sarcastically.

"Probably another five miles or so."

"Jeez. Seriously?" She turned to look at him "Did you *want* to make things as scary as possible for me?"

The car began to drift to the side of the road.

"Watch out!" James cried.

A second later the car hit a giant pothole. There was a horrible *crunch* and Jenny lost control of the steering. The car was still traveling at about fifty miles per hour when it left the road, bumping along the grass verge.

Jenny slammed her foot on the brake, but they were still going too fast. Amidst all the chaos, James tried to reach over and steer the car away from the roadside drainage ditch they were approaching at alarming speed. Before he could manage it the nose of the car thumped up, then dropped, as the car nose-dived into the ditch, sliding to a stop with a jolt that rattled metal and bones. Jenny screamed as everything went black.

~ ~ * * ~ ~

James opened his eyes. Everything looked out of focus. He put his hand up to feel for his glasses. They were there, but when he took away his hand he saw blood. He touched his nose and confirmed it was just a little nosebleed, not a gusher. The details of the crash slowly came back to him. He had no idea how long he had been unconscious. Once he realized where he was, he looked over at Jenny. She wasn't moving.

"Jenny? Are you okay?" His voice trembled. "Are you injured?"

She finally woke and shifted in her seat. Slowly, painfully, she turned to look at him. Her long hair was tangled, and there was a bruise on her cheek, but otherwise she appeared uninjured. She tried to reply, but only whimpered.

James released his seat belt and reached over to her, patting her arms, ribs and legs. She flinched but he took her lack of an anguished cry as evidence she wasn't seriously injured.

"You're fine, quit being a baby."

He turned his attention to their surroundings. The vehicle sat at an almost forty-five degree angle. All he saw on the passenger side was the gully wall, tree roots and rocks poking out of it.

"That was the most horrible thing ever," Jenny said. "I had no control."

"Because you're a *terrible* driver. That's the last time I take *you* anywhere."

"I just want to get out."

"Good. Maybe you'll get run over and I'll be free of babysitting you."

"Stop being a jerk!"

She opened her door and slowly climbed out. James was forced to slide across the seat to follow her. They both walked around the car to assess the damage. One whole side of it was buried in the ditch. It was hard to see what condition the tires were in with the darkness and mud obscuring everything, but James guessed it wasn't good.

Teeth chattered loudly, and he turned to see Jenny trembling, tears on her cheeks. He put his arm around her.

"I'm sorry, I shouldn't blame you. It was only *mostly* your fault."

"Why did we have to take that stupid shortcut?" she hissed.

"Hey," he said, backing away. "I was just trying to save us time! Don't take it out on me."

She glared.

"I better call home," James said. "Let them know you've got us stuck out here."

He took out his mobile phone and pressed the power button, the little green screen glowing.

"Shit," he said softly.

"What is it?" There was a note of panic in Jenny's voice.

"Can't get a signal here."

"So we're stranded?"

"Don't be stupid. Even if I can't get the phone to work, someone will drive by eventually."

Jenny looked at him doubtfully. Suddenly, they heard something rustling in the woods above them.

"What was that?" Jenny asked, alarmed.

"A badger?" James replied in as relaxed a tone as he could manage.

The rustle and crunch came again. It sounded like a large animal.

"I think we should get back in the car," Jenny said.

"Yeah," James agreed before she even finished speaking.

Jenny jumped in and slid across to the passenger side. James sat behind the wheel. He turned the key in the ignition.

"What are you doing?" she asked.

"Seeing if we can get out of here on our own."

The engine started, giving him a glimmer of hope. He hit the pedal, and hope quickly died. The car didn't move an inch, the tires finding no traction on the muddy slope.

He banged his fist on the wheel.

"Fuck!"

"How are we going to get out of here?" she said, starting to cry again.

"It's okay," he reassured her. "Someone will come along eventually."

"We're not that lucky."

He noticed her shivering.

"Want me to put on the heater?"

"No. It's not the cold. I feel … weird."

"Weird how?"

"Like I'm not really here. Like this is a dream."

"My dreams involve a threesome with Katy Perry and Jennifer Lawrence, not being stuck here with my brat of a sister."

"Don't call me that!"

"What, sister?"

"Moron."

"I'm going to see if there's any house around here we can call for help from," James said.

Jenny grabbed his arm.

"Don't! It's not safe."

"What are you talking about?"

"We have to get out of here."

"Why?"

"I… I just have a bad feeling about it. Don't leave, please?"

"This may be our only chance. Are you coming?"

She stared at him defiantly.

"Fine. Stay here and get raped and killed."

He got out and slammed the car door, feeling slightly guilty about his choice of words. But she was so difficult to deal with, he couldn't help but be harsh. Before he could find the easiest path up the muddy hill, Jenny appeared beside him.

"I've decided to come with you," she said quietly.

James just smiled and nodded and started to climb the slope. He slipped several times, but managed to grab a branch or stone before falling. Once safely at the top he called for Jenny to follow, then reached down and pulled her up. A flickering light from deep in the woods caught James' attention.

"Did you see that?"

"No."

"It looked like a house."

"Can't we just go back to the road and flag down a car?"

"Don't be such a girl. Come on."

Clutching his sister's hand, James led her deeper into the woods, down a trail leading toward the mysterious light source. Twisting tree roots threatened to trip them up, but eventually they reached a clearing.

Inside the clearing was a cabin that looked like it hadn't been inhabited in years. The wooden walls were rotted through in places and most of the windows were broken. Several logs were missing from the roof. The only sign of life was the light that glowed inside.

James pounded on the door with his fist.

Silence.

He tried again, with the same result. He turned the handle and found the door unlocked.

"What are you doing?" Jenny whispered.

"There might be a phone or something in here. Come on."

He pushed the door open and stepped into the darkness. Jenny belatedly followed him.

The room was in an even worse state of repair than the outside of the cabin. The wallpaper was peeling, the floor cracked, and the furniture broken. There was mold and dust everywhere, a rancid smell flooding his nostrils. The light came from a single candle burning on a desk.

"We shouldn't be here," Jenny said, her hand over her nose.

"I just want to see if there's a working phone."

"How can there be?" Jenny cried. "No one's been here for years!"

"Then who lit the candle?"

His eyes found a tattered old portrait hanging on the wall. It depicted a stern-faced woman who looked to be about a hundred years old. Her eyes sparkled, but not in a pleasant way.

"Look at that old bat," James said to himself.

He searched the filthy room. Spiders and other bugs scuttled away from his touch. His hands passed over several curious objects, including a stone paperweight in the shape of a tiger. Finally, just as he was about to give up, he found an old rotary phone. He frantically picked it up and put it to his ear.

"Is it working?" Jenny asked.

"No," James replied. "Shit!"

He slammed the phone down.

"Let's get out of here," Jenny begged.

"Okay."

They started to walk out. James stumbled in several places where small objects lay hidden in the shadows. Jenny, however, moved with ease, almost as if she had been there before. Just before he reached the door, James heard a loud thump.

"Oh my God!" Jenny screamed, clutching at him.

They both turned to look at the source of the sound—a wardrobe in the corner of the room.

"Who's there?" James asked.

No reply. He prised Jenny's fingers from his arm and walked toward the wardrobe. He paused only to pick up the stone paperweight he had noticed earlier. It wasn't much of a weapon, but it gave him some comfort. He reached the wardrobe and his hand closed on the door handle.

"Don't open it!" screeched a voice he barely recognized. It was less a warning, more a command.

He turned. Jenny stared at him with a cunning expression.

"What's going on?"

"You're ruining the plan," she said, coldly furious. "You weren't supposed to find this place. I just wanted to come home with you. When I found you unconscious in the car, I knew it was my chance. My chance for a new life."

"What the hell are you talking about?"

She sighed, a faint smile on her lips.

"Open that door if you really want to see."

James opened the wardrobe—and screamed as a naked body fell out. He stumbled away, choking on bile.

It was Jenny. He knew right away, even though the body was barely identifiable. The top of the head had been peeled back, revealing an empty cranium. Her throat had been ripped out and her nose removed. The rest of the body was similarly mutilated. It didn't look like the result of any human attack. It was pure animal savagery.

James stared in horror at the dead body, then turned to the thing that looked like his sister standing before him. Under its imitation skin, something … *rippled*. Ancient, sparkling eyes studied him greedily.

The useless paperweight fell from James's hand and crashed on the floor as he slowly stepped away until his back collided with a wall. The thing cocked its head to one side and studied him, licking its lips.

"I warned you not to come here!" it cackled. "I could have been just like your sister. I consumed her mind. You would never have known the difference. But now it's too late."

The thing's body began to twist, stretching into inhuman positions, as if something was fighting to break its way out through the skin. It wagged one finger, suddenly an elongated claw.

"You should have been a nicer brother while you had the chance."

James was frozen in place as the thing approached him. He closed his eyes and heard a wet ripping, something tearing like cloth. Maybe if he wished hard enough, he would wake up from this nightmare. But the demonic laughter was soon drowned out by something far worse.

The sound of chattering, hungry teeth.

32. SENTINELS OF THE ENDLESS UNKNOWING BY DJ TYRER

When you are dead, do you know what it is that you might feel and see? Is it torture and torment, or a perfect serenity? That was the question that they posed to me, and my answer was that I did not know; and they replied that soon I would join them in ignorance ...

~ ~ * * ~ ~

"Honey, you're screaming." Marge shook me awake and I looked up at her in confusion.

"You were screaming," she repeated, "that's why I woke you. You were thrashing about and screaming and having one hell of a nightmare. What was it about?"

"Uh, I was dreaming." It was a needless statement, yet it was the first clear thought I could muster. "Um, yeah, I was dreaming that there were these figures, dark, shadowy figures, and ..."

"And what, honey?"

"Uh, well, ah, they were asking me questions."

"And that had you screaming? Why? Were you losing a fortune on a quiz show or something?"

I'd started to wake properly, and while my head was clearer, the dream was fading.

"No, nothing like that. They were ... asking me about death or something. I can't quite remember. But ... whatever it was, it was horrible ... nihilistic, I suppose you could say."

"Nihilistic? That's a big word. When I have nightmares, it's usually something chasing me. Straightforward."

"Well," I laughed, "I'm sorry that my complicated, philosophical dreams disturbed you. I'll try to keep my nightmares on lighter topics in future."

But even as I laughed, something cold and fearful lingered within my guts that I just couldn't shake. Whatever my nightmare had been about, it had really rattled me.

~ ~ * * ~ ~

When I woke in the morning, Marge was there with a tray of coffee and toast.

"Well, it's your day off," she told me as I looked up at her in surprise, "and after your nightmare last night, I thought maybe you could do with a little pampering."

"Oh, thanks. That's very kind of you." I took a bite. "Nice toast."

"Soon."

"Sorry?"

She looked at me, confused. "Honey?"

"Uh, what did you say?"

"Um, that you could do with pampering."

"No, after that."

She shook her head. "I didn't say anything else."

I took another bite. "That's odd, I—"

"Don't talk with your mouth full; it's disgusting."

~ ~ * * ~ ~

I'm not sure what happened next.

It was as if I blinked my eyes and, in that nanosecond of darkness, everything changed. Instead of lying in bed with a tray of coffee and toast on my lap, I was lying on a sunless shore, upon a beach of grey sand or ash. The strangest thing was that while there was no sun, moon or stars in the shadowed sky, nor any other source of light, I could see my surroundings, if but murkily.

"Marge? Marge, are you there?"

There was no reply. There was no sound. The place was as silent as the proverbial grave: there was no breeze, and the water to my right was utterly still. Even when I began to walk, the soft, ash-like sand meant my footfalls made no sound. It was eerie. Bizarre.

"Marge? Marge, are you there?" I called again. Again, there was no reply, only silence.

I had no idea where I was or how I'd gotten there. Had it been a normal beach, I might have assumed I was the victim of some prank. I couldn't imagine Marge drugging me and taking me somewhere, but some sort of practical joke was the only logical explanation … only there was no way a prankster can put out the sun. To create this place— and it appeared huge—would've required a movie-sized budget, and I really couldn't see anyone spending a fortune just to make a fool out of me.

Then, I began to wonder, was I the victim of some weird reality TV show? I mean, there was that one show where they convinced the guy that the world had come to an end … only, you'd have to sign some sort of release form, even if you didn't realise just what was planned, and I was certain I'd signed nothing. Which made me wonder if this was all some sort of crazy Area 51 thing. Had I been kidnapped by the government and taken somewhere for some crazy research project? But surely there would be some kind of experiment, *Men In Black* and all that? I supposed some weird conspiracy made as much sense as anything.

"Okay, so what do you want?" I shouted to the air. "Tell me what you want! Why you're doing this to me!"

There was no answer.

I suppose I could have just stood there, waiting; perhaps it would have been for the best. But I felt as though I ought to be doing something, so I started to walk. Lacking any better plan, I chose to walk away from the water, "inland," as it were, stopping every so often to call out to Marge and the universe in the hope of some explanation for what had befallen me.

I don't know how long I walked. At times it seemed like mere minutes, at others it felt like an eternity. Eventually I became aware of figures in the distance. Something about them unnerved me, yet I continued to walk toward them, scared to remain alone. I had to hope they might be able to answer my questions.

Drawing closer, I saw the figures were tall and thin and seemingly swathed in black robes. Only, as I drew closer still, it seemed to me that they wore not robes, but had long hair that fell down about them on all sides, shrouding them. I finally reached the nearest of the immobile figures. I stopped before it and looked up. Through the falling hair, through narrow gaps, I saw not the face of a man, but a hollow-eyed skull. I shivered. I didn't understand.

"Who are you?" I asked, my voice weak and timorous. "Who are you? I need to know!"

The head tilted slightly, an empty socket staring down at me through a narrow gap in the hair. There was a long silence as it regarded me.

"Truly, I do not know," it said in leaden tones, its fleshless jaw not moving.

"How can you not know? Surely, you must know?"

"Truly, I do not know, and why I know not, I do not know. I believe I am ignorant of all things, although I cannot be certain of that."

"I don't understand ..."

"Nor do I. Perhaps that is why you are here ..."

"Is it?"

"Possibly; I do not know."

"And where is this place? Do you know?"

"No, I do not. We have given a name to it and a name to ourselves, but they were not the names we or it truly bear, unless by some accident of fate."

"You are of no use to me!" I shouted, angry.

"Possibly so. I could not say for certain."

I swore and strode past the tall, thin figure toward another wreathed in long, flowing black hair that obscured its features.

"Who are you?" I asked it. "And, what is this place? And, why am I here?"

"Truly, I do not know," the figure replied. I could not see a face beneath the shroud of hair.

"Your fellow there said you have given a name to yourselves and to this place. Can you tell me?"

"We call this place the Endless Unknowing, for there is no knowledge here, only ignorance unending. As for us, we call ourselves the Sentinels of the Endless Unknowing, although I know not why. We stand here in eternal ignorance, never knowing how or why."

I remembered my dream. It had been these dark figures who had questioned me, asking about the afterlife and telling me that soon I'd be joining them in ignorance. As I remembered their questions and what they'd said, I shivered. Did this mean that I was dead? Was this Heaven or Hell—or Purgatory?

I asked the Sentinel.

"Truly, I do not know. I yearn to know, but know not."

"Were you once a living man? I have to know!"

"Truly, I do not know. None here can recall our origin, nor know the reason why we stand here."

"But, what am I to do? I just don't understand …"

"Then, stand beside us …"

I blinked. It was strange. My vision was growing obscured. It was as if a veil had fallen across my eyes. I reached up and felt a long fringe of hair.

"What is happening?" I asked myself. Then, answering, I said: "Truly, I do not know."

And I didn't.

I turned and joined the ranks that stood there upon the ash-like sands that stretched to infinity, and despite their presence, was alone in my ignorance. And, there I stand yet, uncertain as to truth, a Sentinel of the Endless Unknowing, gazing into forever and never understanding why.

Why?

Truly, I do not know …

33. THE DEVIL'S SPOTLIGHT BY VINCE LIBERATO

The cabin was half empty, with only thirty-eight passengers remaining on the once-full flight. One of their number was condemning them all: this they knew as 30,000 feet below the Devil's Spotlight was clearly visible, shadowing the old Boeing, drawn to the one that was acting as a beacon to it. The beacon knew who he was by the burning pain that wracked where he had accidentally touched it during their last refueling stop, but the other thirty-seven on board could do little more than guess as they frantically tried to find out who it was that the Devil's Spotlight was after.

Whether it was out of cowardice, or some sort of misguided justification steeped in revenge or malice, the motivations of the liar were irrelevant at this point. Those that had been marked before him had admitted to it, and put as much distance as they could between themselves and the remaining passengers as a final act of kindness. By now the flying ark was one of the largest remaining clusters of human beings on the planet, and their survival depended on finding the one the Devil's Spotlight wanted and removing him from the jet as soon as possible. Baseless accusations continued to fly from one passenger to the next, and when it came time for the liar to speak again, for the third time he said he felt nothing.

For days, United Airlines Flight 2523 had been circling the United States, stopping for food and fuel at vacant airports across the country before continuing its Sisyphean journey to prolong the lives of its remaining passengers. The air was the best place to keep away from the Devil's Spotlight, though there were a few pockets of life left living deep underground, high up on mountains, and in arctic areas of the ocean. A handful of people had even figured out how to avoid its attention and still lived, albeit in extreme caution, alone in areas once populated by millions. And now, the one thing all the survivors had in common was that they understood how the Devil's Spotlight operated; knowledge they had gained by watching billions get taken in only a few short days.

It was called the Devil's Spotlight because, from above, it looked like a dark-beamed flashlight shining from an indeterminate point in the sky. The dark nucleus that currently stalked the airplane below was just a fraction of the creature as a whole, the acidic portion of its body it used to digest food. In reality it was much larger, the vast majority an imperceptible, microscopic membrane hundreds of miles in diameter that covered most of the earth's surface. If the bare flesh of something the Devil's Spotlight could consume made contact with this clear portion, the victim was marked, and would be followed by its dark eye until they were caught. Thick clothing and other materials could act as a buffer, but one mistake, one accidental touch or moment of carelessness, and nothing would keep the Devil's Spotlight away from them. Everything that touched the Devil's Spotlight burned on the inside with a fire that would only die when they did.

The pilot came out to speak with the group. The time for talking was reaching its end as the plane was running out of gas, and they were going to land soon. Because he had remained inside when it landed last, he was the only one who was guaranteed not to have been marked, and he had a solution to the problem at hand. The passengers would draw lots numbered one through thirty-seven and be ejected out of the plane until the Devil's Stoplight stopped following them. If they refused this, he would crash the plane himself. A game of roulette, he explained in a grim tone, in which the odds would get a little better every time the wheel was spun. Otherwise, every one of them was already dead. None protested when he finished, all believing that disagreeing with this method could be a false admission of guilt. After a short pause, the captain told them they had fifteen minutes to decide while he numbered scraps of paper to use.

The arguing renewed with even greater intensity in a last effort to find the liar before the captain's return. One man suggested they check clothing for holes or some other telltale sign that would identify the marked. The liar was prepared for this, however, and had replaced his frayed gloves at a gift shop when he was scavenging for food in the empty receiving terminal. He had not noticed the small hole in the fingertip of the glove until it was too late. It happened so fast, his fingertip grazing the tile while tying his shoe, and in an instant his flesh lit up at the contact. He ran back with the food he had scavenged, picking a new pair of gloves from a ski shop before boarding the plane. Hundreds of miles away, the black nucleus of the Devil's Spotlight began throttling toward him, and had made it not long before the plane took off.

After the clothing check, unsubstantiated accusations continued, founded on nothing but suspicion and desperation. When the captain emerged with the lots to be drawn, they all went silent, lining up to pick one from where they were concealed in his hat. One by one, they pulled slips of paper out to see the order they would be going. The people with numbers past the halfway mark seemed confident that they would be spared and the liar found, while those on the other side of it took some comfort in the fact that they would not be the first to go and still stood a chance of survival.

It was the liar's turn now. He held his breath and picked a number while the internal burning raged on. His fist closed on his choice, and slowly, he unwrapped it to see where in the line he would have to stand.

Thirty-five.

He was third to last, and this brought him comfort.

The next person was a middle-aged man, who had started the trip with jet-black hair that by now had gone completely grey. His hands shook when they dipped into the hat, and he turned away from everyone to see what number he drew.

The person behind him refused to draw until it was revealed what the grey-haired man had picked. The scrap of paper that he had been clutching fluttered to the ground in response, all eyes on it to see a single, rigid stroke of ink that stretched from the top of the paper to the bottom. When they looked back up at him, all stared into the barrel of a pistol the grey-haired man held with shaky hands.

"Hey, listen …" the liar was the first to speak. "Fair's fair. You drew the one, and …"

The grey-haired man cocked the pistol in response and the liar shut his mouth. He pointed it at the liar, and asked if he was the person that the Devil's Spotlight was chasing. Without pause, the liar lied a fourth time.

The barrel of the gun darted from suspect to suspect, and every time the grey-haired man asked the same question: every time he was given the same answer. Then the gun pointed at the captain, and the look in the eyes of the grey-haired man told all who could see it that his intentions had shifted. The marked man, who knew he was the one they were looking for, suppressed a smile with the same difficulty he did with the fires raging inside him.

"Please … please don't shoot. I'm the one it's after." A voice broke the silence, causing the grey-haired man to lower his weapon in surprise. Several of the passengers tackled the grey-haired man and disarmed him before he could get a shot off. The liar, barely able to contain his shock, turned, looking for the owner of the voice.

A young girl, no older than twenty, accepted responsibility, claiming she had been the one to touch the membrane after stumbling and falling.

She said the burn had not begun until they were in the air and she was sorry she had waited so long to confess. Tears welled in the corners of her eyes, and she apologized again and again to her stunned audience, asking only if they would allow her a parachute when she jumped. Some wanted to refuse, and eject her now as punishment for waiting so long to confess. More arguing over this luxury occurred, but it ended when she suggested that if she had a slow descent, it would give them time to move further away from the black eye of the Devil's Spotlight. Even without a victim, their hunter still crept along the surface of the earth, and if she kept it stationary for a few extra minutes, the airplane would be able to put more distance between them.

This was agreed upon, and she was given the parachute. Before the door was opened however, the liar blocked her path.

"I'm sorry," he said, hoping to understand why she had said what she did.

"No. No, you're not," she replied, and jumped out of the cursed airplane.

The parachute opened, jerking her with a hard pull. Below her, she could see even more clearly the pitch black heart of the Devil's Spotlight. It rushed below her, and a few seconds later, continued on its trajectory under the airplane, following the living beacon on board. She hit the ground, took off her parachute, and continued to live.

I cut a piece off Jane's arm, placed the soft pink flesh in my mouth, and chewed it slowly. She didn't even flinch.

"Too salty?" she asked when she saw my lips twist slightly. She rubbed a finger over the wound I had made with the knife. Seconds later, another piece of flesh draped it like a veil, then attached itself to her arm. The wound was healed.

"No," I lied. "You always taste good."

Jane sat in her chair, robe open to show off her naked body. We had just had sex, which, it dawned on me a year ago, is why her flesh can cure most ailments, even bring some people back from the dead.

"How's your headache, now?" Jane leaned in and kissed my forehead.

"Better," I said. Lately the rains have been bringing in dust from the chemical plant the next county over. It wreaks havoc on my body as well as the others in town. Ever since the Town Corporation began creating their own human beings—a synthetic body with a chemical brain—those particles spread everywhere and we regular humans have acquired … problems. For me, it's not so bad; for most, brain tumors and other cancers have developed.

Some babies have been born with strange side effects. I recently delivered a child here in town that was born with an extra hand. Two days later the mother smothered it to death with a pillow, screaming that it was a monster. A week after that I found out she hung herself in her cell. Where did she get the rope, since all inmates are stripped of their clothing, not to mention their dignity?

Others, such as Jane, have evolved into Healing Mistresses. Their bodies can be used for medicinal purposes, though it is outlawed in forty-seven states, including here. I'm not sure why it is against the law. Is it the sex part? That's what helps these Healers produce the chemicals that cure. Or is it the fear of these inhuman properties?

I don't have an answer.

Jane lowered my head to her breasts. I kissed her left nipple, licked gently. Then her right, sucking it some. She sighed.

There was a knock at my front door. She pushed me away, wrapping her robe around herself quickly. I fell out of my chair laughing. Out of the corner of my eye I saw Jane run past. Whoever it was kept knocking, softly, slowly, then rapid and fast.

"Answer the door, will you?" Jane yelled from the bedroom as she slammed the door.

I picked myself up and went to the front door. My neighbor, Walter, stood there, looking frantic. We served together in the Second East Coast War between New England states and New York. We were even in the same POW camp in Attica.

"Heyyyy…Walter." I smiled. "Come on in and have some stew Jane made—"

"Steve," he said, then bit his lower lip. Walter always did that when he was nervous about something. You don't spend two years together in Attica without learning to know a guy real well. "I need your help." He pushed past me and started walking in circles. "It's bad, man. It's bad."

"Calm down," I said, closing the front door. "Sit down and tell me about what's bothering you."

"It's Sissy." Walter held his head in his hands as he sank slowly into a seat at the table. Sissy was Walters's wife. We met her in the POW camp—she the only one that was healthy in that place. Sissy helped tend to the sick, and when I brought Jane here she was motherly to her, so it was heartbreaking to hear something was wrong with Sissy.

I sat beside him and put a hand on his shoulder.

"Something is wrong, Steve. She's not herself. She's become something I don't recognize." He looked up at me. "I'm telling you, it's frightening."

"Tell me: what's wrong with Sissy?"

"She's changing," Walter said. "Changing into something … I don't know what it is." He choked on his tears and shook his head. "I don't know what to do."

"Okay. Maybe I can help. When did all this start?"

"A few weeks ago, really. I started noticing small things. Bumps on her back. She said it was an allergy. Remember?"

"Yeah," I said. "You brought her here, and we fed her a piece of Jane. They didn't go away?"

"Just for a day or two." He thought a minute. "But … a few months ago, when Sissy cut herself on that metal pole when we were running from Gugs, Jane healed her then too."

"I remember. What are you getting at, Walter?"

"Nothing, I was just thinking out loud. Damn those Gugs. They poisoned us with that corporate shit from the chemical plant. Turned us all into some sort of freaks."

Gugs were these people who lived by the swamps where the plants dumped unwanted chemicals. These people used to live in the suburbs until they lost their jobs and then their houses and had to move out to the swamps. The chemicals they'd absorbed had caused some form of random devolution—a strange form of caveman: some with three arms, and some with no limbs at all; some with loose, over-sized jaws that hung to their chests. Some with glowing red eyes in the backs of their hands, and some who had strange umbilical connections to one or two other people.

Walter was right. We were all becoming horrible freaks in this godforsaken world.

"She's been to the Circle," Walter said. "I asked why she was there. She said she was hungry."

My face fell. "My God," I said. "You have to keep her from going there."

"I've tried. I had her locked in the cellar. She broke out this morning. I looked for her at the circle. I couldn't stay there, Steve … I couldn't do …"

"Okay," I told him. "We'll look for her."

The Circle was a low rent apartment building, owned and funded by the state, called Circle West. Made famous when city police, at the behest of the mayor, rounded up all the so called "degenerates" and moved them out. The mayor wanted to knock it down and build a new football stadium for the college next door, but the police took it too far. They murdered over 150 men, women, and children, of all races, and simply left their bodies *in situ*. After that, it became a place where they brought bodies and torched them. Soon enough they just dropped off the unwanted, dead or alive, left them locked in the basement of the building. Within a few years, more than a thousand had occupied the Circle and its surroundings. All sub-genres of humans, dead or alive. . . or none of the above, reside there.

The Circle was a dark gray four-story building standing on the edge of town, just across the train tracks facing the synthetic food packaging plant. A wire fence had been erected to keep the undesirables in the building, but it looked like those undesirables had other plans: the battered fence barely clung to the metal poles attached to the large stoops in front of the entrance. It was grotty. Horrible smells snuck inside your nostrils, and never let go.

We were out front, Walter and I, scared shitless. The sounds rising from the Circle were inside prisons or POW camps. People being savaged, stripped of any humanity. We didn't want to go in there. Twice I had to stop Walter from leaving me.

Inside the Circle there was no electricity. Pitch black. Walter had just a penlight on his belt. As we walked, slowly, my hand firmly on his shoulder, we had the sensation of the walls moving beneath our hands. Occasional sounds seemed to come from them: a grunt, a yelp, or a blood curdling scream.

Finally, we stumbled into light. It was a boiler room, and hotter than hell. Steam rose from the walls, forming a thick mist that surrounded us. We saw shapes in the mist, hands reaching out—not grasping or groping, just reaching out. In a corner of the place, beside two huge water heaters, we found Sissy. She crouched on the concrete floor, devouring a man's face. Although he screamed, arms flapping like a fish out of water, he made no effort to stop her.

Walter took a breath. "Sissy!"

She turned, hissing. Her mouth was filled with the man's blood, dripping from her chin. Her eyes were like two half-moons, the color of burnt umber.

"Sissy," Walter said. "Please come home … we can cure this … Jane can cure you."

"No." Jane stepped out of the thick mist, naked, showing how the pink flesh on her thin body moved like hands on satin sheets, leaving shadows on it like scars. "I can't cure what I have created."

"What?" Walter said, confusion on his face. "Created what?'

"An extension of the human race. It ensures their existence … just not as recognizable to you. All over the world, we healing mistresses have become new deities—goddesses—for these new humans to worship."

Sissy gurgled, body shaking like an epileptic being electrocuted. Her skin slowly peeled away. Two large humps appeared at the shoulder blades, then morphed into folds of new, see-through skin. In one burst of energy, wings expanded from that clear skin. Her jaw extended down past her neck. She opened her jaws to scream, and a forked tongue rolled out of her fanged mouth. Her face was flattened, as if someone had smacked her with the smooth part of an iron. Her long blond hair began to recede, the brittle strands falling to the concrete as her fingers curled into elongated claws.

Sissy stopped shaking. She got to her clubbed feet, standing hunched over.

Walter wept.

"What have you done?" he asked in a whisper. "What have you done?" He shook his head.

"It's for the best," I told him. "We will survive. Rise up and take the world back from those who keep us down."

"Steve … this is wrong in so many ways. Jane wasn't curing people. She didn't have the cure … she had the disease."

"I shrugged. "You say tomato, I say tomahto. Nothing you can do about it."

Walter had lost all hope. It was in his posture, the way he stood. No hope.

But I had one surprise for him.

My skin began to move. A massive pain grew in the pit of my stomach. I was hungry, hungry for flesh.

Hungry for Walter.

There was a resounding click, followed by flickering as the bulb fought to capture the spark. The light expanded, cone shaped, like what you would see in a B-movie interrogation room. The light caught Jo just right, hunched over her broadcast setup, matter-of-factly taking in her essence as she stared into a blinking screen.

Dark Goth bob over pale, vampire skin. Perky tits pushing through the tattered remains of a Ramones T-shirt. If the screen went any lower it would show her naked from the waist down, her body curled snake-like around a squeaky revolving chair that had done more damage to her extremities than anything the CIA could dream up.

Jo smiled as she adjusted the dials, amping up the frequency. Most men would find her eminently doable; but most men, or women for that matter, were not what her audience was all about, which was why sex for her was anonymous hookups in faraway places. She never gave her real name. They most likely did not give theirs. She had one rule. No cameras. No cell phones.

And yes she did frisk them.

Because distrust and disbelief was what Jo was all about.

Jo grabbed the monster of a microphone, something left over from the Cretaceous age of technology, and gave it a few love taps. The sound levels were spot-on. She glanced through the darkness to a far wall where the luminescent numbers on an old style industrial clock showed 11:59. Jo took a final drag on a smoldering cigarette and tamped it into an overflowing ashtray.

The clock went twelve midnight, straight up. It was show time.

Jo moved within inches of the microphone. She whistled a raw erratic snippet of *The Twilight Zone* theme, then segued into a high pitched hum that peaked in a bloody banshee scream.

"Good evening my children," she cooed into the radio ether. "Welcome to *The Land Beyond Beyond*. The place where trust is a myth, conspiracy is the life-blood, and belief is what you make it because you know better than everybody else what is truly out there. I'm Jo. Or at least that's who you *think* I am."

Jo twisted another knob hard to the right, sending a *squawk* and *squall* out along the airwaves. She slammed the dial to the left as the static shot to black. Jo's mouth smoothly caressed the metal appendage.

"Talk to me, my children." Her tone was a breathless whisper. "Tell me your dreams, your wishes, your magic tales. Tell me what you believe and disbelieve. Don't be shy, my pets. We all dwell in dark places. We have nothing to fear."

Jo was answered by silence. Ten minutes into her show, and nary a sound. She knew they were out there. But for a long time there had been nothing to say.

She sighed.

"Come on," she softly admonished. "Give me something. A memory of the times. A theory that only a few of us understand. Is there anybody out there? Did the world suddenly end just before I came on the air? That's it. It's apocalypse now. Most of us are atomic ash. But I'm sure a few of you made it to the bunkers. Tell me what you see. Tell me what you hear. Tell me what you believe."

Ten minutes later and still nothing.

Jo reached for the pack and another death stick. She lit up and dragged deep. She leaned back, her creaky chair emitting a raw death rattle amid the silence. Her body passed easily out of the light and into the dark. Jo took another drag …

… and remembered the time. When fantasy and reality were abroad in the land.

The Loch Ness Monster, UFOs, Bigfoot, the Kennedy assassination. People gathered to speculate, to explain and, most importantly to believe and not believe. They believed in a conspiratorial way. They knew the truth as nobody else did. Area 51, Chupacabra, Bat Boy, the screams of Hell heard coming from the center of the earth by a passing Russian trawler.

Their mantra was the possibilities that lurked in the darkest corners of night.

Their numbers grew. They were the isolated, the socially inept, the just plain psychotic and crazy. But they all found a common cause, refusing to believe and not believe what the status quo insisted was right, good, and just plain not there.

Jo mentally marveled at how their numbers had grown to legions over the years. They came together at larger and larger unions. They seriously recounted how they had been abducted by aliens, and nobody laughed. They listened intently as the rancher proudly proclaimed that he had a live dinosaur roaming his back forty. One woman claimed she had seen the bodies of the Roswell aliens. Another said her morning toast had an image of Elvis in it. There was the earnest, overweight and excessively sweating nerd who always dressed in a suit, and who, through endless books and speaking engagements, had convinced his believers that the death of Kennedy and the 9/11 attacks were the work of rogue CIA operatives known simply as The Blacks.

Jo was one of them. The unexplainable had been her companion from an early age. It had been ingrained in her DNA, to believe only in the fantastical possibilities. She was big on cryptozoology, even claimed to have seen a Bigfoot during an outing in her teens. Reality did not get her through her day: the truly unbelievable did.

And so she begot *The Land Beyond Beyond*.

The show began life as a microscopic watt on the far left side of the FM dial. The format was simple. *Tell me your stories. I will not judge. I will believe.* The format was so different from anything else on the dial that it soon picked up steam and the all-important ratings. As the guide, listener, and sympathetic conduit to the unknown, Jo was a natural: her teasing, prompting, and somewhat sultry tones were ideal for the late at night, for an audience that most perceived as emotionally marginalized from the workaday world.

Callers had found their savior. Their tales of encounters, sightings, and personal beliefs about what the government was *really* adding to the water morphed into a campfire roundtable of the airwaves. Experts were not shunned, but were rarely given more than cursory time to hawk their wares. It was the people calling in from darkened rooms, trucks barreling through the night, or dealing with age and loneliness by calling Jo and telling her what they knew that was important.

The Land Beyond Beyond soon went viral, becoming an internet sensation. Before long syndication came calling, and Jo was able to quit her day job as a barmaid in a low rent strip mall dive and turn up the frequency on what was really important …

To her and to them.

And then something really strange happened.

The Loch Ness Monster flippered its way out of the depths and onto a loch-side dune and basically sunned itself in front of more than fifty astonished tourists, all of whom had cameras, before casually turning and sliding easily back into the loch. Long story short: yes, it was a Plesiosaur.

Right in the middle of an overcast Washington D.C. morning, a UFO, doing its best *The Day the Earth Stood Still* imitation, settled down on The White House lawn, and over an advanced sound system that reportedly reached around the world, it broadcast in perfect English "Take me to your leader."

Bigfoot made an unexpected entrance at a mountainside mom-and-pop store in the Pacific Northwest. Locals captured it and were astonished to find that, through primitive sign language, they were eventually able to communicate with it. The creature, a Neanderthal-looking thing, was surprisingly cooperative, letting the human race know that they had been around since before the Ice Age and, to the shock of many, had become more human than human by mating with modern day women. The sound the world heard was that of a million anti-evolutionists hitting the floor. But there they were, brothers and sisters under a hairy skin.

Jo took another languid drag and laughed softly into the night. The Philadelphia Experiment. Invisibility tests on big ships to aid the war effort. Nobody believed it... until some yahoos with metal detectors scoping a stretch of land near the legendary naval base struck something very rough, metallic and invisible. A year later a researcher with sensitive fingers discovered it was a ship's title plaque, etched with the words Eldridge. The jig was up.

The Kennedy assassination. After nearly sixty years of fingering everybody from Castro to the CIA to the janitor who emptied Congress' ashtrays turned up nothing but a billion words of speculation that indicated everybody on the planet we really knew who blew JFK's head off... who would have thought the French and the Swedes were capable of such a thing? But a deathbed confession took care of that one.

Within a couple of years all of the great mysteries that had eluded hard science for centuries and gave true believers a reason to get up in the morning had been proven. The world was in amazement, tying itself in and out of emotional, sociological, and political knots. The people who listened to her show puffed out their collective chests.

Jo's people had been right all along. Their withdrawn, desperate lives had been worth something after all. But their triumph was short lived …

Because soon there was nothing left to believe in.

More often than not *The Land Beyond Beyond* had evolved into an immature, bitch session with thinly veiled discourses on how letting all the true mysteries out of the bag had been the devil's work or a plot by the Illuminati to strike at the very fiber of humanity. But soon things changed. The calls to Jo turned into rambling, often psychotic and thinly disguised cries for help. The people whose questionable lives hinged on the drug of belief had suddenly had their drug taken away from them.

And most were not detoxing real well.

The calls were tinged with alcohol, coke and meth. Jo could tell. And any doubt that many in Jo's listening audience had replaced pure belief with pure heroin was removed one night when one of her regulars, a gentle soul who claimed he was Jesus and that it was a heretofore unknown twin brother who actually died on the cross, called up and, in a mumbling monologue, described in detail how he had just scored some pure shit, was digging around in his arm with the spike to find a virgin vein and finally jammed the horse into an obliging line. Jo was just a touch freaked, but listened intently as the caller described how the blood had surged up into the syringe before a moment of orgasmic relief and, finally, the sound of his body hitting the floor.

Jo was momentarily speechless but not without a sense of dark irony.

"Ok. I give that a 7.5 for originality. If you can top an OD give me a call."

And they did.

The woman with many alien abductions under her belt called in. The line crackled with crisp, thin static, a sign that the caller was outdoors. The caller was tearful. She sounded high, or was it a final sigh of resignation that she now was dealing with a reality that did not include her ideas about UFO's, sea monsters and *Men In Black*? As Jo listened, the woman jabbered incoherently about the aliens coming for her. They had instructed her to jump, high wide and far and that they would catch her in their interceptor beam and take her aboard the mother ship for a ride home. After a moment of silence, there was a low whisper.

"Goodbye."

The *New York Tattler* led with the story the next day. "Woman Takes Suicide Solution In 20 Story Leap."

Jo sighed and smiled tightly as the silence in the night continued. As did the memories.

She recalled a fairly regular caller who called himself Rod who would regale her listeners with tales of how H.G. Wells' *The Time Machine* was based on fact, and that he had spent years of researching and fine tuning what he would one day unveil to the world as the first actual time machine. Two years after the "Time of big discovery," with the calls coming fewer and further between and bordering on extreme nut job, Rod called in.

There was excitement in his voice. He had finally figured out what made time work, had put all the elements into the engine of a 1967 Mustang and was about to rocket out of the present and into the future. The revving of the engine shattered the airwaves. A screech of transmission and Rod was off. Those who still listened called in with enthusiastic encouragement. Rod reported in one more time. The speedometer had just hit 105. By his calculations another 20 miles and he would pass through space and time. Finally he reported that he had hit the magic number. He gave a manic cowboy "yeeha"…

… as he rocketed through space and head-on into the 9:25 express coming in from Oshkosh. There was not enough left in the wreckage to identify the remains. Jo would silently hope that Rod had truly made it and was somewhere in the time to come.

Jo was certain that the demise of those who suddenly had nothing left to believe in had not always been so dramatic. Most probably died alone in their rooms on the business end of a straight razor or a bottle of downers. Some were probably cop-assisted suicides. She was certain a lot had become institutionalized. They were the lucky ones. She feared that the vast majority were still out there, walking the streets, searching in vain for something to believe in. And doing who knows what in the process.

She wished them luck.

Jo leaned back into the stagnant cone of light. She hunched over the microphone. *The Land Beyond Beyond* was going on 45 minutes without a sign of life. It was time to bring up the heavy artillery.

"So you have nothing to say?" she feigned boring disgust. "Maybe this will loosen your tongues. From now until I sign off you will have to contend with "In A Gadda Da Vida." The extra-long version on a never-ending loop. The only thing that will save you is a call. Insult my ancestry. Talk about the shape shifters that are hiding in your flower bed. Give me something people. Here comes Hell."

The haunting keyboard intro and the fuzzed-out guitar heralded the arrival of one of the most obnoxious songs ever created by man. Jo pulled a tattered roach out of her pocket and lit up. Then she leaned back to enjoy the ride.

One hour and four-and-a-half plays later. Then out of nowhere came a blip on the screen. It was brief, faint but persistent. Crank calls and hang-ups usually did not register that kind of fingerprint. Jo knew the difference because she could remember how, before everything in the night was suddenly out in the open, she would have those kind of signs lined up around the block. Jo took a final drag and pressed some buttons.

"It's Jo. You know the drill. Talk to me."

"First off, I hate 'In A Gadda Da Vida,'" said a low sinister male voice. Jo smiled. "Yeah everybody's a critic. It's your dime."

"The name's Deep Throat. Yeah I know. But I'm the real Deep Throat."

Jo stifled a laugh. Making fun of a caller was a no-no in this business. "I'm listening."

"I used to work for the space program. You know Armstrong, the first man on the moon?"

Jo played along. This was the first live wire she'd had in almost six months.

Deep Throat hacked out an aged, rasping cough. "Well what the world does not know was that there were four astronauts on that mission. Three came back. Need I say more?"

Deep Throat clicked off. Jo relit the stub of her joint and inhaled. What a rush. She barely had time to exhale before another blip of a caller made its presence felt.

"I was diagnosed with terminal cancer eighteen years ago. I'm still alive. The pharmaceutical industry is trying to shut me up because what I know would put them out of business. I can't say much more at this time because my line is constantly tapped." *Click.*

There was a flicker of hope in Jo's blitzed expression. Was a second wave of whacked-out believers out there, waiting to make their move? Over the next hour, the calls began to once again take hold on the possibility and impossibility of it all.

A stereotypically scummy stock broker made a deal with the devil and claimed he had the whole transaction on video. A left-wing nut literally screamed that he had proof that the head of the NRA had a criminal record a mile long. A right-wing wacko balanced the ledger when he claimed that the scripture clearly outlined how liberal thinkers were the spawn of Satan. Jo was convinced that desperation and the futility of life for so many had brought her people back. Quite simply it was believe or perish.

The rest of the show raced by with waves of argumentative, rational and irrational ravings. It was like the time before the discoveries dampened the spirit. Everybody was right and everybody was wrong. Which is the way it should be.

"Okay, my children," Jo enthusiastically crooned into the airwaves. It's good to have you back. We've got time for one more call. Zelda, welcome to *The Land Beyond Beyond*."

"Oh am I on? I know you're running out of time, so I'll make this quick. My name is Zelda and I come from the future. You are going to die in ten days. Just thought you'd like to know."

Jo faded the show out in an abrupt shock of static. She leaned back in her chair and contemplated what might be a limited future. She could believe or disbelieve. She was content to just let it play out. One thing was certain.

If Jo was around on day eleven it would be one hell of a show.

~ * ~

God could not be everywhere, and therefore he made mothers—
Rudyard Kipling

~ * ~

Some might call her a curtain-twitcher. Day in, day out she watched the children playing out in the street. *Nosey old bag*, the parents might say. *All she does is stare all day. She's a bloody witch if ever I saw one.* Such malicious references caused her no harm. The old adage about sticks and stones had always held a special place in her heart; a decades-old tapestry hanging above the kitchen door said as much. The bad things they said always got back to her, though, for she had tiny eyes and ears everywhere. The children *trusted* her—why wouldn't they?—and she compensated their loyalty with sweets, and stories of faraway lands and magical creatures. Of course, the parents were oblivious to such activities. Despite not caring what they thought of her, she knew stealth was of the utmost importance; therefore a clandestine path had been cleared to the right of her house, beyond the bins, and the back door was kept slightly ajar whenever the children were out front.

They called her *Ma*, a wonderful sound that simply rolled off the tongue. Even the youngest of children could say it, and so they did, with great satisfaction, whenever they were around her. "Why do you enjoy smoking so much, Ma?" That had been Billy Cooper, one of the more ostentatious children of the neighbourhood, just yesterday. His question was followed by calls of *yeah, Ma and why, Ma?* She should have been embarrassed, perhaps told them the truth; that she was hopelessly addicted and more likely to stop urinating than quit smoking. Instead, she'd sat back in her creaky armchair and smiled, listening to their affectionate keening as though they were her pets. In a strange way, that's exactly what they were.

She lit a cigarette and watched as Paul West bullied his little sister into handing over her favourite doll. She thought about tapping gently on the window, just enough to let Paul know she was watching. It would be enough; he would hand the doll back to his sniffling sister, hold an apologetic hand up to Ma before mounting his skateboard and whizzing hastily off down the street. By the time she'd considered a light rapping upon the glass, though, the taunting had ceased. "He's a good boy, really," Ma mumbled, her parched voice and the rattle of her throat startling even her.

She made her way into the kitchen, put the tin kettle upon the stove and set it boiling, then headed back to the window. The twins, David and Deborah Blake, were tossing a ball at one another across the road; she'd watched them play this game before, and knew the rules, or at least got the gist of them. There were celebrations whenever the ball popped up from the kerb, so Ma conjectured the aim of the game was to hit the kerb. It was, she thought, a silly game, but the Blake twins seemed to enjoy it.

Children, so many of them, came and went. Often, they simply aged, outgrew their dear old Ma, but sometimes they were unceremoniously packed up and moved across the country, where they were no doubt forced to join schools mid-term and make an entire set of new friends. She'd never understood why children were made to endure such terrible and sudden revolutions, and took it as a personal assault whenever one of her favourites (not that she would ever profess to such unfair partiality) relayed the news of such a transfer.

Still, she got to watch the majority of them grow up, have their first kisses, achieve good grades, explore their options, have their second and third kisses, eat blue cheese for the very first time, the list went on and on …

After several minutes of kerb-ball—she didn't know if that was what the game was called, but as a name it was as good as any—the kettle began its strident whistle and she made her way toward the kitchen, where she hoped to find a nice piece of cake to accompany her tea.

~ ~ * * ~ ~

It was half-past two when Geoffrey Saint waltzed into her living room, a slight cut upon his forehead. He wasn't crying, for he knew that tears wouldn't get him anywhere, not with Ma, but she could see he was in a certain amount of distress.

"Oh dear," she said, smiling, ushering him forth so that she might take a closer look at his blossoming wound. "Been in the wars, have we?"

Geoffrey practically ran toward her, almost tripping over the rug in the centre of the room, which had lifted ever so slightly at one corner. "I fell off my bike," he said. "That's a funny saying, ain't it? Been in the wars?"

Ma chuckled. "Yes, I suppose it is." She brushed his copper hair away from his head, teasing it this way and that, trying to locate the source of the thin rivulet of blood staining one cheek. "And what have I told you about being careful on that bike? You're like a boy possessed; I've seen you, pedalling up the street as if your life depends on it. Surely you don't have anything that urgent to attend to?"

Geoffrey hissed as Ma's long unkempt fingernails brushed against the thin slit in his scalp. "You have to go fast," he said, "otherwise you just fall off."

Now Ma, who had been upon the earth fifty years longer than Geoffrey Saint, couldn't help finding the irony in his statement, and stifled a laugh, lest he feel more ashamed than he already did. "This isn't too bad," she said. "We'll get it cleaned up and it'll be fine. Does your dad know you're here?"

Geoffrey shook his head. Of course he hadn't told his father; he knew—they *all* knew—Ma's policy on the back door: all were welcome through it, so long as they didn't have their parents' permission. It wasn't that Ma worried about what people thought of her; quite the opposite, in fact. They could think her a witch, a haggard old busybody, or even a paedophile—even though she despised such monsters and believed they should be castrated with rusty scissors before beginning their life sentences. Her reason for wishing to keep her association with the children a secret was more plain: it was nobody else's fucking business.

Once Geoffrey's wound had been staunched (he was what Ma's own mother would have referred to as a bleeder) Ma signalled for him to sit opposite. "How are things at school?" She lit a cigarette, ignoring the smell of surgical spirit upon her knuckles; she doubted it was possible to go up in flames from such a small amount. "Still getting good grades?"

He nodded, a little too enthusiastically for Ma's liking. "Better than ever. And I made it into the football team, though it's just the reserves, but if one of the other kids breaks a leg or something, there's a good chance I'll get to play."

"I'll keep my fingers crossed for you." She sucked long and hard on her cigarette, her mouth puckering until her lips disappeared completely. Not once did she take her eyes from the boy, who seemed to be getting eaten alive by the huge chair and its overbearing cushions. He looked, she thought, more and more like his father every day. Roger Saint (whose surname couldn't have been more ill-fitting) had been married more times than Richard Burton, though for the life of her Ma couldn't see how; he had a crafty look about him, as if he was constantly considering how to fuck somebody over. And Geoffrey was starting to inherit his bastard father's expressions, those sleazy eyes and that sinister grin. *Such a shame*, she thought.

Within an hour, the living room was filled with children. The Blake twins had become bored of kerb-ball, and Paul West had tired of frustrating his little sister. Then there was Kevin Eads, who was just on the right side of sixteen, and Shaun Hunter, who liked to swear a lot, especially when Ella Green was around as it made him sound tough, or so he believed. Ella was sitting on the arm of the chair upon which Geoffrey would soon be taking root, sipping at her lemonade. She was, Ma thought, a very pretty young lady, but they always were at that age.

Even *she* had been.

But it wasn't David or Deborah Blake that had Ma's attention, nor was it Geoffrey Saint, Kevin Eads, Paul West, Shaun Hunter, or Ella Green. Standing behind the sofa—nervous too, Ma couldn't help but notice, as if she had been thrust before the king of some faraway place to receive judgement for some atrocity or other—was a girl of nine or ten, a child absent of notable features, apart from her short hair, which jutted out of her head at obscene angles. Upon entering, Ma had mistaken the poor girl for a boy. It wasn't until David Blake had said, "This is Kim, Ma. She's just moved in on Myatt," that Ma realised she was gawping at a girl.

"Oh, they finally sold that house, did they?" Ma had asked. "Been empty for a while."

The girl—Kim—had opened her mouth to speak, but nothing had fallen out. Instead, David had proceeded to tell Ma how Kim's father had made an offer way below the asking price, and that desperation had forced the buyer into accepting.

"Well, it's nice to be knowing you," Ma had told the unremarkable girl. "You stick to these kids like glue, Kim. Ain't none better around here." She'd lit a cigarette, the one she was now putting out on the over-spilling ashtray on the floor beside her chair.

"So, what do you want to hear about?" Ma asked no one in particular. Kim appeared confused, something Ma was quick to rectify. "Oh, sorry," she said. "I always tell a story, usually something about my life. Sometimes I help with problems. Ain't nothing you can't come to me about, Kim. I've been passing wisdom down for longer than I can remember, though why anyone would want to listen to a decrepit old crow like me is a mystery."

"It's because you say it how it is," Kevin mumbled.

"Fucking *right*, she does," Shaun added before winking surreptitiously at Ella, who rolled her eyes. Ma thought about reproaching the boy for his cussing, but there was no point. He was like a recalcitrant toddler; if you tell them to stop picking their nose they do it even more, often with both fingers simultaneously.

"Ain't no point in lying to children, that's what I was always taught by my own ma." She adjusted herself in her chair; bones cracked audibly. In the corner, Deborah Blake sniggered. "So come on. One of you must be in need of guidance, something you can't go to your folks about." When nobody offered anything, Ma turned her face to the girl partially hidden by the sofa. "Kim, you're new to the area. Is there anything I can help you with?"

The girl looked shocked, positively terrified that the attention had been thrust upon her so suddenly. Ma thought, for a moment, the girl might turn and run for the door—or even the window, where she would leap up and through, shattering glass and cutting flesh as she made good her escape. Her tiny mouth had fallen open to reveal a toothless *O*; the poor girl had seemingly never been acquainted with a dentist. Ma realised the girl was shaking, as if she'd been asked to perform something impossible in front of the rest of the group, or else feel the wrath of the curmudgeonly old bat whom everyone else in the room appeared to cherish.

Not wanting to put the girl under any unnecessary stress, Ma said, "That's okay. Not to worry. In time, maybe, you'll be ready to share something. *Anything*." She smiled, and the girl—*Kim*—nodded.

"Why don't you read us the story about the whale?" Kevin said, visibly excited.

"Yeah, the one with *dick* in the title," Shaun added, snorting. To him it was the funniest thing he could have heard; if Herman Melville could only see the joy his story brought to the world …

And so Ma, chain-smoking her way through a twenty pack, read *Moby Dick* to the children, who *oohed* and *ahhed* at all the right moments, none of them interrupting—there would be a chance for questions later. Occasionally Ma would scan the faces turned toward her, and was unsurprised to discover she had enchanted them all …

… all except one.

When the house emptied an hour later, leaving Ma feeling suddenly deflated and at a loss as to what to do with herself, all thoughts of the new girl—the way in which she had vacantly stared toward the wall during the recital, the way her eyes twitched if Ma raised her voice ever-so-slightly, and the way she hunched, as if in preparation for something, some unthinkable brutality that would require sturdy feet and even sturdier shoulders—troubled the ageing lady. Sure, Kim was new to it all; it was like starting a new school, but with a teacher that copiously smoked and friends that got away with profanities. And yet there was something else, something other than timidity, burning away at the scruffy young girl's heart.

What was her last name again? Had any of the other children told her? Did any of *them* know? If it had been mentioned, Ma had certainly forgotten, though she knew where the girl lived should the concern get to her, as it so often did.

She's not your problem, a voice inside Ma's head reminded her, and yet she disregarded it, as she had on so many occasions. Besides, what if the girl had nobody else, nobody to look out for her? What if Kim was all alone, as Ma had once been before the children had started to pay her mind, to bring her back to life with tales of their exploits and grazed knees? There was a reason they chose her over their own parents, a rationale as to why they took their bleeding wounds to her, their instances of bullying, their concerns over members of the opposite sex …

She's not your problem…

And yet Ma knew little scruffy Kim needed her more than any of the others.

~ ~ * * ~ ~

Three days later, Ma was caught in a particularly inclement storm; she'd needed bread and milk from the shop, and it hadn't been raining when she'd left. Walking as quickly as she could, the rain painting her silvery hair to her cheeks, Ma made her way along Myatt, past the old tyre-swing that was now just a piece of rope flapping maniacally in the wind. The bags were cutting her hands to ribbons, for bread and milk had become bleach, dishwasher tablets, sugar, a bottle of gin, and sodas for the kids. With each step she took—it was almost impossible to see through squinted eyes—she had to remind herself that stopping, if only for a moment, would favour no-one. No, she would fight through the pain, ignore the soreness in her fingers and soldier on.

That was the intention.

A sudden yelling to her left changed that.

" *… fucking think I WON'T! Get the fuck out of here, you little BITCH!"*

And now, Ma *did* put her shopping bags down, just as a shape
erupted from the front door of the recently sold McKenzie place.

Kim.

Crying hard, and yet so eager to rush out into the rain, to put some
space between herself and the house from which she had so hastily
emerged. She didn't see Ma (if she had, might she have run to her, threw
her arms around her and begged for asylum?) as she raced along the
pavement to Lord knows where. Seconds had passed since her sudden
materialisation, and yet she was already sodden, a drowned rat, Ma
thought, scuttling away, helpless, hopeless, destitute …

At the edge of Myatt sat a passageway. As far as Ma knew, it led to a
series of abandoned garages. She watched as Kim scurried along the
path, disappearing behind a leafless hedge; her sobbing was audible
even above the howling wind and incessant pitter-patter of heavy rain.

Ma took a deep breath, lifted her bags—her fingers almost screamed
out in protest—and crossed the road.

She's not your problem …

"Oh shut up!" Ma grunted, and entered the passageway after Kim.

The alley opened up into something much larger. On either side were
corrugated structures, some in better condition than others. Graffiti
covered several of the derelict erections and a burnt-out car—how had
she not been here before?—jutted from one of the garages at an odd
angle. It wasn't until she got closer that Ma realised it wasn't a car at all,
simply the back end of one. It struck her as funny. Where was the front
half? Were her children responsible for this mess?

The rain continued to hammer down, peppering the crenelated roofs.
A persistent drumroll that should have been annoying and yet wasn't
spurred Ma on; if you listened really closely, it sounded like *findthegirl,
findthegirl, findthegirl, findthegirl* … at least, that's what Ma heard.

Where *was* Kim? Was there another way out, one that only the
children knew of? Ma glanced around, but couldn't see any egresses,
other than the one at her back. She was sure the girl hadn't passed her,
which meant that she was there somewhere, hiding, sheltering, crying
until her tears ran out.

Ma edged forward. The last thing she wanted to do was upset the girl
further, and suddenly appearing—without so much as a whispered
forewarning—might send poor Kim into a deeper state of despair.

For a moment the rain abated; Ma could fully open her eyes. Truth
be told, she hadn't noticed she was squinting until then.

She cornered one of the deserted garages, slowly, still wary of her own movements and how they might impact upon the poor girl. If she'd have looked down in that moment, she might have seen the … too late. A plastic wheel-trim crunched beneath her foot, and although she didn't weigh eight stone, wringing wet, the noise it made was like something from an old war movie.

"Shit!" she muttered, glancing around, expecting the girl to suddenly rush across the opening. She didn't; Ma sighed, relieved.

She tucked her shopping bags in a dry corner of the garage; she would pick them up once she'd found the girl, once they'd had a little chat—something that Ma was strangely looking forward to. Maybe Kim would open up to her while the others weren't around; either that or she would tell Ma to fuck off and leave her to sob in peace. The old woman was ready for both outcomes.

An old bicycle was on its handlebars in the next garage. If it had once had wheels, there was no sign of them now. It amazed Ma how the children spent their free hours. When they weren't sitting in her living room, entranced by one of her stories, they were mangling old bits of machinery, putting bits and bobs together as if they might, one day, stumble upon the intricate design for a car bomb.

Not *her* kids, though. Her kids were good.

"Why are you following me?" a tiny voice said. Ma turned, making certain her smile was in place before finishing the manoeuvre.

"Oh, Kim, I thought I saw you come this way." Ma held a liveried hand to her chest, as if the girl had frightened her to within an inch of a coronary. "Are you okay?"

The girl shrugged. "Been worse," she said. "You didn't answer my question."

Now it was Ma's turn to squirm. "I thought you were upset. I wanted to make sure you got in out of this bloody rain." As if to verify that it was, in fact, bloody raining, Ma reached up and pulled her hair apart in the middle, like opening hoary curtains. She hoped the juvenile gesture would elicit a laugh, or even a smile, but neither were forthcoming. Instead Kim looked at her with a modicum of uncertainty, as if she believed their little unheralded rendezvous to be intrinsically wrong.

"Was that your father I heard back there?" Ma relaxed. What was the worst that could happen? Kim could tell her to fuck off, and off she would fuck, but Ma doubted that would happen. When the girl nodded, she relaxed even more. "You know you can tell me anything. I'm not just some nosey old biddy with nothing better to do than pry into other people's business." Now that she'd said it, that was *exactly* what she was, but it was for the greater good …

"Geoffrey says I can trust you," Kim said, shuffling nervously from one foot to the other, as if trying to avoid the raindrops.

Ma smiled. "Clever boy, little Geoffrey, though of course he's not as little as he used to be. Kid gets wider every time he comes round."

Finally a smile; a soupçon, but enough to warm Ma's freezing innards.

"What do you say we get in out of this torrent before we end up floating off down the street? I don't know about you, but I've not surfed in some years."

Kim—the girl who had been speechless before today, at least in Ma's presence—nodded and said, "Sounds like a plan to me." Any signs that the girl had been crying were washed away with the rain, and yet Ma knew it was the beginning of a very long and arduous afternoon.

She had no idea what she was getting herself into.

~ ~ * * ~ ~

Kim told Ma everything: how her mother had died two years ago following a short battle with bowel cancer; how her grandmother—on her mother's side—had died two months later after falling down a particularly tricky set of stairs in the hospital, where she was receiving treatment for myriad problems, including multiple myeloma; how her father had taken it upon himself to "make ends meet" however he possibly could, and it was this that almost caused Ma to choke on the digestive she'd pushed into her mouth.

"Sonofabitch," was all Ma could muster, such was the anger she felt in that moment. She was about to add to it when Kim suddenly stood, took a step toward the door. "Where are you going?"

"Home," the girl said. She said it as if it was the last place she wanted to be, and it probably was. "I shouldn't have said anything."

Ma stood, swallowed what remained of her biscuit. "You can't go back there," she said. "Not with all … *that* going on."

"It'll be a thousand times worse if I don't go back soon," Kim said. A solitary tear rolled down her cheek, leaving a shiny trail in its wake. Her bottom lip quivered as she said, "It's not just him. It's his friends, his brother, his nephew, anyone that can afford it. Dad says it's to keep a roof over our head; that's why we lost the last place, why we had to move here."

Ma didn't know what was worse: the fact that Kim was being put through such terrible things, or that she had somehow come to believe that it was all her fault. *You shoulda just done what Daddy wanted, you little bitch, and you'da still had your aquarium ...*

"No," Ma said, shaking her head so violently that something cracked. For a second, pain coursed along her spine, pain that she had no time for. "How do you think I'm going to sleep tonight, *knowing* ...?" She trailed off, unable to finish the sentence.

Kim sighed, shrugged her tiny shoulders. "The same way you've *always* slept," she said, and with that she turned and disappeared into the kitchen. By the time Ma traversed the coffee table and reached the door, the girl was gone.

~ ~ * * ~ ~

It was three days before Ma saw Kim again, and even then it was brief, a pane of glass separating them. As the girl rushed along the street (on the other side, of course) Ma hammered at the window with frail fists. The girl turned to see where the thumping was coming from before realising her mistake; she quickened her pace, as if Ma was the monster, not her father, not her uncle and her cousin. By the time the girl was out of sight, Ma's hands were sore; it was all she could do not to scream out in pain ...

"What's the matter?"

Not expecting anyone to be standing behind her, it was quite a shock when the voice came. Ma turned, her trademark smile nowhere to be seen on this occasion. Geoffrey Saint stood before her, looking tremendously concerned. It was strange to see such an aspect upon his countenance, as it was *her* job to worry, to fix things as they came up. Geoffrey looked nothing like his ne'er-do-well father in that moment— Roger Saint had never worn such an authentic expression, not even to try it on for size.

"Come and sit down," she said, gesturing to the sofa. "I've got something I need to talk to you about."

Geoffrey had never looked more lost, and yet Ma made sure to give him the once over before he found his way to the sofa. She was relieved not to find a mark on him, for she had enough on her plate without stemming the flow of more blood.

"Do you have any of those nice biscuits? The ones with the coconut?" He gawped at her, expectantly, as if changing the conversational tone would somehow prevent the imminent discussion. It was as if he could sense the significance of what Ma was about to share with him.

193

"In a little while," she said, sitting in her armchair. Something creaked; she wasn't sure whether it was her or the ancient cushions beneath. And now, sitting facing Geoffrey—who only wanted a nice coconut ring and a chapter from *Moby Dick*—she was at a loss for words. She lit a cigarette, exhaled a plume of blue-grey smoke into the room; Geoffrey watched as the fug contorted against the sliver of light shining through the window. "You're not a kid anymore," Ma said—it wasn't much, but it was a start.

"That's what my dad keeps telling me," said Geoffrey, "usually when I do something wrong."

A noise erupted from Ma's throat; it was as close to cussing as she could get without actually doing it. "You take no notice of your father. He's no right to give you tips and tricks on what's right and wrong." She took a long, hard drag on her cigarette before sighing. "I'm not getting any younger. Living around here will be the death of me; I always knew that, but—"

"You're not *dying*, are you?" He looked appalled, shocked at the sheer notion of death coming for his dear ol' Ma. If he didn't look so distraught, Ma would have fallen into fits of laughter.

"No, I'm not dying, Geo—"

"But it's something bad, isn't it? You've got something and you need to go into hospital—"

"I've never been healthier," she interrupted, though the smouldering cigarette in her gnarled hand suggested otherwise. "Look, if you'll just let me finish what I've got to say … it's very important."

The boy relaxed, though not wholly. He still perched precariously on the sofa's edge, his eyes were so wide they looked apt to drop out and roll across the carpet.

"What do you think of the new girl?" The question threw Geoffrey, such was its unexpectedness.

"She's okay," he said, a comical frown wrinkling his brow and nose. "I don't *fancy* her, if that's what you're getting at."

Ma chuckled. "Not at all," she said. "I was just wondering if she'd told you anything about herself. A secret, perhaps, something she wouldn't be comfortable sharing with a grown-up?"

Shaking his head, Geoffrey said, "I know she doesn't like beetroot, and that she had a cat, once, but it got squashed by the bin-men."

Ma squashed her cigarette into the over-spilling ashtray on the table, knocking several butts onto the floor. It didn't matter; none of it did, not anymore. "She hasn't told you anything about her father? Or her uncle, maybe?"

"Nah, all I know is that her dad sleeps and drinks a lot." He shrugged, as if sleeping and drinking a lot was a normal occupation. In the current climate, Ma supposed it was, but the *other* thing … well, there was nothing normal about that, and it had to stop, one way or the other.

Realising that she'd moved off track, somewhat, Ma took a second to light another cigarette and compose herself. Once again, Geoffrey watched the tendrils of smoke as they danced across the room; Ma wouldn't be surprised if they didn't, somewhere along the line, diagnose him with ADHD. "Anyway, what I meant to say was that I might be … moving soon." That wasn't strictly the truth, but it wasn't a lie either.

"Where are you going?" Geoffrey said. He looked more concerned than when he thought she was dying. "You can't go … I'll … I'll *bleed* to death."

"You'll be fine," she said, stifling the laughter that threatened to emerge. "You *all* will. I just wanted to make sure that you knew I was going before … well, before I went." Glancing into his wounded face, she imagined him growing up, what he would become—nothing like his father, she hoped—and how he would deal with life as it threw obstacle after obstacle at him. She *hoped* he would do just fine, and yet she would never know, not for sure …

"What about the whale?" Geoffrey was clutching at straws now. "We'll never know how it ends." He poked nonchalantly at the air, parting the smoke that drifted past him.

Ma sighed. How easy it would be to simply tell Geoffrey it didn't end well for the crew of the *Pequod*, to ask him to pass the tragic denouement on to the others like some sort of grave emissary. Perhaps she could rework it, make it so the whale and the crew all lived happily ever after. Almost immediately she pushed the thought away; they would hate her for it should they ever read it in their adulthood, and Ma had never lied to a child; she wasn't about to start now.

"I'll tell you what." She sat forward on her chair; the creak came once more, and this time she knew it was her own desiccated bones. "Why don't you go call for the others? We'll finish that story this afternoon, all of us."

Geoffrey managed a smile and pushed himself up from the sofa. "Coconut biscuits?"

"Only the best," Ma said.

And with that, Geoffrey raced for the back door, their saccharine conversation forgotten in an instant.

~ ~ * * ~ ~

Rain-drenched and tired, Ma stepped into the house and closed the door behind her. The clock upon the wall was concealed by shadows, but she didn't need to know the time; she was simply going through the motions. Somewhere, out on the street, a fox keened. A chill ran the course of Ma's spine—there was something inherently unnerving about a fox's mewl; *too much like the screams of a crying baby*, Ma thought, and made her way into the kitchen, where she placed the kettle upon the hob and lit the gas with a match.

She returned to the living room, where *Moby Dick* sat finished upon the coffee table. It had been a wonderful afternoon, filled with laughter and delight, though it seemed so distant now, as if nothing more than a dream she'd had once. She picked the book up, leafed indifferently through the pages. It was beautifully illustrated throughout by Rockwell Kent, and Ma's fingers traced over one of the book's more infamous images: the whale's tail whipping up and out of the ocean, an overturned boat in mid-air, spilling out its crew. The illustration was monochrome, and yet Ma could see traces of red upon the page.

Smears of crimson that did nothing to compliment the beautiful sketch.

Ma closed the book and headed back to the kitchen, where the tin kettle had begun to shrilly whistle. She noticed the dark smudges against the patina of the kettle; now that her eyes had adjusted to the dark, the blood stood out like inkblots on a white canvas.

She made her tea—ignoring the stickiness on the palm of her hands as she did—and carried it through to the living room, where the faint dopplering of distant sirens told her she might not have time to finish her Earl Grey.

She wasn't your problem, the voice inside her head said so matter-of-factly. And as the sirens neared, and the mewling fox hurried off to find somewhere safe and sheltered to hide until it was all over with, Ma smiled to herself, knowing that little scruffy Kim would never suffer at the hands of her tormentors again.

37. A WHISPER IN THE STORM BY ROBERT FRIEDRICH

(Taken from *Enlightened by Darkness* - Vol. II *The Invasion*)

It was the last day of the holiday vacation for a group of friends. Their flight home the next day gave them a chance for a last night adventure. They decided to make full use of it in ways possible only in Las Vegas; a night full of partying, treading from bars to strip clubs.

The night progressed exactly as the group wanted; they got so intoxicated they could no longer tell the difference between a drink and a hot lap dance. Their euphoria continued 'til the early morning hours. They had no worries, and planned to sleep on the flight. The last strip club finally threw them out after closing, and they returned to the hotel to pick up bags before heading to the airport.

The group still felt the craze of their last night as they boarded the flight home on a Boeing 747, or as they called it: "Sex Queen of the Skies". Twelve hours in a plane didn't bother them, since all were so drained they would sleep the whole way home. Not even the fact that a storm was picking up on their flight route troubled them as all finally dozed off.

~ ~ * * ~ ~

The turbulence woke Isaac as the airplane passed through the rough weather; he immediately puked on the seat in front of him. Fumbling his seat belt open, he struggled up from the chair.

"God … I am never going to take a drink from a stripper again!" he muttered as he tried to walk to the restroom.

Still drowsy from the hangover, and with blurred vision, he didn't realize that he was alone. All the seats were absolutely empty as the airplane flew through the storm. Isaac tripped over his own foot, landing in a nearby seat. He reflexively attempted to apologize, but at last noticed that there was no one. His vision was slowly improving as he looked around. Turbulence made the plane shake once more, knocking him to the floor and making him puke again. Finally, he crawled to the restroom.

He spoke to his mirror image as he washed his mouth and face. "I must be dreaming … seriously, the plane was full as we boarded."

Cautiously he exited the restroom, but the scenery had not changed: he was there all alone, lightning bolts passing both sides of the aircraft.

He slapped and pinched his face in attempts to wake up, but nothing helped. The place was the same: a deserted airplane. Frightened and confused, he aimed to return to his chair, avoiding the puke on the floor. Before he could reach his seat the plane shook again–violently, knocking him again to the floor as more lightning flashed by.

"What is the matter … scared of the solitude?" said an oddly distorted voice.

"What the … who is there? Where is everyone? Where are my friends?" asked Isaac, but his questions remained unanswered.

Isaac finally managed to get to his feet and set off on his walk through the plane. Bound on finding someone or something to explain the events that surrounded him, he passed aisle after aisle.

"There have to be pilots!" He continued his search all the way to the front compartment of the aircraft. The turbulence was picking up again as he finally reached the flight deck door. He was going to knock, but the door opened at the first touch, revealing that even the flight deck was empty, no one flying the plane through the heavy storm.

"Shit," said Isaac, running inside. He tried the headset, he screamed for help, but all he could hear was static. After hesitating he attempted to operate the aircraft, but the controls were not responding. He kept looking around the cockpit for anything that could help him.

"I'm so cold, Isaac," said the distorted voice as it appeared to come from behind the door.

Isaac ran out into the cabin, yet once more he found no one. He was about to walk back to the flight deck when the door slammed shut. He screamed and kicked the door, but it was locked and would not open for him.

"The … are showing Isaac …" said the deformed voice.

"What? What the hell do you want?" Who are you?" screamed Isaac, looking around, frantic.

"I am here to help you …" said the distorted voice.

As the voice faded, the airplane began to shake. Slowly but surely it twisted into a roll. Isaac strove to hold on to something but as the aircraft turned he tumbled among the seats. The plane smoothly inverted; Isaac fell to the ceiling which was now his floor.

"Forgive … for I am sin …"

"What the fuck are you?" asked Isaac as he tried to crawl.

The airplane maintained flying upside down as Isaac fought his way through the cabin. He didn't know where he was going, but he kept on searching for any other sign of life. He reached the stairs that normally would lead to the lower deck, but now the only way he could go was up. Bit by bit, he climbed the stairs.

"What did you do with everyone else? Where did you put them?" asked Isaac, as he reached the upper floor.

The voice remained silent as Isaac continued his search.

"Ring around the rosie … a pocket full of posies … Ashes! Ashes! … We all fall down!" sang the distorted voice as the plane started rolling, inverting again.

"No, not again!" screamed Isaac tumbling among the seats as the airplane turned up.

All of the oxygen masks dropped as the aircraft returned to its original orientation. Isaac was lying on the floor, dizzy from all the rotations. Out of the blue, a red liquid began to ooze from the oxygen masks and the overhead compartments. As Isaac was trying to get up, a few drops landed on his hand. They were warm and thick. He rubbed them between his fingers and smelled.

"Blood … what the fuck is going on here?" asked Isaac, as more and more blood oozed.

As he stood up the blood flowed underfoot, amassing on the floor. He could hardly walk, his feet submerged in the blood puddle. Frightened and confused, he yelled for help. Endlessly he kept on yelling and whimpering, but his cries remained unanswered.

"I just want to go home ," he sobbed.

"Listen to them … the … the night … what sweet music …" said the unclear voice.

"What do you want from me?" cried Isaac.

As he walked, he started to feel short of breath. He coughed, feeling he was choking. He dropped to his knees in the blood as he continued to choke. Without warning, an invisible force grabbed hold of him. He could not move, just coughed. The invisible force threw Isaac, slamming him against the ceiling. Shocked and breathless, he hanged there for a few seconds before falling back to the deck, and the pool of blood.

He was panicking, and still breathless, as the force grabbed hold of him again before tossing him across the cabin into a wall. Once more he fell to the floor and continued to choke and cough. Inexplicably, water began to come out of his mouth.

~ ~ * * ~ ~

Isaac woke up fastened in his seat. He could not breathe, for the airplane was underwater. He tried to loosen up the belt as he looked around. Everyone around had drowned. Among the floating bodies were a few small children. His friends were dead beside him. All he could do was scream before choking as the water entered his lungs.

He drowned there, along with everyone else, as the plane kept descending deeper and deeper into the endless watery grave.

38. THE REAPING OF THE SEAWEED BY MEGAN N. WATSON

Ethel Yorke shivered in the breeze, the memories of the horrors that took place here still fresh in her aging mind. As the sun set, casting auburn rays across the colorful foliage still clinging to windswept branches, the large, empty hole below looked unearthly. Hard to visualize when the space was actually a lake, with water the color of ice tea and stumps of dead cedar trees piercing the surface. Nature's sculpture garden. She smiled as a single tear ran down her cheek, wishing she didn't have to make this trip every year, but knowing the possible consequences if she stopped.

~ ~ * * ~ ~

The community of Cedar Lake, nestled in the middle of the New Jersey Pine Barrens, was once a typical small town. Most families had lived there for generations, though the last couple of decades found a growing number of retirees and young families from the city, escaping the stress of metropolitan chaos. Simple wooden docks speckled most of Cedar Lake's shoreline, with the Central Clubhouse sitting prominently in the center. Near the far end, the lake connected to a swampy area with a small creek fed by the dam. The edge of the lake here was most popular among the canoe and fishing crowds. The majority of the swimming and boating occurred at the opposite end. A small road encircled the entire lake, one only paved in recent years. Just a few houses were located directly on the lake, the rest scattered about in a type of wagon wheel pattern.

Summers tripled the local population, the surrounding quiet and eerie pine forest invaded by echoes of youthful laughter and boat motors. Not that one would hear any complaints from the locals, as those throngs of people pumped enough into the local economy to keep everyone solvent through the off-season months. Their biggest issue was the constant battle against the seaweed invasion every year.

People hated the seaweed. It entangled swimming limbs, caught on blades trying to propel small fishing boats, made the lake floor slimy (only an issue in the shallow parts), and it smelled funky. Thus began the annual ritual of clearing the lake known as the Reaping of the Seaweed, a festival celebrating the unofficial kickoff of the tourist season. Seven days of fun-filled activities: fireworks, lakeside barbecues and late night shenanigans. And hundreds of gallons of toxic, untested chemicals and herbicides thrown into the once-pure cedar waters. Not every citizen of Cedar Lake agreed with this particular tactic. Ethel Yorke was among the loudest of the critics, never letting a Reaping go by without a fight.

Then came the 50th Annual Reaping of the Seaweed. Despite the waters not yet being cleared of the pesky aquatic plant life, people couldn't wait to jump in and wash away their winter blues. Long, cold and snow-covered, the frigid weather marked the first time the lake had ever frozen completely over, solid enough to walk the three miles across, shore to shore, with ease. Cabin fever had raged. As soon as the weather turned mild, the lake was full of people. The seaweed population was abundant. Never had the lake been so choked. But soon sugar highs and liquor buzzes set in, and all that mattered was that it was warm and winter was mercifully over.

Ethel was in full force, her long silver hair braided down her back and her voice filled with strength and authority; she passionately spoke about the dangers of continuing to poison the lake. She handed out pamphlets and literature full of scientific studies, though most ended up in the recycling bin outside the Central Clubhouse.

"You're killing the ecosystem!" she pleaded. "You're killing our paradise!"

No one listened. People just streamed by, eager to get to the opening celebrations, the free spread of food and ice-cold beer calling them. A few stopped out of sheer politeness, but Ethel could see right through their well-intentioned gestures. As the afternoon progressed, she sighed and packed up her things, hoping to have better luck tomorrow. Despite her protests, she proceeded toward the clubhouse to grab a beer. Her taxes helped pay for the seaweed genocide party; she might as well help herself to some hard-earned rewards. She took her beer and a small plate of food to the main dock. She sat staring at the seaweed plants floating on the surface, tracing them to their roots underwater. A sunfish swam by, tickling her toes as it passed.

"Poor things, you have no idea what's about to happen, do you?" A piece of seaweed brushed the side of Ethel's foot. She yipped, "Ouch! That stung." Feeling it was a sign, she finished her beer and left.

On day two of the Reaping, Ethel stood in the parking lot of the Central Clubhouse, her usual signs and literature in hand, and this time, she reminded passersby that she was a retired scientist. No one flinched. Sheriff Spike Curtis and Councilman Sam Harding approached Ethel. She stared them down.

"If you two think for one moment that you can make me leave. . ."

"Calm down, Ethel," said an empathetic Sheriff Spike. "Just making sure you know we read your studies. Sam here says there's nothing to worry about."

Nodding, Sam added, "Don't forget the sacrifice is at six o'clock tonight. It's the most popular event of the whole festival!"

Smiling, he gave Ethel a condescending pat on her shoulder as he and Sheriff Spike continued into the clubhouse. Spike's deputy, Devi Loomis, followed a beat behind. Devi, used to a bit of teasing herself thanks to her alliterative job and name combination, looked over. She too smiled at Ethel, but it was filled with kind sincerity, her eyes glimmering with unspoken but pleasant understanding. Ethel smiled back, thankful for the brief but uplifting encounter.

That day, swimmers, getting in their last moments before the poisons were added to the water, started to report a strange tingling sensation on areas grazed by seaweed. More than a few inquired about the possibility of jellyfish, or some other animal, that may have joined the ranks of the lake's underwater population. That notion was quickly dismissed with the simple explanation that the swimmers probably just got scratched by the branches of submerged cedar stumps. The celebrations continued, leading up to the main event for the night: the Ritual of the Seaweed Sacrifice.

Large pieces of seaweed were gathered and hung up, along with strands of white lights, to tastefully decorate the top of the Central Clubhouse lamp pole. Next came a toast of thanks for the sacrifice the seaweed had made to ensure the prosperity of the community for another year, as the deadly concoction of herbicides (mostly experimental thanks to the questionable ethics of Councilman Harding) was poured into the waters of Cedar Lake. The ritual concluded with a community feast by candlelight, usually full of vegetarian fare in jest of the massive slaughter of seaweed that had just begun. By the end of the night, drunken revelers would wave pieces of lettuce or fresh seaweed at the lamp pole, as if teasing the dying plant, rubbing in the ingestion and murder of its brethren, laughing as they stumbled away. Some kinder souls would thank the seaweed, and quietly apologize for their more brutal counterparts. And every once in a while, one person, usually a child, would claim to have heard the sacrificial seaweed weeping as it died on the pole overlooking its former home in the lake, as if crying out for help. Unfortunately, those lone voices of reason, Ethel Yorke among them, were ignored.

Days three and four were raking days. People in full rubber suits waded into the water to rake the seaweed up and remove it from the lake. This took care of the larger areas of seaweed concentration, as well as the loose plants, many already dead. Once the water was reasonably clear, sand was brought in to cover up the naturally slimy lake floor. Day five was a day of rest and fireworks over the lake, counting the minutes until it was officially safe to swim again. The morning of day six, the entire community gathered on the shore of the Central Clubhouse under the still-decorated lamp pole to declare the clubhouse open for the season. On the final day, the waters were cleared for swimming and the summer officially began. The festivities always continued into the wee hours of the morning, this year under a full moon sparkling on the lake and making the white sands of the Pine Barrens glow in celebration.

The 50th Annual Reaping of the Seaweed had been the best one yet, at least until the missing persons desk at the Sheriff's office became inundated with reports. A week after the celebrations had concluded, ten people had been reported missing, and the list was growing. On the other side of town, the clinic overflowed with people suffering from bizarre maladies. One group had mysterious stings and red tendril-shaped marks on their limbs, people swearing there must be some type of jellyfish in the lake. The other group had more severe cases: toe-and fingernails peeling off out of nowhere, leaving tips raw and bloody, resembling hamburger meat. The worst cases evolved into tooth and hair loss. The only common variable was that every person, whether missing or ill, was at the Reaping and all had swum in Cedar Lake in the past two weeks. With the tourists already starting to pour into town, officials, especially Sam Harding, were worried and trying to come up with some cover story to keep the money flowing in, not tourists fleeing out.

Mutterings about the seaweed being responsible spread around town, especially at Mini's, the local diner. A part of the wall right by the front doors was covered in missing persons posters. Seaweed only made sense, as it was a common denominator, except for the fact that seaweed didn't sting. Sally White swore the seaweed was trying to drown her, that she could feel it pulling her down, fighting with her, the painful stinging getting worse the longer she fought. Her boyfriend, Jack, had managed to pull her away before exhaustion caused her to go under for good. The day after relaying their tale at Mini's, which caused quite a stir among diners, Sally went missing. Jack, who had been stung while rescuing Sally, ended up at the clinic two days later, completely bald and missing most of his finger and toenails.

A town meeting was held, panicked citizens asking "Why are so many sick, and where are our missing loved ones?" The clinic began sending patients to the general hospital, an hour outside of town. People were waking up choking on their own loose teeth, pillows sprayed with blood. The town council's explanations were no longer calming Cedar Lake residents. The people were scared and they wanted real answers.

Ethel Yorke stood up. "I know what's going on."

Silence fell over the frantic crowd.

"It's the damn chemicals. I've been warning all of you for years! No one listened. So, being that I was an aquatic biologist and botanist for thirty years, I took it upon myself to run some tests on the water and especially the seaweed. The seaweed has mutated into a new species. The so-called 'environmentally safe' herbicide Councilman Harding insisted we use contains animal and plant DNA. It altered the seaweed causing the plants to …well, fight back by stinging anything it determines is a threat. Like a snake biting when cornered. And though further testing is needed to know for sure, I think its sting is causing all these other horrific symptoms. The new formula, which I'm sure is top notch," she glared at Harding, "is the only explanation that makes any sense." Ethel looked around and was met with looks of confusion and disbelief.

"I am not insane. Please! Listen to me!" But she feared her efforts were futile, especially as a woman with the undeserved reputation of being the town crazy person—a reputation earned only from being educated and trying to impart that knowledge to her fellow Cedar Lake neighbors.

Councilman Harding was the first to speak. "Uh, we appreciate your insights, Mrs. Yorke, however, your explanation seems highly unlikely."

The room erupted; people were shouting, most in disbelief, or rather denial, at Ethel's explanations. Sam banged the gavel, while Sheriff Spike called for order. Ethel walked out with her head down, knowing the worst was yet to come and seeing nothing she could do about it. Sheriff Spike called to her to stop, but she didn't hear him. Promising solid answers, a frustrated council adjourned the meeting until further notice.

Sheriff Spike Curtis was not equipped to deal with the issues plaguing his town. Tourist revenue was already unusually low and with so many missing and ill people, not many were picking Cedar Lake as their summer getaway. He had few resources, over twenty missing people, and a medical facility overflowing with patients suffering from bizarre and disfiguring ailments of unknown origins. He sat down on his own private dock, beer in hand, surveying his home. Though new to being sheriff, he wasn't new to Cedar Lake. He was local, born and raised, and in fifty years nothing like this had ever happened. As the sun began to descend over the calm, mirror-like water, he stared down at his reflection, dangling his feet over the dock edge. His toes tickled the surface, thoughts racing, until something wet and slimy jerked him back to reality. Some seaweed had gotten caught on his toe. He tried to shake it off, but it was climbing across his foot, making its way up his calf. He watched in a terrified daze, until the plant started to forcefully pull his foot. Shaking his head, he ripped it off. Stinging and burning had started, red streaks marking the contact spot. Spike, knowing—*knowing*—he had felt it pull him, stood up unsteadily. It was then he noticed how much seaweed was in the lake. It was as if the Reaping had never happened! How had no one noticed?

Ethel Yorke. Ethel had noticed. Sheriff Spike, shaken but determined, hopped in his car and headed to Ethel's house.

Ethel was already on her way to Deputy Devi Loomis' house. The two knew each other from Devi's graduate school years. Ethel still occasionally taught, and Devi had been one of her interns in aquatic botany. Devi would have gotten her doctorate but changed careers when she was forced to move home to care for her sick father. While Ethel was sounding the alarms at the town meeting, Devi had been concluding the necessary tests to prove the seaweed was to blame.

When Sheriff Spike saw Ethel on Cedar Lake Road, he turned on the lights and pulled her over.

"Mrs. Yorke … uh, Ethel, I need to talk to you. I got stung."

Speaking with a curt and urgent tone, Ethel replied, "We need to go to Devi's."

They arrived at Devi's place shortly after. Devi answered the door, confused by the presence of her boss. Ethel nodded, letting Devi know it was okay to speak freely.

"I'm still waiting on a few results, but there is no doubt it is the seaweed. I improved my earlier serum and it appears to stop the spread of the venom."

"Give some to Spike," declared Ethel, who had tested Devi's initial serum on her own stings.

Devi applied the serum to Sheriff Spike's stings and to the relief of all, it appeared to clear the red streaks. Spike exhaled a sigh of relief. The three sat and talked, discussing what they knew, and the more dreaded topic, what they didn't know. The fate of the missing people weighed heavily on them all, and none of the test results provided the needed clue to the final piece of the puzzle.

Cedar Lake was closed down, no swimming, fishing, boating, or just dipping toes. The warm summer months wound down into a cold and dreary autumn. None of the missing people had been located and there had been no leads, no clues, no nothing to their whereabouts. Most of the sick people had gone missing shortly after being sent home. The rest died after losing all their hair, nails and teeth, though many had been found sleepwalking near the lake shortly before death. There were no new cases once the lake was closed. Sam Harding resigned and left town.

Winter arrived with a bang, in the form of a major blizzard at the beginning of November. It dumped three feet of snow, and was followed by two weeks of subzero temperatures. Cedar Lake froze over. Sally White's little brother, Randy, was curious what it looked like by the small dam on the lake's edge. Knowing the lake was frozen solid, he went exploring. Most of the lake's surface was snow-covered, any ice itself opaque and nearly impossible to see through. As he cautiously made his way closer to the dam, aware the ice would be getting thinner due to the current, the ice also became clearer. Peering down, he swore he saw faces. As quickly as he saw them, they would disappear as if pulled down, away from the light of the cold, frozen day. The dam was about fifty feet in front of him when something bright red caught his eye. Slowly Randy made his way to the source, carefully bending down on the ice to get a closer look. It was Sally, a bright red scarf wrapping her now bald head, framing her face beautifully in her watery grave. He banged on the ice, his grief immediate. Sally's eyes opened, meeting her brother's tearful gaze. Bubbles hit the ice as she screamed. Randy fell backwards, not sure of what just happened. He went back, leaned over, and sure enough, there was Sally, eyes open and mouth screaming, alive but paralyzed thanks to the seaweed venom. He began pounding the ice, praying it would break just enough to save her but not kill him. A tiny crack opened as he continued to hit the surface, screaming once he had found his voice. A couple walking their dog ran to the shoreline closest to his position, but didn't understand why he was screaming. The ice began to splinter all around Randy and in his panic he saw Sally wasn't the only person under the ice, just as he realized he was about join her. A green tendril slithered through one of the cracks and made its way toward him. It wrapped around his leg like a python, and in a flash pulled him under, bending his slender body in ways it was never meant to move. It happened so quickly the couple was hardly sure he was even there.

Sheriff Spike and Deputy Loomis arrived with special rescue teams. No one knew for sure, but it seemed that all the missing people from the previous Reaping were there, bald and missing their teeth and nails. The seaweed had attached to the bodies as if feeding from them; the aquatic plants had never looking so lush and plentiful. No other life was left in the lake, just paralyzed bodies tied to the lake floor by seaweed. Not one person survived being extracted from the lake, and the seaweed attacked anyone who entered the water, causing rescue teams to abandon their task, knowing the victims were being left to suffer an unimaginable fate. As soon as the water thawed, the lake was drained and families showed up to claim their loved ones … or what was left of them. The seaweed had continued its attempted takeover, but without water and the special chemicals, it soon dried up and disappeared. The few people left physically unharmed moved away, leaving Cedar Lake another ghost town, tucked away in the middle of the New Jersey Pine Barrens.

39. OPRAH FUNDS "END OF THE WORLD" PROJECT IN MEMORY OF SAVANT CHILD AUTHOR BY TRISHA J. WOOLDRIDGE

PROVIDENCE (AP) – Oprah Winfrey, with the backing of Harpo Print, LLC, is partnering with Brown University Ancient Studies Program to translate the handwritten manuscript of the late Isaak Prouty of Spencer, Massachusetts. In the past six months, Prouty wrote over 500 pages of Ancient Sumerian in crayon on construction paper before his untimely death three days ago. Prouty was only 8-years-old.

Parents Bill and Maria did not realize what their son had done until their niece, Lisa Hammond, noticed the work after the boy's funeral. Ms. Hammond, a student of Brown University's Ancient Studies Program, thought she recognized the crayon scripting. She took a copy to Professor Erishkigal En-Kur, recently hired by Brown for her specialty in Ancient Sumerian language and culture. En-Kur immediately began putting together a team to translate the text from the original manuscript.

"We really didn't want to give it up," says Mrs. Prouty. "But Professor En-Kur said that it would change the world… what our son wrote, so I let her take it. Isaak was a special boy; clearly there are greater forces at work here."

Knowledge of Ancient Sumerian culture, and especially language, is limited, so funding was required to bring experts from all over the globe. One of the students working on the project sent the story to *O, the Oprah Magazine*, which brought it to the attention of Ms. Winfrey.

Spokesperson for O and Harpo Print, LLC, Gabriel Nidaba, says, "Ms. Winfrey sympathizes with the loss of the Proutys and looks forward to preserving the work of their amazing son through her support of 'The End of the World.' This project looks like it will have a major impact throughout the world and Oprah Winfrey and Harpo Print look forward to being part of that."

Isaak, who suffered severe autism, struggled to speak or even write. However, the boy's parents share his detailed drawings of ancient and fantastic cities and creatures. They say he would throw a tantrum whenever they interrupted any of his projects. This recent project had caught their attention because of its English-written title: "The End of the World."

"I originally thought he copied it from something," Mr. Prouty says. "He would copy things he saw, usually ghastly things, but he could copy them perfectly."

The cause of death is cited as "inconclusive," but a medical examiner who wished to remain anonymous said the boy's lungs were full of water, as if he'd drowned. The boy was found dead in his bedroom with no signs of being moved. No charges have been brought up on any count of foul play.

En-Kur's team estimates that the translation will be complete within the next three months. A memorial service on campus is already being arranged for the team to read the translation in both English and the Ancient Sumerian during the solar eclipse, just as Isaak drew on his papers. The Prouty family is touched and honored that so much attention and effort are going into their son's work.

The Ancient Studies department of Brown University is handling all the details of the memorial. They have released the following announcement for those interested in attending or taking part in the ceremony, "Attendees, celebrants, and all worshippers who wish to Honor the Subject of the Great Revelation and Welcome a Master to our humble realm should send their True Names directly to Erishkigal En-Kur, along with a blood sample for the Purpose of Security."

Contact information for En-Kur is available on the Brown University website. The Prouty family thanks the community for their support and has even reserved all rooms at all the local hotels for anyone who would join the in honoring their son's life's work. Most generously they have allowed us to print the translation to the opening pages of what experts are calling the "Sacred Manuscript of Isaak Prouty." In both English and phonetic Sumerian, sponsored by Oprah and Harpo Print, LLC, is the opening passages to, "The End of the World."

It is suggested you read the passages aloud to best appreciate their power …

I never apologized at the blackjack table. Didn't matter if it was a father one bust away from putting his family into a cardboard box, or a whale I gutted with the sharp turn of an ace. Never saw the point. They knew the possibilities when they sat down in front of me. I wasn't their friend. I wasn't there to cheer them on, or see their dreams come true. On the other side of that, I never congratulated the winners. Again, no point. They were going to leave my table regardless of how the cards fell. There and gone.

A line of little deaths, one after the other. They sat down, won or lost, and faded away.

That didn't change a whole lot with the new job, to be honest. A lot more losing, though. All losing, in fact.

The powers, abilities—whatever the hell they're called—that came with the job made it impossible for the merely human to resist my … suggestions. There was also whatever it was that made it possible for me to move wherever I wanted at a whim. Yeah, that sounds really good, doesn't it?

But I miss driving.

I miss being at the wheel, and stomping the gas pedal. Miss that feeling of finding the perfect stretch of long country road and opening it up, hitting those hills just right.

Which was why I wasn't all too happy with the next Take in my career. He sat at the wheel of his 1970 Charger like he was with a Mormon girl. Sure, she was clean and pristine, but all the excitement of tea party in Utah. Hearing that .440 barely purr when it wanted to roar brought to mind watching the tigers pacing at a zoo. Trapped, but still ready to tear apart any fool not showing proper respect for the power waiting to be set free.

Meaning the Take was all flash. A goddamn guest at Gatsby's party. Only took a second for his life story to come to my mind. One of those debt lawyers: no lie too big, no trick too dirty, no judge too ethical for a fat bribe of cash or favors. This piece of garbage had led hundreds to ruin … broken lives, homelessness, or worse. All over old debts bought for pennies.

I didn't recognize the area, but it was all commuter gray, with horns, exhaust, and the frustration of people wanting to be anywhere but where they were. The Take's cell rang … "Money" by Pink Floyd.

Asshole.

"This is Ross," he said.

There was a long silence as the person on the other end spoke. The Take shook his head. Never understood that particular tick of people, making facial expressions and gestures while on a damn phone. Another of the million little rages that put me in the passenger seat next to the bipedal leech at the wheel.

"Move the date up," he said. "This is SOP, goddammit. The more you move the dates around and keep stalling, the more likely the losers are to miss a date, giving us the default. Or they give up. How long you been with us? Keep it up like this, and it won't be much longer."

He tossed the cell phone on the passenger seat. Which meant the damn thing went right through me. Not something I'd gotten used to at that point in my tenure as a killer of scumbags. Unnerving as all hell, seeing physics just say fuck it and throw up its hands.

"How will you do it this time, Suicide King?"

Didn't need to turn around. Didn't need to think about it at all. The air turned cold, razors using my nerves as a dance floor.

"You have a thing for me?" I asked Mr. Gone.

He stared at me from the back seat. I wasn't looking at him, so how would I know what he was doing, some smart ass might ask. When something like Mr. Gone is looking at you, you just fucking *know* it— and hope like hell you're something close to invulnerable, which I was as long as I was … whatever I was.

"You don't know how your own power works, do you?" asked Mr. Gone.

He had me there.

"I want them dead, whisper them the how, they figure the rest out," I said, still not giving him the satisfaction of turning around. "Easy."

His laugh was the same I imagined oozing out of a pedophile at a McDonald's birthday party. "I do so love it when a new one is flailing away."

"Bite my ass, Gone."

A shiver went down the Take's spine. Something in the bastard was responding to the shift in Mr. Gone. He was lucky. *I* felt the whole damn thing, as pure violence radiated from the thing behind me.

Then he—it—was gone.

I stared out the Charger's windshield, astounded. No beating, or threats of future violence. He was right, though, there was a lot I didn't know.

Pink Floyd erupted again.

The Take reached for it.

It was at that point the thought of this asshole reaching through my junk provoked something I wasn't expecting. I popped into my old reality, right next to him. He froze in place, hand stopped midway. Couldn't fault him that, what with Stranger Danger showing up out of thin air.

"What? How?" he said. His instincts kicked in and he righted the Charger before it became an accordion.

Sometimes all it takes is the smallest thing. One word to end a person, to steal away that grasp on life so many people cling to with all the tenacity of an exposed priest to his faith.

"Melissa," I said. It rang inside the Charger like a death knell.

Without a single word, he stopped the car, causing a symphony of protesting horns, opened the car door, and calmly stepped into the path of a city bus.

Yes, there was a lot I didn't know … about what I was, and what I could do. Some things never change, though. I never apologized for what happened in my time. I did, on the other hand, have a cherry new ride.

41. ENTRAPPED BY K. TRAP JONES

I don't consider myself a violent person. I see no point in physical confrontation when a perfectly executed trap does the job just fine. With two barrels pointed at my head, I wasn't about to start getting physical. I could hear their fingers rubbing against the triggers. Any sudden movement I made probably would've turned my skull into a soda can on a shooting range. They were angry. I didn't blame them. Their raised voices tempted me to resist, but like I said, I'm not one for confrontation. Instead, I merely sipped on my coffee and gazed down the porch at my dirt road. Their dead comrades were scattered about as a result of the previous successful traps.

With my face slammed against the wooden planks, I stared at the still-smoking cigar lying next to me. It seemed like a waste of a perfectly good cherry, but I knew it wasn't going to return to my mouth. With a knee against my neck, they bent my arms back. I felt no pain, but became agitated seeing their wet boots dripping mud all over the porch, contaminating my land with their city filth. While I watched the others being slaughtered by the traps in front of the house, these two bastards were flanking me from behind. A lapse in judgment on my part, or just plain laziness; either way I found myself in quite the jam. It was only a matter of time. With so many people missing on the mountain, their arrival was predictable.

They lifted me up where I could get a good look at their pristine city faces; clean shaven, without an ounce of labor-worn skin. The dip in my mouth was drying. Any excess spit was used to cleanse my bottom lip. Down the porch steps I went. Every aggressive shove made me smile more. As we passed between several of their dead comrades, the hidden guns, once buried, were still pivoting on the contraptions. That particular trap was always my favorite, the way the triggering mechanism released the pressure causing the guns to pop from the ground and fire. They were tricky to set up, though, because of the unreliability of the pressure within the springs. I remember failing a few times trying to get the tension just right. Damn near lost an arm one time; the bullet just grazed me. I learned my lesson quickly and never stood in front of a trap again when setting them up. The flicking of the triggers could still be heard, and the grinding of the pivots was intoxicating; a well-oiled machine that worked like it should have. There's not much I ask from the traps, except to work when I need them to. The bullets tore through the men with ease, gutting them at such an angle their stomachs served as the entry zone. One guy was almost completely cut in half. If anything needed adjusting, I would probably raise the angle slightly so that the aim was a little higher, around the chest area. The smell was God-awful, but the wind also carried a hint of oak.

Walking further down, we came to the edge of the pit where two more men were skewered at the bottom. One was daggered through the neck. The other was staked right through the back; the wooden tip was protruding through his chest. Brutal way to die, but the way I look at it, it was all chance. I didn't actually push them into the pit; they walked into it under their own free will. Honestly, if I was guilty of anything, it was sitting on my porch and watching the whole thing unfold. Not really sure if that would stand up in court or not, but I had no blood on my hands. The bad luck was really on the side of the trespassers: they chose their fates when they decided to drive up my dirt road. I paused briefly to admire the contents of the pit. The skewered bodies of their allies stared up at us.

"Well, look at that," I said sarcastically. "Their eyes don't even blink against the bright sun; not even a squint."

They didn't like that too much, and I felt the handle of a gun collide against the back of my skull. It wasn't a square hit, but it did blur my vision and sent me falling face first to the dirt. Chuckling in a confused state, I spit mud from my drooling mouth.

"You're going to rot in Hell, you sick bastard," one of them replied.

"Wait, this isn't Hell?" I said with a smirk.

That's about when the boots rained down upon me. I lost count how many times I was hit, but I remember seeing the sole of one of the boots blotting out the sun. I woke up cuffed to a tree. I was sitting on my ass with my arms wrapped behind the tree. Standing before me were two men with their guns drawn. Seemed like I had pushed the limits to their civil duty of *protect and serve*. Spitting blood, my tongue felt chipped, jagged teeth. Fuckers. Teeth are hard to keep up with, especially on the mountain.

They were arguing with themselves about who was to do the dirty deed of ending my pathetic life. It appears that neither of them brought their balls with them. It was frustrating; my right eye was swelling shut, bugging the shit out of me in the process. They were pacing and talking about what to do. They were conflicted, as they really hated me but the small remnants of loyalty to the legal system were causing hesitation. Their feet were shuffling about like squirrels searching for an acorn.

That's about when I saw a glimmer of light reflecting off of metal. My head ached badly, but I was able to remember.

I consider traps to be similar to pets: sometimes they roam off then reappear out of the blue. The sun highlighting a small portion of metal was like Spot coming home after a long stay away. My busted lip curled and hurt like a mother fucker as I watched their feet getting closer. Like watching a roulette wheel as it slows, I tried to predict where the ball would land. They were about five feet away from me when contestant number one stepped on the trap.

Grenades are an interesting item to use for traps; the way the pin has to be in there and such. They really are a very unstable firecracker with a short fuse. Regardless, I was very content due to my distance from the trap. Still cuffed to the tree, I really could not do anything to prepare, except close my one good eye and tilt my head to try to shield my face.

The blast was brutal. When I opened my eye, I had one of the men lying upon my legs. I'm guessing he was the one who didn't step on the trap because he was somewhat intact. The other man, well, fuck, he was all over the place, like using a blender without the lid. Everything was red and sludgy. My shoulder was burning something crazy. Rotating my neck, I was able to see that my shoulder had taken some shrapnel, but any pain subsided when the man lying on me began to move. Moaning in pain, he rolled over and looked to me with half of his face missing. Blood was gurgling out of neck as his lungs fought for air. After a few minutes of annoying coughing and confusion, he bled out.

Again, I don't consider myself a violent man. Honestly, the traps are the bad guys. I'm just a slave to bloody innovation. Secured to the tree, I couldn't have possibly done any of this mess, but unfortunately I'm always the one who has to clean it up. I'm sure they will send more in time, a lot more to be honest, but just like the others, they too will have a choice whether or not to drive up my dirt road and interrupt the peaceful tranquility of my mountain.

With a corpse atop of me, the mountain wind never felt so good. Dangling out of the man's pocket are the keys to these damn cuffs. It'll be quite a feat to maneuver those keys from the pocket and get them behind the tree to my hands. Seems like a lot of work. Definitely won't be getting out of here before sunset. Fuck.

Agent Holt's world had been turned upside down. Literally.

His fingertips brushed the concrete floor, his feet encircled by a noose high above his head.

He cursed himself at having stepped on the scattered newspapers that had hidden the age-old trap—a device set by his nemesis, Simeon—who sat before him, handcuffed to a rusting radiator on a dilapidated wall.

"So, Mr. Holt," the wiry man smiled, his dark skin and the low-lit room emphasizing the whites of his large eyes and strangely long teeth. "What do we do now?"

"Screw you," Holt sneered.

Simeon rattled the chain holding him fast to the metallic heating appliance. "Oh, you could, but I am somewhat indisposed," he said, his voice calm and melodic.

Holt swung from his tether, the slow rotations occasionally showing him Simeon's smiling face like an upside-down moon orbiting the earth.

"I need to get down from here," he said, gritting his teeth as he felt bile rise in his throat … or descend, given the position he was in.

"I would love to aid you, Mr. Holt," the criminal said through his grin, "but since you chained me, I'm afraid I'm not much help to anyone."

"You ain't gonna be helping anyone from the electric chair either, Simeon," Holt said, anger making his face redder as blood rushed into it. He tried to pull himself up his own legs, hand-over-hand, fists grabbing handfuls of his trousers.

Reaching the thick rope around his ankles, he struggled to free himself, but his own weight was pulling the trap tight. He let go and fell back to his original position, swinging wildly, not helping his physical or mental discomfort.

"Oh please," said Simeon, holding his hand up to block the view. "You'll give me motion sickness."

"I'll make you feel a whole lot worse when I get myself down," Holt snarled, fighting to keep the contents of his stomach under some semblance of control.

"And—pray tell—how will you achieve that?" Simeon asked. "You've hunted me for so long that you haven't been a 'real' agent for months. Discharged, I believe? No one knows you are missing, *Agent* Holt. No one knows where you are, and you were very lucky to stumble upon my home out here in the sticks. We are a long way from civilization, so I am intrigued to find out just exactly how you plan to free yourself or to take me in."

"I assume that, seeing as you have not produced it yet, your phone is in your vehicle?" Simeon continued, brow furrowing as his mind flowed smoothly. "You could not have called back-up as you are forbidden from continuing this case …" His eyes sparkled as he leaned forward ever-so-slightly and whispered: "And I know that you have no *partner* to follow behind you anymore …"

Holt stared at Simeon; the hulking former agent of the FBI glaring at the frail, thin, almost ill-looking rapist, pedophile, and murderer of over a dozen men, women and children.

"Mr. Holt," the tombstone teeth grinned, his voice rising an octave. "I believe that I may well have a solution to our problem. However, it does require an element of trust … at least on my part."

The blood pulsed in Holt's temples, his face burning as his body tried to adjust to the world being the wrong way up.

"Ok," he said, his voice strained. "Consider me a captive audience."

"You have been chasing me for, what … six years?" asked Simeon, closing one eye, his tongue poking out of the corner of his mouth in a gesture that looked anything but childlike.

"Eight years!" Holt spat, knowing the man was taunting him. "I've been chasing you ever since you gutted little Evie Miller."

"Ah, yes," Simeon seemed to focus on some far away thought, his voice quieting. "Mrs. Miller's pride and joy …" He snapped out of his reverie. "I had to convince them to let me work on their farm just so I could get close enough to the darling little—"

"I know the details!" Holt shouted, writhing uselessly. "Get me down from here!"

Simeon raised his free hand, indicating an apology his face did not convey.

"Forgive me, Agent Holt, I digress." He waited until Holt's fury had diminished, the whole time watching the sway of the former agent as if hypnotized, his body rocking gently in rhythm.

"I have a knife on my person that will cut your rope," Simeon said. "But in return I need you to help me with something … some information."

"What sort of information?" Holt asked, hatred barely simmered beneath his words.

"Do you recall Louisiana, approximately two years ago?" the maniac asked, eyebrow raised.

Holt nodded, his body swaying slightly with the motion. "Russell Martin, twenty-four years old, from Akers. We found some of him in Lake Maurepas, and the rest in his home." said Holt. "He was a male prostitute … I didn't think he would be your type."

"Oh please," Simeon said, eyes fluttering. "*Anyone* is my type, dearie," he said and winked.

"What about him?" Holt said, desperate to change the direction of the conversation.

"Well," said Simeon, all pretense vanishing as he sat, cross-legged, hand firmly attached to the radiator. "After you had walked in and seen my … 'artwork,' if you will, and then finished emptying your stomach out the back window, you found something of mine that you took."

"How would you know?" Holt asked, his eyes widening.

"I was under the floorboards, my pet!" Simeon squealed, enjoying the look of torment in the other man's eyes. "You were so close to catching me that day! Ha!"

"I found your bag," Holt blurted, his mind working furiously to ignore Simeon's words. *You could have saved countless lives if you had caught him!* his mind screamed.

"Yes," Simeon said, smiling. "My bag of tricks."

"There were knives, hooks, hammers …"

"Yes, my bag of tricks." The smile was gone. "Where is it?"

"In … in an evidence locker."

"Ha!" Simeon pointed a finger at him. *"You lie!* When I strung your partner up—much like your good self right now—and tortured him for hour after long hour, he admitted that he had never seen nor heard of my bag!"

Holt's head pounded as he twitched on his rope. Simeon had killed his partner over a year ago and Holt had been the one who found him; hung from a ceiling and barely resembling a human being. The floor had been slick with blood and entrails, and Holt had slipped, falling into the remnants of his partner.

"Actually, he told me right away that he didn't know where my property was," Simeon said. "But I skinned him all the same …" His smile returned. "So, Agent Holt. Where is it? I bet it's somewhere you can sit and stare at it from time to time, trying to get in my mind, no?"

Holt swung impotently.

"It's hidden in my garage," he said finally. "And when we get out of this and you're sitting smouldering in the chair, I'll destroy it and you'll be nothing more than a footnote in a training manual."

Simeon's smile broadened, encompassing his whole face. He stood up, rubbing his wrist as Holt stared dumbly at the empty handcuffs attached to the radiator.

The killer looked down at them, smiling. Always smiling.

"If the combined forces of the FBI, CIA and police in every state of our fair country couldn't catch me," he said. "How the hell do you think I'd let you just walk up to me and cuff me if I wasn't able to free myself? Now, if you'll excuse me, I have to go and retrieve something that belongs to me," Simeon said, opening the door.

He paused at the entrance, his smile sly as he looked over his shoulder, speaking quietly:

"Are your wife and son home, Agent Holt?"

The door clicked shut.

43. GRAVEYARD GAMES by J.T. Seate

The half moon created ominous shadows as the four of us trundled through a field complete with a menacing scarecrow. Ahead was the cemetery, beyond the view of farmhouses, waiting for us like a quiet sentinel. It looked like a dark obstacle course, with its high weeds, tombstones, and a few crypts serving as challenges beckoning to be traversed.

I looked at my sister, Steph, the youngest of us four. For she and I, the luster of crossing the graveyard alone had lost whatever shine it may have possessed while we were whittling the stakes.

"We should have brought a flashlight," I said.

"Naw, the girls will be easy to see in their nightgowns," Glenn answered. "Each of us will walk across, stick the stake in the ground by the fence on the other side, and come back."

"Uh huh," the girls said.

"Who's first?" Glenn asked.

"This was your idea," his sister said.

"No problem." Glenn picked up one of the stakes and scrawled his name on its shaft with a ballpoint pen. "I'll see you scaredy-cats in about ten minutes." He jumped over the black iron spears and was gone.

I suddenly felt … no … I *knew* we were violating some unwritten rule, and tempting fate.

Ten minutes passed; then fifteen.

"BOO!" Glenn hollered, springing from the darkness.

I'm sure I levitated a foot. Steph's frightened eyes squirted tears.

"God damn it, Glenn!" Barbara yelled at him.

"No more of that crap, or we're going back," I said.

He changed the subject. "Walking across is a piece of cake. Just look out for the footstones."

"I'll go next," I said. I wrote my name on my stake and jumped the fence as Glenn had done. I just wanted to get it over with.

It was darker than I'd expected. Halfway across, something moved—a figure rose above a gravestone. Its body undulated, then crawled to the side of the stone, revealing its spiked pelt. *A porcupine, for Chrissake*. I proceeded to the far edge of the cemetery. I looked for Glenn's stake, but didn't see it. I plunged mine into the ground and started back, careful to avoid the low stones and equally careful not to run.

I imagined squirmy, creepy-crawlies on the stones, and sensed the presence of the dead, their troubled spirits still active. A mausoleum door was ajar as the wind picked up to a nasty whine. In my mind, rotting corpses prepared to walk about, stirring from their dark sleep.

I'd had all the graveyard games I wanted for one night.

When I rejoined the group, Barbara wanted to go next. She picked up a stake and got over the fence easier than either Glenn or I had. I'm not sure how long we waited for her; one minute can seem like ten when you're waiting for something.

"Do you think Barb's messin' with us?" Glenn asked.

"Dunno. She's *your* sister."

"I'm going after her," he said, then jumped the fence again, and ran into the dark.

"I feel like we're being watched, Davie," Steph said.

I ignored her for several more minutes, until—

A scream tore through the night, like something out of a horror movie.

Then: "Help!"

"Go see what's wrong. I'll wait here."

"Promise you'll stay right here," I said, then traveled back along the path I would've given anything not to travel again.

Barbara lay on the ground next to the far fence. Glenn knelt over her.

"She's not breathing!" Glenn wailed.

I looked at Barbara's gown. It stretched to the foot of the fence. Her stake was driven through the hem of her nightgown. When she turned to leave, it must've pulled taut. She thought something was grabbing her. Can someone be scared to death, I wondered?

As I bent over Barbara, her eyes flew open. She made a horrible, guttural sound like the bride of Dracula. I stumbled back and grabbed Glenn's legs. An indefinable sound came from my mouth. Barbara rose up and reached for me.

Someone screamed. It must have been me, because Barbara's expression changed. She began to laugh. I looked at Glenn. He broke into laughter and fell to the ground, his arms around his sides, laughter coming in waves of delight.

I looked back at Barbara, tears streaming in amusement.

"You should've seen your face," Glenn managed to choke out. "You looked like you'd seen …" He couldn't continue, holding his sides, yucking it up.

Barbara hooted. "We didn't mean to give you a heart attack. Can you talk?" she said, her laughter subsiding a bit.

They had gotten me good, and that's all there was to it. I returned to where we'd all started as quickly as I could, not wanting Steph to be alone, but when we got back, my sister was gone. I saw something that petrified me: Steph's clothes, her nightgown and her underwear, stacked in a neat little pile on top of her tennis shoes. I think I sort of went into shock at that point. The joke on me had been numbing, but this—my little sister gone. I feared the real terror was only beginning.

We all called for her. I picked up the clothes and ran down the road toward our farmhouse. I wasn't sure if this was another elaborate hoax, but I prayed to God it was. I was responsible for Stephanie, yet here I was, running back from a cemetery where she'd been left alone. My second prayer was that she would be at the house waiting for us in her jeans and tee-shirt.

~ ~ * * ~ ~

Local people and State Troopers searched for days. I never went near that graveyard again because if I had, I was afraid I might hear Steph calling for help, calling for me to find her.

Weeks later, I remembered something: *The unused stake.* It was missing, vanished into thin air just like my sister.

If those responsible for my sister's disappearance read this, I beg you to take pity and tell me exactly what happened. I know you're out there. I know because of what I found in my mailbox yesterday—an old, weathered stake, with the letters S-T-E-P-H crudely scrawled on its shaft.

44. THE ELEVENTH PIPER BY REBECCA FUNG

On the first day of Christmas, he sent to the gates of our kingdom a partridge in a pear tree.

"It's so beautiful!" I squealed. "Look, those pears are so luscious and big … I'm in love! Bring them in!"

My mother slammed that idea fairly quickly. "Are you a fool? You barely know the man. A few dates does not mean he's your destiny. You read far too many romance novels. Send that ridiculous plant away!"

As she was the queen and I only the humble princess, the guards did as she ordered. The pear tree was marched away and I never even got to finger a single leaf.

"You don't want me to have any fun," I grumbled. "I want to have boyfriends. I want to get presents from admirers. That was my chance. And I love birds, and pears. That was perfect!"

"Stupid girl," chided my mother. "You need to learn more about acting like a Queen. There'll be more presents another day."

There were. The very next. Two turtledoves—and the partridge returned.

"He knows I love birds!" I said. "Oh Mother, it wouldn't do any harm, they're just … please?"

"No," said my mother. She dismissed them. The offerings grew the next day, and the next, and still she remained adamant.

But on the fifth day, a courier arrived not just with the line of birds in tow, but with a little purple velvet pillow. Upon it sat five gold rings.

"Pure gold, your Highness," said the courier, sweeping a bow.

I reached through the bars of the gate and fingered them. They seemed to warm and glow even brighter under my touch.

"He sends his respects, your Highness," said the courier.

"That's quite enough," said my mother. "What on Earth do you think you're doing, girl? Didn't I tell you … oh … gold!"

"Symbols of eternity, Mother. Rings! I'm sure he is my true love now. What else could it mean?"

Mother pursed her lips. "Send them back."

"Mother!" I exclaimed. "You saw them. Real gold. And I know you loved them too. What were you thinking? After all this time, you must see … he really is in love with me."

Mother smiled and pulled me aside so the guards couldn't hear. "A man besotted is a man to be played, my dear daughter. As you grow up you will learn this. Look at how his gifts increase in number and in glory every day. If you hold out a bit longer I wouldn't be surprised if we don't see a whole trunk full of diamonds here one day. So don't be too hasty to accept a man. Keep them wanting a little more and it'll pay off. I know men."

"Mother, you are wicked."

"We all have a little wickedness in us. You'll thank me, my dear. Now watch those gates and see if I'm not right."

I watched those gates each morning. Mother was very good at predicting certain things. Six geese, seven swans, and eight little girls carrying pails of fresh milk came trotting out to me over the next days, bearing messages that my lover begged me to accept his gifts as symbols of his undying passion. He was wasting away with love, they told me. He would die if he could not hold me in his arms, and all he wanted was to whisper sweet nothings into my perfect pink ear. It was all the meaning his life held for him.

I swooned a little and started to check my ears out in my mirror each morning, but Mother helped me to reject all the gifts. However, even she seemed to weaken a little each day. The scent of fresh milk in the morning—oh my!

"When do we know when to accept? At some time, we must accept. The presents won't go on forever."

"A few more," said my mother. "Just a few more. Oh, I wonder what's in store for tomorrow!" She sounded more excited than me.

Nine ladies trouped out the next day to perform a complex acrobatic dance outside the gates. Their arms waved, their legs kicked and I gazed at them in awe, wondering how anyone could manage to move their limbs so quickly and in such a formation. They blew me kisses and tried to entice me to welcome them in, but I shook my head sadly. So the next day ten young men joined their exhilarating exhibition, jumping, leaping over the ladies as they danced, higher and higher into the air, some of them managing to incorporate somersaults into their leaping! Mother and I clapped and clapped.

But it was on the eleventh day that we capitulated, when eleven pipers marched up beside the dancers and leapers and began to play a musical accompaniment.

Their fingers flew up and down the pipes, blowing out a tune in time with the rhythmic dances of the ladies. Or did the ladies dance to the pipers? For as the pipers sped up, so did the ladies, and as the pipers chose a slower, smoother melody, the ladies moved to flowing, elegant dance moves to contrast the high energy snaps their limbs had been delivering only moments ago. Who was following whom?

Several notes were given—long, high and sharper than usual—and I watched as the young men flipped higher and higher, twisting in the air and landing neatly over the ladies.

"Higher!" I screamed, and the pipers adjusted their pitch and the gentleman leaped even further from the ground.

"Such talent, such skill," cried my mother. "The music goes straight to my heart."

It was such perfect piping. Every lady and gentleman dancing was reacting to it, and I could even feel it tugging at my own feet. The piping pulled at my heart and spoke of loneliness and despair, as well as reminded me of beauty. The notes drove themselves into my brain and flashed so many gorgeous images in front of me I could feel my lips trembling, and before I knew it, I was at the gates, pounding at them, screaming, "Let them in, let them in!"

Mother was walking up behind me, as if in a trance. A smile played on her lips. "Such beautiful music. Indeed, open the gates, guards. Let them in. Let them in."

"Let them in. Let them in," we both chanted, in time with the pipes.

"Let them in, let them in," repeated the guards. The gates were flung open, and in marched the pipers. The ladies laughed and danced in, and the lords leaped over them. Every part of the parade danced, marched, waddled, flew, in, and I smiled. All my presents, at last, at last!

"My true love," I said. "No trunkful of diamonds, Mother. But we mustn't be too greedy."

"Indeed not," agreed my mother, slurping up the milk from one of the pails offered by a maiden. "Ahh, there's the stuff!"

I took a luscious gulp as well. It was rich and sweet. I couldn't stop smiling and thinking about my true love, and wondering what he was doing. Why did he keep sending gifts, but never come to visit me? What a tease! Surely he would have to come now, now that I had accepted him? Surely we would be together. Surely he would come to my side and hold me in his arms and …

"Oh, he'll be here all right." One of the pipers was standing next to me. He lifted his pipe and began to pipe a melody so sweet I could hear my lover pining for me. "He knew you couldn't resist forever," whispered this eleventh piper.

He raised his pipe again and blew on it. A piercingly high note, but this time a puff of purple smoke was emitted. The other pipers followed the signal.

I gagged, coughed and screamed as the smoke inflamed my nose and eyes so I couldn't breathe or see for a moment, but then it cleared. In those few seconds, the happy little world I was used to seeing had changed.

Lords and ladies were ransacking my kingdom. Their athletic bodies scaled walls, leaped over barriers and through windows. They did not tire. A lady reached a very high wall and simply stretched out and her long arms extended to its top. The gentlemen adjusted their springs to account for the higher windows of certain buildings so they could crash through. They were looting machines.

I heard the screams of my people, and the gentlemen and ladies silenced them with sharp blows and kicks of those swift legs I had so admired. The hard metal limbs of these robot ransackers easily took out my people, who cried in pain and lay crippled in the street, and most of the others fled with very little. The thieves moved in robotic time to efficiently break my furniture and fill boxes. Turtledoves and collie birds flew this way and that, pecking at anyone who remained, urging them out.

"Perfectly programmed," smiled the piper.

I heard a scream and I saw my mother staggering along the road, chased by a goose with gleaming red eyes. She fell to the ground and vomited a pool of whiteness.

"Mother!" I screamed, but as I jumped to my feet I could feel the milk in my stomach. It felt horrid and cold, and I started to move uneasily. I sat back down.

"No, no," I whispered, looking around me at the havoc. People were running as mechanical birds chased them down the streets. Houses crumbled. And the pipers played on.

I could feel the rings clenching my fingers, growing hotter and tighter, and the eleventh piper warned, "A finger will fall off for every scream. So keep your mouth shut. But keep watching the performance, my dear. Oh, and he sends his regards. He says, please think of him."

I stared ahead sullenly. I wished I'd never met the bastard. "Why? Why me?" I whispered.

"You're a princess, of course. We all love princesses. To make, to take, to break. He promised twelve drummers tomorrow," said the piper.

"I wonder why." He reached out, placing his hand on the right side of my chest. "Ba doom. Ba doom."

45. THE COLOR OF PEPTO BISMOL BY JOHN ALFRED TAYLOR

"What's the point?" Henry says. "Dinky carnival. Went last year. Stupid rides and the world's smallest Ferris wheel."

His cousin turns off Front Street. "This is something else, something you should see now that you're old enough."

"The sideshow? I've already got plenty of classmates with tattoos. And as for the Fat Lady—you should see the girls."

"This is different," Fred insists.

Henry gives his cousin the hairy eyeball, but Fred's too busy watching the road to notice. "Maybe like a geek biting the head off a live chicken?"

"Not that kind of thing," Fred says. "Something wonderful. You can't imagine."

Parking is in a fallow soybean field. The late afternoon sun hits them the instant they're out of the air-conditioning, and they stumble through the dust toward the world's smallest Ferris wheel.

The midway is every bit as tawdry as Henry remembers: speakers on poles blaring calliope music, popcorn and cotton candy, hot dogs turning on metal rollers, a shooting gallery, a ring toss, milk bottles stacked to knock down. Next comes the long canvas front of the sideshow, crude paintings of THE GIANT TRENCH RAT, THE LOBSTER BOY, THE HUMAN PRETZEL grinning through her thighs, with a sweating barker trying to convince the few people listening. Henry cringes when his cousin swerves toward the barker. "I thought you said no freaks."

"Not here," Fred announces, passing the barker and images of HE DRINKS FIRE HE BREATHES FIRE, ALLIGATOR MAN, and THE LITTLEST EQUESTRIAN. He leads Henry past the corner and through an arch labeled THE SIREN.

They're between two canvas walls, one the blank end of the sideshow tent, the other side a new image: black outlines on a red field that show a naked man tied to a mast. Head tilted back so his beard sticks out horizontally, he looks up at a huge bird with a woman's head dive-bombing the ship. "Copy of a Greek vase painting," Fred says.

Henry doesn't think that's an explanation, but follows his cousin down a path marked off by construction tape. Ahead is a long travel trailer with its front lip anchored to the bed of a massive pickup. "Glad we came early," Fred says, indicating the four men waiting ahead. "Negroponte only lets in fifteen at a time."

"You've been before?"

Fred smiles beatifically as they join the line. "Last year." Others show up behind them, so fast that Henry understands why Fred wanted to come early. "Hurry up and wait," his dad used to say, and now they're waiting. With the sun this hot on his head, he wishes he'd worn a hat.

Then the front door of the trailer opens, and a dark-haired man steps out. "Here we go," Fred murmurs.

"Twenty dollars admission." Negroponte announces, and Henry winces. Not your ordinary freak show price. Fred sees his expression. "Don't worry—it's on me. Pay me back afterwards, if you think it's worth it."

Working his way up the line, Negroponte counts out loud as he takes admissions. Henry sees his cheek is deeply scarred when he nods to Fred. He tells the first fifteen to wait at the trailer while he sells the late-comers rain checks for the night show.

~ ~ * * ~ ~

"You'll be absolutely safe inside," says Negroponte before he opens the door. "Not that you'll care in a minute. You'll be too happy. But afterwards you'll be glad I made sure."

The trailer settles under their weight as they enter. Henry blinks in the dimness. The front half looks like any house trailer—a bed, a bathroom, a tiny kitchen and table—but the back is hidden by a curtain. Negroponte puts on a pair of earphones. "Noise-canceling. You'll see why."

He opens the curtain, revealing a sliding security gate like those on mall store entrances. "You can go right up to the grill," he announces, "even put your hands through. Only risky past the yellow and black line on the floor."

They all surge forward when the lights come up on the other side. Henry and his cousin have their heads together in the press, but they can both see through the bars. In one corner there's something the violent pink of Pepto-Bismol curled up on a foam mattress.

When she sits up he sees the woman is wearing a pink cap and jacket with ostrich feathers on the shoulders and jagged fringes on the forearms. As the creature comes to her feet Henry stares, realizing it's not a jacket. Except for the down on her shoulders and the bright plumes on her forearms, she's naked and obviously mammalian, with skin the color of honey. Instead of hair, she has a crest like a jay, but with feathers the wrong color.

A chain rattles behind her as she strides toward them, attached to a canvas girdle around her waist. Henry wonders if this is some kind of S&M thing 'til the chain stops her. The inhuman planes of her visage break into a smile that opens wider. Her teeth are long and pointed, and the inside of her mouth dead white as a water moccasin's.

She opens her arms and begins to sing. A song from before there were words, a song that makes words unnecessary. A low note, rising and gathering in strength, then breaking from pitch to pitch in dazzling glissandos 'til there are no separate notes, only a continual trilling, yearning, demanding, calling. Henry is outside of time, straining toward the song while it lasts, and the song seems to last forever.

It stops with terrible abruptness, leaving Henry trembling. He's clutching the bar of the gate so hard his hand is numb, and Fred has a mark on his face where he pressed against the next upright.

The woman-thing is down on the floor, tearing at a butcher-paper package. Red meat spills out and she crams it into her mouth.

"Now you've heard the song of the siren," Negroponte announces. "I always feed her afterwards. It's only fair. Cruel to let her see potential prey who can't come at her call."

"She'd attack us?" someone says.

Negroponte grins. "Wouldn't need to. The song draws you. You happily walk into her arms. 'Til she stopped singing every one of you was straining against the security gate." He taps his earphones. "Why I wear these."

~ ~ * * ~ ~

On the drive home Henry is lost in himself, trying to reconstruct the melody, but it slips away, too variable and alien to hold. He might remember if there had been separate notes instead of a constant changing. Only the feeling lingers, exhaustion after the agony of joy and the ache of its ending. He remembers a thread, begins to follow it. First this, then that, then—

"Glad I took you?" Fred's question crashes in, breaking the thread.

"Yes," murmurs Henry, too shaken to say more.

"Had to go back after I heard the siren last year. Worth it. But only once a year. More would be too much."

"No," Henry says. "Never too much."

"Probably drive you nuts. A person can only stand so much."

"I could listen to her again this instant."

231

"Lucky you can't," Fred says. "The evening show's already sold out. And that's all there is."

"Not if I went back and paid him enough. He'd make a show just for me."

"It would drive you crazy. Or something worse."

"Try me."

"The hell I will. Not going to drive you out there again. Next thing to murder."

Henry's still raging when Fred drops him off. Such a wimp. He must hear the song again before the carnival is gone. If he pays Negroponte enough he can have his own show.

~ ~ * * ~ ~

Mom's out and Dad's still at work.. Henry writes a big note and props it against the salt and pepper grinders in the middle of the kitchen table: *Home late. Invited to supper at Fred's.*

Fred might as well be good for something.

He gets out his bike and heads for Front Street, where he hits the ATM outside the bank for a hundred dollars. There's plenty in his account, thanks to his four-week stint detasseling corn. Then he's pedaling off the long miles toward the carnival, heart beating fast.

He dismounts at the midway and walks his bike. The space is mostly empty, and the sideshow barker has vanished. Nobody notices when he goes through the arch of THE SIREN and down the path marked off with plastic tape. If only Negroponte will listen—

Then he hears the music. He can't resist, dropping his bike and rushing to the trailer door. It's unlocked, and he's already in when the song stops. The security gate stands open, the ceiling spots are on. He freezes in mid-stride: back there the woman-thing crouches over her master, with Negroponte's noise-canceling earphones fallen a yard away.

She flashes her terrible smile as she rises. Henry is caught at the first trill. Ecstatic, drawn by delight, he crosses the yellow and black curve of the safety line. Her feathered arms and clawed hands open for him as the song rises around him. Disregarding the smear of blood on her cheek, he walks down the music toward the open mouth, the white tunnel of her throat.

232

46. SMOKE BY RICK A. CARROLL

To be motionless is fire and pain, so I run.

People scream, letting free panicked cries that terminate in strangled coughs. By the time I pass, they fall to their knees and clutch their throats, fighting with all they have to draw one last breath. The air is scorched and clogged, burning with outrage. The Smiling Man has judged this world, and only smoke remains.

It is thick and grey, dry like summer but smelling of autumn. It's the scent of a campfire in the woods, natural and healthy and carrying a hint of rain. The city and its stink of oil and gasoline is absent. The smoke is pure; the smoke cleanses. It trails behind me, washing away the sins of a dying world.

When I began to run, I knew nothing but fear. How could I not? I was lit on fire, a woman ablaze. The flames died out and left only smoke and ash. Before that? My world was one of beauty, days of love and happiness until the dreams began. Until the Smiling Man came.

There is no experience like burning, no agony like feeling your skin as it blisters and cracks. The body convulses and the muscles strain before they sizzle and pop. When I tried to scream, the heat burned the air from my lungs. My eyes boiled, blinding me until even that was taken away.

Nerves take the longest to die, so vibrant, bringing the kiss of flame with every impulse.

They chanted. They cheered. They would not suffer me to live. Kill me for my own good, so I could kneel before the Jesus and pay for my sins. They are false witnesses all, led astray by the holy man and his hanged god.

When the flames died there was no agony or sight or sound or anything to anchor me to this world. Existence was a waft of smoke, a dream drifting through ash. There was no heaven, no warm embrace of the Jesus to shepherd me home.

And they couldn't suffer me to live. That truth pulled me back from the abyss.

Not once in my life had I lifted a hand against them, never spoken an unkind word. I was no more a witch than the baker in this trendy store, with his well-trimmed beard and unpronounceable wares. I kept to myself and my house, tending my garden and delighting the neighborhood children with stories my Nan told me. They called me "kooky" and "crazy cat lady," but I was neither unwelcome nor shunned. The neighborhood enjoyed my teas: they loved the flavors, so healthy and natural, each lovingly crafted to leave the body vibrant and pure.

Purity. If there was anything I worshipped, it was purity.

How long did it take before I began to run? It's so hard to remember. My head has burned away, the thoughts it once contained now scattered and free. Had I become smoke, or was I trying to escape it? Does one drive the other, or is the latter the former's result?

So many questions, so much confusion. I stop for a moment and smoke engulfs me, spiraling around in chaotic tufts. For a moment I see the Smiling Man and his wicked white teeth, watching me through the haze. It flows around me, spreading and expanding. Shops and homes, alleyways and streets, it moves in all directions, stealing breath and snuffing out life.

The smoke is killing so many. I begin to run again and it follows, withdrawing from the buildings and centering on me. I can't let it catch me; I can't let it consume me. I run down city streets and leap across the vehicles that scurry along them. They screech and crash, destroyed as they careen into one another. Those that can pull themselves free of the wreckage only to fall over and choke, smothered by my smoke. I want to laugh, for surely madness has taken me. But if I stop to laugh, the smoke will catch me again. The smoke has changed; the purity is threatened. There are streaks of oily black in its form, as if burning the wicked has stained it.

Never again! I was choked once, my lungs filled with smoke and ash; I know that pain, that terror. There is no peace beyond, just agony followed by the abyss. I am too fast; it cannot catch me. But it tries, reaching for me as I fly through buildings and jump through windows. Everywhere I go, people die. Those not ravaged by sickness try to flee, but some just lie there and accept their fate.

A man steps from a store, untouched by the plague. He doesn't notice me or the smoke, and even stops long enough to light a cigarette. I run a circle around him, the smoke at my heels. He inhales, looking for the release of his drug, but what he draws in is so much more. He chokes and I laugh as he is engulfed in the cloud. When the smoke clears, only his bones remain.

The holy man led them when they came to take me. Disease festered in the city, but those who drank my teas were untouched. A sickness like the world has never known, unleashed by the weak will of a woman of science. It ravaged the earth, a nightmare from legend. Doctors in their sterile hospitals promised a cure, but their science is soulless. It could no more defeat the plague than it could love a sunset.

The disease touched everyone and everything, and all knew fear. I brewed my teas and shared all I could. That's what brought him to me, the holy man. Word of my remedies reached his ears, and he came to beg me to assist his flock. I was taken with his sweet smile and his kind words. He was taken with the look of me.

The church! That's where he would be.

I race through an intersection, and glass bursts from a storefront as I pass. There is more smoke now than ever before, as if the thought of the holy man has increased its volume. When they took me, he watched, him and his joyless wife. The woman spent more time on her knees praying to the Jesus than she did loving or caring for her husband, a cruel woman who replaced love with piety. He was a proud man, but completely bent to her will. Even the brief passion I showed him could not break her hold, and she hated me because I could cure the people that her hanged god seemed indifferent to.

That was when the whispers began. They said the disease was my doing, and came for me. They cracked the door of the house my father built, sending my cats scattering for safety. I was asleep when the door split, and the mob dragged me from the comfort and warmth of my bed. They cast me out into the cold, unclean world and tore me from the revelations of my dreams.

When the sickness began, I started to dream of the Smiling Man. He was all shadow and hate, completely hidden save the blinding white teeth of his wicked smile. I dreamed of the world undone, where death rode the highways and war sprang in his wake. Pestilence gripped the land, replaced with famine once the disease ran its course. There would be hunger and the dead would live. My dreams told me what was to come, and every day my dreams became real, broadcast back to me by twenty-four-hour news networks.

In front of the house of the Jesus they piled the wood high and recanted scripture, faces lifted to empty heavens and searching for approval in the void. I cried. I was so very scared. When the flames touched my feet I could see her smile, see the hate in her eyes. I pleaded for mercy, I begged for forgiveness and he stopped singing, looking from the flock to me. Did he feel regret as I burned? Was he repulsed by the sins of the mob before the hanged god? Or was it the sweet smell of cooking meat that caused his voice to falter?

I sweep through the streets. Over fences, through homes; everywhere I run the smoke pours from me. It is my shadow, my pursuer. I, who was meant to cleanse the world, now only spread death by smoke. I run and they die, and I feel sorry for them. It isn't their fault, they do not understand. They have no will anymore; they barely have hope. They grasp for what remains, but in the end, the only salvation they receive is my choking death. The promises of false men have damned them all.

Men who lie and lust. Men who burn innocent women out of shame.

My rage becomes unbearable and I scream. The smoke rips free of me, so powerful and violent it obliterates everything in its path. It is black and angry, dark tendrils choking out the pure grey and engulfing all. High buildings shake on their foundations and are blown away and the smoke consumes them. The anger burns in me so hot that the asphalt below bubbles and melts, my footprints blazing hot even though I don't have feet.

What have I become?

My anger fades and the smoke recoils, recalled like a child summoned by a mother's voice. It drifts from what buildings remain and forms into streams, flowing down city streets to gather around me once more. I can see the roads clearly, the people on their knees and burned to ash, frozen like statues until the wind sets them free. Death surrounds me. I have become its agent, its angel on smoky wings. Somewhere I can hear the laugh of the Smiling Man.

This was not my destiny. I hiss through lips that have no form, my rage building again as I start to run. The smoke gives chase and I can feel it on my back and in my hair. I play with its substance with spectral fingertips. It is no longer my pursuer, it is my miasma. It has power but no cause, and I am cause without power. Together, we are complete.

The house of the Jesus is lit from within. The flock kneels around the building on a manicured lawn, perfect save for the circle of ash where they burned me away. They pray for deliverance, so I close in and deliver them. Their prayers turn to coughs, the songs to shrieks. As they die I circle the house. The door is closed, barring me from inside, but I cannot be denied. It may be the house of a god, but it was built by the hands of a man.

I press against the doors and the wood begins to sizzle. My smoke engulfs the house of the Jesus, surrounding it and scouring the pretty colored windows, turning them black with soot. They are screaming inside, so very scared. Smoke assaults the building, pressing in through cracks, finding entry in the tiniest holes. Their screams sound as mine did. The wood warps and sags, so very close to catching fire, but I am not hot enough. The smoke gathers around me, tense and waiting.

As they lashed me to the stake, I saw the holy man clearly. His face, so serene, reading from his book. His sweet voice lifted in song to the hanged god above, full of love and devotion while his flock doused me in gasoline. His wife, smiling as she pulled a red-tipped match from a wooden box.

My scream is rage and hate, expelling smoke from ashen lungs and letting loose the fire within. The doors are consumed in seconds, and those beyond perish in the blast of heat. Smoke rushes through the ruined entrance, flowing around me, my outline clear with arms stretched wide. It is unstoppable; *I* am unstoppable. We claim each pew in rapid succession, eating away their fear and sins without mercy. I walk the aisle as the flock is burned away, my eyes on him at his podium, a terrified shadow of the man I once knew. Above him, the Jesus watches with uncaring eyes.

He begs as I approach, crying for both his mother and his god. His wife is absent, but I don't care. He is the one who betrayed me; he is the one who summoned the flock to burn me away. He is the one who caressed me in the night and then tore the curtain away, discarding me when he was done.

I lift my hand and the smoke coils, hungry and ready. Black tendrils wrap around his body, lifting him into the air and dragging him before me. His jacket is stained black with ash, and his god's house is ablaze. I wonder what he sees when he looks into me, into the space where I once lived. Does he see my beauty and youth? Or does he see that charred corpse that I became? He stares into me and I see recognition in his eyes. I don't know what he sees, but I am certain he knows me for who I am. He knows what he has done, and why I have come.

If I were any less of a woman, I would laugh. Instead, I reach for his face with phantom hands and kiss him one last time. Smoke drifts from what were my lips to his, filling him before burning him away.

Dust to dust, and ashes to ashes.

I fall to my knees, letting my smoke have its way with what remains of the house of the Jesus. I am done now, I can die and drift and find my way back to the abyss … but the smoke lingers, coiling around me. Instead of running free, it caresses me.

I open my eyes and see the Smiling Man, his sharp teeth and the mocking laugh. He is free of my dreams, and it is his will that kills the world.

Beyond the house of the Jesus, the sickness lives on. The world is filthy, diseased. Even those that survive the plague will be covered in filth. My smoke is clean. Where once I might have cured the world, now I can cleanse it. I can take the breath of the dying and burn away the infection. I can accept the cold embrace of death, or let my fire free and purify the world that is to come. I rise and begin to run.

When the Smiling Man laughs, I laugh with him.

47. PAYING AT THE PUMP BY KEN MACGREGOR

Mike maneuvered the rig around the tight corner into the gas station. There were only two diesel handles, one on either side of the same pump. As Mike eased the cab around, checking the mirrors to make sure his trailer was clear, a midsized BMW whipped in and took the spot. Mike braked hard to avoid hitting the car. Sighing, Mike leaned forward to catch the guy's eye through the windshield. The BMW logo caught the sunlight, bouncing it into Mike's eyes. He blinked.

The driver of the Beemer didn't even glance up. Mike put it in neutral and set the brake. He let the truck idle and looked down from his cab.

The guy sat in his car wearing dark sunglasses, a top-of-the-line smartphone pressed to his ear.

"Hello, Mr. Businessman," Mike said quietly. Minutes crawled by. Mike's truck partially blocked the gas station driveway, but the man in the BMW still sat in the driver's seat.

Finally, Mike undid his seat belt and killed the engine. Pulling the keys from the ignition, Mike stepped out of the truck. He strode over to the Beemer with a smile on his face. When the businessman noticed him, Mike waved and made his smile bigger. The window slid down with a slight hum.

"Yes?"

"Hey there," Mike said. "You probably didn't notice my truck there when you pulled up, but um, this is the only pump with diesel, and I was wondering if maybe you were gonna fill up anytime soon so I could use it next."

The man exhaled sharply through his nose and told the person on the phone to hold on.

"I'm going to fill up," the man said. "This is a public gas station, you know?"

"Right," Mike said. "Sure it is. Just, you know, you kind of cut me off there and now you're spending a lot of time *not* pumping gas ..."

Tilting his shades forward on his nose, the man rolled his eyes up at Mike. Mike gave him another smile, but not without real difficulty. The man pushed his shades into place and the window slid back up as he returned the phone to his ear.

Putting his hands out in the universal sign for *seriously?* Mike stood outside the BMW for another full minute.

"Hey," Mike said, raising his voice so the guy could hear him. "I've been on the road a long time, and I just want to get home and see my kids. Have a heart, buddy."

Mr. Businessman ignored him.

Shaking his head, Mike got back in his truck.

For the next ten minutes, Mike sat in the cab, glaring at Mr. Businessman. The son of a bitch just sat in his car, blocking the pump, chatting away on his phone. Mike saw the man laughing. One pump over, a green Jeep pulled up. A woman got out and filled her tank. She glanced back and forth between the BMW and Mike's truck, frowning. When she met Mike's eye he gave her a little wave. Her hand twitched, but she didn't quite wave back.

Mike watched her drive off, then thumped his head against the headrest a few times.

"You think this is funny, little man?" Mike was getting hot. He scratched at his scalp behind his ears. Mike's left leg was bouncing up and down and his right hand tapped on the steering column, the impact jangling the steel keys hanging from the ignition.

Another minute crawled by. The businessman took the phone from his ear.

"Finally," Mike said.

The man looked up at Mike's truck. A slow, nasty smile crept over his face and he leaned back in his seat, putting his hands behind his head.

He didn't get out to pump gas. He just sat there.

Mike clamped his teeth together. His hands clenched into fists. Once. Twice. He reached for the door handle but stopped. Instead, Mike turned the key halfway to warm up the plugs. The yellow light on the dash popped up and told him to "wait to start." When it went off, Mike cranked the key over and the big engine roared to life.

Below Mike, Mr. Businessman pulled his hands from behind his head. He leaned forward and smirked. With one hand, the man gave Mike a little wave.

"Oh, I'm not leaving," Mike said. He shifted into first and took off the brake. The tractor-trailer, totaling twenty-four tons, inched forward.

Mr. Businessman's smirk fell away as his jaw dropped. Scrambling for the keys, the man tried to get his car started.

The front bumper of the truck was an inch thick plate of solid steel, painted black. It pushed the BMW back a few feet before sliding up over the hood. Inside the Beemer, the airbags deployed, shattering the designer shades and cutting the man's cheek.

Mr. Businessman stopped trying to start the car and grabbed the door handle. He opened the door hard—but it only went six inches before stopping against the steel arch that protected the gas pump from collisions.

Mike kept it in first gear, easing the truck forward until he could no longer see the Beemer's windshield. Smoke poured upward around his grill. The sound of crumpling metal was barely audible over the big engine.

A guy who had been about to pump gas into a purple Neon ran a few feet toward Mike's truck, yelling "What are you doing?" at the top of his lungs. Mike didn't look at him.

Mike heard the door slam into the barrier again and again.

"Fuck you, fuck you, fuck you, *fuck you* goddammit," Mr. Businessman shouted.

Mike kept the truck going forward another few feet and stopped. Taking it out of gear, Mike set the brake. Taking his time, he killed the engine and pulled out the key. He had pushed the BMW far enough forward he could now get to the pump.

"Fuck you, too," Mike said.

Mike went into the station where the clerk, phone to his ear stared at Mike and said nothing. Mike handed him two fifties.

"I need a hundred on pump six," he said. The clerk took the money with a shaking hand and pushed buttons on the register.

"I'm on the phone with the police," the clerk said. His name-tag read *Vinny*.

Mike nodded.

"Just the diesel. Thanks."

After filling up, Mike replaced the nozzle and locked the fuel cap again. Only then did Mike look at the mangled car still under the front of his truck.

Inside, Mr. Businessman was a mess. The BMW's engine was in the front seat with him, pushed halfway through his abdomen. Underneath, his legs were so much shredded meat. The businessman's chest and head were above the worst of it, but he didn't seem to be breathing. The driver's door was open an inch or so, and blood streamed out onto the asphalt.

"Next time," Mike said, "don't be a dick."

Mr. Businessman didn't reply.

Mike grinned at the man and gently slapped his cheek. Three police cruisers screamed into the gas station lot. The cops were out with guns drawn almost before the cars stopped. Mike, still grinning, put his hands behind his head for the cuffs.

He knew the drill.

48. MARGIE DON'T KNOW WHAT SHE WANTS BY
R.L. UGOLINI

Nothing wrong with Margie a little bowl of ice cream couldn't fix. Her sugar got low between meals. Didn't everyone's? Made her a little cranky. A little testy. Between meals she didn't like nobody, leastwise him. Got to talking about how she might just pack up and go to her sister's. Leave him, and see how he liked that.

Well, he wouldn't like it. Not one bit. They were married, and that meant they stuck together. Sickness and health. Her health was not good. He'd take care of her.

Even from downstairs he could hear her fussing. Moving around up there, making the timbers groan.

He opened the icebox. Three scoops of chocolate ripple should do the trick. Then she'd be his sweet lady again.

Three? Maybe one more. Just to make sure.

Generous, he was. A provider. He snapped the lid back on the bucket of ice cream—it came in gallons. He got a good deal on it at the S&P.

Nuked the bowl for eight seconds. His Margie liked her ice cream on the soft side. Made it go down all smooth. Put the spoon in—the big one, a soupspoon, not the teaspoon. Teaspoons never would get the job done.

Upstairs then, and down the hall. The door to Margie's room didn't meet the jamb anymore; the floorboards were warped. He pushed in, the air so heavy with her scent.

She frowned at him something ugly. Beads of sweat sprouted along her hairline. Her breaths came heavy, but oh, so quiet. So sneaky.

"You've been up to something," he said, rounding the bed to stand before her. He was not surprised. Margie often got up to mischief if she wasn't watched.

This time, she'd pulled up the comforter and wadded it behind her, boosting her to an almost seated position on the bed. One pale drumstick of a leg dangled off the side. Milky white skin veined with stretch marks, both pink and new and gray and old, made her look like marble. Like a statue, back in the day when more men liked their women with substance.

Margie was a woman of much substance.

But not much sense.

"I think I can get up—"

"Now why would you do that?" He set the ice cream on the nightstand. The spoon clinked against the bowl.

Her gaze darted to the sound. "I don't want that."

"Sure you do."

"You don't know what I want."

He did. She wanted nothing to do with him. But that was just her low sugar talking.

He pushed the bowl closer to her. "It's your favorite."

"Get that shit away from me."

It wasn't shit. He bought the good stuff. But, at least in one sense, she was right. Coming out, it would look about the same as going in. Didn't smell half as nice, though. However, ever since he'd had the idea to put puppy piddle pads beneath her on the bed, he hadn't had so much of *that* to deal with.

It was a learning process.

He tried to ignore her hurtful tone. It was hard, but over the years, he'd come to ignore a lot. Pissing and moaning was what she did. He took her leg and heaved it back into bed.

"Want anything?"

She turned away. The cold shoulder.

He let her be. For now. Later, when he walked her lunch upstairs, the bowl of ice cream was empty. She still wasn't her sweet self, though.

"You're lucky I don't call the police," she said.

He followed her gaze across the room, where an old princess phone landline gathered dust on her vanity table. Where she kept her makeups. All sorts of paints and creams. He'd opened the lipstick once, dabbed it against his bottom lip. It was both dry and sticky. Something in it had gone rancid. He'd wiped his mouth, but the smell had stayed with him.

"You won't," he told her. Not 'cause he was a mind reader, but 'cause he'd canceled the landline two years ago. She wasn't going anywhere. He didn't get married so one day his wife could leave him.

That's why he had to take care of her. So she would stay. He made sure she ate right and stayed off her bad feet. Bad knees. Bad back. He was the responsible one. 'Cause the way things are, with her sugar so low, Margie don't know what she wants.

Not like he does.

Our marriage vows said " 'Til death do us part," —but some vows are made to be broken.

My husband, Ronnie, is dead, but he still stays by my side night and day. When I go to the store, he rides in the top of the cart, where other women put their babies. When I'm driving, he's in the passenger seat, safely strapped in. I've seen the looks and heard the murmurs, but I don't care if people think I'm weird, or that it's some big joke. He's still my husband. He'll always be my husband—and what else am I supposed to do? Leave him in the car? I wouldn't even do that to a dog.

I love my husband more than anything in this world, and that is why I carry a box around with Ronnie's picture taped to the lid. It's where he sleeps. It holds him.

I hold him.

And, for the last two months, I've been eating him, too.

My problem started three months ago, shortly after his death in a hit-and-run accident.

He was cremated in accordance with his wishes, and I bought him a nice box of dark, carved wood. I know he would have liked it, if he'd ever gotten a chance to see it.

When I transferred his ashes from the funeral parlor's temporary cardboard box into his nice new home, some of Ronnie puffed out and settled on my hand, light as a butterfly. I stared at the ash on my skin and fought hard not to cry. It felt like Ronnie was trying to hold my hand one last time.

I tilted my hand over the box and brushed him back inside, but a thin grey layer still clung to my skin. I couldn't just wash him off. He was my husband. I wasn't going to send him down the drain. So I did the only thing I could think of. The only thing that felt right.

I brought my hand up to my lips, and I licked my husband's ashes from my skin.

He didn't taste anything like he used to, all salt and musk and healthy man.

He tasted like sand, dust, and bad eggs. Like nothing I'd ever tasted before.

Since then, I've licked my finger and dipped it into his ashes several times a day, just to feel him on my tongue again, to bring him deep and hold him inside me.

I never taste him around other people. That'd be just as inappropriate as dropping my pants in public. It's a very dear, intimate moment for us, whenever I bring him inside. And I can't stop.

I'll wake in the middle of the night and reach over to his side of the bed, expecting just for a second to feel him lying there, warm and broad and breathing. He's not though, and my hand lands instead on the cool, hard box he sleeps in. And I take a taste.

He calms me.

He soothes me.

He lets me know he's here with me, and he'll never leave.

Some nights I wake from nightmares, certain that I've taken too much, and that when I look over, his box will be empty. Those dreams break something inside me every time. I feel it falling away in flakes, and I fear that one day soon, the nightmare will come true.

In the time since that first grey sprinkle touched my skin, I've already consumed a pound of Ronnie.

I don't know what I'll do when I reach the bottom of the box. Part of me prays that if I stretch my hand down through the ash, I'll find that there is no bottom, and that Ronnie will be here for as long as I need him.

Another, stronger part of myself feels sure that the day I run out of ashes, my heart will stop. Or else I'll stop it. From the first day we met, I knew I couldn't live without Ronnie.

But that's okay, because I have a plan.

The first part, unladylike as it is, is that I've stopped using the toilet. I don't think my body absorbs the ashes anyway, and the thought of flushing away any trace of Ronnie is unbearable. All solid waste is collected and rolled flat between two pieces of wax paper, then set out to dry in the sun. Once it's dried, I powder it in a thrift store food processor and store it in an empty coffee can.

The second part is that, since Ronnie was cremated, he never had a grave.

I made him a headstone and placed it in the backyard, then spent a weekend digging his grave. I filtered out the rocks, roots, and impurities, until I had a wheelbarrow of clean earth.

Then I mixed half of the remaining ashes with the grave dirt and my collected powders, and refilled the hole.

It will take some adjustment, but I'm certain I can adapt. I didn't like the taste of Ronnie at first, but I grew to love it. I'm sure the same will be true for his grave dirt, and I am comforted by the knowledge that there's a little bit of him (and me) in every handful. I dug his grave deep, so there's no fear of burning through it like I did with his ashes. And it is, in a way, self-replenishing.

Ronnie and I will never be parted again, no matter what our wedding vows said.

Some things were made to be broken.

But not us.

50. HERE BE VAMPYRE BY JOHANNES PINTER

"Mom, why are we different?"

It's Liv who asks. But Mom doesn't respond. She cannot collect two thoughts at once when she has a blown-out chest in front of her, sprawling ribs like a smoldering fireplace grate. She cannot lose focus when she has exactly five seconds to annihilate the black heart of the beast.

Afterwards, Mom stands next to the girl, Liv, who looks out over the landscape that extends around the pine-covered hill they are on. She glances at her; the girl seems to have a lot of thoughts in her thirteen-year-old head. It's maybe not that odd to have existential ponderings as a teenage monster-butcher.

"Did you get in contact with Bielke?" says Mom.

The girl points past a low rise twenty feet away.

"What is he saying? Are they here?" Mom wonders, without getting more answers.

She cocks her rifle, goes around the rise—and halts in her steps.

There Bielke hangs, skewered on a moderately thick tree trunk running in through his bottom and out through his mouth. The skinned torso is ripped open and gaping, hollowed out like a slaughtered animal, completely gutted of intestines. No residue on the ground more than blood-red soil indicates it has been brought here. Or eaten. His tongue hangs, grotesquely long, out of a mouth with no lower jaw and a neck gnawed to the vertebrae. The appalling remains of the tracker and former colleague effectively demonstrate the statement: *Here be Vampyre!*

Down the hill, through the small community and up to their destination; the Rolfstorp church. Liv points and describes as they both stand on the top of the hill, considering their intended path through their rifle scopes.

A kilometer away they actually see a glimpse of the Bocksten bog, where the ancestor of the Vampyres was found long ago, pile-driven to the bottom. The idiots who found it never came to burn its heart, and look where they are now: fighting an uneven battle in a country besieged by bloodsuckers—and we're not talking about politicians or moguls.

The year is 2114. The year of the Vampyre. Like every year.

Piles of branches effectively cover the burrow where the killed Vampyre is hidden. Mom thinks she surprised it before it had the chance to warn the others, but one cannot know for sure. Caution is a virtue.

She takes the shotgun from her back, holds the pistol grip while test pumping it a few times, then reloads it with silver slugs. The girl checks her Desert Eagle, taps the .44 bullet-filled magazine to her leg before sliding it back into place. They check each other's silver chainmail, ensuring that it covers neck, wrist and ankles properly; the spots Vampyre go for at the first strike. The rib blasters sit in their belts' special holsters. They finish by checking the sensitive high-tech equipment, measuring instruments and sensors around their heads hidden by their hoods. Everything is hunky dory. They're ready.

~ ~ * * ~ ~

Weapons raised, mother and daughter move smoothly and synchronously into the long-abandoned small town of Rolfstorp. Both have the same silver-white hair, standing like a plume behind them as they run. They cross an overgrown football field, move through the dead silence in the backstreets of the small town idyll, and rush past rusted car wrecks on the larger Skällinge Road. They crouch in the ditch, scout, then move further.

They halt for a drink break in the shade of a burned down school. In the rubble they spot the remains of what was probably the main course on the Vampyre menu: scattered bodies in severe decay. But no Vampyre. What would they do outside, in the sunshine?

Onward, past another overgrown football field. Two football fields in such a small town—how bizarre! They reach the slope and the grove at the church's west fence. Hiding, they look over the cemetery: silent like a grave. Lawns like jungle undergrowth between inclined tombstones. The church, whitewashed and stately, and the assumed dwelling for twenty Vampyre. Liv points at the gate to the clock tower.

They slip over the fence. Avoid the rustling gravel paths. Circle the church, weapons always ready. They get a brief overview of the haunted neighborhood. Reaching the clock tower, Mom tries to push open the gate, but something blocks it. Through a small gap, they see a carelessly piled stack of pews barricading the entrance. Liv crouches and succeeds in squeezing her small body sideways through the gap.

Inside the gloomy church she removes the pews so Mom can get in. They remain standing, slowly turning, letting the sensitive measuring instruments under their hoods take in the surroundings. The silence is deafening.

"No movement registered in any direction," confirms Mom.

"But the smell."

Liv looks around. A sickening stench has fallen over them like a rotten blanket. They zoom in on the tower's curved wooden staircase. The lower half's missing, so Mom helps Liv up and then stands guard.

Liv reaches the arms room, immediately locating the source of the stink: piles of decayed human bodies, more or less grown together after being stacked for an indefinable time. With disgust, she gets out a small flashlight and looks over the room. Dead bodies. Nothing else. She quickly climbs down again.

~ ~ * * ~ ~

They move through the church's sanctuary as fast as they can without being careless, passing the remains of the pulpit and the nave, where the pews stood before they were used as doorstops.

Liv rounds the impressive Hammarberg organ, repressing an impulse to try a dusty key. Mom stops at the vestry in the north gallery, peeking through the door, shotgun close and ready to fire. No bodies, no Vampyre.

Liv climbs the loft along the west wall. She gets a good view of the church as she advances, twenty feet above the ground. She walks on her toes, not putting her heels down, avoiding the vibrations it could send through the Church body. Her eyes alternately search the wooden ceiling barrel vault and every corner of the interior.

Mom passes the soapstone baptismal font, its entire inside covered with dried blood. She stops in front of the altar. Its design, with various images of the history of the tormenting of Christ, fits well where humanity is right now. The illustrations are flanked by images from the Garden of Eden, and it makes her grin; whose Eden are we?

Then Liv signals up on the platform. In a corner of one of the church's transept aisles, she has caught sight of an excavation covered with temporary tarps.

They remove the tarp, and find a hole into the basement revealing the remains of the old round building beneath, which was later built over by the newer cruciform church. But it might as well be the gateway to Hell.

The sun shines flat. They have maybe half an hour before darkness sets, and with that, a growing number of uncertainties. After a short assessment, they decide to do the job now anyway; they just have to keep track of the reflections of the sun halfway up the wall.

The girl goes first, moving lithely down the stale steps. It is pitch black down here, so she switches on her IR goggles. In the goggles' flickering green images, she sees how the existing foundation under the church floor is composed of a large room, divided in three smaller spaces by the remains of stone walls. She immediately locates five *cocoons*—Vampyres carefully wrapped in their thick, light-tight coats. In the next bay she spots four more cocoons, and in the farthest, ten. She signs to Mom, who confirms.

Liv stands over a cocoon, Mom behind her with the rib blaster ready. Then, the girl shoots an ampoule of holy water into the body of the first Vampyre. It immediately begins to tremble with a rattlesnake's dry sound. While she moves to the next cocoon, Mom unwraps the coat from the first one. Sweet Jesus, they're ugly: hairless, emaciated humanoids with veiny, livid, leather-dry skin. Disgusting over-sized mouths, with thin lips retracted from constantly exposed fangs. It is paralyzed by the holy water boiling in its bloodstream, making Mom's job easy. She impales the rib blaster into the middle of the creature's chest and turns on the switch. With a muffled sound, the rib blaster lives up to its name—it expands with a *crunch*, opening up the chest like a flower, exposing all of its sick, tar-black interior. As the Vampyre still screams, Mom ladles up the heart and destroys it in an instant with the acid pump.

They work like that. Systematically. Liv injects the holy water while Mom blasts chests and burns hearts. Two done. Then five. Nine. Fourteen. It is hot as Hell down here. The work is strenuous … and they forget to check the reflection of the sun on the wall above the hole. Suddenly, the church goes dark. Mom and Liv look at each other anxiously, hearing the characteristic rustling of Vampyre about to wake up. Slowly, coats unfold, and five pairs of hateful, red eyes look at them from the dusk of the first bay.

Liv and Mom gather and cock their weapons.

As five Vampyres simultaneously bolt out of the bay, mother and daughter let the hellfire break loose on the scavengers. Silver slugs tear large pieces from gray bodies, paralyze muscles and murderous minds. When the smoke clears, the two Vampyre hunters are the only ones standing, and they continue to rib-blast and heart-burn the last monsters.

~ ~ * * ~ ~

"Shouldn't there be twenty?" Liv later ponders, walking down the church's nave, removing her neck armor to wipe her sweaty nape. "It was just nineteen down there."

Mom opens the door. She's about to suggest that maybe it was twenty down there, they may have miscalculated. Or that it was number twenty that she killed up on the hill. Or …

Then a shadow falls over them from the arms room above the clock tower. Before they can react, the twentieth Vampyre is over Liv, unfathomably quick, striking the girl to the floor in the doorway to the cemetery. Mom rises her rifle and pumps, seeing Liv draw her gun, but also that the creature already buried its fangs into the girls unprotected neck.

Bam-bam-bam!

Liv's gun blasts into the Vampyre's chest as its fangs work her neck.

Ka-boom, ka-boom, ka-boom!

Mom sends the devilish creature struggling into the church's interior, emptying the rest of the silver slugs into its body until it is just a steaming pile of black meat.

Mom kneels, taking her daughter in her arms as the girl lies on the ground, her hand over her bitten throat. She silently swears at herself; why did she relax before they were out? Why didn't she keep count? Some things cannot be asked of a thirteen-year-old. With her free hand, out of the girl's view, she sneaks out a pointed tool.

"Mom, are you crying?" Liv asks. "Will I be a Vampyre now?"

"No, sweetie, I'm not crying. And you will not become a Vampyre."

Mom removes the hood, uncovering the girl's head—and all the high tech sensors and measuring devices that are attached directly to the girl's titanium skull, connected straight into her nervous system.

Liv quietly hums some unrecognizable tune as Mom, with the sharp tool, opens a small hatch in the girl's nape and locates the broken IR transmitter on the left motion sensor of the neck.

No, she does not cry. And the girl won't become a Vampyre this time, either. Cyborgs don't. But she never gets used to seeing the monsters biting her girl. Eighty years of adjustments and repairs and "new parts and it's back up on your feet again," but you never get goddamn used to it. She wants to protect her thirteen-year-old daughter … even though the girl's been thirteen for a while now.

"Mom … why are we different?"

"We are the ones who feel but cannot cry, sweetie." She kisses the girl on the forehead.

Mom supports Liv as she gets up, shaken after the attack. Moaning, the girl stretches her back while slipping a new magazine into the pistol and puts it in the holster.

As they walk along the gravel path they soon hear the helicopter coming over the hill. Mom glances at Liv, then toward the church, one last time.

Here be no longer Vampyre.

THE END

To be continued in…

Demonic Visions

50 Horror Tales

Book 6